NO ONE
LIVES TWICE

JULIE MOFFETT

NO ONE
LIVES TWICE

To Debbie—
May your life
be filled with
romance! :)
Julie
Moffett

W🌐RLDWIDE.

TORONTO • NEW YORK • LONDON
AMSTERDAM • PARIS • SYDNEY • HAMBURG
STOCKHOLM • ATHENS • TOKYO • MILAN
MADRID • WARSAW • BUDAPEST • AUCKLAND

To my dad, William F. Moffett, Lexi's number one fan!

Recycling programs
for this product may
not exist in your area.

No One Lives Twice

A Worldwide Mystery/June 2015

First published by Carina Press.

ISBN-13: 978-0-373-26948-8

Acknowledgments

I would like to thank Dr. S. Rosenberg for taking the time out of a very busy practice to answer my questions on in vitro fertilization and related medical questions. Thanks also to my sister, Sandy Moffett Parks, for her help with various math equations and lots of editing; my mom, Donna Moffett, for proofreading and story suggestions; my terrific Carina editor, Alissa Davis, for tightening up the book and keeping it consistent; and my husband, Robert, for assistance on all computer-related questions and brainstorming the plot with me from the beginning. You guys are incredible! However, any mistakes (technical, medical, scientific or otherwise) are mine alone.

ONE

WHEN I WAS LITTLE, everyone who knew me thought I was odd. I never wanted to play with dolls and I didn't enroll in ballet or gymnastics. Instead my paramount interest was numbers. For years I carried around math flashcards and liked to entertain my parents' friends by adding, subtracting and multiplying in my head. As I grew older, I quickly moved on to more mature themes, devouring linear algebra, differential equations, quadratic reciprocity and stochastic processes. Computers were my only friends and the internet, my playground.

Today, some twenty years later, I'm still fascinated with numbers, computers and code. But this time around, I'm getting paid for it as an information security technologist with the U.S. National Security Agency, or NSA for short. Most of us call it the "No Such Agency" because we are so secret. I heard somewhere that less than five percent of Americans even know we exist.

Basically, I do a lot of web surfing and looking for bad guys. Using methodical, mathematical and logical techniques—and when that fails, sheer imagination—I'm supposed to stop hackers from compromising America's national security.

Although I work for a top-secret agency, I've unfortunately never participated in even one exciting car chase, had a sip from a stirred (not shaken) martini, or shot a poison dart from an umbrella. That kind of action belongs to the spooks at the CIA. Some of us at the NSA joke that we are the brains of the nation, while the CIA is the brawn. I don't imagine CIA employees would be amused to hear that.

In fact, at this very minute, I was sitting in my cramped, government-issued cubicle checking out a popular chat room. My boss, Jonathan Littleton, hovered behind me, doing what we computer types call shoulder surfing. Jonathan had joined the NSA in the seventies—before computers were commonplace. Although he now officially headed the Information Security Department, better known as InfoSec, he was more a manager than a techie.

Jonathan whistled under his breath as he perused the data displayed on the twenty-five-inch color flat panel monitor on my desk.

"Having fun in there?" he asked.

The *there* Jonathan referred to was a creepy chat room called Dark Hack where I was currently imping a brash, male teenage hacker. I'm not the type of girl who typically hangs out in the dark and eerie underbelly of the internet in rooms with names like Dark Hack, Mute Slay or Crack-Hack, but sometimes we do what we have to in the name of national security, and today that meant impersonating a social misfit with a grudge.

I was pretty sure I was currently chatting with the guy who had hacked into the NSA's Public Affairs website a couple of weeks ago using some pretty robust and unusual code. Utilizing fairly colorful language he defaced the site, drew a mustache on the president and urged teen hackers to unite to breach the electronic barriers that separated people from the free flow of information.

Since I'm a fairly junior member of the team, Jonathan thought this particular assignment was right up my alley. So last week he tossed the case file onto my desk with a sticky note on top that read "Lexi Carmichael—Urgent" in bold red pen.

Lexi Carmichael. That's me—a computer geek with a name better suited to a bubbly cheerleader. Lexi isn't even short for something more dignified, like Alexandra or Alexis. And to make matters worse, I look nothing like a Lexi. Imagine a delicate-boned, pink-cheeked girl with long, curly blond hair, blue eyes and an adorable, pert nose…and that's exactly what I *don't* look like. To my mother's great dismay, I inherited nothing of her remarkable looks except for a pair of exceedingly long legs. By the seventh grade I was five foot eleven—skinny and all legs with a short torso, no boobs and ordinary brown hair like my dad. I'd also been given his facial genes—a thin nose, wide mouth and hazel eyes. At age twenty-four, not much has changed, including the fact that I still have zip in the boob department.

"Is PhearU the target?" Jonathan asked, leaning closer to the monitor to read what we had been chatting about.

"Yep, he's the guy," I explained. "I've been casing him for a while. Today I made contact. We're instant messaging. I'm Disease2, and I'm running a trace on him."

There was a pause and then the words popped up on my screen.

PhearU: I've seen you here a couple of times before. Where ya at, dude?

I glanced at my other monitor and saw that PhearU was using a major internet service provider in Charlotte, North Carolina.

"Gotcha," I murmured under my breath.

Disease2: Iowa. Told the rents i was too sick to go to school. They bought it. ha, ha. Be right back.

I quickly tracked down the number of the internet provider in Charlotte and punched it in on my phone. I requested a manager and after providing my security information was told that the number was a public dial-up— meaning Phear probably sat at an internet café somewhere. That meant if I wanted more information, I'd have to provide a court order to the phone company to further trace the exact location in Charlotte.

"Crap," I said to Jonathan. "He used a dial-up."

"Clever," Jonathan offered. "A slower connection, but a more secure one."

PhearU suddenly started typing.

PhearU: U still here, Disease?

Disease2: Right here, man.

PhearU: Good, cuz I just nailed your ass.

Disease2: What?!?!?

PhearU: U aren't calling from Iowa.

"Uh, oh," I murmured under my breath. "What raised his hackles?"

Disease2: Whatcha mean, dude?

PhearU: U think I'm an idiot? I know you're calling from southern Maryland. YFGI!

"No way!" I uttered, the pencil I held between my fingers snapping in two. "He made me. How did he do that?"

Phear abruptly logged out of the chat room. I banged my forehead against the monitor.

"What did I do wrong?" I moaned in disbelief. "Even if he ran a trace back on me, he shouldn't have been able to make me so easily. I was protected."

Instead of being angry, Jonathan seemed amused. "Apparently the protection was inadequate. What's YFGI stand for?"

"You freaking government imposter," I said with a sigh and tried not to be offended when Jonathan stifled a laugh.

"Better luck next time," he said and left just as my phone rang. I yanked the receiver out of the cradle and jammed it against my ear.

"Carmichael," I said in an irritated voice.

"Lexi, darling," my mother said in her soft southern drawl. "I've been thinking of you all day. How would you like to come to dinner tonight?"

My mother, Clarissa Carmichael, is a former first-runner-up in the Miss America contest, and the winner of a slew of other beauty pageants including Miss Teen USA, Miss Virginia and Miss Colonial Blossom. She is gorgeous at age fifty-four, a statuesque natural blonde with a body to die for and a face that stops strangers dead in the street. She's the kind of woman who can bend men to her will with her looks alone and who makes other females downright catty with envy.

Her main objective in life after marrying my father, who is now a wealthy corporate lawyer in Washington, D.C., was to have a sweet, adorable girl she could mold into a clone of herself. It took her three tries and two rambunctious boys, but I finally popped out one hot summer day. I think Mom liked Lexi because she thought it sounded cute, bubbly and perky—the perfect name for a future Miss Teen USA. Unfortunately I was a disappointment to my mother the moment I made my appearance in this world. But that didn't stop her from trying to mold me into a miniature version of herself.

"Your birthday is coming up and I thought we might discuss your party over dinner," she continued, her drawl deepening with excitement. That always seemed to happen when she planned social events and the mere sound of it turned my blood to ice. I was turning twenty-five, but my mom still wanted to plan my birthday parties.

"I'm not going to have a party this year," I said in the most nonchalant voice I could manage. God forbid that she sensed I was appalled by the idea because then she'd latch on to it like a dog with a bone. "I want to turn twenty-five in a quiet, peaceful, *alone* sort of way."

"Nonsense," she said, clucking her tongue in that disapproving way. "Turning twenty-five is an important milestone. Come to dinner, sweetie."

"I can't, Mom. I'm busy," I lied. "I've…uh…got a really hot date."

My mom fell silent and I knew she didn't believe me. Okay, so I didn't even believe it myself. First of all, it was a Tuesday. What kind of people had hot dates on Tuesday? Second of all, it had been eons since I'd had a hot date. Or a cold date, for that matter..But I didn't need a man to make my life complete. My life was complete enough as it was, thank you.

All I really wanted to do was stare at my computer screen for another two hours and then get into my spiffy red Miata convertible and sit in traffic for a half hour on the parkway before arriving home just six miles away. Then I remembered the pile of dirty laundry waiting for me on the floor of my bedroom, and the fact that I had nothing in the refrigerator for dinner. I'd eaten only a pathetic garden salad with fat-free dressing for lunch, so that meant I was ravenous, cranky and vulnerable. Thirty miles away in her upscale Georgetown home, my mother zoned in on my weakness with that annoying secret radar only women with children seem to have.

"We're having your favorite…beef stew," Mom coaxed. "Sasha made fresh bread, too."

Sasha Kovalev is my parents' personal cook. He came to America when Russia was still the Soviet Union. He was a former nuclear scientist or something like that and managed to defect with his wife and two kids. In America he seemed to have found his niche as a personal cook to the rich and didn't seem to miss his high-profile scientific job. Which is lucky for me because he's a whiz at physics and I'd often picked his brain for help with my homework while he whipped up Chicken Kiev.

Just the thought of Chicken Kiev made my stomach gurgle loudly. I sighed, knowing I'd lost the battle. "What time?"

"Six-fifteen sharp," my mother said, practically purring. "And, Lexi, wear something nice."

"I'm wearing what I have on," I protested. "I'm coming straight from work."

"Okay, darling," she said, and then hung up before I could question her further. Why did it matter what I was wearing?

I looked down at myself and then grimaced. I wore a pair of wrinkled black slacks and a purple blouse with flowing sleeves. I guess I'm not much of a fashionista, whatever that means. Any clothes purchased with something other than comfort in mind intimidate me. If I have to buy stuff for work, I buy whatever is on sale in my size. I was pretty sure my outfit wouldn't be what my mother had in mind when she envisioned something nice, but we all do the best we can.

On the other hand, image means everything to my parents. They live in a gorgeous redecorated townhouse in colonial Georgetown. Their neighbors are some of the most powerful and richest people in the world—senators, congressmen, Supreme Court justices and former Enron executives. You can't touch real estate in that area for under two million dollars. Since I work for the government, you can well imagine I don't live anywhere in the vicinity. But I did go to Georgetown University, so I have a fondness for the area in an it's-a-beautiful-place-to-visit-but-I-could-never-afford-to-live-there sort of way. My parents moved to Georgetown the year I entered the university. It was also the year my dad got a full partnership in his law firm. His new position required new living arrangements. God forbid that they be seen mingling with common folk anymore.

Don't get me wrong; I love my parents. My dad worked hard to get where he is today, and my mom was born to the role of rich, gorgeous, slightly bored housewife. But they embraced their new life a bit too enthusiastically for my taste. I could never see myself living out that kind of fantasy even if it's what my mom obsessively envisions for me. After three years she still talks about my job at the NSA as if it is only temporary. I think she still hasn't recovered from the fact that I double-majored in mathematics and computer science when I should have been enrolled in the finding-a-suitable-rich-husband program.

But I had committed to go to dinner at my parents', so I was stuck whether I liked it or not. Before I knew it, my watch beeped five o'clock. I leapt from my chair, darted out to my car and drove south on the Baltimore-Washington Parkway.

spent another half hour circling around looking for a parking space. I was walking about two blocks away from my parents' house when a big white guy in a dark blazer suddenly materialized out of nowhere from behind a parked car and strode right up to me. He had a huge, beefy neck, a brown crew-cut and pockmarks on his face. He didn't look friendly. I smiled brightly even though my heart was doing the tango in my chest.

"Good evening," I said politely and tried to walk past him.

He blocked the way, crossing his thick arms against his chest and saying nothing. I glanced up the street and watched as a couple of cars whizzed by, but no one gave us a second glance. It was just my luck that the narrow sidewalk was empty of other pedestrians.

Sighing, I held out my purse. "I've got thirty-two dollars, an over-maxed credit card and four tampons. If it's not too much trouble, can I keep the car keys? That way I'm spared the double humiliation of being robbed and then driven home by my parents."

His mouth fell open as he stared at me. Then his mouth slowly curved into a grin.

"I'm not here to rob you, little girl."

I took a shaky step back. *Little girl?* Oh God, I was being accosted by a pervert who probably intended to rape, maim and torture me. I saw the exact same scenarios week after week on the television show *America's Most Wanted,* hosted by John Walsh. I tried to remember what I was supposed to do and wondered if I could outrun him in my pumps on these damn cobblestones.

"Look, buster, you can't assault me right here in the middle of Georgetown," I said, my pulse jumping faster than a ping-pong game at the Olympics. "It's still daylight.

Besides I'll scream bloody murder and someone will call the cops."

The grin remained plastered to his face. "I'm not going to hurt you." I noticed he had a gold front tooth that sparkled. "As long as you cooperate."

"Cooperate? With what?" I asked, now pathetically clutching my purse to my chest as if it were some kind of protection. I glanced up the street again. My new plan was to scream the next time I saw a car and hope for the best.

"You've got something I want. Your roommate sent you some papers," he said. "I need them."

That threw me for a loop. "Roommate?" I hadn't had a roommate since college, and that was four years ago. I laughed in relief. "Oh, thank God. I don't have a roommate. Sorry, you've got the wrong person. I'll just be on my way now."

Beefy didn't look amused. "Your former roommate," he corrected. "Does the name Basia Kowalski mean anything to you?"

He'd mispronounced both Basia and Kowalski, but I knew whom he meant. She had indeed been my roommate at Georgetown University and also happened to be my best friend. My stomach knotted up again.

"No, I'm sorry," I lied. "I've never heard that name before. So, can I go already?"

He frowned and a red flush crept from his neck up his chin, cheeks and forehead. "Don't play me for a fool," he growled.

I heard a noise behind me and glanced over my shoulder. Someone was walking a dog in our direction. Before I could do anything, Beefy grabbed me by the arm, yanking me off the sidewalk and into a patch of grass beneath a nearby tree. He poked me beneath one of my ribs with something hard, then lifted his jacket and showed me it was a gun.

"The papers," he repeated ominously.

"I don't know what you're talking about," I protested. "Really."

He poked at me with the gun again and this time it really hurt.

"Ouch! I mean it," I said, trying to shift away from the gun. "Okay, I do know who Basia is, but I haven't heard from her since last week. She didn't give me any papers. Is she in some kind of trouble?" A rather dumb question, actually, given the fact that some guy was upset enough to poke a gun at me while asking questions about her. God, I really hoped she wasn't considering him as boyfriend material. We'd have to have some serious girl talk.

The guy walking the dog came closer and Beefy leaned his head down near mine. "Scream and I'll pop you both," he whispered. "Then I'll finish off the dog for dessert."

I swallowed hard. I had a gut feeling that this guy was fully capable of popping us *and* eating the dog. And I always trust my gut feelings.

The guy strolled up to us, carrying a plastic bag full of poop and tightening his hold on the leash. The dog, a cute cocker spaniel, lunged toward us, wagging his tail. You could see he was disappointed we were blocking his access to the tree.

"Nice evening," the guy said, dipping his head at us. The pooch woofed in agreement.

"It's too humid for me," Beefy replied with a casual nod, putting an arm around my shoulder. The gun dug into my side and I had to swallow hard to keep from yelping. At the same time, I was morbidly fascinated by the fact that the Beefster actually had some sort of conversational skills.

"Believe it or not, Miami is more humid," the guy said with a smile. "I'm transplanted here."

Beefy grunted and I tried to draw the dog walker's attention by pasting an "I'm-being-held-at-gunpoint-by-a-psychotic-maniac" look on my face. To my dismay, the guy didn't seem to notice. Instead he smiled sheepishly as his dog did wee-wee near Beefy's foot and then he sauntered away with the dog trailing, neither knowing just how close they had come to meeting their Maker.

As soon as they were safely out of earshot, Beefy returned his attention to me. "The papers," he growled, the gun still pressed against me menacingly. "Where are they?"

I shook my head, really confused now. I usually saw Basia every other week or so, depending on what was happening in our lives. Why in the world would she mail me anything when she could just drive them over and give them to me?

"Scout's honor," I said, holding up three fingers. "I don't have any papers from Basia."

He looked at me for a long moment as if trying to decide if I were telling the truth. I cringed as he put his hand into his pocket, reaching for God knows what kind of torture device. Instead he pulled out a business card and handed it to me. It was blank except for a phone number. No name, no logo, no address.

"If you get those papers, you call this number before you do anything else," he instructed, patting the gun beneath his blazer. "If you don't and I find those papers have fallen into other hands, I'll hold you personally responsible, Lexi."

Oh, God, he knew my name. In this day and age, it probably meant he knew my address, phone number, sexual preference and weight. I nodded and stepped back, rubbing my ribs where he had poked me with the gun. I was going to have a wicked bruise there for sure, but at least I was alive. For now.

"So, what's the big deal about these papers?" I asked, trying to keep myself steady.

"Nothing," he snapped. "And don't get too nosy. I'm protecting them for a client. And I'm gonna see he gets them back safely or else…"

I didn't want to know how I figured in the rest of that sentence, so I backed away, holding up my hands in front of me. "Well, it's been fun, but I've got to go now," I said brightly.

"You tell anybody we had this little meeting and I'll be unhappy," Beefy warned. Then he made a little pistol with his fingers and fired it at me. "Bang."

Jeez, he was a psycho *and* stand-up comic wannabe. "What meeting?" I said innocently, lifting my hands.

He narrowed his eyes. "Want a useful piece of advice, little girl?"

I didn't, but I'd never say that to a man with a gun. "Okay."

"Lose the shirt. Purple isn't your color."

With that, he walked across the street and down the sidewalk. I watched until he took a hard left and disappeared behind a row of townhouses. I needed desperately to sit down, but was afraid he might come back. Bending over, I removed my pumps and ran the rest of the way to my parents' house in bare feet with the cobblestones cutting painfully into my soles.

I was out of breath and nearly crying when I reached the front door. Frantically I twisted the knob, but it was locked. After all, this is Washington. Decent citizens lock themselves in their homes and put bars on their windows. I dropped my pumps and fumbled in my purse for the key when the door magically opened. My mom stood in the doorway, dressed in a stunning peach dress with glittering diamonds at her neck and ears. She took one look at me and nearly fainted.

"Lexi, what happened to you? Where are your shoes?" she gasped.

I scooped my shoes off the porch and darted inside barefoot, yanking the door from my mom's hand and slamming it shut. My heart was pounding so loud, my ears hurt.

"I'm sorry I'm late but there was this guy and he stopped me on the street, asking about some papers and…"

My sentence trailed off as I realized she was no longer looking *at* me, but *behind* me. I got this horrible sinking feeling as I turned around and saw the entranceway to the dining room was filled with people staring at me curiously. My dad stood there looking cool and collected in a pressed suit and tie, and I recognized Senator and Mrs. Marshall. Beside them stood a young blond-haired man I didn't know.

My eyes swung back to my mom's. "You didn't tell me it was a dinner party," I said under my breath. I had been set up, and I was angry.

"You're late," she whispered. "Wherever did you get that horrid purple blouse? Have you been shopping at Wal-Mart again?"

"Don't change the subject," I growled, but my mother shut me up by air-kissing both my cheeks. She put a hand on my shoulder, turning me around.

"Tom, Diane," she said, "I believe you've already met my daughter Lexi." They smiled weakly at me, no doubt scandalized by my attire, the flushed condition of my face and wild hair.

"What a delight to see you again, Lexi," Diane said politely.

My mom then turned to the young man, dazzling him

with her thousand-watt smile. "Lexi, I don't think you've yet had the pleasure of meeting their son Thomas Marshall III," she said. "He's a CPA at Price, Waterson and Morris over on Connecticut Avenue."

I looked over my shoulder at my mother with a raised eyebrow. Her typical set-ups for me involved lawyers or politicians in the making. A CPA was a real departure for her and I suspected there was more here than met the eye. To my ever-annoyed chagrin, she was completely convinced I would never get married without her help and had made it her life's mission to take charge of my love life. I should have smelled a set-up when she called. I just hadn't expected it to happen on a Tuesday, which is undoubtedly why she'd planned it that way.

I glanced back at Thomas and saw he was not quite able to hide the disappointment in his eyes. I was used to it by now. Guys took one look at my mother and thought they were in for a treat with her daughter. Instead they got me—brown-haired, flat-chested and geeky.

Sighing, I bent down and slipped on my pumps, my appetite having long ago fled. I was angry at my mother and still shaken from my bizarre encounter with Beefy. This day was going to hell in a handbasket faster than I could blink.

After a moment, I excused myself to go to the bathroom. Once inside, I splashed cold water on my face and combed my hair, hoping I looked reasonably presentable. My first instinct was to tell my parents what had just transpired on the street, but I wasn't sure I even understood it myself. What I did know for certain is that my parents would freak out if they knew I'd been accosted by gunpoint, forcing me to stay at the house with them for protection. I was pretty sure I'd rather face down a gold-toothed homicidal maniac than be maneuvered into that.

I returned to the table and sat down at a seat that had conveniently been left open beside Thomas. He was probably about twenty-five and was well-built, impeccably groomed and dressed in a navy blue coat and tie. He had good skin, good teeth and wavy brown hair that looked like it had been strategically highlighted. Handsome, if you liked the preppy, gleaming, I'm-the-son-of-an-important-politician kind of guy.

I snatched a hot roll and put it on my plate, figuring him for having attended a private boy's academy, Ivy League for an undergraduate degree and an MBA. You know, the typical rich-kid routine.

Thomas, apparently trying to be polite and engage me in some kind of conversation, leaned toward me while our fathers argued politics. "Nice shirt," he said in a low voice.

Jeez, who knew one shirt could elicit so much conversation? "Nice tie," I countered.

He laughed. "Touché," he said, taking a bite of his stew. "So, Lexi, where do you work?"

"In Maryland," I answered. "For the Department of Defense." It was my standard song and dance, seeing as how I wasn't allowed to mention the words "I work" and "NSA" in the same sentence—not even to my gynecologist, who knew more about me than I did.

"DOD?" Thomas said. "Are you a secretary?" Then before I could reply, he added hastily, "I mean, administrative assistant. We can't be too politically correct these days, can we?" He laughed, looking around the table, his gleaming white teeth nearly dazzling me.

Disappointment swept through me because, for a nanosecond, I'd thought he might have potential. I tried to swallow my annoyance at his condescending tone, but it kind of stuck in my throat.

"Actually, I'm into computers," I said.

He looked surprised. "Oh, really? Programming and stuff?"

He was *so* totally not a tech-head. "Um, something like that."

"I see. Well it sounds…quite unusual."

I didn't know what he found so unusual about me working with computers, unless my mom had led him to believe I was a lingerie model—something I wouldn't put past her. She always chose guys like Thomas who put a heck of a lot of stock in appearance and big hair. Frankly, those just weren't my strong suits.

"Are you the lone woman in your office working on computer stuff?" Thomas asked.

I gritted my teeth, wondering for what earthly purpose he had decided to drag out this conversation.

"No," I said, shoveling in a mouthful of stew and wondering how he would react if he discovered I actually worked at the NSA as an anti-hacker. I bet his next question would then be to ask how many women dabbled in *that* kind of profession. I considered offering him a statistical essay on the number of women involved in the technology field when my mother shot me one of her warning looks.

"So what is it exactly that you do?" Thomas persisted. "I mean you don't actually fix stuff, do you?"

If he said "stuff" one more time, I was pretty sure I'd have to clock him with my water goblet. I held my breath and counted silently to ten before plastering a perky smile on my face.

"Actually, Thomas, I try not to do anything too technical since I'm a female and it's a miracle I can even read."

Thomas looked taken aback for a minute, and then he laughed. "Hey, that's a good one, Lexi. You're funny."

My mother intensified her glare and I smiled back sweetly, dipping my spoon in Sasha's delicious stew.

"So, Thomas," my mother said, apparently deciding she had better take control of the conversation. "Why did you decide to pursue a career as a CPA?"

Thomas dabbed his mouth with his napkin. "Well, I majored in business at Yale and then went on to graduate school at Dartmouth to get an MBA," he said. "I graduated top of my class with full honors, passed the CPA exam and pretty much had my pick of accounting firms at which to work here in Washington. My ultimate goal, however, is the Senate, just like Father."

I choked on my stew and gagged until Thomas thumped me hard on the back. I *knew* my mother had something up her sleeve. Thomas Marshall III was a politician in the making, and my mother hadn't been able to resist trying to set me up. She knew I had a personal rule to never, *ever,* date anyone wanting to be in politics, which, of course, made Thomas irresistible to her.

I mumbled something and excused myself from the table. If I didn't get out of there now, I would certainly say something to ruin the evening. I slipped into the kitchen and saw Sasha, a slight, blond-haired man with a big, Slavic nose, working at the counter.

"Lexi," he said, holding out his arms and hugging me. "How's the food? Is there a problem with dinner?"

I liked the fact he greeted me with questions about dinner. He didn't waste time asking me about my health or my fashion sense. He went straight to what mattered—food. I love a man with a one-track mind, especially one who can cook. Too bad Sasha was already happily married.

"Dinner is perfect, as usual," I said, patting his arm. To prove my point, I tore a piece off a loaf on the counter and took a bite before he could snatch it back.

"You little thief," he scolded, but in an affectionate way.

"Look, Sasha, there's something I want to ask you," I said, my mouth half-full. "Have you seen Basia around lately?"

"Basia?" Sasha said, puzzled. "I haven't seen her in a month. She no like my bread anymore?"

"Perish the thought," I said, appalled by the very idea. "She loves your bread. I guess she's just been busy."

"Finding you another job?" he quipped.

I laughed it off, but actually he had a point. It *was* Basia who had got me hooked up with the NSA in the first place. She dragged me to the job fair when the agency was recruiting at Georgetown because she had always dreamed of working as a linguist for them.

The problem was that after the Cold War ended, no one needed linguists with Slavic or Romance languages anymore. If you wanted to get hired by the NSA these days, you needed to speak Arabic, Farsi or Somali. Since those were like the only three languages in the entire world she didn't speak, she hadn't been hired. And in an ironic twist, I had.

But that hadn't dampened Basia's spirit at all. She started her own freelance translation business and worked part-time at Berlitz—those guys who make those nifty little phrasebooks. It wasn't a bad living and she got to be her own boss. It was good for me, too, since I get a new phrasebook every Christmas. I'd racked up Spanish, French, Russian, Italian and German so far. I was hoping to get Romanian this year—if I lived that long.

"What's wrong with my job?" I asked. "You used to think being a techie was a cool job."

"It is…but not for you. You need to start living life outside your comfort zone," Sasha said, stirring something that smelled like hot fudge in a pot on the stove. "A girl like you doesn't need to sit around in front of a computer all day. You need to experience real life. Find someone *outside* the internet, and have actual, sweaty sex."

I opened my mouth to argue, but he was right. I needed to experience *real* life as opposed to my virtual existence. I didn't necessarily want it, but I admit to curiosity about the excitement part, especially in regards to sex. I'd only had sex one time in my entire life and it was definitely *not* exciting. It wasn't sweaty either. In fact, it hadn't even been interesting.

"I think you're made for adventure," Sasha continued. "But you need to go for it in a big way. Basia will help you."

Maybe Sasha had a point. I wasn't going to meet a guy by sitting in front of the computer all day. I needed to pay more attention to pesky little details like my wardrobe and grooming. If anyone could help in these areas of my life, it was Basia.

In all truth, she had already made a tremendous impact on me. First of all, because she was the only close girlfriend I had ever had. She'd befriended me at Georgetown when we were randomly selected to be roommates. Basia was the antithesis of me—a real girl's girl who liked dating, fashion, the social scene and expensive haircuts. My mom adored her and so did my brothers. But I soon learned that Basia was as smart as a whip beneath that feminine exterior, speaking several languages and having a flair for architecture and biology.

Compared to me, exciting was Basia's middle name. But I certainly didn't want the kind of excitement that came with a guy like Beefy.

I sighed. "If you happen to run into Basia, you tell her to call me right away, okay?"

Actually I considered calling her right now from my

parents' house, but after thinking about it some more, I decided it was too risky. I refused to own a cell phone, so that meant I'd have to use my parents' phone. My mom was a top-rate eavesdropper and I had decided I didn't want them to know about my encounter with Beefy. I wasn't sure what was going on yet and needed more input.

I heard the murmur of voices coming from the dining room, and then another one of Tom's annoying laughs. I decided I *really* didn't want to go back in there.

"Look, I've got to get out of here," I said to Sasha. "Do you think you could retrieve my purse from the sofa in the living room and bring it here?"

"Why don't you get it yourself?"

"Long story, but I'm afraid I'll be trapped. Then I'd have to be horribly impolite to ensure my escape. And you know how my mother hates it when I'm impolite."

He gave an exaggerated sigh. "I think this means you don't like the young man in there. Truthfully, me neither. He's too full of himself."

Sasha wasn't a nuclear scientist for nothing. "My thoughts exactly."

He nodded and went out the side door to the living room to retrieve my purse. I snatched an entire loaf of his bread from the counter, rolled it in a dishtowel and shoved it under my blouse just as my father walked into the kitchen. He saw the guilty look on my face and I knew I'd been busted.

"Making a break for it?" he asked calmly.

I exhaled a breath. "Do I really have to stay and talk to Mr. Preppy?"

Despite his attempt to look stern, his lips twitched. "Your mother will be disappointed."

"I know," I mumbled. "But I was ambushed. And trust

me, Thomas isn't going to call even if I stay for dessert. And honestly, I don't want him to."

To my surprise, my dad came over and ruffled my hair. "All right, go. I'll tell everyone you weren't feeling well."

"Thanks, Dad," I said, standing on tiptoe and giving him a kiss on the cheek. "I owe you big."

"I'll keep that in mind," he said. He looked down at me, worry lines creasing the corner of his eyes. "You're looking a bit pale. Are you sure everything is all right?"

"Never been better," I lied.

At that moment, Sasha darted back into the room with my purse. He saw my dad and stopped in horror. "Mr. Carmichael," he said in a breathless rush. "Lexi wanted me to get her purse and…"

"It's all right," my dad said, sighing. "I know what Lexi talked you into doing."

"Can I borrow him for a few minutes more?" I asked since my dad seemed so accommodating. "I'd like him to walk me to my car."

He frowned. I'd never asked for an escort to my car before and I could sense more questions hovered on his lips. But he nodded. "Of course."

"Thanks, Dad," I said, trying to push Sasha out the door before my dad could change his mind or ask me questions I didn't want to answer. "Tell Mother goodbye for me and that I'll call her tomorrow. We can go…ah, shopping or something." I cringed as the words left my lips. Did I just say I'd go shopping with my mother? Sheesh, guilt was hell.

"What a lovely idea. I'll tell her," Dad said before I could retract my statement.

Sasha walked me to the car, keeping a brisk pace. Thankfully no huge forms lurked in the shadows ready to grab me. Just the same, I checked the backseat of my convertible, under the car and in the trunk. Sasha probably thought I was crazy, but he's always thought that about Americans, so nothing new here.

I drove home to my apartment with the top down, the precious loaf of bread sitting in the passenger seat, moonlight streaming across my arms, and the radio blaring. I had pretty much calmed down by the time I got home and was ready to have a heart-to-heart chat with Basia about the Beefster via the telephone and then drop dead into bed. It had been that kind of day.

I zoomed into the parking lot and found a space not too far from the complex entrance. It's not a fancy building, just standard colonial brick with about forty-five apartments with small balconies. I live in the small, rural town of Jessup, Maryland. There are only a handful of apartment complexes in town. Out of the approximately eleven thousand people who live here, half own their own homes. The rest of us work for the NSA. Our talents lie in the area of national security, not gardening, home improvement or lawn mowing. It makes sense since we are largely math, computer science and language majors—great with numbers, linguistics and outsmarting the bad guys, but at a complete loss with a plant.

My mother was horrified when I decided to move to Jessup. In her mind it is serious redneck country and I might as well have moved to West Virginia. Now when friends ask her where I live, she is nonspecific and says near Baltimore.

After checking the parking lot for any suspicious characters, I covered the top of my Miata and locked it. Usually I'm bold enough to leave it unlocked, but unpleasant images of Beefy still played in my head. I secured the bread beneath my arm and keyed in the code to the front door of the apartment complex. When it buzzed open, I trudged up

the three flights of stairs to my apartment. No fancy eleva-
tor in this place. I unlocked the door and fumbled for the
light switch. But when I flicked it on, nothing happened.

Alarm bells went off in my head, but "uh, oh," was all I
had time to say before a man stepped out of my apartment
and yanked me inside. He clamped a hand down over my
mouth, the other snaking around my neck. Instinctively I
clawed at his arm, feeling thick muscles and hair. I caught
the faint scent of mint aftershave. My purse and the stolen
loaf of bread dropped to the floor with a thud. I kicked my
legs ferociously as my attacker slammed the door shut with
his foot and dragged me into my living room.

"Sit down," he said against my ear, but didn't remove
his hand from my mouth. "If you scream, I'll shoot you.
I've got a gun with a silencer, so no one will hear a sound
and you'll be dead before you hit the carpet. Do you understand?"

I nodded, my heart thudding in my chest. This was the
second time today I'd been confronted with a gun and I
didn't like it much.

Slowly he removed his hand from my mouth and I half
fell, half sat on the couch. I got my first clear look at my
attacker thanks to the moonlight streaming in through
the window and saw dark hair and dark clothing. I didn't
recognize him. But the soft accent I heard when he spoke
made me pretty sure he was of Middle Eastern descent.
Moonlight also glinted off the steel barrel of the gun he
pointed at my chest.

"Where are the papers?"

"Papers?" I squeaked.

He shoved the gun into my chest, painfully squishing
one of my breasts. "Don't play dumb with me."

Like I had to play at it.

"Answer me," he demanded. "I know she sent them to you."

She? As in Basia? Oh, God, I thought, my heart hammering. What in the world had she become involved in?

"Look," I said as calmly as I could, given the fact that my nipple was in imminent danger of being blown off. "I don't know what you're talking about. Perhaps if you could be a little less cryptic it would help."

"Basia Kowalski," he growled. "Is that clear enough?"

I considered for a moment. "Yes," I said. "Actually, that's quite clear."

"So, where are the papers? You are trying my patience."

I exhaled noisily. "I haven't spoken with Basia for about a week and she didn't mention any papers. Look, I already told the other guy I don't have them. I don't even know what you are—"

"What other guy?" he interrupted.

"I don't know. Some big white guy with a beefy neck, gold tooth and dark blazer. He accosted me in Georgetown and said he was trying to retrieve the papers for his client."

My attacker said something under his breath. I didn't understand the language, but it sounded like he was using lots of swear words. Then he strode to where I had dropped my purse in the entranceway and rifled through it. Apparently he didn't find what he was looking for because he turned his attention back on me.

"What were you doing in Georgetown?"

"If you must know, attending a miserable dinner party at my parents'."

"How did he know where you were going?"

I considered for a moment. "Good question. I don't know. He could have followed me from work, I guess." The thought gave me the creeps.

"Did you give him the papers?"

"I just told you, I don't have the papers," I said in exasperation. "I don't even know what *the* papers are. Besides, why would Basia mail them to me anyway? She doesn't live that far away and she could drive them over if they were that important."

"I know she mailed them to you," he said, his voice angry again. "But they weren't in your mailbox today. Did you get them yesterday?"

"Hey, isn't mail supposed to be private?" I said, a nanosecond later realizing what a dumb statement it was given the fact that this guy was assaulting me in my own apartment with a gun. Snooping around someone else's mail was probably small peanuts for someone like him.

"You didn't receive any packages from her today?"

"No. I swear. Cross my heart and hope to live," I said, trying to sound cheerful. "You can look around if you don't believe me."

He exhaled a deep breath. "I already did. And so did someone else."

While I pondered that, he stood quietly, apparently thinking. The gun still was pointed at me but at least it wasn't pressing against my boob anymore.

"If you receive the papers, call me immediately," he finally said. "Don't call anyone else. If you do, I assure you, you'll pay with your life and the life of your friend."

I swallowed hard. "Okay." I could be mega agreeable when a gun was pointed at my chest.

He pulled a pen from his shirt pocket and then grabbed my arm. He scrawled a number on the inside of my forearm. "Don't wash that off," he warned.

"Who me? Take a bath?" I joked weakly.

He leaned down close to my face. "I know you work for the NSA," he said, his voice low and threatening. "This has nothing to do with them. I have friends in high places that work there, too. If I hear that you've reported my visit here to anyone in your office or to the police, I'll find you and kill you no matter where you are. You will not be able to hide from me. Do you understand?"

His matter-of-fact tone chilled me to the bone. I totally, *absolutely* believed him.

"I understand," I said. "My lips are sealed."

He tucked the gun away beneath his jacket and I breathed a little easier. "This is no joke. The minute those papers arrive, you call me no matter what time of the day or night."

With that, he walked to the door and let himself out. I hyperventilated for a few minutes sitting there in the dark before I was able to determine what I should do next. Finally, I gathered enough courage to stand and turn on the lamp next to the couch. Light flooded the room and I blinked, realizing that my electricity was fine and that the intruder had either smashed or removed the bulb in the entranceway.

I blinked again and my vision cleared.

I wished I had stayed in the dark.

My apartment had been completely trashed. Books had been dumped from my bookshelf, pictures removed from the walls, magazines and papers scattered across the carpet. A quick cursory glance seemed to indicate that nothing had been stolen—just rifled through.

Dazed, I wandered into the kitchen and bedroom, finding a similar disaster there. Thank God my most precious possession, my sleek new laptop, had not been stolen. It was turned on, however, and someone had apparently tried to peek into my hard drive. He must not have been much of a geek because it looked like my password had stopped him cold.

It's not that I have any matters of national security to

hide on my computer or anything. At the NSA we're not allowed to bring our work home. I do have all my financial information there, although anyone clever enough to hack in would get a good laugh at my checking account balance. Just the same, I logged on, whizzed about my hard drive and checked my email. Other than the usual spam, there was nothing exciting, including no email from Basia telling me what the hell was going on.

Anger rising, I stalked into the bathroom. Even it had been ransacked. Tampons, make-up and rolls of toilet paper had been scattered about.

"Well, crap," I said, sitting dejectedly on the toilet lid. This had been one hell of a day. I'd been set up on a date with a politician in the making, accosted twice by men bearing guns, and my apartment had been trashed. It totally bit the big one.

After a minute of wallowing in alternating anger and self-pity, I stood and went to the phone in the kitchen. I dialed Basia's number, but her answering machine picked up right away.

"It's Lexi. Call me immediately," I ordered and then hung up. Then I dialed her cell number, but got her voice mail there, too. I left the same desperate message and hung up.

Returning to my bedroom, I searched for about ten minutes before I found my address book underneath a pile of underwear on my bedroom floor. I thumbed through it until I found Basia's parents' number in Chicago. My bedroom phone had been thoughtfully stuffed in one of my black flats. So after I extracted it, I sat on the bed amid a bunch of clothes and dialed the number.

A woman answered the phone. "Hallo?"

I immediately recognized Basia's mother's voice. The Kowalskis were from Poland and had emigrated to America about twenty-five years earlier. They were the sweetest, most down-to-earth people I'd ever met. But for some unfathomable reason, even though the Kowalskis had learned English in America, they spoke all fancy, just like the Brits.

"Hello, Mrs. Kowalski?" I said. "It's Lexi Carmichael. I'm sorry to bother you."

"Lexi, dear, how nice to hear from you. You're not bothering me. How can I help you?"

"It's nothing really. I was just wondering if you had heard from Basia lately."

Mrs. Kowalski must have been doing the dishes because I could hear her shut the water off in the background. "Basia? Well, let's see, I spoke with her a few days ago. Is something wrong?"

"Oh, no," I hurriedly reassured her. "I just need to reach her right away and she's not answering her phone or cell. I thought maybe she had mentioned to you that she had planned on going on an extended trip or something."

"Not to my knowledge. She might just be out with other friends. Unfortunately, Basia never keeps me abreast of her social life. I thought that was your department."

It was, but apparently I wasn't doing a bang-up job of keeping on top of it. "Oh, well, I'm just trying to get in touch with her about something, ah, possibly related to work. Did she happen to mention anything new she was working on?"

"Now that you mention it, she did say she had started a new project. Some new translations had apparently come her way. She did say it was in Polish for which she was glad since it could be done relatively quickly."

"Did she happen to say who the work came from?"

"No, dear, she didn't. I was more surprised that she'd recently started karate lessons."

My mouth fell open. "Karate?" I repeated, completely

dumbfounded. Basia doing karate was about as feasible as the pope turning Protestant. She *hated* exercise and would drive her car to the 7-Eleven to avoid having to walk across the street. If the escalator was out of service at the mall, she refused to shop there. Something weird was definitely going on here.

"Karate. Well, that's news to me, too," I said in the understatement of the year. Had I dropped off the face of the earth? Why hadn't she informed me, her best friend, of all these shocking new developments?

"Did she say where she was taking these karate lessons?" I asked.

"No, she didn't. Should I be worried?"

"No, not at all," I said hastily. "But if she happens to give you a call, will you tell her I'm trying to reach her?"

"Of course, dear," Mrs. Kowalski said, and I could hear a hint of worry creep into her voice. I hoped I hadn't spooked her, but mothers had that second sense thing going, and I had a feeling I'd been nabbed.

"Well, thanks, Mrs. K. I gotta go," I said as cheerfully as I could fake and hung up.

I stood and returned to my front door. I opened it and examined the jamb, but I couldn't see any marks where Mr. Middle Eastern Guy must have broken in. Not even a scratch. He must be one heck of a burglar.

I checked all the windows, but they were closed and latched from the inside. The balcony sliding glass door still had the piece of wood wedged into it that served as an extra lock. Honestly I didn't think he had come in either via the windows or the balcony. But that meant he had easily picked both my lock and deadbolt. Sheesh. Wasn't anyone safe these days?

I really, *really* wanted to call the police. I'd been accosted by armed thugs twice in one day, which ranked high on my list of reasons to call the authorities. But if Mr. Middle Eastern Guy and Beefy were still watching me, they'd see the police car arrive. I remembered their threats and changed my mind. I needed to talk to Basia first. Besides, nothing had been stolen, and as far as I could tell, nothing major had been broken. The place was just an unholy mess.

Sighing, I fastened the safety chain on the front door, wedging a chair beneath the doorknob for extra security. As soon as I got off work tomorrow, I was going to buy some mace and have an alarm system installed. No more surprise visitors. No more guns pointed at me. No more playing the victim.

I retrieved the loaf of Sasha's bread from the entrance-way floor, brushed it off and carried it into the kitchen. I nuked a couple pieces in the microwave and slathered them with butter and jam. I'm really into comfort food and this seemed the appropriate time to indulge.

After I'd finished stuffing my face, I felt better. I found a pen and piece of paper and jotted down the phone number Mr. Middle Eastern Guy had scrawled on my arm. Then I pulled down all the shades on the windows when there was a loud knock on my door.

My heart jumped to my throat and stayed there. I grabbed a heavy, ugly vase that my mother had given me for Christmas and cautiously approached the door. Without speaking, I peered out the peephole and breathed a sigh of relief when I saw it was my neighbor Jan Walton.

Jan was a cute, single mom with a seven-year-old, high-functioning autistic son named Jamie. The boy was the most handsome kid I'd ever seen, with thick, dark hair, sky-blue eyes and a dazzling white smile. He was super smart, but often had odd fixations. He'd once named every single part of my vacuum cleaner. In return, I'd listed the entire mathematical equation for the Mandelbrot Set. We'd been buddies ever since.

I quickly removed the chair from beneath the doorknob, unfastened the chain and unlocked the door.

"Hey, Jan," I exclaimed, sticking my head out. I didn't open the door all the way in case she saw the mess inside and asked questions to which I didn't yet have answers.

Jan looked puzzled that I hadn't invited her in. I *always* invited her in.

"Why is it so dark in your entranceway?" she asked.

"Oh, that," I said. "The light burned out, I guess. I'll have to replace the bulb."

A look of surprise crossed her face. "Hey, you don't have a guy in there, do you?"

Sometimes it astonished me how invested everyone, except me, was in my love life. Maybe turning twenty-five was some kind of blazing social milestone that meant if you didn't have a significant other, you'd better find one. In my case, dating meant change and I *hated* change. Change was different. Change was scary.

"No. Unfortunately, there is no guy in here, hot or otherwise," I said.

"Well, I came by earlier, but you weren't home."

"I was at my parents' for dinner."

"On a Tuesday? Special occasion?"

"Just my mom trying to set me up. Again."

Jan laughed. "How awful. You poor thing."

I laughed, too, but it was forced and I still didn't invite her in. Apparently sensing I wasn't in the mood for company, she held up a large FedEx mailer.

"Anyway, this came for you tonight. Since you weren't home, Jack dropped it off at my place. I forged your signature, and Jack said it was okay as long as we don't tell anyone. He didn't see the harm in it, seeing how we're good friends and all."

Jack was our FedEx guy. Jan was on a first-name basis with him because she insisted her ex-husband send his alimony check that way. Jack had become quite friendly and Jan often invited him in for coffee.

My hand trembled as I reached out to take the mailer from her. I didn't need to look at the return address because I already knew what it would say. But I had a morbid need to see, so I glanced down at the sender's address.

Not surprisingly it read "Basia Kowalski."

TWO

I NEARLY PEED in my pants right there on the spot, but instead smiled and thanked Jan, hastily closing the door. She probably thought I'd gone round the bend. Maybe I had.

I turned the deadbolt, fastened the chain and wedged the chair underneath the doorknob again. Then I stood with my back pressed against the wall, trying not to hyperventilate.

Why had I ever agreed to dinner at my parents'? If I had come straight home from work like I was supposed to, Jack would have given the mailer to me, and Beefy or Mr. Middle Eastern Guy could have stolen the papers from me, perhaps even before I got a look at them. Then I would have been happily clueless about this whole mess. But no, my mother had to pick this day—out of three-hundred and sixty-five choices—to try and set me up with a Senate-bound, preppy CPA.

Taking a deep breath, I darted into the kitchen. I sat at the table, pushing aside the silverware that had been dumped from a drawer. I gingerly set the mailer on the table.

I sliced open the top with a knife and shook the package a bit. Some papers slid out onto the table. I picked up the top sheet. It was a note hurriedly scrawled in Basia's messy handwriting.

Dear Lexi
Keep these papers safe for me. Hide them some-
where no one will think to look. I've got to go away

*for a few days to help a friend. I'll be in touch soon
and explain everything. Be careful and look closely.*

That was it—a strange cryptic message from my best
friend. I flipped through the papers, but found no further
explanation of what these papers were or why two people
had already accosted me at gunpoint for them.

Shaking my head, I set the note aside and picked up
one of the papers. It looked like a bunch of legal documents in a foreign language I didn't recognize. I thumbed
through the rest and counted seven neatly typed pages. I
could see letters with a bunch of funny accents and wig-
gly lines both above and beneath the letters. I recognized
the Roman alphabet in play here, so the language wasn't
Arabic or Russian. That narrowed it down to a few dozen.

I glanced over the papers again more carefully and managed to pick out an address. The city read Warszawa. That
meant Poland. No surprise here. Polish was Basia's first language and she did a lot of translation work in the language.
But why had she sent them to me for safekeeping? And why
were two armed men desperate to get their hands on them?

"What's this all about, Basia?" I murmured aloud.

There had to be a clue somewhere. Determined, I studied the papers again, this time more closely, line by line.
Not that I knew what I was looking for, but I had a hunch.

Then I saw it. At the bottom of page three, someone
had penciled in something so lightly, I almost missed it.

I squinted and held the paper up to the light. It looked
like a phone number.

(138) 518-1514

I didn't recognize the area code. However, it definitely looked like Basia's handwriting, and I was sure it
was important.

I snatched a piece of paper from a kitchen drawer and scrawled down the number even though I had already committed it to memory. Then I located the phone book amid the mess in my kitchen and searched through the listed area codes. There was no such U.S. area code as 138.

It could be a foreign number, but it was missing the critical country and city code. Besides, despite the layout, it just didn't feel like a phone number to me. I tapped the pencil against the table, studying the number. My mind searched through several possibilities before I realized I was breaking a code. It took me less than a minute. Each number represented the position of the letter in the alphabet and when I was finished I had written down one word on the paper: *Acheron.*

I had no idea what the hell that meant, so just to be on the safe side, I tried several other, more complex, codes. But nothing else made sense and the amateur code felt right to me because I was pretty sure it came from Basia. While she was a whiz with languages, writing code was definitely not her forte.

I looked carefully through the rest of the papers once again in case I missed something, but saw nothing else of interest. Of course, I couldn't read the other pages, so I could have been missing something incredibly vital. I was about to put the documents away, when I looked again at the page with the bogus phone number at the bottom. Without even knowing why I did it, I grabbed the pencil and erased the number. Call it instinct, call it long-distance telepathy between best friends, but I was sure that the number, whatever it meant, was for my eyes only.

I gathered the papers and put them back in the mailer. For a minute, I sat at the table, my chin in my hands, thinking what to do next. The phone number Mr. Middle Eastern Guy had scrawled on my arm seemed to blink under the florescent glow of the kitchen light. I reached into my pants pocket and pulled out Beefy's card. The number scowled back at me as if it were the Beefster himself. I compared the numbers and saw they were different. I frowned, disappointed. I guess a part of me had hoped they were working together. Then I could consider them one big threat instead of two separate ones.

I exhaled a deep breath. No way would I call either one of them until I had a better idea of what these papers contained. Basia had apparently been desperate enough to mail them to me and then disappear. She might be in trouble and these papers could be the only way to save her.

Resolutely I stood and went back to my bedroom. I switched my slacks for jeans and the purple blouse for a dark blue T-shirt. I pulled my long hair back into a ponytail, put on socks and tennis shoes and then rummaged around until I found my black tote bag. I shoved in the FedEx mailer, my wallet and keys and then added my address book just in case, jotting down Mr. Middle Eastern Guy's phone number there, as well. Then I took the paper with the phone number Basia had written on the papers and stuffed it in the back pocket of my jeans. I'd figure that out later.

For about fifteen minutes, I walked around my apartment turning lights on and off and pretending that I was getting ready for bed just in case I was being watched. Just after midnight I turned off the light in my bedroom. I slinked out the front door, locked the door and the deadbolt—not that it was keeping anyone out lately—and dashed down the side stairs of the complex. Not too many people knew about this exit and I hoped if I were being watched, my observers wouldn't expect me to come out there. Tonight I was afraid to use my car, so I slipped outside into the sticky summer air and headed out on foot to another apartment complex about two miles away. I cut through fields and backyards, checking continually to see if I were being followed.

Twenty minutes later I reached the Oakton Woods apartment complex and rang the buzzer for apartment 6D. It took about three minutes of frantic buzzing before I heard a sleepy voice through the intercom.

"Who is it?" he asked.

"It's me, Lexi Carmichael," I whispered, even though there was no one about. "It's urgent. Can I come up, please?"

A long silence. "Lexi? It's after midnight."

"Please, Paul. It's important."

There was a moment of hesitation before the buzzer sounded. Quickly I yanked the door open and slipped inside. I climbed all six flights and found Paul Wilks standing in the doorway in a rumpled T-shirt and shorts. He was forty-two years old with blond hair and a pretty good body. He was also divorced with three kids.

Paul was a linguist at the NSA and we'd been teamed together once on a project that we'd successfully completed. He'd gotten his job at the height of the Cold War when all the agencies were in the market for Slavic linguists. He was a decent guy, but slightly annoying. He'd asked me out once and I'd gone, but I hadn't felt any chemistry. Too much of an age gap, I guess. But apparently he'd felt something because it had been awkward between us for about two months while I politely turned down his requests for more dates. Then he had asked out Carla Romanov and things had gone back to normal.

Frankly I didn't care about any of that now and hoped he didn't either. Paul spoke fluent Polish and I desperately needed for him to translate the papers for me.

"Nice of you to visit," he commented, closing the door behind me. "Perhaps you could call ahead next time."

"Sorry," I said, shrugging my bag off my shoulders. "I know this isn't the most convenient time, but I have a bit of an emergency."

"Work related?"

"No, it's personal."

He ran his fingers through his hair and sat down on the couch. "What's up?"

"I've got these documents I need you to look at," I said, pulling out the FedEx mailer. I shook out the papers and handed them to him.

He leaned over and flicked on the lamp next to the couch. He took the papers and held them under the light. "Are you sure this can't wait until tomorrow?"

"I'm sure," I said, deciding it wasn't a good idea to bring him up to speed on the psychos with guns. He already thought I was nuts as it was.

Sighing, he leaned back on the couch and started to read. After reading the first page and setting it aside, he started the second. I couldn't stand the anticipation so I interrupted him.

"Well?" I asked. "What does it say?"

He shrugged. "It looks like a contract of some kind."

"A contract? What kind of contract?"

"It appears to be a contract providing for living arrangements. It outlines the conditions for a one-year lease on an apartment in Warsaw, a daily living stipend and car." He set the second page aside and kept reading. "Pretty generous actually for this part of the world."

"That's it?" I said in disbelief. "Who's the recipient?"

Paul flipped through the rest of the papers, scanning the documents. "It doesn't say. It looks like this is just the generic form. There are no names mentioned, just 'client' and 'recipient'."

I stood behind the couch and looked over his shoulder. "Are you sure? No names anywhere?"

He lifted a pale eyebrow at me and then resumed reading. I paced back and forth behind the couch. Why in the world had Basia sent me this strange document? What in the hell was so threatening about a contract without any names?

Paul finally set the papers aside and stood. "Sorry, but I don't see anything else exciting. But it is strange that the everyday details of the 'recipient's' life are very clearly spelled out. He or she has to agree to live in the apartment for a minimum of one year, be available for unannounced visits from so-called 'client,' go to specifically named doctors and medical institutions, withdraw money from one specific bank account and not to travel outside of Poland for the duration of the year."

"It sounds like an agreement between a man and his mistress," I mused aloud. "But why have a contract in the first place? Is this a new kind of guy thing?"

"You're asking me?"

"You're a guy, aren't you?"

"Yeah, but since when do I have mistresses lined up?"

"I don't know. I thought guys stayed current on this kind of thing."

He rolled his eyes and then spread the documents on the coffee table. "Lexi, there is one other thing of possible interest. I think I recognize the name of the company named here." He ran his fingertip beneath two words in Polish on page two.

"There's a company name?" I asked. "What is it?"

"I'm not one hundred percent sure of the translation. Let

me check it out tomorrow and I'll get back to you. May I ask where you got these?"

"Ah…from a friend," I said, remembering what Mr. Middle Eastern Guy had said about letting anyone at the NSA know about the papers. "Look, Paul, I need you to be especially discreet when you do your check tomorrow."

He looked up at me in surprise. "Why?"

"I can't go into it right now. But it's important. Discretion is imperative."

He sighed. "What have you gotten into this time, Lexi?"

"Nothing I can't handle," I said with a confidence I didn't feel. "I owe you big, Paul."

He stood and walked over to a nearby desk, pulling out a pad of paper. "Yes, you do. And I fully intend to collect. Dinner and dancing."

"What?" I squeaked, taking a step back. "Oh God, you don't want to see me dance. I'm telling you, it's not a pretty sight."

He smiled. "Remember, you owe me *big*. Big requires dancing for an equitable payoff. Besides, seeing how you woke me from a good dream, I think I've earned the right to see your fancy footwork. This Friday."

"This Friday?" I almost screeched. "That's blackmail."

"Take it or leave it," he said calmly.

I fumed for a moment while he leaned back on the couch and crossed his arms against his chest. "Well?" he asked.

I was desperate. "I thought you were going out with Carla Romanov."

He lifted his hands. "I haven't seen Carla for a couple of weeks. It didn't work out. We didn't have much in common."

"And we do?"

He leaned forward. "Look, I'll be straight with you. I'm hungry for female companionship. It's hard for me to get a date. I know it's hard for you, too, so think of it as me doing you a favor. Don't take it personally."

In some perverse way he was right, but on the other hand, he had insulted me. It didn't really matter which because I needed his help, so I was stuck.

"All right, dinner and one dance. No disco stuff."

"At least four dances, whatever music I want, and a minimum of one slow one."

"Two dances and one of them can be slow," I countered. "The music is up to you. That's my final offer."

"Deal," he said and then carefully copied the phrase down. "I'll stop by your cubicle tomorrow with the exact translation of the company name."

I thought for a moment, making an executive decision. "Actually, I'm not going to be in tomorrow. I've got a…ah, doctor's appointment. Can I call you instead?"

He narrowed his eyes. "I guess."

"Thanks. And, Paul, one more thing. Can I get you to give me a lift somewhere?"

"A lift? Right now? What's wrong with your car?"

"It's on the blink," I lied.

"The Miata?"

"The one and only."

"How did you get here?"

I pointed to my feet. "It's only a few miles and a good cardiovascular workout."

He looked at me as if I were crazy. Maybe I was. "Jesus, Lexi, why didn't you call me? It's the middle of the night. I could have come and got you. There could be all kinds of unsavory characters out and about at this time of the night."

Yeah, if he only knew. "I didn't want to trouble you too much," I said. "But, how about that ride now?"

He sighed. He seemed to do that a lot with me. "All right. Let me put some clothes on."

He disappeared back into the bedroom and returned wearing a pair of faded jeans, a white T-shirt and sandals. A set of car keys was in his hand. I gathered the papers and my bag. He locked up and we walked out to the parking lot. He had a nice car, a black BMW that he'd somehow managed to keep in the divorce settlement. I rode in it on our one and only date. It happened to be the most exciting thing about him.

Paul opened the door for me like a gentleman, which I liked, and I settled back against the soft leather cushions. He got in and started the car.

"If it's not too much trouble, could you take me to Guilford Street instead of my place?" I asked.

He looked at me for a long time and then turned off the engine. "Guilford Street? At this time of the night?"

"I've got to see some friends," I said.

"At one in the morning?"

"They're expecting me," I lied.

He raised an eyebrow at that. "They?"

"The Zimmerman twins," I explained. "I've got a computer problem."

Everyone at the NSA knew the Zimmerman twins. They were extremely odd people, identical twins marching to the beat of a completely different drummer. They were also incredible math and physics geniuses and had been the stars of the InfoSec department until they were lured away by a huge computer security firm in Baltimore for boatloads of money. Although they could have afforded a mansion the size of New Jersey, they still lived in the dinky town of Jessup in the same two-story house off Guilford that they had purchased a few years earlier when working for the NSA.

I had bonded with the twins at first because I was the one person they knew who could whip them both at Quake.

We also liked hanging out together, eating greasy pizza with anchovies, talking code and playing pinball. In fact, other than Basia, the twins are my closest friends.

Paul looked doubtful, but remembering we were talking about the wacky Zimmerman twins, he probably figured it was possible I wasn't lying. He tapped his fingers against the steering wheel, thinking.

"It will cost you," he finally said.

"Cost me?" I exclaimed. "More? For God's sake, Paul, I already agreed to dine and dance with you. What else could you possibly want?"

He smiled, his lips parting slowly. "A kiss."

I rolled my eyes, leaned over and pecked him on the cheek. "There. Can we go?"

He sighed. "No, Lexi. A *real* kiss. A good one. Friday night after dinner."

I shook my head. "Dinner, dancing and now a kiss? You've got to be kidding."

He took the keys out of the ignition and dangled them in front of my face. "Nope. No kidding. That's how much it costs for a one-way ride to the Zimmermans' house at one o'clock in the morning."

He had me good and he knew it. "Okay." I was really, really desperate. "One kiss, no tongue."

"No deal. I said a *good* kiss."

"All right, all right. A little tongue. But that's it!"

He smiled, put the keys back in the ignition and started the car. "I can work with that."

It was my turn to sigh. I was going to kill Basia the moment I saw her. She had no idea what she was putting me through.

Paul drove us in silence to the Zimmermans' house. I was relieved to see a light on in one of the windows. The twins had nocturnal tendencies, not unlike many computer geeks I knew, including myself. I got out of the car, smiled at Paul and told him I'd call tomorrow.

"I'm looking forward to Friday," he said, leaning across the passenger seat. "Wear something sexy."

Yeah, fat chance I'd do that. I pretended I didn't hear and waved as he backed out of the driveway and sped away.

I walked up the gravel driveway and rang the doorbell. After a minute, Xavier answered the door. I knew it was Xavier because he had a small scar over his right eyebrow where his brother had clocked him with a keyboard when they were arguing over the answer to a monalphabetic code. They were only four at the time.

"Hi, Xavier," I said. "Can I come in?"

He didn't seem surprised in the least to see me and held the door open. "Hey, Lexi," he said as I stepped across the threshold. "What's up?"

"I'm having the worst day of my life, and I need your help with something."

Xavier's twin, Elvis, walked into the room. I never ceased to be amazed that their mother had actually chosen the names Elvis and Xavier for her two boys.

Tonight the two brothers were dressed identically, which is really a miracle because they were two of the most absent-minded people I knew. I was surprised that they even remembered to dress, let alone coordinate what they wore. But it was just another mystery about the two of them that had already spawned a legend of mega proportions.

"Hey, Elvis," I said. "How are you doing?"

"You here to play Quake?" Elvis asked as if it were normal to get visitors at one o'clock in the morning who wanted to play computer games. Maybe they did.

"Not tonight, thanks," I said. "What I need is a favor."

"Okay," Elvis said. "What's up?"

I slid the bag off my shoulder and took out the documents from Basia. "Could you scan these and keep a copy on your drive?"

Elvis took the FedEx mailer. "Sure. But why can't you do it yourself?"

"Long story," I said, following Xavier and Elvis into the command room.

They called it the command room because they had transformed the living room/dining room into a high-tech operating center. They worked out of their home, going in to the firm in Baltimore only on rare occasions when the CEO required it. It worked well for everyone since the twins preferred their privacy and the big shots at Com-Quest would do anything to keep their star employees happy.

No matter how many times I'd been here, I still marveled at the setup. Large tables crowded with dozens of computers ringed the room. There were three or four spectacular flat panel displays per computer that permitted them to do several operations at once without switching windows. In the left-hand corner was the Linux cluster of thirty-two computers that Elvis and Xavier used to break encryption and do serious number crunching. To the left of those was an area with laptops, all running different systems in order to simulate and test a variety of software. The rest of the room was taken up by single computer units with multiple monitor displays of various sizes, boxes containing firewalls, and a huge number of routers, switches and cables. There were wires everywhere—snaking across the floor, lying atop the tables and even hanging from the ceiling.

The room was arctic cold with a specially ordered air-conditioning unit running twenty-four hours a day. I was frozen within the first two seconds in the room, but Elvis and Xavier wore short sleeves and didn't even have goose bumps. The room was filled with the comforting sounds of humming, blinking, whirring and clicking. In terms of their work, Elvis and Xavier complemented each other quite well. They were the legendary co-architects of computer security at most of the government's top-secret organizations. They were also stellar cryptologists, although neither had officially pursued that particular field. Yet.

Elvis was the network guru and Xavier the system's expert. Separate they were formidable. Together they were impregnable. Sheer and unadulterated computer geniuses. Even now I felt a twitch of envy.

"Want a beer?" Xavier asked me as I started to shiver.

"Yeah, and a blanket," I said. Actually I could have used a shot of alcohol a lot stronger than beer, but didn't think it was a good idea to suggest it at this point. Just in case I was accosted again at gunpoint for the third time today, I didn't want to be half-tossed.

Elvis brought me a beer and draped a blanket over my shoulder. He propelled me to an empty swivel chair and I sat down, extracting the papers from the mailer. I handed them to Elvis, who stacked them up on a nearby scanner and pressed a button. The soft whir of the machine started, pulling the paper through. I took a swig of the beer and watched as the material came up on the monitor.

"Polish," Elvis commented.

"Yeah," I said, surprised. "I didn't know you speak Polish."

"I don't. I just recognize the alphabet."

"Oh." I took another swig of the beer as my teeth started to chatter.

"What is it?" Xavier asked curiously, looking at the monitor over Elvis's shoulder.

"A contract of some kind," I said. "I think."

"You get them from Basia?" he asked.

Xavier had a major crush on Basia, but she never paid him the time of day. Granted he was a bit odd—okay, *really* odd—but by no means unattractive. Both he and Elvis were in their early twenties, tall and slender with brown hair and piercing blue eyes. Contrary to the unfair computer-geek stereotype, neither wore glasses repaired with tape or funky, oversized clothes. Okay, so they often dressed alike and weren't great conversationalists. Those things weren't my strong points either.

On the up side, they were filthy rich and could afford to keep any woman in the style of her choosing.

The problem was they didn't suffer fools easily. They were also strange in that intense, genius sort of way where they could talk about something for an hour and you wouldn't understand a single sentence of what they said. I guess it was a turn-off for some women. Since I sort of share their profession, I mostly understood what they said, but a lot of the time they left me in the dust, too. I suppose it would be a bit demoralizing day after day to realize the clear confines of your intellect in comparison to theirs.

"Yeah, Basia sent them to me," I said dejectedly. "Now, if I could only find out why."

"So what's with all the secrecy?" Elvis asked. "Is this something work-related?"

"No, I think Basia got mixed up in something real bad and I'm trying to help her out."

"Basia? What could Basia get mixed up in?" Xavier asked in surprise as if she were a virginal angel from heaven.

"I don't know," I answered. "But she sent me these papers for safekeeping. I've been…ah, approached by some people who want them. I'd like to keep at least one copy safe. And, in my opinion, there is no place safer in the world than your computer."

Of that I was absolutely certain. No one could possibly hack into their computer. It was better protected than the president's. I knew this for a fact because they were pretty much the sole architects of the president's computer security, among other things.

Then I pulled the piece of paper with the numbers Basia had jotted on the contract out of my jeans pocket and handed it to Elvis.

"What do you think this means?" I asked him.

"Is it code?"

"I think so."

"Who wrote it?"

"Basia, I think."

He eyed the numbers. "Acheron," he said and handed me back the paper.

"How do you do that so fast?" I asked, impressed.

He shrugged. "Practice."

Watching these guys work always floored me. "Well, do either of you know what Acheron means?"

"There is an Acheron in ancient Greek mythology," Xavier offered.

"Greek mythology," I said. "I thought it sounded vaguely familiar. What was his story again?"

"Acheron is not a person," Xavier replied. "It was one of the rivers of the Underworld. At the confluence of the rivers of Acheron and Styx, it is said that the hero Odysseus dug a pit and poured sacrificial blood into it to summon the ghosts of the dead."

"Ghosts of the dead," I murmured. "Weird."

"Acheron is also the name of a river in modern Greece, still reputed to give access to Hades," Elvis said.

Sheesh, how did they find room in their brains to store this kind of stuff? Who needed a Google search when they were around?

"I should add that Acheron is also a Belgian heavy metal band, famous for its violent sounds of apocalyptic rage," Xavier added. "Pretty dark stuff. Not for the faint of heart."

I made a mental note not to buy one of their albums. I had obtained more information than I bargained for and none of it particularly helpful.

"Do you think it could be something else in another code?" I asked.

Xavier took the paper from me. "I'll give it a thorough run-through in a bit."

"Thanks."

Elvis finished the scan, encrypted the file and handed me the papers in the mailer. I stuffed it in my bag.

"Could I get one of you to give me a lift home?" I asked, setting my empty beer bottle on a table and standing.

Elvis nodded and walked over to the table, picking up a pair of car keys. He didn't once ask how I had arrived at his house without a car in the middle of the night. Details like those didn't faze these guys. Which was one reason why I liked them so much—no extraneous conversation.

I asked Elvis to drop me off about a half mile from my apartment complex. He didn't raise an eyebrow, simply pulled the truck over to the side of the road and let me out. He gave me a cheery wave, did a U-turn and sped out of sight.

I crept up to my apartment complex, entered the side door using my key and dragged my tired body up three flights of stairs. I opened my apartment door, keeping the keys in my hand to use as a weapon. Thankfully no one tried to grab me or assault me with a gun.

Yet.

I flipped the lock, set the chain, turned the deadbolt and wedged a chair beneath the doorknob. I wasn't taking any chances. I made my way back to the bedroom and turned on the light in the bathroom. If anyone was watching, it would seem as if I'd just awakened to go pee. The same mess was there as when I left, but at least I didn't see any strange men with guns in my shower.

I breathed a sigh of relief and sat down on the edge of the bed, removing my shoes and clothes. I dug around in the piles of clothes on the floor and found a T-shirt and pulled it over my head. I brushed my teeth, threw everything off the bed and jumped in, stuffing my bag with the FedEx mailer under my pillow. A quick glance at the clock showed it was two-thirty. I was exhausted.

Thank God, tomorrow was a new day. I just hoped I lived long enough to see it.

THREE

My ALARM WENT off at six-thirty like it always did. Except this morning I could barely pry my eyes open. I slammed down the snooze button and returned my head to the pillow, marveling at how comfortable and soft it was. That's when I remembered it should be lumpy since the FedEx mailer and my bag were there.

I sat up so quickly I got dizzy and snatched away the pillow. No bag. Wide awake now, I removed the other pillow. Nothing. I leapt out of bed and searched around the floor for my bag or the mailer.

Nada.

I stripped off all the sheets, looked beneath the bed and waded through the mess on my floor, even though logic told me the papers were no longer in the apartment. Then an even more worrisome thought crossed my mind. I ran to my front door. The deadbolt was locked, but the chain dangled loose and the chair sat neatly to one side. My black bag sat on the chair, but when I looked inside, the FedEx mailer was gone. My wallet, keys and address book hadn't been touched.

"No way!" I exclaimed. Had someone sneaked back into my apartment while I was sleeping and stolen my bag right out from under my head?

Not only did the sheer audacity of it shock me, but it also royally pissed me off. I felt violated, invaded and pretty darn stupid. How could I have slept through an intruder entering into my bedroom and sticking his hand beneath my head? Sheesh. And I work for the nation's top security agency?

Just to be sure, I did a more thorough search of my apartment. No FedEx mailer in sight. I sat down on one corner of my bed and surveyed the room's mess. It seemed to be a reflection of my life, and I wasn't any too happy about that.

Sighing, I picked up the telephone and made a call to my boss. I knew Jonathan wouldn't be in yet, so I left a message on his machine that I wasn't feeling well. I wanted to spend the day hunting Basia down and getting to the bottom of this mystery.

I took a quick shower and managed to find a clean pair of underwear among the mounds of stuff on my floor. I pulled on a sleeveless T-shirt sans bra and a pair of shorts. Since it was likely to be another sweltering summer day in the nation's capital, I scraped my hair back in a ponytail and put on a pair of sunglasses and sandals.

Before heading out, I tried Basia's number again, but her machine picked up. This time I didn't leave a message.

I walked out to where I had parked the Miata. It was still there. Thank God, at least that hadn't been stolen while I slept. I checked the trunk and underneath the car before opening the door, then slid in and popped the hood, thinking it might be prudent to check for a car bomb. I braced the hood open and stared at the guts of my car. There were lots of black metal cylinder thingies among the tubes and wires. It smelled like grease and exhaust. After a few minutes of thoughtful contemplation, I decided all those wires and cylinders could indeed be a car bomb or, on the other hand, just the engine to my car. Since I didn't feel much like staring at it all morning, I decided to live dangerously.

I slammed the hood closed, got back in the driver's seat and, taking a deep breath, put the key in the ignition and

turned it. The car roared to life. No kaboom. I took that
as a good sign.

Since it was a hot, sunny morning, I put the top down
and drove directly to the only Dunkin' Donuts in Jessup.
I hoped no one from work would be there to see me and
report to my boss that I was playing hooky. That was no
joke, because the NSA almost single-handedly supports
the place. Thankfully, there was no one I knew except the
people behind the counter, who call me by name. After
perfunctory greetings, I purchased a large Diet Coke and
a chocolate éclair. Nothing like a little chocolate to start
the day right. I ate the éclair in the car, licking the cream
off my fingers while I formed a plan of action. After a
few minutes of contemplating, fueled by a serious chocolate rush, I decided to start at the source of the problem.

Basia.

Driving into Washington so early, I missed a good
chunk of the morning rush hour. Traffic isn't so bad if
you can slip into the city before seven-thirty. However,
upon reaching my destination, I drove around for fifteen
minutes looking for a parking place before giving up and
parking illegally in an alley. I didn't intend to stay long,
but the parking police in Washington have noses like radar
and can sniff out an illegally parked car five miles away.
The tickets cost something outrageous like two hundred
dollars and your first-born child. Most people don't pay
them out of principle, but that isn't so easy to do when you
work at the NSA.

I hiked the two blocks to Basia's apartment complex
and let myself in with her key. She had mine and I now
began to wonder if Mr. Middle Eastern Guy hadn't stolen
it from her and used it to let himself into my apartment.

Basia lived on the first floor in apartment 1A. I rang the

brass knocker. No one answered. I tried the door and found it locked. I used the key to let myself in and was not overly surprised to see her place as trashed as mine.

I felt anger rise inside me as I walked through her tiny place, looking at the books, papers, clothes and junk on the floor. There was no sign of Basia and no sign of where she might have fled. I flipped through some papers on her desk, but nothing jumped out at me. Her computer was turned off, so I turned it on to see if there was anything interesting on it.

Her password stopped me for a full twenty-seven seconds—my third try at guessing it was the charm. She'd used her birthday as a password. I'd have to talk to her about that. I scanned her hard drive but wasn't sure what I was looking for and nothing screamed "important."

I then rummaged about in her closet and noticed that one of her suitcases was missing. I didn't see her purse anywhere either. Walking into the kitchen, I saw the phone message light blinking.

The first message was from her boss at Berlitz, wondering why she had missed work yesterday. The second one was from me, the third from some guy named Finn who said he really, *really* needed to talk to her, and two more from her mother. Uh, oh. I guess I had set off the mother alert after all.

There were a few hang-ups in between and the last message was from someone named Lars at Anderson's Karate Academy reminding her about her lesson on Thursday night. Again I felt a sweep of surrealism. Basia and karate? What was wrong with this picture?

I found the Yellow Pages tossed in a heap on the kitchen floor and looked up the address for Anderson's Karate Academy. It was located in Laurel, Maryland, not too far from my neck of the woods. I jotted the address and phone number down on a piece of paper and stuffed it in my jeans. And since I had the book open, I flipped through the pages until I came to the section on burglar alarms and monitoring. No way was I going to spend one more night in my apartment that, even locked, apparently had a revolving door. Since the phone was handy, I called a few of the firms listed in the book, finally choosing a home security device from the one company that could install it later in the afternoon.

I left Basia's apartment, carefully locking it up behind me—as if it made a difference. After yesterday, I'd never feel the same about a lock and key again.

In my car I pulled out a map and noted the location of Anderson's Karate Academy. Pulling my shades back on, I headed north on the interstate. Since the traffic was coming into the city and I was going out, there was no back up.

It took me about twenty minutes and I drove slowly, looking carefully at the street numbers so I wouldn't miss it. I soon saw a small strip mall and a sign for the karate studio. It wouldn't be open at a little after eight o'clock in the morning, but I wanted to check it out anyway.

I parked in an empty spot and walked up to the building. The place was dark, but I pressed my nose against the glass and peered inside. It had ceiling-to-floor mirrors, several large mats and a bunch of cool-looking trophies with guys kicking their legs above their heads. Just as I was about to leave, something moved inside the studio. I squinted and pressed tighter against the glass.

To my surprise, a huge blond-haired guy walked in and sat on one of the mats. He was dressed in one of those white karate outfits with a logo on the back I couldn't make out. He positioned himself cross-legged on the mat, closed his eyes and didn't move.

I banged on the window and after a moment, he rose

and walked to the door. He unlocked it and shook his head, clearly annoyed by my interruption.

"We don't open until one o'clock," he announced.

I detected the faint trace of a Scandinavian accent. "Sorry to bother you, but I'm looking for a guy named Lars."

He stared at me. "I'm Lars," he finally said. This guy was really huge—six feet four, at least. Thick corded muscles stood out on his neck. He had clear blue eyes and a nice tan, and good health practically radiated from his pores.

"Do you own this place?" I asked.

He looked me up and down, probably noticing the smear of chocolate I'd gotten on my T-shirt from the chocolate éclair. "Who are you?"

"I'm a friend of Basia Kowalski's," I replied. "She told me she'd signed up for karate here."

I was pretty sure I saw a flicker of surprise in his eyes. "I've got a lot of students," he said casually.

"Basia has short brown hair, brown eyes and is very outgoing," I offered. "She has a class on Thursday."

He shrugged. "Sounds like a lot of girls I know. But even if I did know who you were talking about, I don't discuss my clients."

I decided to play it straight with this guy. "Look, I'm her best friend. She's missing. I'm worried and I'm trying to find her."

Lars stared at me for several seconds as if measuring my honesty, then stepped aside, silently inviting me in. I entered and he closed the door behind me and locked it. I pushed my sunglasses to the top of my head and followed him to a small office in the back of the building. The place smelled of sweat, hard work and dirty socks. He motioned for me to sit in a nearby chair, so I did.

"Now, what's your name?" he asked, sitting behind a desk and clasping his hands together.

"Lexi Carmichael," I said, holding out my hand. I had this urge to touch him to see if his muscles were real. I was also starting to get a fairly good idea why Basia had signed up for karate.

He reached across the desk and took my hand. His skin was warm and he had a firm handshake. I held on a little too long and flushed in embarrassment when he pulled away.

"So, why do you think Basia is missing?" he asked, leaning back in his chair.

"Then you do remember her."

"I usually remember all the pretty girls I meet," he answered, shrugging. "She's a new student."

"Yes, well, she left me a certain matter to attend to and things are sort of falling apart. I need desperately to talk to her, but I can't find her."

"Why would you think I might know anything about her whereabouts?"

"It's a long shot," I admitted. "I just thought it odd that Basia didn't tell me about signing up for karate. If you knew Basia well, you'd understand that undertaking karate is a life-altering decision for her and one she'd positively have to share with her best friend—me. See, she's not the athletic type. So I thought maybe her disappearance might somehow be connected to her very odd decision to sign up for karate."

Lars leaned forward, his big elbows on the desk. "Do you know what Tae Kwon Do is?"

I lifted an eyebrow at the abrupt subject change. "A tasty chicken dish?"

His lips twitched. "Tae Kwon Do is a system of unarmed self-defense that originated in China and was further refined in Korea. In Japan it evolved into the form we now know as karate. I teach both of these martial arts, as well as Wing Chun—a kind of Chinese kung fu."

"Wing Chun? Wait a minute, I thought they were a rock band."

He chuckled. "That was Wang Chung, and they have nothing to do with martial arts. And for that matter, nothing to do with good music, either."

"That's no kidding," I agreed emphatically.

"Anyway, karate is more than just a sport to many people," Lars said.

"So, you're saying that you don't have to be athletic to do karate."

"It certainly helps to be athletic, yes. But it's not necessary. Many people, especially women, don't see it as just a sport. They see it as a self-empowering exercise, and in some cases, an exercise in self-protection."

That stopped me cold. "You mean Basia might have been afraid of someone?"

He lifted a blond eyebrow. "It's possible, I suppose. Frankly, she never said so to me. Whatever the case, martial arts are excellent ways of improving self-discipline and self-defense, as well as a good way to stay in shape."

I studied him thoughtfully. "Are you Swedish?"

He smiled. "Good ear."

"So I'm right?"

"I was born and raised there until a few years ago. I'm an American now, so it's politically correct to refer to me as Swedish-American."

"How did you meet Basia? Did she just show up here one day and ask if she could start lessons?"

Again I saw something flash in his eyes. Whether it was alarm or wariness, I wasn't sure. But it was something out of the ordinary and it made me a bit uneasy.

"She called me, I think. I'm in the Yellow Pages after all."

Call it feminine instinct or a gut feeling, but I was certain he was lying. But why?

I leaned back in my chair and crossed my legs. "So, she looked you up in the Yellow Pages and then called you to sign up for classes? That's strange. There are several karate studios a lot closer to her place than yours."

"I've got a good reputation and an excellent word of mouth among my students."

Yeah, like Basia would mingle with people who took karate. If only he knew how ridiculous that sounded. "How many lessons has she had so far?"

"One," he said. "Last Thursday."

"Do you call all your students to remind them of forthcoming lessons?"

That question took him by surprise, but he recovered quickly. "Sometimes," he said. "Especially the new ones."

I stood up. There was no more information I could get here. "Well, thank you for your time, Mr...."

"Anderson," he supplied, standing and walking around the desk.

"Oh, as in Anderson's Karate Academy," I said. *Stupid.* I was really an amazing detective. "I guess that makes sense."

He smiled and I realized just how big he was. He towered above me, every inch solid muscle. "You must call me Lars."

"Okay, Lars."

He stood next to me, studying my form. "Have you ever considered trying the martial arts, Miss Carmichael?"

"Me?" The word came out as a snort. "I don't think so."

"Why not? You have the body of a martial arts expert, you know. Long legs, long arms and a graceful way of carrying yourself."

Graceful? Me? My cheeks warmed. "Well, no… I—I couldn't…" I stammered. Did he really think I was graceful?

"I'll tell you what," he said, leaning close to my face. "Come in for a couple of free lessons. It won't cost you a thing, and you can see if you like the challenge."

I was still amazed that he thought I was capable of co-ordinating my body movements. I had never been much of an athlete and stamina was a word that didn't exist in my vocabulary.

"Are you serious?"

"Tomorrow night, eight o'clock," he said in a firm voice. "It's Basia's class, too. Maybe you'll see her here. Wear a soft T-shirt, sweat pants and no socks. I think you'll enjoy yourself."

He put a hand on my shoulder and I could feel the heat emanate all the way down to my toes. "Okay," I said. I just kind of hoped he would never move his hand.

Before I knew it, he had propelled me to the door. I took a step outside and Lars locked up behind me. I blinked in the sunlight, pulled my sunglasses back down on my nose and walked to the car.

Graceful, I thought, adding a spring to my step. Maybe after a few karate lessons, I could even be dangerous.

"I'm Lexi Carmichael, black belt in karate," I said to the Miata. "My hands and legs are licensed killing weapons."

I slid behind the wheel, liking the feeling of being in control—especially after what had happened to me yesterday. Maybe a couple of lessons in self-defense wouldn't be such a bad idea.

Feeling better, I pulled into a nearby McDonald's drive-thru, ordering a Diet Coke and a large order of hash browns. I ate the crunchy potatoes in the car, sitting in the parking lot. After the last one was gone, I wiped the grease from my hands with a napkin and got out to use a pay phone in front of the building.

I called the main number of the NSA and rattled off Paul Wilks's extension. After two rings, he picked up.

"Hi, Paul," I said. "You got that translation for me yet?"

"Sure do," he said, his voice cheerful. "You ready for this?"

"Fire away," I said. An ambulance screamed down the road, so I pressed a finger to my ear to hear him.

"Hey, I thought you had a doctor's appointment," he said.

"I do," I lied. "I'm on my way there now. What's the translation?"

He paused. "Look, you're not going to back out of our date Friday night after I give you this info, are you? I already told half the office."

I groaned. "For God's sake, Paul. Why did you do that?"

"Insurance. You gave me your word, Lexi. Friday night and all the trimmings. I'm looking forward to it."

I rolled my eyes. "I know what I promised. I'm good for my word. The company name, please."

"Okay. I'm pretty sure it's Bright Horizons. I considered a couple of other combinations, but this one seems right to me. Just in case, I checked out the address on the contract for you and it fits. A company with the same name is registered there in Warsaw."

"Bright Horizons? It's a Polish company?"

"No. American."

"Well, that's interesting."

"Why? There are hundreds of American companies operating in Poland."

I supposed that was true. "Where is their home base in the States?"

"Richmond, Virginia."

Rather close to home. "What kind of company are they?" I asked. "Technology?"

"Sorry, I don't know."

"Did you check the internet?"

"Do I look like your personal secretary?"

I sighed. "Guess not. Well, I gotta go. Just tell me you were discreet."

"It's my middle name."

"Thanks, Paul. I mean it."

"Thank me on Friday," he said and hung up.

I replaced the receiver and headed back to my car. I sat there for a few minutes, trying to piece together all the strange pieces of information I had gathered. I thought I was pretty darn good at finding threads and putting them together to form something that made sense. But I just didn't have enough information to get a big picture here. More input was needed.

I drove home, trying to figure out what to do next. Upon my arrival, I did a thorough search of the apartment to make certain no unauthorized persons had entered while I was gone. The place was clean of lurkers, but still a disaster area. Even more depressing, I knew I had to do laundry today or I'd have nothing to wear to work tomorrow. But first things first. I needed to check the internet.

I sat down at my desk and booted up the system. I may have a tiny apartment and not much in the way of furnishings, but I was damn proud of my computer. My laptop was considered "geek chic" among most computer aficionados, myself included. I liked it because it was sleek, elegant and lightweight. Next to Basia, it was my best friend.

I Googled "Bright Horizons" and "Richmond, Virginia" and came up with one hit.

Bingo.

I clicked on the link and the Bright Horizons website

appeared with a pretty logo of a sun rising over the horizon while a happy couple held a smiling infant in their arms.

"Well, lookie here," I murmured. "A fertility clinic."

The Bright Horizons clinic was actually part of a larger medical research company called CGM, Inc. CGM had been founded in 1952 in Richmond as a medical clinic and expanded into a research facility in 1964. In 1984 Dr. Geoff Sandberg launched the Bright Horizons fertility clinic in Richmond, using various techniques of in vitro fertilization. It appeared that Bright Horizons had been quite profitable for CGM, boasting a sixty-five percent pregnancy rate per embryo transfer over the past two years, which must be good if they bragged about it online.

In 1990 CGM expanded into biotechnology, receiving a slew of prestigious academic grants and attracting top medical names in the field. The company had expanded internationally and currently had offices in London, Morocco, Genoa, Amsterdam, Warsaw and Paris. They currently employed over twenty thousand people worldwide.

I sat back and linked my fingers behind my neck. Okay, there was nothing necessarily sinister here. Bright Horizons had apparently contracted Basia to translate some documents for their international clients. No biggie, right? Except why had she sent the documents to me, why were two guys with guns ready to kill to get them, and what did the word Acheron written in code at the bottom of page three mean? Just thinking of Acheron prompted me to do another search of that word, but I came up with nothing more interesting than what the twins had told me.

It was clear I needed further expert assistance.

I drove over to the Zimmermans' and knocked on the door. Elvis answered this time and smiled when he saw me. He still wore the same clothes he had on last night and I wondered if he had slept. In fact, I wondered if he ever slept. Maybe geniuses didn't need sleep. Funny how he didn't look the worse for wear, whereas I was sure I looked like death warmed over.

"Hey, Lexi. Long time, no see. Come in."

"Sorry to keep bugging you guys," I said, stepping across the threshold. "But things are getting weird."

"Yeah?" said Xavier, coming out of the command room. "What kind of weird?"

I went to the couch, picked up the blanket and wrapped it around my shoulders. I decided to be straight with the twins and told them everything that had happened to me since yesterday evening.

They listened with their usual intense focus, and when I finished, Elvis leaned back against the cushions, stroking his chin. "Bright Horizons is the name of the company, you say?"

"Yes," I answered.

"You know anything about the people who work there?" he asked.

"Only what's in their bios on the website."

"Was the name of their IT guy listed?"

"I don't know," I admitted, feeling as though I'd failed a homework assignment. "I didn't check it."

But I instantly knew why they wanted to know. Elvis and Xavier would check to see how good the IT guy was— possibly tracing him to his home, finding out what kind of broadband service he was running and what kind of firewall and routers he had in place. It's much easier to break into someone's home computer, steal a password and then log on to the company's server using that method. If not, they wanted to know if they'd heard of this guy and how capable he was. They would look and exploit any vulnerability, including personnel, without being detected. It's what they did best.

I liked the fact that the twins were careful and thorough; they did their homework first. I guess that's what made them the best in the country, perhaps the world.

"You say that the parent company CGM, Inc. is big," Xavier murmured, speaking more to himself than to us. "And international. They've likely got lots of money. My bet is they've got a good IDS system."

Any company worth their salt had a good intrusion detection system, but some systems were better than others.

"Unless they outsource for their protection," Elvis said.

"True," Xavier acknowledged. "Only one way to find out."

"Let's take a look," Elvis said, standing.

That's what I love about these guys. No challenge too big, no company too impenetrable.

The twins sat down at adjacent computer terminals. I hovered behind them, watching with awe as Xavier quickly accessed an account in Singapore, and Elvis one in Budapest. From there they hopped across the country, leaving a trail that would lead nowhere. Then they began their investigation of the computer security of CGM, Inc.

At this point, the twins' rapid and unconventional maneuvering left me in the dust. I knew theoretically what they were trying to do, but had no understanding how they were going about it. I guess that's why they get paid the big bucks and I don't.

During the session, Elvis and Xavier brainstormed constantly in a computer language I didn't understand, their fingers flying over the keyboard so fast they were a blur. I was afraid to speak in case I interrupted their flow of concentration. So I just stood there uselessly—ready to offer moral support if needed.

After about ten minutes, Xavier suddenly slammed a fist on the keyboard.

"Backspace, backspace!" he shouted to Elvis. "Abort!"

Elvis's fingers hammered out some rapid-fire commands. Then he swiveled around his chair and looked at me.

"Abort what?" I said nervously. "What happened?"

"Someone was scanning us back."

"Shoot. I guess that means the company has a good IDS system," I mourned.

Elvis frowned, looking slightly offended. "Good, yes. But it won't keep us out."

I believed that one hundred percent.

"No it won't," Xavier agreed, stretching his arms above his head like he had just run a marathon. In a way, I guess he had. "We'll get in sooner or later. The question is—how much time do we have?"

"I don't know," I answered. "Based on the fact that I'm being chased around by guys with guns and Basia has mysteriously disappeared, I'd say the sooner the better. But truthfully, even if you do break in to CGM, I don't know what I'm looking for."

"How about a file called Acheron?" Elvis suggested.

I glanced over at Xavier. "Find anything different with that code I gave you?"

He shook his head. "No and it feels amateur, so I'm going with Acheron, as well."

That had been my feeling exactly. "Okay, then let's stay with Acheron. Right now, it's my only clue. I don't know how it's connected to what's going on, but Basia wrote it on those documents for a reason."

Elvis sat back, thinking. I know he was thinking because he always puts his finger against his chin and taps it while staring into space. Even Xavier didn't interrupt him, although I suspect he was thinking, too. I guess I was the only one in the room who wasn't thinking. I was too busy worrying.

"You know, Elvis, we could do this a lot quicker if we brought some help on board."

"Help? What kind of help?" I asked. I didn't want to get anyone else involved, or for that matter, in trouble. I was already up to my neck in deep doo-doo for asking the twins to hack into a private company. And frankly I didn't want to sink under completely and disappear into the dark void of criminal activity, dragging everyone else along with me.

Elvis looked at his brother and shook his head. "No way."

"Why not?" Xavier said.

"Too risky."

"I've been wanting to meet him."

"Not under these circumstances."

"Excuse me," I broke in, exasperated. "Can someone tell me what the hell you two are talking about?"

"Slash," Xavier said simply.

"Slash?" I repeated in disbelief. "As in *the* Slash? Come on, you guys really don't believe this guy exists, do you?"

They both looked at me as if I were a child. "Of course he exists," Xavier said.

I wasn't so sure. There was a running legend at the NSA about Slash, who was supposedly a brilliant hacker and computer programmer. The story went that the NSA brought Slash aboard after the Zimmerman twins defected to the public sector. His duty—to modify the government's security programs enough to protect them from the two young men who essentially created them. Most people believed Slash was really a team of thirty or more computer experts working around the clock on the best equipment money could buy. Others said Slash was a twelve-year-old genius kid who was protected 24/7 by the FBI like some kind of national treasure.

I happened to be among those who didn't believe this so-called Slash was real and suspected the government had made him up solely to provide an illusion of security to a system that was hopelessly compromised after the twins left. But I suppose that if the government could make the twins believe Slash existed, then half their job was done.

"Have you two lost your freaking minds?" I said, aghast. "If he is real, he could turn us in. He'd be compelled to turn us in. We could go to prison. Forever."

Elvis looked amused. "Don't be so macro-dramatic, Lexi. Slash is one of us."

Us was apparently the exclusive hacker club. To them, it was that simple. To me, it wasn't.

"I'm not kidding, you guys," I said. "It's not worth it. It's not *that* important."

Elvis's blue eyes focused on me thoughtfully. "Your life is at risk here, Lexi, and Basia's, too. People are aiming guns at you and breaking into your apartment. Slash could easily help us with this."

I was touched by their concern, but scared to death that I was going to get them into serious trouble. "I thought you just said this was too risky," I pointed out to Elvis.

"I changed my mind," he said, shrugging.

"Then change it back. I've got a bad feeling about this," I warned.

"You've got to trust us, Lexi," Xavier said. "You need a quick, thorough look at that company and this is the fastest way to do it."

"I *do* trust you," I said emphatically. "But what if Slash is not trustworthy? What if he really is a consortium of federal computer experts ready to arrest our butts for hacking?"

Xavier laughed. "You think we'd go into this without protecting ourselves first? Come on, Lexi. Have a little faith. We'll just send Slash a message…drop an invitation, to say so."

"An invitation?" I repeated suspiciously. I had no idea what he was talking about. "In what way do you plan to do that?"

"The *right* way," Elvis said, his eyes softening. I guess he kind of had a soft spot for me. Especially when I was completely clueless, like now.

"Do you even know how to reach him?" I said. "You just can't send a message blindly." I think I started to sound hysterical. "And what if this so-called invitation falls into the wrong hands?"

Elvis sighed. He did that when he got tired of explaining things to me. Which, unfortunately, happened more often than I cared to admit.

"I'll leave a message that only Slash can read in a place only he would find it," he explained. "If Slash is a consortium of experts, as you believe, they will neither find nor understand the message. But if he is one of us, he will. And I guarantee you, he'll come."

He spoke with such confidence, I almost believed him. But by now my stomach hurt and was well on its way to developing an ulcer.

Elvis gently touched my cheek. "You're so cute when you're worried. But you shouldn't question our methods."

He turned back to the computer and typed for a few minutes. After a moment, he stood and stretched his lean form, arms over his head. "Done. We'll see if he comes."

I looked from Xavier to Elvis and realized I'd been summarily dismissed. "So that's it?" I asked uncertainly. "Now what?"

"We wait," Xavier said. "Either he shows or he doesn't.

And in the meantime, we keep looking for a way into the company."

Elvis walked me to the door. "You've got your car today?" he asked.

"I do," I said, pulling my sunglasses out of my bag and putting them on. "Thanks again for everything, Elvis. I mean it."

"For you, Lexi, anytime. You're pretty optimum for a chick."

That was probably the nicest thing he'd ever said to me, even if it was in a backhanded sexist kind of way, and it made me feel better. Especially since guilt was eating away at me for having involved them in the first place.

I left the house and hopped into my car. It was past noon and I decided my stomach hurt not because of nerves, but because I was starving. I drove to Taco Bell, went through the drive-thru and ordered three tacos and a Diet Pepsi. I ate one taco in the car at a stoplight, spilled some hot sauce on my T-shirt and sighed because now I *really* had to do laundry.

I pulled into the parking lot at my apartment complex and picked up the bag with the remaining two tacos and my Diet Pepsi. I juggled the bag and cup while opening the complex door and then trudged up three flights of stairs. I unlocked my door and peeked in cautiously. I didn't hear anything suspicious and no one reached out to grab me, so I stepped inside and breathed a sigh of relief. I closed and locked the door and then walked into the kitchen.

Sitting at the table, drinking one of my Diet Cokes, was Beefy.

"Hey, Lexi," he said, smiling at me. "About time you got here."

FOUR

I DROPPED THE bag with my tacos on the floor and heard a sickening splat. Beefy waved a hand at the empty chair, motioning for me to sit. I didn't see the gun, but I was one hundred percent certain he had it underneath his tacky polyester blazer.

"Sorry to startle you," he said. "You weren't around, so I let myself in. You really need to get a maid, you know. You live like a pig."

My initial fright faded, turning into anger. I was tired of my apartment turning into Grand Central Station.

"What do you want?" I snapped, picking my tacos off the floor and plopping into the chair. I opened up the bag and frowned at the mess that had once been my lunch.

He feigned a hurt look. "Have you forgotten our little talk yesterday? And why didn't you go to work today?"

"What are you, my mother?"

He held out his hand. "The documents."

"You're too late," I said. "Someone already stole them."

"What?" he exclaimed, leaping out of the chair. For a terrifying moment I thought he'd lunge across the table at me.

"Someone stole them," I repeated, trying to calm him. "I thought it might have been you, but now my money is on Mr. Middle Eastern Guy."

"Mr. Middle Eastern Guy?" He stared at me in surprise. "What the hell are you talking about?"

I tried to act casual even though my heart was pounding. I stuck my fingers in the taco mess and licked off some sour cream. "I kind of hoped you were working together, but now I see that isn't likely."

His eyes narrowed. "I work alone. Who the hell is Mr. Middle Eastern Guy?"

"How would I know? He was here in my apartment waiting for me when I came home from my parents'. He wanted the documents from Basia just like you. He held a gun to my chest and had evidently tossed the place searching for them."

"What did he look like?"

"Dark hair, dark skin, dark clothing. Accent. Big gun."

"And from this you extrapolated Middle Eastern descent?"

"Hey, I've been to college. I took world geography."

Beefy didn't look convinced. "So you just gave him the papers?"

"I didn't give him anything. I didn't have the papers. My neighbor gave them to me after he left. They were apparently delivered while I was at my parents'. He must have doubled back and stolen them after I went to sleep."

Beefy slammed his fist on the table, causing me to jump. "You went to sleep without calling me to tell me you had the papers?"

"It was the middle of the night," I said, a little of the fright coming back. "I thought you'd be asleep. I didn't want to disturb you. I had planned on calling you first thing in the morning. But once I discovered they were stolen, I was too afraid. I didn't want to make you angry."

He growled, his gold tooth looking like some kind of weapon that could shoot out of his head. He had started to turn red, too, which wasn't a good sign.

"I told you to call me before you did anything," he yelled.

"I know, I know," I said, holding up my hands. "I'm sorry. I fell asleep. Sue me. It had been a long day."

He swore under his breath. "And this man just stole them from you while you slept? You didn't hear anything?"

"Not a peep."

"You left them out in the open? Didn't you at least have the foresight to hide them?"

I shifted uncomfortably. "I tried."

He narrowed his eyes. "What's that supposed to mean?"

"I, ah, put them under my pillow for safekeeping."

He stared at me, clearly flabbergasted. "You mean to say he stole them out from under your head while you slept?"

"That would be the winning scenario."

He shook his head. "And you call yourself among those who protect America's security and freedom? How in the world did you get a job at the NSA?"

I lifted my shoulders. "Can I help it if I take tests well? And might I mention that appearances can be deceiving? Ronald Reagan made movies with chimpanzees and he still led us out of the Cold War."

Beefy stood and started pacing in my tiny kitchen. It meant he took two steps forward and two steps back. It started to make me dizzy. Finally he stopped and looked at me.

"Did this Mr. Middle Eastern Guy say why he wanted the papers?" he asked.

"He wasn't exactly chatty. But, like you, he knew Basia had sent them to me." Apparently everyone else in the entire universe had known except me.

He stared at me for a long moment, assessing, weighing his options. "Did you take a peek at the papers?"

"No way," I lied. "After my encounter with you and then Mr. Middle Eastern Guy, I didn't even want to know what was in there."

"Are you telling the truth, little girl?" he asked, bending

down close to me. I smelled garlic on his breath and tried not to gag. "I can tell if you're lying."

"I'm not lying," I said, hoping I sounded convincing because I had this weird feeling that my life depended on it.

Before he could say anything else, the doorbell rang. Startled, I looked at him, unsure what I should do.

"Answer it," he said. "And no funny stuff." He patted his blazer and I got the message loud and clear.

I opened the door. A young, skinny guy about nineteen stood there. He had a bad case of acne and reeked of High Karate aftershave. I knew it was High Karate because my brothers had once drenched me in it as punishment when I told my dad they'd been sneaking out. The scent of it haunts me to this day.

"Hello, Miss Carmichael," he said, looking at a piece of paper attached to a clipboard. "My name is Jesse Kirkpatrick and I'm with SuperProtect Alarm Systems. You requested a system to be installed?"

"That would be me," I said, trying not to wrinkle my nose. "Jesse, would you mind waiting here just a sec?"

He looked puzzled, but shrugged. "Sure."

I shut the door and walked back to the kitchen. Beefy was standing with his back against the refrigerator, his hand resting beneath his blazer. "Who is it?" he asked.

"Home improvement," I said. "Look, would you mind if he came in and did his thing? It will only take a few minutes and I really need to get this done this afternoon."

His eyes narrowed. "What are you having done?"

I didn't see how I could lie about it. "A home security system."

He looked at me incredulously and then laughed. "You're a real card, Lexi. All right, let him in."

I returned to the door and let Jesse in. "Thanks for coming on such short notice," I said.

"No problem. We aim to please every customer at SuperProtect." He lifted a paper. "You want the standard alarm system?"

I looked over at Beefy who had walked into the hallway and leaned casually against the wall, watching us. "Not anymore. If possible, I want the best system you have."

"That would be our wireless system. But it doesn't come cheap."

"I'm sure I'll get my money's worth," I assured him.

"All right, ma'am. The wireless system it is."

I felt depressed when he called me "ma'am". I was going to turn twenty-five next week with nothing to show for it except that kids now called me "ma'am".

"Where shall I put the main pad?" Jesse asked.

I motioned to the wall near the front door and he nodded, returning to his truck and coming back with a large toolbox and an alarm pad.

Beefy jerked his head to the side, motioning that I should return to the kitchen. He had a gun, so I did what he wanted. He sat down at the table, so I opened the fridge and got out a Diet Coke.

"Hand me one, too," Beefy said.

"I've got regular Coke, you know," I said.

He patted his stomach. "No, thanks. I'm watching my weight."

Sighing, I tossed him a can. He caught it and popped the top. "We need to finish our conversation," he said.

"Okay," I agreed. Anything to get him out of my apartment. Then I could turn on my spanking new alarm system and keep him, and everyone else, the hell out.

"So, you know how I can reach this Middle Eastern guy, Lexi?" he asked.

The question took me off-guard because my hand shook,

spilling Diet Coke on the table. "What do you mean?" I asked, wiping up with a napkin.

"Did he leave you a way to contact him if you received the documents?"

"You mean, a business card?"

"Stop playing dumb."

Why did people keep saying that to me? Was it that obvious? "Yeah. He gave me his phone number."

"I see. And are you sure you didn't call him first to come get the documents? You can trust me with the truth."

Yeah, and pigs flew, too. "I am telling you the truth," I insisted. "I didn't call either of you. Someone came and stole the papers last night while I slept. Check my phone records if you don't believe me. No phone calls to either your number or his."

Beefy smiled slowly. "I already checked. One call to Basia's apartment and one call to her mother in Chicago. Neither overly productive, I presume. You don't own a cell phone, so you're clear on that front. Unless you got one of those pre-paid jobbies."

"Hey, you snooped around in my phone records?" I said, outraged even though I had just given him the suggestion to do so. First the mail and now my phone records. Wasn't anything sacred in America anymore?

"I snoop a lot of places," he said. "Now be a good girl and go and get his number for me."

Standing, I stalked back to my bedroom, past Jesse who was wiring the window in the bathroom, and grabbed the piece of paper with Mr. Middle Eastern Guy's number on it. I jotted it down for Beefy and strode back into the kitchen.

He took the scrap of paper, studied it and then carefully put it in his shirt pocket. "Well, I guess this concludes our business," he said.

"Forever?" I asked hopefully.

He smiled and his gold tooth gleamed. "That remains to be seen."

"I was afraid you'd say that."

Beefy stood just as Jesse came into the kitchen.

"You're all set, ma'am," Jesse said to me.

"So quickly? Are you certain you covered every possible entrance? What about the sliding glass door on the balcony?"

Jesse smiled proudly. "I install fifteen of these systems a day, ma'am. You are completely covered. Like I told you, we aim to serve at SuperProtect."

"I'm impressed," I said, taking a sip of my Diet Coke.

"You want me to show you how it works?" Jesse asked.

I looked at Beefy and then shook my head. "Not yet. My, ah, friend is just leaving." I turned to Beefy. "Right?"

To my dismay, he stepped to my side, putting an arm around my shoulder and squeezing. "Oh, honey, I can wait. I wouldn't miss this demonstration for the world. Go ahead, young man, show us how it works. We have no secrets from each other."

I spewed a mouthful of Diet Coke on Jesse and then choked. Beefy slapped me hard on the back until I could breathe again. Jesse removed a tissue from his jeans pocket and calmly wiped his face as if women spewed on him every day.

He handed me the alarm manual. "I'll show you how the pad works. You can read about the fine details of the system later."

Jesse very professionally and adeptly explained how the system worked and then told me my security code. I practiced punching it in, watched it turn red and then learned how to disable it. Probably thinking he was a riot,

Beefy tried it a couple of times, too, until he got the hang of it. Then I wrote Jesse with the High Karate aftershave a check for money I didn't yet have in my checking account and he left.

Beefy exited shortly afterward, as well. Thank goodness he hadn't shot me. Yet. I wasn't so optimistic about the future.

As soon as my apartment was empty, I turned the deadbolt, set the chain and turned on the alarm. Then I flipped through the manual trying to figure out how to change the password. I had just found the instructions when my phone rang.

"Hello?" I said.

"I'm trying to reach Lexi Carmichael," a deep male voice said. My mind instantly recognized a soft brogue, Irish perhaps.

"This is Lexi," I said.

"I'm sorry to bother you. My name is Finn Shaughnessy and I've been frantically trying to reach Basia Kowalski. I've been unsuccessful so far. I wasn't sure where to turn next when I remembered she spoke of you often."

"All good stuff, I hope."

"Actually she spoke of you in quite high regard. I apologize for sounding so desperate, but frankly, I am. Do you happen to know where I can reach her?"

Finn. I remembered the name from Basia's answering machine. Just another person looking for Basia. Take a number and get in line, buddy, I thought.

"I'm sorry, Mr. Shaughnessy," I said politely. "I don't know where Basia is."

"Well, I'm very sorry to hear that," he said. "Would you mind passing on a message to her if she does happen to contact you? She was doing some translation work for my company and I really need to speak with her as soon as possible. It's most urgent."

My interest perked at that. "What company do you work with?"

"CGM, Inc. I'm a lawyer. The company is based in Richmond, but I work out of a satellite office here in Washington."

"Ah, Mr. Shaughnessy, would you be willing to meet me for a drink sometime this evening? I know it seems odd, but I'd like to talk to you in person about Basia and the kind of work she was doing for your company."

He paused on the other line. "So you *do* know where Basia is?"

"Not exactly," I admitted. "But I've got a little problem and it turns out that we might have something in common here."

Another pause and then he answered, "All right. Can you come into D.C. this evening?"

"I think so. What time?"

He was silent for a moment and I heard him shuffling some papers. "I'm busy with a client until seven. How about we meet at seven-thirty at Murphy's Pub? It's not far from Union Station. You know where it is?"

"I know. But how will I find you?"

"I'll be the only real Irishman there," he said with a chuckle. "Don't worry, I'm sure we'll find each other."

"Okay dokey," I said and then wondered if I could possibly sound any more juvenile. I seriously needed to get out more. "And thanks for agreeing to meet me."

"If it helps me find Basia, it'll be worth it," he said and hung up.

I replaced the receiver in the cradle and leaned against the wall. My life just kept getting stranger and stranger.

I sat down at the kitchen table and read the instructions

on how to change my alarm password. When I figured out what I was supposed to do, I keyed in the code 25ME. It wasn't brilliant, but I could remember it. Anyway, I planned on changing it weekly, just to be on the safe side.

After that, I picked up the phone and dialed my brother Beau's work number. Beau is the middle child and now a robbery detective in Baltimore. My mom named him after fashion icon Beau Brummel. That's Mom for you.

I'm lucky I didn't get named something worse. She named my oldest brother Rock in honor of her favorite actor Rock Hudson, a move that she later regretted after learning that Mr. Hudson was gay. But the deed had been done and the name stuck.

It's weird for me to admit it, being their sister and all, but my brothers are pretty cool despite their surfer boy good looks—tall, tan, athletic and dark blond. Frankly, I consider it rude that they completely commandeered all of my mother's beauty genes, leaving none for me. Oh well, some of us have to live with the knocks life deals us.

Yet in spite of my envy, I am close to my brothers. There is a five-and six-year difference respectively between us, but they are decent guys. Neither one of them is married, not that they have ever once in their lives lacked for female companionship. My mother makes a point of reminding them about their bachelor status every time they come home. They laugh and say she's the only woman for them. Then she melts and forgets all about nagging. I still haven't figured out how to do that.

My brother's phone rang and rang and I wondered if the robbery division of the Baltimore Police Department really had employees or it was just a front to discourage burglars. I counted eleven rings before someone picked up.

"Burglary Squad," I finally heard. I recognized Beau's voice. He sounded out of breath.

"I'm glad this wasn't a real emergency," I replied. "What were you doing? Chasing a robber around the squad room?"

"Yeah, someone took off with my donut. How the hell are you, sis?"

"Hunky dory, as usual," I said cheerfully. "Look, Beau, I've got a favor to ask. I wondered if you could run a name for me through the system."

"Christ, you're the one who works at the NSA," he said irritably. "Run it through your own system."

"It's not a matter of national security. I just want to know if this guy has a criminal record."

"What guy?" He paused and then laughed. "No, wait… let me guess. You're thinking about dating again."

"Ha, ha," I replied. "Beau, it's important."

He sighed. "We're not supposed to run unauthorized checks, Lexi. You know that."

"You owe me," I reminded him.

"For what?"

"I lent you two hundred bucks last Christmas so you could buy that ruby bracelet for your girlfriend."

"It was a hundred and I paid you back."

"Two, and no you didn't."

"Did too."

"Did not."

He fell silent, obviously remembering that I was right. "All right," he said in a resigned voice. "What's the name?"

"Lars Anderson," I said, spelling it for him. "He runs a karate studio in Laurel. I think he's a naturalized U.S. citizen from Sweden."

"A karate instructor? You sure know how to pick 'em, sis."

"I'm not going to date him," I insisted.

"Yeah, whatever. You now owe me big."

I wished people would stop saying that to me because it had started to be the story of my life. "Thanks for being so accommodating, Beau."

"Just a public servant at work, ma'am."

I cringed. I'd been called "ma'am" twice in one day and it stunk. "Glad to hear my tax dollars are hard at work."

Beau snorted. "I'll call you when I've got something."

"Thanks, bro," I said and hung up.

I wandered back to my bedroom and surveyed the mess. Beefy was right. My apartment was a pigsty. I needed to clean it up big time. But even more pressing, I had to do laundry or I wouldn't have anything to wear tonight to meet with Finn nor to wear to work tomorrow. But I didn't have any quarters and I *really* didn't have the desire to sit in the laundry room for two hours waiting for the cycles to complete. That left only one dreaded option.

Shopping.

I was *so* going to make Basia pay for all of this when I found her. I grabbed my bag, set the alarm and went out to my car. I drove to the mall, fretting that I'd have to use my already maxed-out credit card for any purchases.

Once there, my first order of business was to buy a cinnamon sugar pretzel and a large ice tea with extra ice. I sat on a bench and watched shoppers go up and down the escalator. At one point, a toddler escaped from his mother's hand and made a dash for the up escalator. In a move worthy of a gold medal at the Olympics, the mother did an amazing long jump and grabbed his arm just before he started up.

After I'd drunk the tea, sucked on the lemon and licked all the sugar from my fingers, the inevitable had arrived. I had to buy some clean clothes. I threw my stuff in the trash and headed for the first clothing store I saw. Better start with the necessities like a new bra and some underwear. I found the lingerie section and wandered through the racks. I found a pack of white cotton briefs on sale, three to a pack, and picked them up. I heard a disapproving voice over my shoulder.

"Men prefer something prettier and sexier," she said.

I turned to see a saleswoman frowning at me. She was middle-aged with short dark hair and black-framed glasses. She was dressed in a navy blue schoolmarm-type dress with a high neck and lace collar. I thought it odd that of all people, she would know what men liked. On the other hand, she worked in the lingerie department and that had to mean something. Her gold store nametag read Norma Jensen.

Not that I had a man to impress, but I was open for suggestions. "What did you have in mind?" I asked.

She smiled and turned, walking to a nearby rack. "This," she said. There were rows of silk and satin, most of it barely scraps of material.

"I can't wear something like that," I said, scandalized.

The frown returned to her face. "Of course, you can, dear," she said, studying my form. "You're young and men go wild over thongs."

I liked the part about men going wild, so I lifted up a blood-red thong and peered at it.

"Which way is the front?" I finally asked.

She turned the material around. "This way."

I studied it harder. "How can you tell? It's just string."

"Exactly."

Uncertain, I hesitated. "Won't it be uncomfortable?"

"Oh, no," she assured me. "They are so lightweight, it will feel like you aren't wearing anything."

I *wouldn't* be wearing anything if I had these panties on, but I figured she was a trained professional, so she knew what she was talking about. I'm not sure how, but she talked me into trying them on over my briefs. The thong wedged right into my behind while a little triangle of material covering exactly diddly went in the front. I'd never seen such impractical, illogical underwear in my entire life. However, I reminded myself that my life needed a change, and change was good.

Thanks to Norma, I bought four thongs in different colors and two push-up Wonderbras in size 36A, red and black. I left the department with big hopes and headed for the clothes area.

I felt more on solid ground here and bought a pair of jeans, two white T-shirts, a black skirt and two white blouses. Apparently I'd used up my exciting quotient with the underwear. But then, on my way out of the department, I spotted a mannequin wearing a red silk dress. It was daring, bold and so not me, but I needed something to wear to meet Finn this evening so I forced myself to try it on. It fit in all the right places and made my lanky form look almost feminine. I'd never owned anything red in my life before today and I didn't have red shoes, so I paid for the dress and then wandered over to the shoe department where I found a pair of not-too-high red pumps. *Done, thank God.*

Relieved I didn't have to do laundry but more worried than ever about my credit card balance, I drove home. The alarm was blinking red and buzzed when I opened the door. I keyed in the new password, the buzzing stopped and the light turned green. What do you know; it worked.

To be on the safe side, I checked my apartment for uninvited guests. Empty except for the mess I'd left. I set my packages down in the bedroom and reset the alarm. No one was going to surprise me now. I was impregnable, defended by the best SuperProtect could offer.

I stripped off my T-shirt and shorts and decided to take a shower. It was getting late and I wanted to give myself an hour to get into Washington to find a parking space and meet Finn. After showering, I toweled off and blow-dried my hair. I stared at my pale face in the bathroom mirror and figured I might as well put on makeup. Reaching under the sink, I pulled out the box that held every bit of makeup my mom had ever bought me. I lifted out the top item and determined that it was an eyelash curler. I held it up to my eyelashes and squeezed, pinching my eyelid. After I had finished screaming, I shoved the curler back into the box and returned it and the makeup to the cabinet under the sink. I combed my hair some more and put on a dash of lip balm. That would have to do for the makeup department.

A bit nervously, I slid into my thong underwear, the Wonderbra and the red dress. I smoothed down the dress and then stepped into my new red pumps. Examining myself critically in the mirror, I wondered how it was mathematically possible to appear flat-chested even with the Wonderbra at work.

Nevertheless, I still felt a little bit sexy and dangerous, especially because it did seem like I was walking around without underwear. In a way, I guess I was. That string didn't cover squat down there. I wasn't sure I wanted to feel that way for a meeting with a lawyer, but hey, you only live once. And the way things were going with me, I might not be living all that much longer anyway. I set the alarm, locked the apartment up tight and left, feeling confident no one would breach my home again.

I drove to Washington with the top down, actually managed to find a parking space not too far from Murphy's and walked into the pub fifteen minutes early. The place was hopping, but I found a small table in the back of the bar. The radio was playing Irish music and I kind of liked the sound of it. I ordered seltzer water with a lemon and cased the place. My red shoe tapped in time to the beat of the jig.

At precisely seven-thirty a handsome young man in a navy blue suit walked through the door. He looked around the place and his gaze settled on me. He looked puzzled and then surprised. I knew it was Finn the moment he started walking toward me.

"Lexi Carmichael?" he asked and I recognized the faint Irish lilt to his voice.

"That would be me," I answered. "Finn Shaughnessy, I presume."

He smiled and sat, shrugging out of his jacket. I don't know how guys managed to wear a tie and a jacket during the sweltering hot summers of Washington, D.C., but they did. After all, this was the city of image. Forty lashes to the lawyer who would dare violate the dress code, although Finn didn't look hot and bothered at all. Just crisp, cool and pretty darn attractive.

He leaned back in his chair and studied me. "You're as pretty as Basia said."

"No way did she say that."

He chuckled. "Well, she definitely implied it."

"You're just being polite."

"Actually, I'm not. You do look lovely tonight in red."

I suddenly felt uncomfortable and wondered why he had brought up the fact that my dress was red. Maybe I looked too much like a hooker.

"I'm wearing a new outfit," I admitted. "It's too much, isn't it?"

"No, it looks great," he said, signaling to the waitress who was instantly at his side. "Really."

"Hey, Finn," the waitress said, smiling at him. "The usual?"

"Thanks, Lucy," he said and she left without writing anything down.

"Come here often?" I asked.

"Lots of business lunches," he said, patting his stomach as if he carried too much weight. Which of course wasn't anything near the truth. From what I could see, he had a flat stomach and a great body beneath that crisp white shirt and dark blue pants.

"Thanks for coming," I said. "I thought you might be able to help me out."

"I'm hoping for the same thing from you," he said.

He leaned forward on the table and I noticed he had nice eyes. A deep green, the color of a freshly mown lawn in summer. They contrasted perfectly with his golden brown hair and eyebrows. He didn't wear a wedding band, not that I noticed on purpose. Well, okay maybe I noticed on purpose, it just didn't mean anything. After all, he could be allergic to gold.

"So, where do we start?" he asked.

"I'm not sure."

"Why don't you tell me about your problem with Basia," he suggested.

I shook my head. "Actually it might be helpful if you could explain in a little more depth your connection with Basia."

I noticed I was tapping my foot a lot more vigorously than the Irish jig music merited and realized I was nervous, though I wasn't sure whether it was due to an instinctive feeling that he might have some clue to Basia's whereabouts that might put an end to my current nightmare or because I felt a weird pull of attraction to this guy just nanoseconds after meeting him. It wasn't typical for me to be instantly attracted to a guy. I fought down the panic. Change is good, I reminded myself. Relax and enjoy the attraction.

Before Finn could say anything, Lucy returned with a dark ale. She set it on the table in front of Finn and then leaned forward so he could see down the front of her blouse. I liked the fact that he kept his gaze averted, and then politely thanked her.

After she left, Finn said, "Okay, I guess I can talk about how I met Basia." He took a sip of his ale and regarded me over his glass. "I initially met her through another company lawyer. She'd been doing freelance translation for CGM for a few years, I guess. We have a lot of foreign clients who require documents translated into a number of different languages."

"Tell me about your company."

"CGM, Inc. is a large international medical and biotechnology research facility. We have clinics, laboratories and research centers across the U.S. and abroad."

"I thought you said you're a lawyer."

"I am. Corporate law. I'm just one of about twenty lawyers employed by the company."

"That's a lot of lawyers for one company."

He laughed. "Actually it's quite small for an international company the size of CGM."

"So how long have you been working with Basia?"

"Our company has been working on and off with her for a couple of years now. I never required her services until recently when I had some Polish documents that needed translation."

"Do you have a lot of clients from Poland?"

He studied me for a moment, a guarded look coming into his eyes. "We have quite a few clients from Poland, actually. That's why Basia has proven to be so invaluable to us. Polish is her first language, after all."

"Yes, I know."

We sat for a minute, both of us sizing up the other and trying to decide if we could trust each other. His next comment surprised me.

"Look, would you like to get some dinner? I'm famished. The pub has a dining room if you'd like to move there."

Some decent food might help me clear my mind. "Sure," I agreed.

Finn stood and took his jacket, motioning for me to go first. As I brushed past him, he directed me toward the dining room, casually putting his hand in the small of my back. Heat shot from his fingertips through the thin material of my dress and all the way to my toes. I yelped in a very unladylike manner. Finn quickly removed his hand and I felt my cheeks burn in embarrassment.

When we arrived at the dining room, a maître d' sat us at a table for two facing the street. It was starting to get dark, so she lit a little candle on our table. I hid my hot face behind a menu until my color returned to normal. Eventually, I decided on a grilled chicken salad and Finn ordered the Irish stew. He said the Irish wine was decent, so I agreed to a glass.

After the waiter brought us our wine, Finn took a sip and looked out the window. "I realize this is an awkward situation for both of us. We don't really know each other. But I need your help and I think you could use mine. I'd like to make a suggestion that we take a leap of faith here and trust each other. What do you say?"

"I usually like to know where I'm leaping before I make the jump."

"Will it help if I go first and tell you what I know?"

"It might," I admitted, taking a sip of wine. Finn was right; it was good. Really good.

"Okay," he said. "Then I'm going to lay it out for you. I don't know much about you other than you're friends with Basia, you're into computers, and live in Jessup, Maryland. If I put two and two together, I'd venture a guess that you're working for the government, CIA, FBI or NSA. More likely NSA since you live in Jessup. I don't care about that. What I do care about is that Basia was involved in an important project for my company when she suddenly disappeared along with the documents she was working on."

"What kind of documents?"

"A contract for a foreign client written in Polish. She didn't happen to send the documents to you, did she?"

I decided neither to deny nor confirm anything. "Why would she send me papers that belonged to your company?"

"Because I think she was afraid. And frankly, she might have good cause to be frightened."

That was a major revelation and I narrowed my gaze as I looked at him. "Why would Basia be afraid?"

Finn leaned forward on the table. "It's complicated. The documents I sent her required a bit of special handling."

"What kind of special handling?"

"The documents were not part of my normal workload and they involved Bright Horizons, our fertility clinic. I don't normally do work with that branch of the company and I had obtained them under, let's say, unusual circumstances from another attorney at the firm. From what I was able to discern, the documents were copies and the original had been written up months earlier. Obviously I couldn't read them, so I sent them to Basia so she could tell me what they said."

"Did you find out what they said?"

"She called me after doing a first draft of the translation and said the contract seemed extremely unusual to her and not at all the kind of thing we typically do at CGM. After listening to her initial concerns, I took my findings to my bosses and everyone got nervous. They yanked me from the case and told me to retrieve the documents from Basia at once and forget I'd ever seen them."

I was very interested now and leaned forward. "Why? What was so unusual about the contract?"

"Well, first of all, the firm never negotiates the kind of deal that was stipulated in the contract. It provided for living arrangements, and a stipend between two parties that were apparently involved in some kind of medical research at the firm. CGM usually negotiates legal contracts that protect the company from unwarranted malpractice suits from clients. There are also other types of contracts that are standard for the operation of a large, international corporation. But the kind of contract that Basia was translating was highly irregular and certainly something I suspect the company shouldn't be involved in."

"You mean it was illegal?"

"No, that's not what I'm saying. I'm just saying that the company is not in the business of conducting personal legal contracts between clients for services not clearly outlined. I considered it quite disturbing."

I thought for a moment. "Was there anything else unusual about the documents?" I was thinking of the code Basia had penciled in on the bottom of one of the pages.

He fiddled with his napkin. "Well, Basia told me she was also concerned because an address in Warsaw on the contract didn't seem right to her. She's quite familiar with the city, so I trusted her judgment on this."

I hadn't expected that. "What address?"

"Actually, there happened to be two addresses in the contract. One was for our branch office in Warsaw. The other was presumably the address of a medical institution used by Bright Horizon's employees. That's not so unusual because we often work out of a country's medical establishments as part of a medical exchange. We offer our expertise in everything from cancer treatments to AIDS research and in return, they permit us to use their facilities. We have agreements like that with several countries, as do many other American medical research and biotechnology institutions."

"So what was the problem?"

"On a hunch, I had a friend of mine in Warsaw check out the second address. Basia was right to be concerned. There is a building there with that address, but no medical institution in sight." He took another sip of his wine. "So, I decided to run the medical identification number of the supposed institution. It was bogus."

I remembered now that when Paul had translated the documents for me last night, he'd mentioned something about the "recipient" being required to go to specific doctors. I hadn't thought it significant at the time, but now I did.

"So, what exactly does that mean?" I asked.

"It means that if this contract was put into place, and presumably it was, CGM's client in Warsaw has been going somewhere other than a licensed medical facility."

I thought for a moment. "Do you know what the client's medical condition is?"

Finn nodded. "She's pregnant."

FIVE

"PREGNANT?" I SAID loudly enough to startle the waiter as he appeared with our dinners. He was about sixty years old, of Indian descent with dark hair peppered with gray.

"Congratulations," he said, putting my dinner in front of me. "How wonderful. Is it your first child?"

I looked at him in horrified shock. "I... I..."

"I had a feeling about you two from the moment I saw you enter the room," he said, beaming. "I feel good karma here. A very strong spiritual connection."

With that pronouncement he left. My cheeks burned again, but Finn sat back in his chair and laughed, clearly amused by my discomfort.

"Well, that was awkward," I said.

"Seeing as how we just met, yes," Finn said, but he didn't seem that bothered. "But an innocent mistake."

"Yeah, innocent," I said as nonchalantly as possible. Like people accused me of being pregnant every day. Anxious to steer the conversation back on safer ground, I asked, "So, how many foreign clients does Bright Horizons typically have?"

Finn sipped his wine. "Thousands. The company is a world leader in the reproductive health field."

"Is the branch office in Warsaw large?"

"Not compared to other foreign locations, but it is comfortable enough, I suppose."

"I presume the kind of medical care and research offered by CGM and Bright Horizons is rather expensive."

"Yes. But if you want the best, you have to be willing to pay for it."

"So, if you have enough money, maybe you could pay extra to have the company set up an unorthodox agreement?"

Finn looked grim. "Until recently, I would have given a resounding no to that assumption. As the company's lawyer, I'd have strongly advised against it."

"That's probably why you weren't in the loop. You said you got these papers from another lawyer in your company under rather unusual circumstances. Do you mind sharing what you meant?"

Finn shoved his fingers through his hair and I thought he looked really troubled. "One of the senior attorneys in the Washington office, Harold Small, was killed about a month ago in a car accident. I was friendly with him and his wife, Chloe. A few days after the funeral, Chloe called me. She said she found some papers in a safety deposit box she hadn't even known Harold possessed. My name was on the outer envelope. Imagine my surprise when I found company documents inside. It was odd because I'd never seen these documents before, never worked this particular case and couldn't figure out why he'd marked them as mine."

Intrigued, I leaned forward, lowering my voice. "Is it standard practice for employees to secure company documents in private safety deposit boxes?"

"Of course not. Aside from the strange fact that my name was on the envelope, there was no accompanying note from Harold saying what the papers were and what I was supposed to do with them. Since they were in a foreign language, I had no idea what they said."

"So you decided to send them to Basia for translation."

"Yes. There was something odd about the whole matter,

so I asked her to be discreet and talk to only me about them. When she eventually got back to me a few days later with her concerns, I realized just how unorthodox and disturbing these documents were."

"And that's when you brought it up with your bosses at CGM?"

"Yes. Except instead of giving me answers they demanded the documents back and told me to keep my mouth shut. But when I tried to retrieve the documents from Basia, I discovered that both she and the papers had disappeared."

"So, you're desperate to get them back to save your job."

"It's not my job I'm worried about. Not anymore, at least. Now I've got a bad feeling about Harold's car accident. It was ruled accidental, but since these documents surfaced, I have sudden misgivings. Add to that Basia's sudden disappearance with said documents and I'm really getting worried."

Those seemed like ominous developments to me and I could see why Finn was concerned. And, as far as I knew, he didn't even know about the men chasing me around with guns.

"I don't get why Harold would put the documents in a safety deposit box," I said.

"I don't know either," Finn said.

We both contemplated that in silence while eating. "Do you know the names of the people involved in the contract?" I asked after a while. Maybe Finn had omitted them before sending the documents on to Basia to protect attorney-client privilege or something like that.

Finn shook his head. "I gave Basia the documents exactly as I had received them. She said the contract was generic with 'client' and 'recipient' substituted for names. It's not that unusual. This is often done to preserve the privacy of the clients when translation is needed. But I'm pretty sure I know at least the first name of the woman in question. And in yet another strange turn, she too has disappeared."

"How did you get the woman's first name?"

Finn finished his wine, refilled the glass and topped mine off. "My friend in Warsaw agreed to stake-out the bogus medical establishment for me," he said, setting the bottle back on the table. "For about a week, he saw a pregnant woman regularly visit the so-called clinic. He followed her home to her apartment, trying to learn all he could about her. About the time I took my concerns to my bosses, she apparently vanished. The neighbors told my friend that she had moved in about eight months earlier, lived alone, kept to herself and was pregnant. They never saw anyone visit and the woman made only two trips outside daily. Then suddenly one day, the woman spills her guts to the old lady next door, saying she is afraid for her life. Shortly after that, she vanishes. The same neighbor said she saw the woman get into a foreign car driven by a dark-haired woman and she hasn't been seen since."

"So, maybe she just went somewhere to have the baby," I offered.

"Maybe. But why tell the neighbor she was scared? And why the contract to make certain she visited the bogus medical establishment?"

I didn't know the answers to those questions, so I shrugged. "None of the neighbors knew her name?"

"Just Judyta, or Judith in English. There are probably a half million or more Judytas in Poland, so it's not much to go on."

I agreed with him. "So what's the bottom line?"

"It seems pretty obvious to me. There's something

strange going on at CGM. Now that Harold is dead, it's fallen to me to figure it out."

He'd said it simply and eloquently. I looked at him with a mixture of admiration and suspicion. Could it be that I sat across the table from a decent human being...and a lawyer to boot? Or did he have some other underlying motive?

"Aren't you nervous doing something like that?" I asked. "What if it's something unethical, or worse, illegal? We've all seen what happens to whistleblowers."

"How can I not follow through? The woman in Warsaw may have believed she received legitimate medical treatment. As far as I know, she didn't. Since she's pregnant, we are talking about two lives in potential danger here. Besides, I strongly believe Harold hid and then marked those documents for me for a reason. I need to find out why. Can you help me?"

I set down my fork and studied him across the table. He met my gaze evenly and without blinking. Again I was taken aback by the startling emerald color of his eyes and the way they seemed to be measuring my worth. I'd bet he was tough to face in a courtroom.

I wanted to trust him, I really did. And it couldn't hurt to let him in on at least part of the truth.

"Okay, my turn. Basia sent me the documents for safe-keeping. Unfortunately, they were stolen from me last night."

Finn gaped at me. "Stolen?"

I told him about my encounters with Beefy and Mr. Middle Eastern Guy and how the papers were taken from my apartment while I slept. I omitted the part about the papers being under my head. The entire universe didn't need to know I was an idiot.

"My God." He whistled. "Were you harmed?"

"No, I got lucky."

"You don't know which of them stole the papers?"

"Nope and it could have been someone else for all I know. I was asleep so I, ah, didn't see or hear a thing. But Beefy was in my kitchen today looking for the documents and seemed pretty upset when I told him someone else got to them before he did. He doesn't, by any chance, work for your firm, does he? Because if he does, can you call him off before he kills me—either accidentally or on purpose?"

Finn looked appalled. "A hired thug? My God, Lexi, I truly don't know what to say except that I sincerely doubt it. I just can't bring myself to believe that my company would hire someone to threaten you with a gun and break into your home, no matter how desperate they were to get the documents back."

From what I'd heard so far about CGM and Bright Horizons, I wasn't so sure of that. "Then what's your take on Mr. Middle Eastern Guy?"

He paused for a very long moment and I noticed he looked decidedly uncomfortable. "I can't say for certain except that we do have a very large Arabic clientele. Tell me, Lexi, did you have a chance to look at the documents before they were stolen from you?"

"I did, but like you said, they were in Polish." I decided not to tell him I'd had Paul look over them for me.

"Was there a note from Basia?" he asked. "Instructions of any kind?"

"She just told me to keep them safe and she was going out of town to help a friend."

He looked interested in that tidbit. "She didn't say who she was going to visit or where?"

"No."

"Was there anything else unusual about the documents? Had she provided a translation, for example?"

"No translation," I said. "Just the seven pages of the

contract in Polish." I got a distinct feeling he was fishing, but decided not to mention the code she had penciled in at the bottom of page three.

"Look," I said. "Something else is bugging me. You said the contract provided for specific living arrangements, special doctors and a stipend. Aside from the fact that CGM doesn't typically handle such legal arrangements, what's up with that?"

Finn shrugged. "I suppose I could take an educated guess. It's no surprise some wealthy men pay women to act as surrogate mothers for their offspring. They have very specific requests to see that the pregnancy and birth goes exactly the way they want. Many insist on no contact with the mother after the child is born. For a few of them, it's a purely business transaction and they purposefully seek out women who understand that well and will perform to those expectations."

That seemed really creepy to me—a business transaction involving human lives. "Yuck. I guess I've lived a really sheltered life."

"I should point out that this is quite rare. Most people who become involved with surrogate pregnancies are just ordinary men and women trying to have a baby. But the point is that to my knowledge, Bright Horizons has never had any involvement in surrogate pregnancies of any kind."

After that, we seemed to run out of things to say on the topic, or perhaps we both needed a little time to digest the information we had learned. We ate and talked for a while longer, eventually discussing other matters that had nothing to do with people trying to kill me or men paying women to have their babies.

I learned Finn was born and bred in Cork, Ireland and had come to the U.S. to go to Georgetown for law school and then decided to stay. His Irish accent was faint, as if he had worked to tone it down, but it came out occasionally when he pronounced certain words. He also had an off-kilter sense of humor surprisingly similar to mine. Of course guys as good-looking as Finn rarely looked twice at a girl like me, but for this night, regardless of the circumstances, I was the one sitting at the table having dinner with him. Since these occasions didn't come my way often, I planned on enjoying every moment. Maybe change wasn't so bad after all.

After we had finished dinner, Finn graciously paid the bill and then walked me to my car. Once in a while his arm would brush against mine until my nerve ends were jangling. I didn't know if the arm brushing was accidental or he was sending me a covert message that he liked me. How could a person tell? Maybe I was supposed to brush his arm with mine to indicate reciprocal interest.

He stood close enough now so that I could smell him, a pleasant scent of male and expensive aftershave. The attraction thing was in full bloom, at least on my side, even though my brain kept protesting that this wasn't a date and I'd just met him. However, my body wasn't even remotely listening to what my brain was saying. For once, I got a feeling of what it must be like to be a guy.

We arrived at my car and I unlocked the door. We turned to look at each other. Finn stood so close that I could see the smile crinkles at the edges of his eyes. He smiled at me and, in a moment of inspiration, I swung out my arm, hoping to catch his in a light brush. Instead I hit the car door and it slammed on his fingers.

"Bugger that!" he shouted as I looked on in horror. Swearing and shaking his fingers, he hopped around like a rabbit on steroids.

"Oh. My. God," I screeched. "Are you all right?"

He looked ruefully at me, gripping his fingers with his other hand. "I'm, ah, fine. I'm sorry. I crowded you."

"No, no," I protested. "I'm sorry. I liked being crowded." My face turned beet red…again.

Finn reached into his jacket. For one weird instant I thought he was reaching for a weapon to shoot me for being a social imbecile. Not that I would have blamed him. But instead, he pulled out a business card and handed it to me. It was embossed in gold and had Finn's name and the impressive title, "Attorney-At-Law." It also had his work address as well as fax, phone and cell numbers. The logo for CGM, Inc. was a double rainbow in front of a snow-covered mountain. Pretty classy looking.

"Can I have your cell number?" he asked. "In case I need to get in touch with you quickly."

"I don't have a cell," I said. Until these past few days, there was no one I needed to call on a moment's notice except Basia.

He looked at me in astonishment. "No cell? And you work for the NSA?"

"I never admitted to that," I said. "Even if I had, my operating hours for protecting America are nine to five. I can give you my work number if you'd like."

"I'd like," he said firmly, so I scrawled it down on the back of another of his business cards. "If you think of anything else, give me a call," he said. "I'm glad we had a chance to meet and talk, Lexi."

I really liked the way my name rolled off his tongue in that Irish brogue of his. "Me, too. Um…sorry about the fingers."

He touched my hair with his injured hand and I held my breath. My heart was beating so loudly, I was certain he could hear it.

"I'll be in touch soon," he said.

I didn't know whether he meant he would be in touch soon to update me on the Basia situation or call so we could go out sometime. I was really hoping for the latter.

Then, to my utter surprise, he leaned over and pressed a soft, gentle kiss on my mouth. It happened so quickly, I didn't kiss him back. For a moment, I think I just stood there forgetting to breathe. Had one of the most gorgeous guys on the planet just kissed me? On the mouth?

He gave me another of those million-dollar smiles and then turned and walked down the street. I gave a quick laugh and then danced around. At precisely that moment, Finn looked over his shoulder and saw me doing my little jig.

His eyes widened and then he grinned, giving me a jaunty thumbs-up before wincing and then wiggling his injured fingers.

Could I possibly act any more like an idiot?

Probably not. Oh, well. At least he kissed me!

Elated, I jumped into the car and turned on the music as loud as my ears could stand. I drove home singing at the top of my lungs and was dead tired by the time I got there. Letting myself in the complex, I climbed the stairs to my apartment. The door was still locked. When I opened it, I heard the soft buzz of the alarm. To my relief it still blinked red, which meant it was working.

Just the same I did a quick sweep of the apartment, thankfully finding nothing or no one else of interest. I did a half-assed job of it, partially because my paranoia was fading. I relocked the door, set the alarm and dropped my purse on the couch. I checked my answering machine and saw I had three messages.

The first message was from my mother asking me when we were going to go shopping. I groaned. Payback was hell.

The second message was from my brother Beau.

"The check on Lars Anderson came back and he's clean," my brother said. "He arrived in the U.S. from Sweden four years ago, was naturalized last year along with his two younger sisters both of whom still reside in Sweden. Mr. Anderson, age thirty-three, is divorced with no children and currently resides in Laurel. He runs Anderson's Karate Academy, located in a strip mall not far from his home. As far as I can tell, he's never had a run-in with the law, not even so much as a parking ticket. He pays his taxes regularly and even contributes to the police annual fund, bless his heart. He's good to go, sis. Have fun, but remember to practice safe sex."

I rolled my eyes. Beau is such a kidder.

The third message contained some heavy breathing and a hang up. Oh God, it was probably Beefy. It sounded like his breathing. Heavy and perverted. Why was he still bugging me?

Somehow I had to go to work tomorrow and act as if my life were normal. All this crazy stuff was killing me. I was in way over my head and I knew it.

Tonight, I just wanted to go to sleep and have wicked fantasies about a handsome Irish lawyer with amazing green eyes. So that's exactly what I did.

I'M PRETTY SURE I was in the middle of a hot dream when my bedside lamp abruptly switched on, the bright light unceremoniously ripping me from my fantasy. I blinked and then tried to scream.

A man stood by my bed, his hand covering my mouth. Not another one! Intruder man was dressed in a black T-shirt and black jeans. Long dark hair had been pulled back into a ponytail, and he had dark eyes and olive-colored skin.

Enrique Iglesias. Yep, that's who he was. But what was Enrique Iglesias doing in my bedroom in the middle of the night holding his hand over my mouth?

I grabbed his wrist and tried to sit up. He held me down easily.

"Don't scream, Lexi," he said softly, not removing his hand. "I'm not going to hurt you. I'm here to help. Do you understand?"

My heart thumped so wildly I wasn't sure I was breathing. Sweat trickled down my back and beaded at my temples. I nodded even though I didn't know what the hell he was talking about. Isn't that how it worked with psychopaths? If you wanted to stay alive, you fed their delusions and pretended you understood what they were talking about. I swallowed hard, watching him warily.

"I'm going to lift my hand," he said. "No screams, okay?"

I nodded again.

Gazing into my eyes as if measuring whether I was good for my word, he slowly removed his hand from my mouth. I promptly opened my mouth to scream when I noticed he wore a leather shoulder holster. Because I really didn't want to get shot, I sat up instead and scooted as far away from him on the bed as I could.

"Look," I said, my voice coming out shakier than I had intended. "I should warn you, I'm trained in karate."

It was a blatant lie, but sometimes guys got nervous if they thought that girls could kick the beejeebies out of their privates. It didn't matter that I hadn't even had my first karate lesson yet, as long as he didn't figure out how weak and vulnerable I really was.

But instead of looking scared or worried, he smiled. "What a coincidence," he said. "Me, too. What belt are you?"

I felt a flicker of panic. Oh, God, this was just my luck. I

had to get an intruder who knew karate. I didn't know diddly squat about karate belts, but I remembered that Bruce
Lee had worn a black one. Sounded good to me.

"Black," I said, raising my chin.

His smile widened. "Really? What degree?"

Degree? As in temperature or as in PhD? "Just take my
word for it. You don't want to mess with me."

He laughed and I noticed he didn't look all that threatening when he smiled. I took another quick assessment of
him, pegging him from anywhere between thirty to thirty-
five years of age with well-defined arms and an amazing
cleft in his chin.

"Look, buster," I said in my sternest voice and then
yanked the covers up to my chin. "Just how did you get in
here? I have a top-of-the-line alarm system, you know."

"A waste of money," he said, shrugging.

Obviously he was right. "What are you doing in my
bedroom?"

"No, the question is why did you summon me and what
do you want?"

"What do *I* want? You're the one who bypassed my
alarm and broke in here in the middle of the night."

He blew out a breath impatiently and made another gesture with his hands. "You requested my presence, *cara,* so
I came. If you have no need of my services, I shall happily leave."

I was really confused now. Either I had completely lost
my mind or this guy was a true-blue psycho. Neither possibility boded well for me.

"Summoned you?" I repeated. "Are you sure you have
the right bedroom?"

He muttered something under his breath and then made
a gesture with his hands that clearly indicated exasperation. "I'm beginning to wonder that myself."

"Why do you keep talking like that? Are you Spanish or something?"

He looked offended. "Hardly, I'm Italian."

"Italian? I suppose this also means I'm not dreaming since I don't know any Italians and I don't think you can dream about someone you don't know." I was blabbering, but there was a strange man in my bedroom, so I felt entitled. "Look, tell me why you're in my bedroom at—" I glanced at the clock, "—two-thirty in the morning. Maybe we can straighten out the whole mess so you can leave and I can go back to sleep. No one needs to get hurt. Cool with you?"

"Okay," he agreed. He had begun to look amused by the whole situation whereas I felt a weird mixture of terror and crankiness.

I took a deep breath. "Let's start at the beginning. You said you got my message. What did you mean?"

He crossed his arms against his chest and leaned forward. "I received a message today from the Zimmerman twins requesting my assistance. Since I knew they would never approach me on a professional matter—pride, you see—I knew it had to be a request for a personal favor, most likely one for a friend. Since, as far as I know, you're their only close friend, here I am. How am I doing so far?"

My mouth dropped open as it hit me. "Wait a minute. *You're* Slash?"

He spread his hands. "You were expecting someone else?"

"I—I—I—" I stammered stupidly. "I wasn't expecting you at all. I didn't even think you existed." My thoughts whirled. "Aren't you supposed to be a national treasure or something, protected around the clock by the FBI or Secret Service?"

He rolled his eyes. "Is that what they say about me now?"

"Is it true?"

He lifted a dark eyebrow. "Maybe."

"Then how come they didn't stop you from breaking in here?" I asked. "Technically, you just broke the law."

He chuckled. "You think the FBI could stop me?"

"They *are* the FBI, aren't they?"

He laughed this time. "*Cara,* they don't even know I'm here. After all, a man needs his privacy when meeting with a beautiful woman in her bedroom at night."

Beautiful? I sat huddled under the covers in my over-sized T-shirt with tangled sleep hair and probably bad breath to boot. He *was* deranged.

"How do I know you're really Slash and not just some guy pretending to be him?"

"How would you like me to prove it? A DNA sample?"

"A test."

"A what?"

"A test. Give me your hands."

"What?"

"Give me your hands."

He stared at me for a moment and then held out his hands. I took them and turned them over palms facing upward. I checked out his fingertips, relieved to see they were hard and covered with calluses.

"A hacker manicure," I said, dropping his hands.

He smiled. "Ah, so there *are* brains behind the beauty."

"Nice try. You still have to take my test. If you really are Slash, this should be a piece of cake."

"Are you *insani?*" he asked, his dark eyes flashing. "Do you know who I am?"

"Slash wouldn't be afraid of a test," I insisted.

He leaned toward me on the bed. "I am not afraid. I'm insulted. Show me this damn test."

Now he looked mad. I wondered about the wisdom of

what I was doing, but at least he wasn't assaulting or shooting me…yet.

"Close your eyes," I said.

"What?" He gave me another dirty look.

"Close your eyes. I need to get to my laptop and I'm not dressed from the waist down."

He sighed but closed his eyes.

"No peeking," I warned as I stepped from the bed, dragging the sheet with me. I grabbed a pair of sweatpants from the floor and managed to shove my legs inside and pull them up one-handed. "Okay, I'm dressed."

"I'm sorry to hear that," he said, opening his eyes. But I saw his lips twitch with what I sincerely hoped was a touch of humor.

I walked over to the laptop, let it boot up and then signed in. I ran a short protocol and when I was done, I unplugged it and took it to the bed where Slash, if that was truly who he was, still sat. I plopped down next to him, balancing the computer on my lap.

I shifted the computer to his lap and he looked mildly interested as I explained what I wanted him to do.

"The twins have got two computers set up on a test network they set up to teach me the finer points of hacking. I just connected to one of them using a secure shell and a digital key. The computer is set up with basic hacking tools. Your job is to compromise the computers on the test network and find one document out of many with a phone number I need. According to the twins, this exercise should take an expert hacker less than ten minutes."

He snorted in disgust. "Are you really going to make me do this?"

"Getting nervous?"

"You wish. So, whose phone number am I looking for?"

"John Phreak," I said.

He raised an eyebrow. "Phreak?"

"You know, a cross between a phone hacker and a cracker."

He sighed. "I know what it means, *cara*."

"That's encouraging," I chirped. "I'll time you."

I leaned over and picked up my watch from the bedside table and held it in my lap. "I guess I don't have to warn you that there are a few traps set."

His eyes narrowed. "Just get on with it before I die of boredom."

I pursed my lips. "Go."

He typed something and then glanced sideways at me. "So, you're into hacking now, are you?"

"Why? Surprised that a woman can do something so technical?"

He laughed. "Ah, I can see it has been a long, hard road for you as a woman in our profession. You must understand that men are, by nature, insecure creatures. Fortunately, that's changing. Only the best survive in our field, and the fact that you have made it this far means you must be very good."

My hostility evaporated. "Well, yeah, that's true."

"Nonetheless, you are prettier than I expected."

I bristled. "Just because I'm into computers doesn't mean I wear thick glasses and have a face that could stop a truck."

"Indeed, you don't," he agreed. "Dare I mention that you have lovely legs?"

"Hey, did you peek? You promised you wouldn't look."

His eyes gleamed with amusement. "Actually, I didn't promise anything."

"Well, forget about my legs. Shouldn't you pay more attention to what you're doing?"

"Ah, but perhaps you are more worried about this test than I am?"

I glanced at the display but for the life of me could not figure out what he was doing. Nothing I saw even remotely rang a bell. He typed in code I wasn't familiar with and did so in a bored manner, barely even looking at the screen. To my dismay he seemed far more interested in giving me a thorough perusal.

"So, you are friends with the legendary Zimmerman twins," he commented. "I am most curious about them. Are they as odd as everyone says?"

"They're not odd," I protested. "I'm really starting to hate that word."

He nodded knowingly. "I understand. People must have called you odd, too."

"The twins are *not* odd and neither am I—the rest of the world is simply out of touch."

He smiled at that. "Unlike you, I embrace my uniqueness. You'll understand better once you get to know me."

"Why would I get to know you?"

"Because I've decided that you will."

I rolled my eyes and his smile widened as he typed some more commands I'd never seen before. Then he did some very strange maneuvers, which, as far as I could tell, brought him no closer to breaking into the computers.

I glanced at my watch. Five minutes had already passed. He'd never make it under ten minutes at this rate. I yawned.

"So tell me, *cara,* what do you like to do in your free time?" he asked.

"The test," I said pointedly. "Keep your mind on the task at hand, please."

"I'll worry about the test," he said lightly. "And you worry about answering my questions."

"Why should I answer your questions, especially when they're personal?"

"It's a nice way to pass the time."

I shrugged. If he wanted to play it this way, I could go along.

"I like to play GURPS, shoot pool and eat pizza," I said. Generic Universal Role Playing Systems are like hi-tech simulation games. They are addictive and I have to be careful not to spend all my free time in front of the computer on them.

"You any good at pool?"

"I'm okay. Xavier is awesome. Every shot is a math-ematical calculation to him."

"What about pizza? What do you like on it?"

"I like the works on my pizza, including anchovies," I answered, glancing at my watch. Seven minutes down. From what I could see, he wasn't even remotely close to breaking in. This guy was toast.

He started humming and glancing around my room as the screens flashed by quickly. I couldn't even figure out where he was, let alone what strategy he was employing. If this was the best Slash could do, he was a total disap-pointment.

He abruptly pushed the computer toward me. "There's your number," he said.

I looked down at the watch—seven minutes and fifty-seven seconds—then back at the screen. There it was, the number for John Phreak.

"How…"

He yawned now. "I did it my own way, *cara*. And now that I've passed your pathetic little test, may I finally learn why I was summoned here?"

I was still staring at the screen. "I can't believe it. You *are* Slash. I'm just surprised you actually came, not to mention that you exist. Will you tell me what was in the message from the Zimmerman twins?"

"That is between me and them. Suffice it to say it piqued my interest."

I took the laptop and set it aside. "Your hacking method was so weird. I didn't understand a thing you did."

"I'm not surprised."

"I guess I am," I admitted. I adjusted the pillow behind my back and leaned against it. "Can I ask a rather personal question?"

"Ah, now the tables are turned. How personal a question would you like to ask?" he said with a suggestive lift of his eyebrow.

"Sheesh, not *that* personal. I just wondered what would happen, you know, if you were to fall into enemy hands?"

"I'd have to kill myself."

I had a feeling that he wasn't joking. "I know how you got in here. You hacked into the SuperProtect computers and figured out how to bypass my alarm."

"It took me less than three minutes," he said. "I left my briefcase in the foyer."

"Optimum," I said. I knew I sounded like a teenager, but I couldn't help it. I was thoroughly impressed and not just a little awestruck. "Well, the twins were right," I finally said. "They assured me you'd come. But they didn't say you'd come directly to me."

"The twins do not know what I will or will not do." There was arrogance in his voice, par for the course for a man like him.

"So, why *did* you come?" I asked. "What exactly piqued your curiosity?"

He looked intently at me. The man had gorgeous smoky brown Italian eyes with long, black eyelashes that most women would kill for. He also had that Colin Farrell, un-shaven look going. And for him, it worked quite well.

"You," he said simply. "I've heard a lot about you and decided it was time to finally meet you face-to-face."

"Me?" I repeated, stunned. "You heard about me? I, uh, hope it was all good stuff."

He smiled. "Before I came tonight, I did a little research of my own."

"What kind of research?"

He leaned back on the bed, putting his arms behind him. They were very nice arms, muscular and well-built, which was unusual for a computer geek.

"You were born in Springfield, Virginia on the twenty-eighth day of July," he said. "That means you are twenty-four, at least until next week. You stand five foot eleven inches and weigh one hundred and forty-four pounds."

"One thirty-seven," I insisted and then blushed. "I've been on a diet. Sort of."

His smile widened as he continued. "Your father is a lawyer in Washington, D.C., for Harrington, Mariball and Carmichael. Your mother is a homemaker and a for-mer beauty queen, active in charity work. You studied at Georgetown University and earned an undergraduate de-gree in mathematics and computer science. Graduated with honors. You currently work as a techie at the NSA and your direct supervisor is Jonathan Littleton, who is totally in-competent, by the way. You have two older brothers, Beau who's a policeman in Baltimore, and Rock, a journalist, in Richmond. You drive a red Miata with Maryland tags ABV333, and you adore Diet Coke and chocolate éclairs. How am I doing so far?"

"Not bad," I admitted. "But that's superficial informa-tion. A kid could have dug up that."

He studied me for a moment. "Your bra size is 36A."

My mouth dropped open. "No way! How did you do that?"

He leaned over and picked my red Wonderbra up off the floor, letting it dangle from his finger. "I'm an excellent observer."

I snatched it from him, my cheeks flaming. "Hey, that's cheating."

"*Al contrario.* That's making good on my talents. And by the way, I happen to like red lingerie on women." He looked at me intently and my cheeks flamed hotter. Grinning at my obvious discomfort, he glanced about at the room. "Another observation—you're not much of a housekeeper."

"My apartment got tossed," I said, hastily stuffing my bra beneath the pillow. "I've been kind of busy and haven't had time to clean it up yet."

"Tossed?"

"Someone searched it."

He stared at me, his smoky eyes shuttered. "Looking for what?"

"Well, that's the thousand dollar question these days."

"Which is why you had the twins summon me, I presume."

"Partially, yes." I crossed my arms against my chest, feeling exposed now that he not only knew my pathetic bra size, but the embarrassing fact that I wore a padded one.

"So tell me the rest, *cara.* Why am I here?"

I exhaled a deep breath. "It's up to the twins to fill you in on the details."

He stared at me for a long moment. "Why? You still do not trust me?"

"I don't know you. True, you passed the test. But I'm

relying on the twins' judgment. If they're convinced you're Slash, that's good enough for me. Come back and talk to me after you've met with them."

"You are dismissing me?" He looked incredulous.

"Look, bringing you on board was the twins' idea. Time is of the essence and they thought you could help. I agreed to go along with it. Frankly, I won't blame you if you decide to back out of this. Things have been a little dangerous lately, and I don't even want to think about what would happen if I put a national treasure in danger."

"Now you think I'm afraid of danger?" He swore under his breath, sounding downright insulted.

"I didn't mean it like that," I backtracked. "It's just I'm not sure what's going on. I don't want to go to jail for endangering you."

He narrowed his eyes, studying me. "I'm not at all certain I have you figured out, *cara.* You openly insult me, but for some reason I think I like you."

"That's a compliment, right?"

He stood abruptly. "Until I hear what the twins have to say, you will not say a word about my visit to anyone, especially not to your boss. Don't trust anyone."

"How did you know my boss is Jonathan Littleton?"

"I work at the NSA, remember? I'll meet you here again tomorrow night and we'll talk. *Si?*"

"I won't be home until after eight," I said. "I have karate. Can you come after that?"

He lifted his hands to the sky in what looked like the Italian gesture for exasperation. "First she summons me, then dismisses me and after that she dictates when I should come again. *Buon dio,* a classic example of how the mind of a woman works."

I rolled my eyes. "So does that mean you'll be here or not?"

He looked pained. "*Si, cara,* I'll be here."

"Thanks," I said. "I think. But tell me one thing, what's with the gun? A new fashion statement for hackers?"

He looked down at his weapon and shrugged. "I live in D.C."

That said it all, I suppose. "But I thought you were protected by the FBI."

"When they know where I am," he replied and then started to walk out of my bedroom.

"Wait," I called out, stopping him. "What's your real name?"

"Sorry, that's classified. Call me Slash. Everyone else does." He paused, crossing his arms and leaning back against the door. "Why do I get the feeling that there is something else you wish to know about me?"

Gee, I'd only known him for half an hour and he could read me like a book. Still, I'm not one to waste opportunity, so I quickly asked, "Are you by any chance related to Enrique Iglesias?"

"That Spanish singer? Certainly not. He's got a big nose."

I looked at Slash's nose and thought it a fine nose indeed. Then again, I thought Enrique had a pretty fine nose, too. Obviously I did not know my noses.

"Um, so I can't tell anyone I met you?" I asked.

"Only the twins."

I sighed. "Gee, it's like meeting Zorro. But if I can't tell people, where's the fun in it?"

"Zorro was Mexican. I'm Italian, and I'm not wearing a mask."

"I know. It was just a figure of speech. And I suppose it's a good thing you aren't wearing tights and a cape either. I might have had heart failure."

He laughed. "You are such a flirt, *cara.* I like it."

I blushed. Me, a flirt? Okay, maybe a little. Who could blame me? There was something dangerous and terribly exciting about flirting with a national treasure. Besides it was three o'clock in the morning and I was punchy. I needed to go to sleep so I could get up and function at work in the morning.

"Buona notte, Lexi. *Sogni dolci,*" he whispered, leaning against my doorjamb.

"Sorry, I don't speak Italian," I said, lifting my hands.

"I said good night and sweet dreams," he said, his mouth twitching. "Perhaps now you'll dream about me, *si?*" With that, he disappeared from my bedroom and presumably my apartment.

Feeling a little testy, I made certain the door was locked and the alarm rearmed. As if it really mattered at this point. Then I picked up the phone and called the twins. Elvis answered on the first ring. It was the middle of the night, but he was wide awake and probably working.

"Hi, Elvis, it's me. I think Slash was just here."

"How do you know it was Slash?"

"I wasn't sure, so I gave him a test. You know, on the practice network you set up for me. I don't know how he did it, but he broke into the computer and found the phone number in seven minutes and fifty-seven seconds. I think it's a record or something."

"Shit," Elvis said and I heard him drop the phone.

"Hello, hello?" I called out. "Elvis, are you there?"

I could hear him talking rapidly with Xavier in the background and then about two minutes later, Elvis got back on the phone.

"You there, Lexi?"

"Yes," I said, worried. "What's wrong?"

He sighed. "Not only did he hack into the computer and retrieve the phone number from said document, he stole all the digital keys from the log-in machine, booby trapped several programs and modified the kernel system so he could break in any time he wanted. We had to shut down the network completely and unplug the computers. We'll have to reinstall everything from scratch. It will take us a weekend's worth of work."

"Your whole system is compromised?" I said, horrified.

"Nah, just the practice network," he answered. "We caught it early enough, so luckily, it's nothing more than a pain in the ass."

I could have been wrong, but amid the irritation in his voice, I thought there was a trace of admiration.

"Oh, God, Elvis, I'm sorry," I said. "I was just trying to make certain it was him. I didn't tell him anything. I left that up to you guys. He said he'll be stopping by soon."

Before he could say anything more, I heard the doorbell ring in the background. "Get that, would you, Xavier?" Elvis said.

I listened intently. "Is it Slash?"

Elvis was silent for a moment. "Nope," he said. "But someone ordered us a dozen pizzas with the works, including anchovies, and charged it to our tab at Avanti's."

Shit. "Oh, well, I gotta go," I chirped. "Call me as soon as you make contact with Slash."

I hung up the phone, unable to believe how stupid I'd been to let Slash into the twins' network, even if it had been in a peripheral way. That was all a guy like Slash needed to get a foot in the door to do some serious damage.

I dragged myself to the bathroom, stripped off my T-shirt and took a long, cold shower so that I could sleep. Suddenly I had gone from famine to feast in the man department. In one day I had met a gorgeous Swedish martial arts instructor, eaten dinner with a handsome Irish lawyer and had an Italian man—not to mention a national treasure—in my bedroom. Not that I meant anything to them, but for me it was an international bonanza.

It was after three-thirty when I finally climbed into bed and turned out the light. Sleep came almost instantly after I sincerely prayed that all this crazy change in my life would turn me into a more interesting, and hopefully irresistible, woman.

SIX

WHEN MY ALARM rang at six-thirty, I stumbled out of bed, brushed my teeth with my eyes shut and got dressed in the new skirt and blouse I'd bought at the mall yesterday. With all the excitement I'd forgotten to shave my legs last night, but there was no way in hell I was wearing hose in humid ninety-plus degree Washington heat. I just hoped no one would notice my hairy legs as I shoved my bare feet into a pair of black pumps.

I swung by Dunkin' Donuts, bemoaned their lack of a drive-thru for the millionth time and bought a large coffee, a bottle of Diet Coke and a blueberry muffin. Taking alternating sips of the hot and cold drinks, I drove to work. After waving my holographic pass at least a dozen times, providing my thumb print and enduring a retinal scan, I finally reported to my cubicle. I hadn't been at my desk five minutes when Joanna Klose, my prissy office-mate, smugly informed me the price tag was still dangling from my blouse. *Sigh.*

My eyes were gritty from lack of sleep, and I hoped the caffeine surge would kick in soon. I looked at the pile of papers in my in-box, checked the slew of messages on my email and wondered how I'd ever get caught up considering all the work *not* related to my job that needed to be done today.

I removed the two scraps of paper from my purse containing both Beefy's and Mr. Middle Eastern Guy's phone numbers and stared at them. I couldn't run a trace on the

phone numbers without producing a court order, but Elvis
and Xavier could. After debating whether it would be pushing my luck to ask for another favor after almost compromising their entire computer set-up, I decided I was
desperate. I punched in their phone number, but the answering machine picked up. After profusely apologizing
again for last night and inquiring as to whether or not Slash
had contacted them yet, I left the numbers and hung up.

I took another sip of my coffee, nearly choking on it
when someone cleared his throat from behind me. Paul
Wilks stood in the opening of my cubicle, grinning. I
hoped like hell he hadn't heard what I'd just said on the
phone to the twins' answering machine.

"Hey, Paul," I said, trying to sound casual. "What's up?"

"Checking up on you," he replied. "Anything new to report on those mysterious documents and Bright Horizons?"

"Not yet," I lied.

"You gonna tell Jonathan about them?"

"Why? This is personal."

"You know, it's standard operating procedure. Something strange is going on."

I really needed to get him off my back. "You're right. I
will tell Jonathan at some point. Actually, I have told someone in a position much higher than me, so I'm not exactly
sitting on this alone." That much was true.

"Greater authority? At the NSA? No shit?" Paul said,
his eyes widening. Paul loved office politics, especially
when it involved higher-ups. Just hearing I'd consorted
with someone upstairs probably raised me in his esteem.
"Who'd you talk to?"

"Sorry. I can't say."

"Why not?"

I kept my expression serious. "It's classified, Paul. And
for now, you need to keep your involvement quiet, too."

Paul looked disappointed but didn't press. "Okay. I respect that. Are we still on for tomorrow night?"

"Sure," I said. If I didn't die or collapse from exhaustion first. And right now both of those were actually looking a lot better than going to dinner and disco dancing with him.

"So how was the doctor visit yesterday?"

"What doctor visit?" I said before thinking.

Paul frowned. "The one that kept you from work yesterday."

I gave myself a mental slap on the head. "Oh, that one. It was fine. Thanks for asking."

Paul narrowed his eyes. "You don't have herpes do you?"

"Paul!"

"I'm just asking. You can't blame a guy for wanting to know. Anyway, keep me posted on the Bright Horizons thing. You know I can help if you need me."

"I will. But for now just keep your lips sealed."

"I will until tomorrow night and then all deals with my lips are off," he said with a sly wink and left.

I rolled my eyes. Had I really agreed to go out with this guy? Rubbing my temples, I returned my attention to the computer screen and started to type when my phone rang.

"Hello?" I said.

"Lexi, it's me, Elvis. I got your message. You got a minute?"

"For you, always."

"I got the info on those phone numbers you requested."

"Already?"

"I work fast."

He wasn't bragging, just stating a fact. "Great. What did you turn up?"

"The news isn't good. The phone numbers were dead ends. One number was registered to a John Jones, address bogus, and the other to a Marvin Cates, also with a fictional address. It looks like both numbers had recently been cloned off legit accounts. I'd guess that the original owners don't even know yet because they haven't got their monthly statements."

"Ouch," I said. "Well, thanks for trying."

"Sure, and by the way, Slash dropped in this morning."

My heart skipped a beat. "So, what do you think of him?"

"He knew his stuff. A true wizard."

Calling someone a wizard meant they were an ace hacker and that is the twins' highest compliment. I was impressed.

"Xavier and I filled him in on the basics, but he'll need to hear more details from you," Elvis said. "He said he's coming by your place tonight."

I sighed. "Yeah."

"Well, we're still working on getting into CGM. Slash had some good suggestions we'll put into play. Maybe we'll get an unexpected break."

"That would be nice," I said. "Thanks again."

I had just hung up when my boss Jonathan arrived at my cubicle. Jeez, I was Miss Popular this morning.

Jonathan looked unusually tired and his mouth was pinched at the corners. He pushed a stray strand of pale blond hair back from his receding hairline and flicked off an imaginary piece of dust from his always-impeccable vest. Jonathan, at fifty-seven, was tall, thin and a member of what we younger generation considered "the old guard" in the computer field. Still, he was an okay guy even though I disliked the way he often micromanaged his staff. Since he was my first boss, I had no one else to compare him to and I tried not to complain about it because I figured there were other people who had it a lot worse.

"Good morning, Lexi," he said and I remembered that Slash had called him incompetent. I wondered how Slash knew that and just how much information he really had on all of us.

"Good morning, Jonathan," I said. "What's up?"

"Just coming to check on you. How are you feeling?"

"Better," I said. "Thanks for asking."

"Is everything all right?"

"Sure."

There was a moment of awkward silence. I felt like he was waiting for me to tell him something and it made me uncomfortable. I couldn't see how he would have any idea what had been happening in my life, but this was the NSA after all. Just the same, I remembered Slash's warning and kept my mouth shut. For now, at least.

"Any new leads on Phear?"

"Not yet," I said.

He gave me a long look and then shrugged. "Okay, then get to it," he said and walked away.

"That was way weird," I murmured.

I'd better do at least some of my work in case Jonathan decided to come back and check. I started surfing around in a chat room called Death Code when the phone rang again. I picked it up.

"Hello, Lexi, darling," my mother said. "I'm going to be in your neighborhood this afternoon and thought you might like to join me for lunch."

There was no way my mother could just "be in the neighborhood." The NSA is located on eighty-six acres of land near the army base of Fort Meade. The establishment is a fortress of its own, and residences, restaurants and major thoroughfares did not surround it on purpose. Since September eleventh, all but one major entrance had been blocked off and a high-wire electric fence and hi-tech security cameras surrounded us with even more sophisticated and super-secret spy equipment.

You were either at the NSA or you weren't.

"You can't just be in the neighborhood, Mother," I protested. "Do you know how ridiculous that sounds?"

"I'm your mother. I can be where I want. Now, are you coming to lunch with me or not?"

"I'm really busy, Mom. What's up?"

"We didn't discuss your birthday party yet."

"Oh, darn," I said, feigning disappointment. "Well, I'll call about it later."

My mother's voice lowered. "You owe me, young lady. You ran out on the Marshalls."

"I didn't run out," I lied. "Not exactly."

"I can't believe you're going to make me beg. Is this what the world has come to? Is it too much for a mother to ask for a little quality time with her daughter?"

I rolled my eyes, as the guilt kicked in full force. "Okay, Mom, I'll meet you for lunch. But it has to be somewhere close. I've only got an hour."

"Then let's make it Le Fromage," my mother said, naming a quaint little French café in the nearby town of Severn. It was a bit beneath my mom's usual fare, but she was determined to see me.

After I hung up, I spent the next several hours earning my paycheck and doing work in the service of my country. A little before noon I left the office and drove to the restaurant. Mom had already arrived and ordered a club soda from the bar. We sat at a table by the window and I ordered the French onion soup and Mom a garden salad with dressing on the side.

"Tell me the truth, what did you think of Thomas Marshall?" my mother asked, nipping delicately at a piece of lettuce.

"Forget it, Mom. He's not my type. He's not interested and neither am I."

My mom smiled her Cheshire Cat grin. I had the distinct and uncomfortable feeling she had something up her sleeve. "On the contrary, darling. He asked for your phone number."

I felt a flutter of uneasiness in my stomach. "He did?"

"He did. He said he found you fascinating."

"For heaven's sake, Mom. He was just being polite. You didn't give it to him, did you?"

"Of course I did. And I might have happened to mention that you had a birthday party coming up."

I choked on my soup. "Please tell me you didn't."

"I did. Come on, Lexi. He's a nice boy with a good future. Couldn't you just *once* consider a man like that?"

"He couldn't even believe I worked for the Defense Department, Mom. Imagine what he'd think if he knew I worked for the NSA."

"I'm sure he could get used to it given time."

"He wants to be a senator," I said, not believing I was even having this pointless argument. "That's completely incompatible with my life goals."

"And your point would be?"

"Mother," I growled.

She dabbed the corner of her mouth with a napkin. "I'm not saying marry him. Not yet anyway. I'm simply suggesting that you invite him to your birthday party."

"There's *not* going to be any birthday party!" I said so loudly that the patrons at the other tables looked over at us.

Mom glared at me. "Lower your voice, young lady. I'm simply trying to bring your attention to a very dire matter. You are turning twenty-five and you're not even dating anyone seriously. You're scaring me."

"*You're* scaring me."

"Natalie Waggoner's daughter is engaged and she is the same age as you," she continued as if I hadn't spoken. "She's marrying a doctor."

I scowled at her. "Mom, for your information, I can manage my own love life, thank you very much. If I want to screw it up, that's my business. If I want to live in the Sahara Desert of dating, then that's my choice."

My mom looked taken aback and I sighed. I had spoken sharply and now regretted it. "Look, Mom, if it will make you feel any better, I actually have a date this weekend."

Now my mom looked surprised. "You do?"

"I do."

She looked suspicious and I guess she didn't believe me. In a way, I didn't blame her. "What's his name?" she asked.

"Paul Wilks," I said. "I work with him."

"Oh," she said, disapproval evident in her voice. "Didn't you already date him once?"

Geez, did my mother keep a written record of every guy I'd ever been out with? "I decided to give him a second chance," I lied.

Mom still did not look happy. "I thought he was divorced," she said as if it were some kind of disease. "Besides, I don't think it's a good idea to date people you work with."

"At least I'm dating."

"That's true. It's just that I worry about you, darling. You have a certain…how do I say it…way with men."

Yeah, I knew I had a way with men, all right. An *ineffective* way.

"Look, Mom, I thought perhaps you, me and dad could go out to dinner for my birthday," I said.

She considered it for a minute and I could see the wheels turning in her head. "No party?"

"No party."

"Then at least bring a date to dinner with you."

I exhaled a deep breath. I knew I'd have to compromise if I wanted to get out of the party.

"Okay, but *I* get to decide who to bring. And under no circumstances are you to set me up on a blind date or promise my hand in marriage to anyone or the deal is off."

My mother took a sip of her club soda. "All right. I can agree to those conditions."

She seemed slightly mollified. I guess she was just happy I'd be quasi-dating again, which I suppose was the real reason for the lunch date. I made a vow right there that if I ever had a daughter, I'd let her date anyone she wanted. Just as long as he wasn't a psycho or a politician wannabe. I had to have some standards.

"...thank God, I'm not the only mother with such problems," my mother was saying. "Miriam Sandberg was just telling me that her son hasn't had a real date in almost two years. I told her..."

"Whoa," I said, interrupting her in midsentence as something clicked in my head. "Did you just say Sandberg? Her husband wouldn't happen to be a doctor at a fertility clinic in Richmond, would he?"

My mother looked at me like I was an alien. To some degree, I sympathized. I suppose sometimes it is hard to follow my train of thought.

"He's not just a *doctor* there," she said slowly, enunciating every word. Maybe she thought if she spoke too quickly it might shatter what was left of my sanity. Now that I thought about it, she might be right. "He *founded* the clinic."

"How do you know the Sandbergs?" As soon as I asked, I knew it was a dumb question. My mother knew everyone who was anyone with money in Virginia.

"They come to Washington frequently and are members of the Hilton Hotel's Capital City Country Club and Spa."

Mom's favorite hangout. "So what do you rich guys chat about in the sauna?" I asked.

She rolled her eyes. "Don't be so bourgeois, Lexi. If you must know, I heard the clinic recently went through some financial difficulties."

I perked up. "What kind of financial difficulties?"

"Does it matter?" Money was money to Mom.

"It could," I replied.

She narrowed her eyes. "I hope there is a good explanation why you are so interested in a fertility clinic."

I took a quick gulp of water and coughed. "I assure you, it's not what you're thinking."

"I certainly hope not."

"I swear this is a strictly professional interest," I said, trying to keep her on track. "Do you know why the company had money problems?"

"I haven't got the foggiest idea," she sniffed. "But your father said they bounced back from near financial ruin last year."

"How?"

"For God's sake, Lexi, I don't know. More clients wanting to have babies, I guess. And it's no wonder seeing as how women are waiting longer and longer to have children these days." She looked at me pointedly and I shifted uneasily in my chair. "By the way, have you met the Sandbergs' son?"

"Forget it, Mother," I said, wagging my finger at her.

She smiled innocently and we finished our lunch. Luckily for my strapped checking account, she picked up the tab.

It was nearly five o'clock when my work phone rang

again. It was Finn. He said my name in that soft Irish brogue of his and a tingle went from my nose to my toes.

"Lexi, can I see you?" he asked.

Naked or clothed was the first thought that leapt into my head. "Sure," I said, trying to keep cool. "Tonight?"

"Yes." He sounded worried.

It would be a tight fit. I had karate at eight o'clock and then Slash was coming after that. It apparently took mortal danger and men with guns to cram my social calendar full.

"It would have to be right now," I said. "I'm booked solid for the rest of the evening."

"Okay," he said. "I'm not far away. I'm in Baltimore on business. Can you meet me at a restaurant called the Fish Market? It's near the Inner Harbor."

"I know where it is," I said. "Be there in about thirty minutes."

"Thanks. See you then."

I immediately left work, drove to Baltimore, cruised down to the Harbor and parked in a covered garage. As I walked to the restaurant a hot, humid breeze drifted in off the water.

Finn was seated at a table in the bar and he waved to me when I entered. He looked gorgeous in a light blue shirt and red tie. He'd removed his jacket and hung it over the chair behind him. He stood, pulled out my chair and I sat down across from him.

"How are your fingers?" I asked.

He held them up. "Perfect. It was just a bump. Accidents happen."

Feeling my cheeks going warm, I grabbed my water glass and gulped half of the ice.

"I ordered you a glass of wine," he said. "I hope that was okay."

"That's fine," I said. "You seem to have impeccable taste in wine."

He smiled. "We can eat in here if you'd like."

I nodded. "Sure, this works for me. Looks like we're making dinner together a habit."

"Not a bad habit, is it?" Finn said with a grin and raised his hand. A waiter instantly appeared, handing us menus.

"How do you do that?" I asked in amazement.

"Years of practice," he said, chuckling.

I took a quick glance at the menu and ordered the grilled salmon. Finn had the swordfish. They don't call this restaurant the Fish Market for nothing.

When the waiter left, I asked, "What's up?"

He leaned across the table and lowered his voice. "I've located the name of the clients that go with the documents Basia was translating."

"Jeez, Finn, how did you get them?"

"It wasn't easy. Technically, this case no longer exists. All the records relating to it have either been destroyed or removed from the regular database. It's as if it never existed, and that's the line I've been instructed to toe."

"So how did you find the names?"

He tugged at his tie until it loosened a bit. "I strolled into my boss's office when he was at lunch with some cockeyed story about needing to consult a file he had in there. Secretary let me in without a word."

"That was pretty bold."

"Well it may yet come back to bite me in the arse. The boss is not much of a techie and had his password written on an index card and taped to his desk. Luckily, I found the names fairly quickly in an email he'd recently sent to one of the senior vice presidents in Richmond. I would've liked to read more, but I was scared as hell I'd get caught. So I jotted down the names and got out of there."

I took a sip of my wine and studied him. He seemed tired, and I could see little lines etched in the corners of his eyes. Yet that didn't at all take away from his classic good looks, and I liked that he lacked the air of pretentiousness that often accompanies guys who are handsome and know it.

"So, do the names mean anything to you?" I asked.

"I thought I'd ask the same of you," he said. He took a piece of paper out of his breast pocket and slid it across the table.

I unfolded it. "Mahir Al-Asan and Judyta Taszynski," I read aloud. Something about the name Judyta Taszynski seemed vaguely familiar, but the reason eluded me. "Were you able to find out anything else about them besides their names?"

"A little. Mahir Al-Asan, age thirty-three, is a member of the Saudi royal family. He's been married for eleven years, served four years in the Saudi military and is now serving as the Minister of Justice. Judyta Taszynski, age nineteen, is a single college student at the University of Warsaw, studying pre-med and English."

I whistled. "Saudi royal family? Okay, I'll ask the obvious question. What do the two of them have in common?"

"You mean besides this contract?"

"Exactly. You couldn't ask for a more diverse coupling. And I mean that in the Biblical sense, by the way."

Finn shoved his fingers through his hair. "All right, since you asked, I'll take a stab at it. From the way the contract was worded, I'd guess that Al-Asan hired Taszynski to have his baby. Again, I feel compelled to point out that this is not the kind of arrangement Bright Horizons typically engages in."

Something seemed wrong with this scenario. "I don't get it," I said. "If Al-Asan and his wife were having fertility problems, why go to Poland for a surrogate through an American company?"

"Good question. Maybe he met Judyta somewhere. She could be his mistress for all we know."

"I suppose," I said doubtfully.

The waiter brought our food and we dug in. The salmon was grilled to perfection. "Then why not employ another Saudi woman, or at the very least, a woman of Arabic descent?" I said after thinking it over. "I mean hiring a young woman from Poland is a pretty big stretch, mistress or not."

He set his fork down. "I agree. But if Al-Asan's got a fertility problem, maybe confidentiality is key here. Perhaps the farther away the better."

I sipped my wine and frowned. "This still doesn't play right in my mind. It seems to me that the Saudi royal family would be concerned about keeping the bloodline, for lack of a better word...pure."

"You do realize that we are speculating blind here, Lexi. There could be a very simple and logical explanation and we're just not privy to it."

I ran my finger around the top of the wine glass, listening to the faint hum. "You're right, of course, but I need more background here. Tell me about the fertility programs at Horizons."

Finn leaned back in his chair. "I'm not a doctor, but usually, it's all very straightforward. Ninety percent of the company's clients are married, just ordinary couples who are having troubles conceiving. They come to us on the referral of their regular physicians. We check them out medically and then decide which of the in vitro methods has the best chance of success."

"And the other ten percent?"

"Some are women without partners who want to get pregnant, and we use donated sperm to help them conceive.

Other clients have various medical issues that require the use of a special technique to get them pregnant."

I raised an eyebrow. "It sounds so clinical."

"It is."

"All right, if we act on the presumption that this is a surrogacy pregnancy for whatever reason, how do you think Judyta and Mahir made their initial connection?"

"Who knows? For all we know, she could have been an exchange student to Saudi Arabia. Or maybe she served as his cocktail waitress at a dinner during a diplomatic visit to Poland. I suppose we could even entertain the possibility that he placed an anonymous ad in a newspaper for a surrogate mother and then chose Judyta when she responded. I just don't know for sure."

Something kept nagging at me and I tried circling around it in my head until I suddenly had an idea. "Finn, may I borrow your cell phone?" I asked.

He looked puzzled, but reached into his shirt pocket and handed me a phone so small it fit into the palm of my hand. It looked like an oversized lighter.

I looked at it in disbelief. "This is a phone?"

He laughed. "I am absolutely shocked that a person as well versed in technology as you does not have a cell phone."

I sighed. "If you must know, I don't want to give my mother the opportunity to reach me anywhere, anytime. And don't you dare laugh, it is so *not* funny."

He laughed anyway as I reached into my bag and pulled out an address book. With the book in one hand and the phone in the other, I headed for the only quiet place in the restaurant, the bathroom.

"I'll be right back," I told Finn over my shoulder.

Luckily the bathroom was empty. I looked up the number I needed and dialed. I pressed the device to my ear and listened, but nothing. No dial tone, *nada*. I peered at the tiny screen. Underneath the florescent lighting, I couldn't even read it.

"And I work at the NSA at the cutting edge of technology?" I muttered.

After another few minutes of dialing and pressing various tiny buttons with no success, I started to get frustrated. At one point, I heard an operator telling me the number I had dialed was not valid and would I please hang up and dial again?

"Dial this," I growled viciously, stabbing the numbers in again just as a little old lady with white hair shuffled into the bathroom.

"What's wrong, honey?" she said, noticing the angry look on my face.

"It's been a tough couple of days," I said.

"What do you have there?" she asked me, peering over her thick glasses at the cell phone.

"A piece of junk," I said, looking at it in disgust.

"Give it here," she said in voice so authoritative that I handed it over immediately.

"Do you know how to work one of these things?"

"Sure," she said, taking the phone. "What's the number?"

I rattled off the number and she adeptly punched it in and then handed it back to me. I could hear it ringing. "How did you get it to ring?" I asked.

"Push the call button," she said, pointing. She shuffled off to a stall and closed the door.

"Thanks," I said, feeling dumb. Good thing she didn't know I worked for the NSA. Maybe I'd have to get a cell phone just to keep little old ladies from showing me up.

On the fourth ring, I heard Mrs. Kowalski answer. "Hello?"

"Hi, Mrs. K, it's me, Lexi again," I said.

"Oh, hello, Lexi," she answered. "Where are you calling from? I hear a slight echo."

"I'm in a restaurant. I'm sorry to bother you. I just had a quick question. Do you know if Basia knows a woman by the name of Judyta Taszynski? For some reason the name sounds familiar to me and the only reason I can think why is because she's a friend of Basia's."

I could hear the clinking of glasses and assumed she was loading the dishwasher. "Of course, she knows Judyta," she said. "Judyta is her cousin."

"Her cousin?" I repeated in surprise.

"Yes. Judyta is the daughter of my husband's sister. The family lives in Warsaw. Has she been trying to contact Basia, too?"

"Ah, not that I know of," I replied quickly. "At least I don't think so." My mind was racing. "It's just I'm thinking of planning a trip to Poland soon and I thought I might look up Judyta. Do you happen to have her address and phone number handy?" I hated lying to her, but it was for a good cause.

"I certainly wouldn't mind giving it to you, but Judyta is no longer living at home."

"Oh. Do you know where she is living?"

There was a pause. "No, I'm afraid I don't. You see, Judyta and her parents had a falling out several months ago."

"I'm sorry to hear that."

"It's embarrassing to admit, dear, but Judyta got herself...well, let's just say, in a family way. Her parents were quite unhappy about it."

"I see. So, her condition was a surprise to them."

"To say the least. Basia might know her new number, though. Perhaps you could ask her when she gets back."

"I'll do that. Thanks again, Mrs. K." I wasn't sure how to end the connection so I just snapped the phone shut.

As I left the bathroom to return to the table, Finn's phone started chirping music. I tossed it to Finn. "I think your phone is playing a U2 song," I announced.

"Irish band," he said, grinning, and popped open the phone. "Shaughnessy."

I don't know how he could hear a thing over the noise in the bar, but he listened intently, asked a few questions and then said thanks. He closed the phone and slid it back into his breast pocket.

"Well, that was interesting."

"What was interesting?"

"That was a friend of mine from the State Department. I asked him to check out whether Basia used her passport recently."

"Good thinking. Did she?"

He nodded. "She left the country last Tuesday."

I felt a sinking feeling in my stomach. "She went abroad?" I said, pretty certain I now knew where she would be going. "Let me guess. She headed to Poland."

He shook his head. "No. To Berlin."

SEVEN

"BERLIN?" I SAID in surprise.

"As in the capital of Germany."

"I know where Berlin is," I said, rolling my eyes.

Finn leaned back in his chair and studied me. "Does Basia speak German?"

"Of course she speaks German, among a hundred other languages. But why would she go to Berlin?"

"Berlin is in the center of Europe. Been there a couple of times myself. Does she have any friends there?"

"Basia has friends of every nationality on every continent on earth. She's the friendliest person I know. But she'd never go to Europe without bragging to me about it first."

"It seems like she just did."

I frowned. "I'm really not liking this at all."

Finn tapped his finger against the table. "I'm more inclined to believe she used Berlin as a springboard. Frankly, she could be anywhere in Europe now, including Poland."

"Actually, I'm leaning toward that theory myself," I said.

Finn looked at me expectantly. "Does this have anything to do with the phone call you just made in the bathroom?"

"It does. Judyta Taszynski happens to be Basia's cousin."

"Her cousin?" Finn said, clearly startled.

"On her father's side."

"Who did you call to find this out?"

"Basia's mom," I said.

"Good thinking."

"Got an address and a phone number for Judyta?" he asked.

"Nope. She's not living at home anymore. Apparently she had a falling out with her folks over the whole pregnancy thing."

"I don't think she would have run back there anyway," Finn mused.

"Why not?"

"Because it would have been the first place they'd have looked for her."

"*They* being the people who want this entire matter to disappear?"

"Exactly," he told me.

"And what if *they* already found her?"

Finn looked grim. "They haven't, at least I don't think so. But not for lack of trying. While I was on my boss's computer, I saw an email dated yesterday to a private detective the company has apparently hired to find her."

I whistled under my breath. "A private detective? Do you think they've traced her connection with Basia like we have?"

"I think it would be safe to assume that."

"Look, you don't think Judyta is in any real danger do you?"

"I don't know. I can't imagine why. On the other hand, men with guns have accosted you twice. It doesn't take a genius to suspect something illicit is happening."

I let out a deep breath. "I think Basia is with Judyta somewhere. My gut tells me she's trying to help her cousin."

"I concur. But I'm not sure what to do next."

I studied him carefully. "I don't understand why you just don't quit CGM. Walk away from all of this. Preserve your reputation. Because if you stay, there's always the chance you might be set up to take the fall if anything rotten comes out of this."

His expression sobered. "Yes, I'm fully aware that I could be implicated in some way, whether I knew what was going on or not. I'm more concerned that if I leave, evidence could be fabricated against me. If I stay and they think I'm being an obedient little employee, I might be able to obtain evidence to keep me in the clear. Right now, I have no solid proof of any wrongdoing, just a hunch. That, of course, won't hold up in a court of law." He exhaled a deep breath. "But beyond that if Judyta or Basia are in trouble, I feel partially responsible."

"How can you feel responsible? You never even officially worked on this case. After all, Harold Small passed it on to you in a rather unconventional manner."

"Which means Harold was likely disturbed by all this, as well. Lawyers just don't go around hiding company documents in safety deposit boxes. I've got a bad feeling. Lexi, there's more at stake here than just a surrogate pregnancy arrangement gone wrong."

"I'm with you on that," I said, feeling more depressed by the minute. "Finn, I heard that Bright Horizons recently went through some financial difficulties. Is that true?"

He looked at me in surprise. "How did you know that?"

"My mother. Her ear is constantly pressed to the rumor mill, especially when it involves money. I guess she's friends with Miriam Sandberg, wife of the founder of Bright Horizons."

Finn reached for his wine glass. "It's true. The company was in trouble because a couple of federal research grants didn't pan out. But they managed to turn around the decline a few months later."

"How?"

"I don't work in bookkeeping, but I presume the infertility business picked up."

"Or maybe a booming surrogacy business."

"Maybe. But there is nothing illegal about it, if done right, so why hide it? And why are men with guns so anxious to get back a generic copy of a document that doesn't even provide names?"

"I don't know. You said there are legal pitfalls to such arrangements."

"Yes, but that wouldn't cause a good man like Harold to hide documents in a safety deposit box."

I considered that for a moment. "All right, let's look at this from another angle. You. Harold put *your* name on those documents for a reason. So, let's try thinking about how you fit into all this. How did you come to work at CGM in the first place and is it typical for companies to hire their own staff of lawyers versus contracting a firm?"

Finn shrugged. "In smaller companies, law firms are typically contracted. But some larger companies prefer to have their own lawyers on the payroll. There are a few middle-aged lawyers at CGM who have been around ten or more years, but the rest of us are relatively young and basically see Horizons as a stepping stone to other more lucrative and exciting jobs. Personally, I took a job at Horizons because I like the close proximity to Washington and because I'm interested in biotechnology. Not to mention it's a relatively stress-free environment since contract law is fairly boring compared to criminal law."

"Until now," I pointed out.

"Well, until now."

"So, what kind of work do you typically do at CGM?"

"Routine work. Drawing up contracts, reviewing regulations and making certain that clients can't sue us for a number of real or perceived infractions."

"What about international clients?"

"The same, only these clients need to have their contracts, questions and various information translated for them."

"And that's how Basia became involved in all this."

"Yes."

I exhaled a deep breath. "So, if no names were involved, how would Basia have made the connection that the contract she was working on was for her cousin?"

"I don't know. Are we sure she did?"

"Honestly, I'm not sure of anything. You said you're pretty certain Judyta is pregnant. I thought the contract would have been drawn up before the actual procedure took place."

"This wasn't a typical contract. This was a contract for what happens *after* the insemination and adhesion takes place—a contract stipulating the actions of the mother after impregnation. This is way out of our jurisdiction. Frankly, I've never seen a contract like it. Had I known about it, it certainly would have been against my legal advice for CGM to involve itself in any way."

I fell silent, thinking over his answers while Finn sipped his wine and then rubbed the back of his neck.

"Did you have any unexpected visitors today?" he asked.

I thought of Slash, but I knew Finn was referring to Beefy or Mr. Middle Eastern Guy.

"Not yet. Did you find out whether Beefy had been sicced on me by your firm?"

"Well, it's not like I can just stroll up and ask whether the company hired an armed thug to harass you."

"Yeah, that's a tough one."

We talked for a short while longer and finished our dinner. I had to leave fairly soon after that to swing by home and change into sweats and a T-shirt so I could make it to karate on time. Finn walked me to the car, keeping his fingers safely in his pockets. This time he only brushed a soft kiss on my cheek. I don't know why I had been hoping for more, but I had.

"Good night, Lexi," he said softly. "Be safe and keep in touch."

"You, too," I said, hoping I didn't look too disappointed.

I drove home thinking about all he had said and what I should do next. When I got upstairs the red light on my alarm was still blinking. I tossed my bag on a chair and checked the phone. There were two messages.

I rewound the tape and listened to the first message. It was my mom saying she'd made reservations for four people next week on my birthday at a swanky French restaurant called Le Rhone. Good thing they were paying.

The second message was from Basia. I dropped in a chair as soon as I heard her voice.

"Lexi, it's Basia. I just wanted to let you know I'm fine. I'm trying to help a friend who has gotten into trouble. We're trying to sort it all out now. I hope you're keeping those documents safe for me. They could be important. Sorry to be such a pain." There was a pause and for a moment I thought she had hung up. Then I heard her continue.

"By the way, if a guy named Finn Shaughnessy contacts you don't tell him anything. He's not trustworthy. I'll try to call again soon. Love ya."

Dazed, I listened to the message again. Finn, not trustworthy? Thanks a lot for telling me *now*.

I leaned back in the chair and thought about it. Actually, it really wasn't shocking news. After all, Finn himself admitted that Basia probably didn't trust him because he was a part of CGM. In the end, I guess I hadn't completely trusted Finn either because I didn't tell him I still had the documents on a computer file. Nor had I asked him if the word *Acheron* meant anything to him. So maybe I was instinctively working this more carefully than I thought.

However, I was a bit peeved that Basia didn't offer a single clue as to where she was, whether or not she was with Judyta, and how I could reach her. Regardless it was a relief to hear, at the very least, that she was safe. And if I was right about her being with her cousin, then by extension Judyta was safe, as well.

Sighing, I changed into sweats and a T-shirt and scraped my hair back into a ponytail. Grabbing my bag, I went to my car. I seemed to be spending a lot of time there lately.

I drove straight to Anderson's Karate Academy in Laurel. Tonight it was all lit up and there were a bunch of cars parked in the lot. When I walked into the studio, I saw about twenty kids aged anywhere from five to fifteen. The only adults were parents. This didn't look like a good ratio to me.

But before I could back out, Lars spotted me. A big grin crossed his face as he strode across the room to greet me. He pumped my hand, towering over me like a great Swedish bear.

"Good to see you, Lexi," he said. "I knew you'd come."

I shrugged like it was no big deal. "Are other adults coming?" I asked hopefully. No way was I going to do this alone with a bunch of kids and their parents watching.

He nodded. "She's right behind you." He waved a hand. "Shelley, come over here, would you?"

I turned and saw a tall woman with brown hair and big hips coming our direction. She had freckles, bushy eyebrows and a friendly, bucktooth smile. "Hi," she said, offering me her hand. "I'm Shelley Hamilton. Are you a new student?"

She had a firm handshake and looked pretty intimidating in the karate outfit. "I don't know yet. I'm not sure I'm cut out for this," I confessed.

"I only come because my son Jeff is in the class," she confided. "I thought I could get some exercise and it would be a great chance for us to do something together." She pointed to a young boy with brown hair and freckles, about ten years old.

How cool is that, I thought. Mother and son doing karate together. I couldn't imagine *my* mother ever doing anything like that.

"It's actually pretty fun," Shelley said. "And gives your muscles a real workout."

My muscles could use a good workout, so I decided to give it a try. "All right," I said to Lars. "I guess I'm up for this."

He smiled. "I knew you would be," he said as Shelley walked away to a wall where she began stretching her legs.

"By the way," I asked Lars as casually as possible. "Have you heard from Basia?"

He shook his head. "No. But this is her class, so she might yet show up."

Fat chance of that, I thought, but weirder things had happened. Especially to me.

Lars walked away and I watched him, willing the connection between him and Basia to leap out at me. I could feel I was missing something here, a link outside of karate that the two of them would have. I wasn't buying Lars's suggestion that she signed up for spiritual or physical reasons. Perhaps she had done it for self-defense, but it seemed more likely to me that she'd buy a gun instead. Exercise was definitely a matter of last resort for Basia. Moreover, as handsome as Lars might be, I didn't believe she had enrolled in karate to initiate a possible romantic encounter or relationship. Miss Popularity could easily have attracted his attention without enrolling in his class. Anyway I'm positive she would have mentioned him to me. We *always* told each other things like that. There was clearly more here than met the eye and I was determined to find out what it was.

But first I had to survive my class.

Lars had all of us sit on the floor for stretches. I discovered pretty quickly that I was about as flexible as a brittle stick. The kids were like little pretzels and even Shelley was fairly adept at moving her body into the positions required. Just sitting on the floor and spreading my legs in a straddle was primordial torture for me.

What came after was nothing short of a nightmare. Lars called them muscle strengtheners. I called them circus contortions and was pretty sure the human body had not been made to do the twists and stretches he demonstrated. Just when I thought I might die stuck with my leg wrapped around my neck, he told us to sit cross-legged and take ten deep breaths. Thank God, I could at least do that.

But I couldn't manage the thirty push-ups. I couldn't even manage one. I had to do them with my knees touching the ground because my puny arms weren't strong enough to push my unwieldy body off the floor. It was pretty darn humiliating.

Finally we were ready for the lesson. Lars walked us through a no-belt routine and then we practiced something called the roundhouse kick. Lars held a bag and we all kicked it. The first time I tried it, I almost broke my toe. But Lars told me I needed to kick with the flat part of my foot. I did it and felt really empowered.

"You're a natural," he informed me.

"I bet you tell all the girls that," I quipped.

He grinned and in spite of myself, I felt proud. At least I was still standing.

When the lesson was over, I left the studio, glad I had brought a small towel. I dabbed at my face and the back of my neck, unsurprised to find I had sweated profusely. It had been one heck of a workout. I drove with the top down, enjoying the warm summer breeze. There was something about physical exercise that made a person feel good. I vowed to do it more often.

Because I felt empowered, I swung through the McDonald's drive-thru and ordered a caramel latte. I drank it on the way home, singing along with the radio to an old tune by Genesis. I swung into my apartment complex parking lot and locked the Miata up tight.

Arriving at my apartment, I stripped, went into the bathroom and turned on my CD player.

Enrique Iglesias was on, so I sang along with him while I soaped up my hair and wailed about being a hero at the top of my lungs. I towel-dried my hair, wrapped the terrycloth around me and exited the bathroom combing my wet hair and holding the towel around my body.

Slash sat on the corner of my bed.

I screamed and nearly dropped the towel. Luckily I dropped the comb instead.

"Is this an Italian thing?" I hissed, trying to calm my galloping heart. "No knocking?"

"I happen to be Italian-American," he corrected, his dark eyes glittering. "One of the perks of the new job."

My heart was still thundering. "Yeah, well when in America, do like Americans do. Knock on the damn door." I was mad because he'd nearly scared the pee out of me and because I was standing half-naked in my bedroom in front of a guy I'd met just last night.

"I did knock, *cara*. You didn't answer and then I heard this horrible screeching noise. I feared for your safety, so I came inside and tracked you to the bathroom where you apparently were *not* being threatened within inches of your life by a psychotic madman, but were singing. Since I was already in, I sat down and made myself comfortable. By the way, why do you have such a thing for Enrique Iglesias? He is such a…boy."

I flushed red, wondering just how long he had sat out there listening to me belt out Enrique's tunes. Sheesh, why couldn't I have put on something agelessly cool like The Rolling Stones? Then at least I could have been singing about getting satisfaction instead of wanting a hero.

"I will *not* discuss my taste in men with you," I retorted. "I don't even know you. Besides, I didn't know what time you were coming. I just got back from karate and had to shower."

I snatched some clothes from the floor and darted back into the bathroom, slamming the door behind me. "Let me get dressed and I'll be right out," I called through the door.

"Take your time, *cara,*" he said graciously.

I hadn't happened to grab a pair of underwear or a bra, so I shoved my naked butt into a pair of jeans and very carefully zipped them up. Then I tugged on a T-shirt, hoping my nipples weren't standing at attention. I walked barefoot back into the bedroom, my hands determinedly on my hips. Damn it, this was my place and I was taking charge.

Slash still sat there, waiting patiently on my bed dressed in a navy blue weightlifter's T-shirt, jeans and a pair of sandals. No holster today and I wondered if that meant the FBI had tagged along. His thick hair hung loose to his shoulders.

"So, you really know karate," he commented approvingly.

I noticed an expensive black leather briefcase sitting next to his feet on the floor. "Yeah, so watch it, buster,"

I bluffed, raising my steely gaze to meet his. "Consider these arms and legs killing machines."

He grinned. "Show me."

"Excuse me?"

"Show me your moves."

"You're kidding, right?"

He shook his head and I liked the way the light glinted off the strands of his black hair. "I'm not kidding."

"I don't think so. What if I hurt you?" I wondered about the penalty for injuring a national treasure.

"I'm quite capable of protecting myself," he said and I thought there was a flicker of amusement in his eyes. "Come on, *cara,* I want you to show me what you can do." This time he used a very commanding tone of voice. Like people didn't say no to him very often.

As I stood there undecided, he slipped off his sandals and flicked his hands toward me in a come-hither gesture. I couldn't take my eyes off his feet. I never knew that feet could be so sexy, but this guy had amazing ones and I don't even have a foot fetish. Or at least I think I don't.

"I'm not sure about this," I said, finally raising my gaze to meet his.

"Scared?"

"Of going to jail if I accidentally hurt you."

He took some kind of defensive position and waited. I remembered how easy it had been to step and kick that bag that Lars had held. If I pretended that Slash was that bag, maybe this karate thing wouldn't be so hard. I concentrated, took a deep breath, stepped forward to give him my best roundhouse kick.

In less than a nanosecond, he'd grabbed my foot and kicked the other one out from underneath me. Before I knew it, I was lying flat on my bedroom floor atop a pile of my clothes, looking up at the ceiling. Slash lay partially on top of me, effectively holding me down with just a fraction of his weight, his muscular forearm resting lightly against my windpipe. One push and he probably could have crushed it. He wasn't even breathing hard.

He looked at me for an interminably long time, his dark eyes searching mine. Then his lips twitched. "You're not a black belt."

"Like, *duh,*" I said from my undignified position. "I only said that because I thought you were a homicidal maniac out to rape, maim and torture me."

He laughed and I pushed his arm aside and sat up, miffed. "You can stop laughing. I had my first karate lesson tonight. I feel like an idiot."

He stood and stretched out a hand. I took it and he pulled me to my feet. "You had courage, *cara,*" he said, still holding my hand. "Impressive. A wise man would be careful of your moves."

"Then why weren't you?" I sniffed, still hurt he'd made such a fool of me.

"Good question…and it may yet get me into trouble," he murmured and then released my hand.

As he moved, I noticed a small gold cross swing out from beneath his shirt. For some reason, the sight of it surprised me. Perhaps because it seemed out of place on a man who practically oozed sex, mystery and danger. Apparently there was more to Slash than met the eye.

He sat back down on the corner of my bed. "So how was your day? Run into any suspicious characters?"

"Except for you, no," I said, still grumpy he had shown me up. "I heard you met with the Zimmermans."

Slash patted the mattress beside him, so I sat down, too. "*Si,* it was a most interesting meeting. I have to thank you for bringing us together."

"You're welcome, I guess."

"The twins told me of your suspicions about CGM and Bright Horizons. When you get into trouble, you get into it big, *cara.*"

"It wasn't like I was out looking for it. It just kind of found me."

"Then it seems trouble is quite adept at finding you. Let's talk about Acheron."

So the twins had told him about that, too.

"There's not much to talk about. For some reason, Basia penciled it in code at the bottom of page three of the document."

"I took a crack at it myself," Slash said. "I agree that this is the best translation. But what do you think it means?"

"I have no idea."

"No operation at work sound similar?"

"None that I'm working on." I ran my fingers through my damp hair.

"I looked around a bit today and found nothing. I will deepen my search."

I didn't know exactly what he meant by a deeper search, and probably didn't want to know. "I'm not even sure what I'm looking for even if we do get into CGM or Bright Horizons," I said.

"We are working on that. It will not be long. If they have something on Acheron in their files, we'll know it soon enough." He paused for a moment. "But I did come up with some very interesting information connected to Bright Horizons from a few other databases."

I realized it would be in my best interest not to ask which databases he'd been poking around in and Slash didn't offer to tell. "What kind of information?" I asked.

"Does the name Hasan El-Karan mean anything to you?"

I thought for a moment. "No. Should it?"

"What about Ahmad Fahil?"

"International affairs were never my strong suit," I admitted. "Is there any reason why I would know these people?"

Slash studied me for a while, then shrugged. "They were bodyguards in the service of His Royal Highness Mahir Al-Asan of Saudi Arabia."

At the mention of Al-Asan's name, I gasped aloud. Slash looked at me strangely. "You know that name, then?"

I nodded. "Yes. In fact, I just heard of him tonight. From a guy who works for CGM."

Slash looked at me as if I had completely lost my mind. "What? You're talking openly to someone on the inside at CGM?"

"Well, sort of," I admitted. "He contacted me yesterday looking for Basia. He was the one who sent her the documents for translation in the first place. He thinks there is something fishy going on at Bright Horizons."

Slash looked at me incredulously. "And you believed him...just like that?"

I started to feel defensive. "Hey, *he* came to *me,* and *he* was doing most of the talking. I learned lots of useful stuff about CGM."

Slash swore under his breath. "You didn't tell him you still had the documents electronically, did you?"

"No, I didn't. I didn't tell him about Acheron either, so quit acting like I did something illegal."

"Foolish is more like it."

"Hey," I protested. "Now you're getting personal."

"Well don't you think it is coincidental that he happened to contact you the day after the documents are mysteriously stolen from you? How did he find you?"

"He worked with Basia and I guess she talked about

me. My connection to her is no secret. It was a logical extrapolation that I might know where she is."

Slash didn't look pacified in the slightest. "Who is this man?"

"His name is Finn Shaughnessy. He's a lawyer for the company."

"A lawyer?" Slash exclaimed, followed by what I think were swear words in Italian.

I held up my hands. "Hey, I know it sounds bad, but he's a *nice* lawyer," I explained and then couldn't believe it myself that the words "nice" and "lawyer" had come from my mouth. "Look, Finn is convinced there's a cover-up going on in the company. He's genuinely worried about Basia and has been trying to get to the bottom of it, at great risk to himself I might add."

"You are unbelievable," Slash muttered.

"All right, that's it!" I said in a huff. "I can handle this myself." I was getting tired of everyone acting like I didn't know what I was doing—even if it were true.

Slash rolled his eyes, sighed and then patted the bed. "Sit down, *cara*. No need to consider this a big problem. Perhaps we can use this lawyer to our advantage."

"That was my plan all along." I sniffed, sitting back down.

Slash took a deep breath. "All right. What does he know about Al-Asan?"

I told Slash everything Finn told me, including Basia's flight to Berlin possibly to rescue her cousin Judyta Taszynski, the apparent connection of Al-Asan and Judyta to the Bright Horizons contract, and the fact that CGM had hired a private detective to find Judyta. Slash listened intently, and about halfway through my story, stood up and started to pace.

He paced for another few minutes and I watched him

walk back and forth across my bedroom floor, absently trampling my clothes, underwear and assorted junk. Finally he stopped and looked at me as if remembering I was there.

"Do you think this Finn Shaughnessy would help us?" he asked.

"Maybe. What did you have in mind?"

"An encryption-breaking program. The twins and I could write it and he could load it onto the network via his computer at work."

"You want him to break into his own company files?"

"Is he looking to protect himself or not?" Slash asked with a raised eyebrow.

"I guess, but what we're asking him to do is illegal. He is a lawyer after all. And if we get access to the network, the files we need may still be encrypted."

"Trust me, *cara,* the encrypted files will be the easy part. We've got to crack the network first. Will you ask him or not?"

I hesitated. Somehow I was casting a wide net, dragging not only my friends, but people I barely knew into murky criminal waters. "I suppose I can ask," I finally said. "*If* the twins agree it's a good idea. However, I can't guarantee he'll do it."

Slash shrugged. "If he doesn't, we are no worse off, and we must then determine why he refuses to help. If he does agree to do it, you mustn't tell him where you got the disk."

"Because you don't exist."

Slash smiled. "Exactly."

I suddenly felt vulnerable, scared and tired. I wasn't sure of anything anymore, including the dark-haired man pacing my bedroom. Was he really who he said he was?

Slash must have sensed the change in me because he

walked over to me and put a light hand on my shoulder. "You're still not sure of me."

I frowned, hating the fact that my thoughts were so transparent. It was time to work on my poker face.

"Well, I think the twins trust you and that is in your favor," I said. "I guess I've just developed an *X-Files* complex—you know, 'Trust No One.'"

He chuckled, apparently also a fan of the old television show. "I assure you, *cara,* there is no government conspiracy here. I came because you needed me. You still do. Now listen to what I have to say and perhaps it will reassure you." Slash sat back down on the bed. "But you must understand that what I will say now is a matter of critical national security. You must promise to keep it confidential."

I looked at him intently. "Do you really work for the NSA?"

"Si."

"Anyone else?"

He smiled slightly. "Si."

"Who?" I demanded.

"The good guys. Don't ask any more, *cara.* I can't tell you."

"But you're sure it's okay to bring me in on an NSA restricted operation?" The last thing I needed to do was add spying or obtaining classified information to my burgeoning criminal activity list. "Are you sure I don't need to fill out some paperwork, have a more thorough background check or take another lie detector test? Even more importantly, are you sure I have the required psychological make-up to withstand torture and starvation if I fall into enemy hands?" I was really worried about the starvation part. The enemy would just have to withhold Diet Coke or donuts for a couple of days and I'd be ready to spill my guts.

Slash rolled his eyes. "If you fall into enemy hands, I'll open the cyanide capsule in your mouth myself."

I searched for a glimpse of humor but didn't see one. "Gee, while that's thoughtful of you and all, I'm not sure I want to go down this path. I really, *really* don't want to be America's weakest link in national security."

Now his lips twitched. "Come on, *cara,* don't you want to know what's happening with your friend?"

"Yes," I admitted.

"Then understand that there are risks involved."

Hello? Like I didn't already know that. Case in point, I had a strange man in my bedroom to prove it.

"I'm well aware of that," I said. "It's just there's a lot more risk than I expected."

"It's up to you."

I sighed. "Okay."

"Good. Then I must start by telling you those two men who were bodyguards for Prince Al-Asan—they showed up dead about nine months ago in Genoa, Italy."

"Dead?" I squeaked and then hated myself for sounding like a scared teenager.

"Murdered, actually. They had just delivered a package to the Bright Horizons fertility clinic and were on their way back to the hotel when they were ambushed and shot in their car."

"Ambushed? Why?"

Slash shook his head. "Their murders have not been solved. But both the CIA and the FBI have taken an interest in the case."

"The FBI *and* the CIA? Why would they be interested in a case of two Saudi nationals in Italy?"

"Terrorism. The FBI requested and obtained the ballistics report from the Italian police and reviewed the other evidence retrieved at the site. There is no conclusive evidence but the CIA is convinced it's the work of the followers of Samir Al-Naddi."

I drew in my breath sharply. "Samir Al-Naddi? Not that terrorist nutcase from Yemen?"

"The one and only."

I suddenly felt sick to my stomach. I didn't like where any of this was going. And I *really* didn't like that it seemed to be going in my direction.

Slash leaned down and picked up his briefcase, pulling it onto his lap. He punched in a code and the briefcase snapped open. I peered inside curiously and saw a precisely organized workstation complete with a sleek-looking laptop, a bunch of neatly rolled cables, computer tools and a sheaf of documents. The briefcase was deep, so I was sure there was more cool stuff in the bottom, including more expensive and top-of-the-line equipment.

Slash pulled out his laptop and I looked with unabashed envy at his ultra slim machine, which looked to weigh about half a pound and was less than an inch thick.

I whistled in appreciation. "Sleek set-up. Can you tell me who makes it?"

"Sorry. That's classified," he said with a shrug.

He probably changed computers as often as he changed clothes, I thought. Sheesh, if I made his paycheck, I'd probably do the same. To him, my laptop was likely a dinosaur.

He opened the computer, booted up quickly and then opened a file. Looking over his shoulder I saw several computer-generated photographs.

"Can you look through these and tell me if you see anyone you recognize?" he asked.

My lip trembled. I wasn't sure I was up to all of this. In my heart of hearts, I knew the unabashed truth—I was a coward. A coward with a degree in math and computer science who liked chocolate éclairs, doing the Sunday crossword puzzle in *The Washington Post* and leading a really boring, tedious life. I wasn't at all equipped to deal with the fact that my best friend had vanished, people were pulling guns on me and talking about superterrorists. I felt like crying.

I closed my eyes and suddenly had the absurd realization that Slash and I had never left my bedroom.

I abruptly stood. "Let's go to the kitchen," I said.

He put a gentle hand on my arm. "I know you're afraid," he said quietly. "You can back out if you want to, *cara*. No one will blame you."

I pulled away from his touch. "Then what happens to Basia?"

"Perhaps nothing."

"Or maybe she ends up dead."

He didn't disagree, and I could see sympathy in his eyes. "You didn't ask for this, *cara*. It's your decision."

I gritted my teeth and tried to screw up the courage to tell him to get out of my apartment. Instead I exhaled. "Okay, set the laptop up on the kitchen table while I brew some coffee."

For a moment it seemed like he might urge me to change my mind and back out. But then he looked down at his briefcase.

"I think perhaps the occasion calls for something stronger," he said. To my astonishment, he pulled a bottle of red wine from the bottom of the briefcase and handed it to me. I wondered if all Italian men carried wine in their briefcases.

I glanced at the wine label. Red, Italian and old. Most likely the most expensive wine I'd ever drink in my life. If my life lasted all that much longer.

"What's the occasion?" I asked.

"Italians don't need an occasion to drink wine, but if

you insist I'll say it's the start of what is likely to be a fruitful partnership."

I wasn't sure what he meant, but I nodded. I seriously needed a drink.

Slash followed me into the kitchen. As I pulled out two wine glasses from the cabinet, he set up the laptop on the kitchen table. I dug out a corkscrew from one of my drawers and handed it to him. He popped the cork and poured the wine. I took a sip. It was light, fruity and full-flavored. Excellent.

"Superb wine," I said, like I was some kind of connoisseur.

He seemed pleased. "I thought you would like it."

He was right and that made me nervous. I sat at the table, clutching my wine glass, and avoided looking directly at the computer. Slash sensed my reluctance because he patted me on the back.

"Courage, *cara*. Come take a look."

I chewed on my lower lip, still refusing to look at them. "Who are they?"

"You tell me," he said.

I steeled myself and stared at the photos. They were all men—different ages and races. I let out a small gasp and pointed to the middle of the third row.

"That's Mr. Middle Eastern Guy! That was the man in my apartment. Who is he?"

Slash looked at me for a long time without saying anything. Then he looked back and forth between the photo and me.

"Look again, *cara*," he said. "It's very important. It was dark in your apartment. How sure are you that this is the man you saw?"

I looked back at the picture. There was no doubt in my

mind that this was the same guy. "It's him," I said. "I'm positive. Who is he?"

Slash rested his chin in his hand. He definitely did not look happy. His finger rested on the corner of the picture and he tapped it slowly.

"His name is Rashid Bouker," he finally said. "He's the military attaché at the Yemeni Embassy in Washington."

EIGHT

"YEMEN?" I CHOKED, nearly spewing the expensive Italian wine all over him. "You're joking, right?" Like he'd joke about this.

Even Slash looked worried. "Those papers, *cara*. Think. What was in them that would have everyone, including a high-ranking official of the Embassy of Yemen chasing after them?"

"You've seen them for yourself, haven't you?" I asked.

"I have, but you and Basia are the only ones who saw the original."

"They're identical, other than the penciled code on the bottom of page three that we decided meant Acheron. I have no idea what an official from Yemen would want with the documents. From what I could tell, it was a contract between unnamed clients generated by Bright Horizons and written in Polish. Living arrangements, including the rent of an apartment in Warsaw, a car, medical services, a bank account and a generous stipend were all provided to an unnamed recipient. Finn thinks it may have been a contract drawn up to provide for a surrogate pregnancy. But he said to his knowledge, the company did not involve itself in such contracts."

"To the best of his knowledge?" Slash asked.

"Yes," I said, irritated that his voice held a note of disdain every time we talked about Finn. "He told me tonight that he found out whose names were part of that contract— Al-Asan and Basia's cousin, Judyta Taszynski."

"Who translated the contract for you?"

I hesitated, not wanting to bring Paul into this. "A friend of mine," I said. "I don't want to involve him."

"You already have," Slash said, but he didn't press further. He shoved his hand through his dark hair in frustration and I felt envious of his fingers. "We need to get more information."

"How?"

"I've already sent a copy of the electronic version of the contract to another expert to have them translated again for us," Slash said. "But it isn't likely we'll learn much more than you've already told me. Maybe your meeting with the lawyer is a good thing after all. He may be the key that breaks this for us."

My anxiety level was ratcheting into the stratosphere. "Look, if this whole thing is now a matter of national security, I should probably tell my boss. At first I thought I was just protecting my best friend. If there is some kind of international intrigue going on, possibly involving terrorists, I could get fired for keeping this to myself. Not to mention I might also get myself killed."

To my surprise, Slash touched my arm in what I think was a gesture of comfort, but instead, I felt a streak of heat race from his fingertips through my skin and directly into my veins. Jeez, guys needed to stop touching me or I was going to die of heart failure at twenty-four.

"You have told someone at the NSA, *cara*. Me. I have informed those persons who need to know. Rest assured that you have completed your duty."

"But I'm not even sure you work at the NSA," I said in frustration. "Not to mention the fact that I don't even know your real name. I mean you could just be some guy who broke into my home and is pumping me for information about this situation. You could even be working for Mr.

Middle Eastern Guy or Beefy." I knew I sounded scared and desperate, because I was. This situation was spiraling way out of my control.

Slash exhaled a deep breath. "You want me to prove that I work for the NSA? Then I shall visit you tomorrow at work. I shall stroll past your workspace and say hello. But you must not call me by name or tell anyone how you know me. Would that make you feel better?"

"It might," I said. Actually the suggestion both intrigued and relieved me. If Slash didn't work for the NSA there was no way he could get to me. You have to be pretty high up to just stroll wherever you want. The complex has a slew of buildings, some adjoining and some not, and is twice the size of the CIA. At the NSA we are strictly compart-mentalized and each of us only has authorization to be in certain parts of the building. And that was after a series of exhausting security checks including holographic IDs, hand prints and retina scans. I had been working at the NSA for two years and I had never seen him on my side of the building. It would be a true test to see if he could actually get to me.

"Eccellente," he said with smile. "Then we shall have no more secrets between us, *si?*"

"I guess," I said uncertainly.

I drained the rest of my glass, feeling a slight bit better. If Slash really was who he said he was, then his help could be invaluable. Moreover, I would fulfill my duty to both my boss and my country. Slash refilled both of our glasses and I felt some of the tension go out of my neck and shoulders. But I still didn't understand something.

"The Yemen connection is still bugging me," I said.

"It bothers me, too, *cara*. I have been unable to de-termine why the FBI and CIA think terrorists under the control of Samir Al-Naddi would kill Al-Asan's two body-guards in Genoa. Al-Naddi and Al-Asan have no obvious connection to each other, no known animosity or political differences. Now you say an embassy official from Yemen broke into your apartment and threatened you with a gun while trying to get his hands on this contract. It does not make sense to me either."

"Maybe I should just call the police and tell them Mr. Bouker broke into my apartment and assaulted me," I suggested.

Slash leaned back in his chair. "Accusing diplomats of a felony is a tricky matter, *cara*. Besides, it would be your word against his. And I have a feeling that he'd have a room full of people swear he was with them at the time you say he was here."

I sighed. "I suppose you're right. So, what do we do next?"

Slash thought for a moment and then logged on to the internet. He had a system going I didn't understand, and had likely rigged his computer in ways I couldn't even begin to imagine.

"What are you doing?" I asked.

"Making notes to myself of things to check out later," he said mysteriously. He pulled up the Linux operating system, typed some unfamiliar commands and then snapped the computer shut. Then he stood, holding the black case in his hand.

"*Buona notte, cara.* Good night. Until tomorrow."

I nodded mutely and he politely waited while I disarmed the alarm before he left. I reset the alarm, locked the door, the deadbolt and chain and then went back to my bedroom where I stripped off my clothes, pulled a baggy T-shirt over my head and, to my great relief, fell promptly asleep.

WHEN MY ALARM went off the next morning at six-thirty, I hit the snooze button twice and then finally swung my legs over the side of the bed. When I stood up and took one step, everything collapsed. Every muscle in my body, including those I had no idea even existed, screamed in pain from my karate workout. Dragging myself to my feet, I stood, swaying precariously and then staggered stiffly into the bathroom like Frankenstein. I splashed freezing cold water on my face and my entire head throbbed in response. I realized on top of everything else, I had a hangover.

Sheesh, two glasses of expensive Italian wine and I was hungover. Of course, there had also been that glass of wine at dinner with Finn. Heck, maybe I was turning into an alcoholic or worse, a cheap date.

Somehow I managed to brush my teeth even though they hurt, too, and combed my hair. Just lifting my arm to brush was hard work.

I shuffled back into the bedroom, snipped the tags off the last of my new clothes purchases and managed to pull them on. The apartment was still a horrid mess—clothes, books, papers, shoes and knickknacks everywhere. I absolutely, positively had to do laundry today. Especially because I had a date with Paul tonight and nothing to wear.

My stomach roiled. A date with Paul Wilks. Laundry aside, how was I supposed to go dancing with Paul when I could barely walk?

I would have to worry about that later. First things first. Just get to work. Somehow I managed to get down the stairs, into my car and drive into the Dunkin' Donuts parking lot. Trying to maneuver my way out of the car took me a full five minutes. I moved like a robot to the counter, where I bought a bottle of Diet Coke, a sesame bagel with cream cheese and two chocolate donuts with sprinkles.

The donuts were comfort food because in the shape I was in now, a little comfort was a definite necessity.

I kept the top on the Miata up because the wind blowing through my hair would just be too painful. Even with sunglasses the sun seemed too darn bright. Worse than that, it was a sweltering hot Washington, D.C., day of nearly eighty-five degrees and one hundred percent humidity at only seven-fifteen in the morning.

I drove to work, shuffled my way through the security checkpoints and collapsed into my swivel chair. Opening a bottle of Excedrin, I took two capsules, washing them down with a gulp of my Diet Coke.

I logged on and then whizzed around the internet, looking for a phone number. When I found what I wanted, I picked up the phone.

"Natty Neatniks," the cheerful voice on the other end said. "We clean, dust, vacuum and take care of the necessities so you can spend more time doing what's important to you. How can I help you?"

"Um… I'd like to hire your company to clean my apartment," I said. "How much do you cost?"

"How big is your apartment?"

"It's a one-bedroom apartment," I answered. "A bathroom, a living room and a small kitchen."

"Where are you located?"

"Jessup, Maryland."

"One hundred bucks," she said in that cheerful voice.

"A hundred bucks?" I exclaimed. "For a one-bedroom apartment in Jessup?"

"That doesn't include windows. Windows are extra."

My headache got worse. "I suppose cleaning the bathroom is extra, too."

"No, that's included."

"What about laundry?"

"That costs extra. You provide the detergent. Ironing carries an additional fee."

Sheesh, this was becoming more expensive by the minute. "Okay, so let me get this straight. You dust, vacuum, and clean the bathroom but no windows. Laundry and ironing are extra."

"Exactly."

I pressed my fingers to my throbbing temples. "Okay. I'd like you to clean the apartment and do the laundry."

"When do you want this done?"

"Today, if possible."

"Today?"

I sighed. "Let me guess. That will cost extra."

"Yes, because we'll have to squeeze you in," she said and I could hear her shuffling around papers. "That means bringing someone extra on staff. It will cost an extra thirty-five dollars."

I heard the sound of money being sucked out a window. But I really, *really* needed some clean, non-thong underwear. "Okay," I agreed.

"Your name, please?" she asked.

She took my name, address, work and home phone numbers. We agreed to meet at the apartment at twelve-thirty, so I could let the maids in. I hung up feeling poorer by the minute.

I waited until nine o'clock before making my next call.

"*Richmond Gazette*. Carmichael."

"Hi, Rock," I said. "How you doing, bro?"

"Lexi," he said, and I could hear a smile in his voice. "What a surprise to hear from you. Let me guess, you need a loan."

"Hey, I don't always call just because I need money," I said and then sighed. "Well, okay, maybe I need money, but I also have something else to ask you about."

He chuckled. "What is it this time?"

Rock works for the *Richmond Gazette* as an investigative reporter. He is a brilliant writer and has an uncanny knack for revealing rotten politicians, health-care scams and a wide variety of other unsavory activities. He's already won numerous awards and a lot of people say he's on the fast track to working for a big-time paper like *The Washington Post* or *New York Times*. He's also a decent and fair guy, which in my opinion are his best characteristics, looks aside.

"I wonder if you could tell me anything interesting about CGM, Inc. down there in Richmond," I said.

"The medical research company?" he asked. I could hear a note of curiosity in his voice and knew I'd piqued his interest.

"Yeah, that's the one."

I heard his chair creak as he swiveled. "Well it's a big company, well respected and generates lots of money for the community down here. They contribute fairly generously to charities and a wide variety of political campaigns and causes. Why? You think something bad is going down with them?"

"I don't know," I said honestly. "I heard they were recently in some financial trouble before they got a healthy infusion of cash. Do you think you could check it out for me?"

"The infusion of cash?"

"That and anything else unusual you might find out about them."

"Sure," he said lightly, but I could hear the cautious excitement in his voice. Rock can smell a good story a mile away.

"Do you mind if I ask why you are so interested in all this?" he asked.

"It's a long story," I said carefully. "I don't have time to go into it now. But Rock, be discreet, will you?"

"Discreet is my middle name," he said cheerfully. "So, how much cash do you need?" He didn't even suggest asking Mom and Dad because we both knew the cost of borrowing from them would be way too high and would involve horrible things like promises to visit and blind dates.

"Five hundred dollars," I said. "I'll pay you back by Christmas."

"Okay," he said without hesitation. That's another thing I like about Rock. He's got that oldest child thing going, meaning he's responsible, dependable and doesn't ask a lot of questions. "I'll drop it in the mail to you today."

"Thanks, Rock. Let me know if you uncover anything of interest with CGM."

"Will do," he said and hung up.

Sighing, I took out some papers from my in-box and began sorting them. After a minute, the back of my neck prickled. I turned around and saw my boss standing there silently.

"Jeez, Jonathan," I said. "You scared me. What's up with the tiptoeing?"

He looked solemn. "Can I see you in my office?"

Uh, oh, I thought. Paul had gone and spilled the beans. Damn, I'd known he couldn't be trusted to keep a secret. Standing, I followed him to his office, all the while trying to figure out how I would explain everything and still manage to keep my job.

Jonathan's office was barely bigger than a box, but it had a window and at the NSA, that alone made him important. He sat down behind his desk and I perched in one of the two chairs angled in front of it. Folding his hands primly on top of the desk, he looked at me for a long silent minute.

"Is everything all right?" he finally asked.

"All right?" I said, my voice coming out a tad higher than usual. "Me? I'm right as rain."

"And your absence yesterday?" he asked, providing me with the opportunity to finish.

"Oh, that," I said, thinking quickly. "I just had a twenty-four-hour flu bug or something. I had lots of stomach problems, as well as problems with the other end. You know what that's like."

He looked kind of grossed out and I cringed inwardly, forcing myself to shut up. I was babbling like a guilty idiot and the fake smile I plastered to my face probably didn't help much either. The problem was I knew *he* knew I was lying and that made me all the more nervous.

"Are you sure there's nothing you want to tell me?"

"Tell you? About what?"

He was silent for a minute. "I want you to know, Lexi, that you are a valued member of my team. *Team* being the operative word here. I'm available if you need me for anything. You can trust me."

I studied Jonathan, but his elegantly pale face was completely impassive. Now I knew what a true poker face looked like. I couldn't figure out if he knew something, suspected something, or whether he was simply concerned about my welfare. Slash had warned me not to say anything to Jonathan, but so had Beefy and Mr. Middle Eastern Guy. Who was a gal to trust?

"Thanks, Jonathan. I appreciate your concern. But everything's okay. Really."

I saw a flash of disappointment in his eyes. "I see. Well, just remember that in my department, we work together. No heroics. Got it?"

Not really, but I didn't say so. "Sure, thanks," I said and stood stiffly, my muscles screaming in pain.

"So get back to work," he said, dismissing me.

I returned to the cubicle, half limping, my anxiety level climbing. His little pep talk had made me really paranoid. He knew something, or at the very least suspected something. But what? And if he suspected something then why didn't he just come right out and say so?

Unless... I picked up the phone and called Elvis.

Xavier answered the phone. "Hey, Lexi," he said. "How are things going?"

"From bad to worse," I said, lowering my voice. "Any progress cracking into the system?"

"Not yet. It's a tough one."

"Bummer. Is Elvis around?"

"How come you always want to talk to him? What am I? Chopped liver?"

"More like a T-bone steak, which by the way, I happen to adore. Look, I just need to ask him a question. I swear I'm not playing favorites."

"If you say so," Xavier said. He was a pretty agreeable guy. "Have you heard from Basia yet?"

He really did dig her, I marveled. I couldn't remember Xavier ever asking about any woman before. Maybe I needed to do something to facilitate that relationship. In fact, the more I thought about it, the more I thought Xavier might be good for the free-wheeling Basia and vice versa. Weird how I'd never thought about that before.

"Yeah, she called," I admitted. "But I wasn't home. Unfortunately she didn't say where she was or what she was doing. She just left this weird cryptic message on my machine."

Xavier was silent for a moment. "When did Basia call and leave this weird message?"

"Yesterday."

"You sure it was her?"

"I think so."

"Then that's good enough for me," he said. "May the Force be with you. Here's Elvis."

Sheesh, sometimes talking with the twins is like an out-of-body experience.

"Hey, Lexi," Elvis said, coming on the line. "If you're calling to chart our progress on the mission, sorry, no luck."

"I know, Xavier already told me. Actually, I've got a question for you."

"Sure. Why are you whispering?"

"Because I don't want anyone else to hear," I said, cupping my hand around the receiver. "I've got a hypothetical question to ask you."

"Fire away."

"Do you know if the NSA ever tests its employees?"

"Tests? As in multiple choice?"

"No, I mean like testing by having someone do something to see how an employee reacts."

He paused. "You mean like you're thinking this whole mess with Basia is some kind of psychological test?"

"That's exactly what I'm thinking," I said. "I mean, I think Jonathan suspects something is going on. He just called me in his office, pumped me for information that I didn't give him and gave me a pep talk about being a team player. But Slash said not to tell Jonathan anything. Am I doing the right thing?"

He fell quiet for a moment. "I don't know, Lexi," he finally said.

I rambled on. "Maybe some higher-ups at the NSA are just seeing how trustworthy I am because I'm up for a promotion or something. If so, I think I'm flunking big time. Given your experience, is any of this even in the *realm* of possibility? I mean you worked for several years at the

NSA and you know how peculiar it can be here. Should I trust anyone?"

Several seconds passed then he said, "There are some strange dudes at the NSA, no question. We know for a fact that NSA methods are often highly irregular. It keeps the bad guys on their toes. Therefore, I suppose the answer to your hypothetical question is…maybe."

There you have it. Wisdom dispensed from a computer genius. I sighed. "My life is a mess."

"Chaos is the true state of the universe anyway."

"My universe was fairly orderly before all this."

"It was only an illusion."

"Oh, God." He was probably right. After all, I was asking for life advice from a guy named Elvis.

"Would you mind if I asked for another favor?"

"I live but to serve you."

"If only. Can you see what you can dig up about an embassy guy from Yemen named Rashid Bouker?" I spelled it for him. "Just in case this isn't some kind of employment test."

"Sure. I got some other stuff to do first, but I'll get back to you."

"You rock it, Elvis."

"Yeah, and don't I know it."

I hung up and stared at the pile of work in front of me. I knew I'd better do something to earn my paycheck. I turned to my computer and got to work. About an hour and a half later, Paul stopped by.

"Hey, Lexi," he said. "Are you ready for the big date tonight?"

"About that date…"

"You're not going to try and back out on me, are you?" he said accusingly. "You gave me your word."

I lifted my hands and the effort of doing so hurt. "Of

course, I'm good for my word. I'm not backing out. It's just I'm not sure about the dancing part of the evening. I've got some serious muscle pains from karate."

"You taking karate? No way."

"What's so hard to believe?" I said, annoyed.

"Well, you're not the type to do karate."

"And what type is that?"

"I don't know. Coordinated, athletic, fit."

"Jeez, Paul, you sure know how to compliment a girl."

He shrugged. "Just telling it like it is. So, how long have you been doing karate?"

"Since yesterday."

"Then you're only stiff because your muscles haven't had much exercise." He had a membership at a gym so I guess that made him a lot more knowledgeable than me. "Dancing will be the perfect therapy. It will warm and stretch your muscles even more. Trust me on this. I promise I'll go easy on you."

I didn't want to warm or stretch my muscles. I wanted to date a guy who suggested a soak in the hot tub and a Swedish back rub. But no, I had to get stuck with a John Travolta wannabe.

"But Paul—"

"No buts. Just trust me."

I rolled my eyes. It hurt. Then I sighed. Sometimes there are things in life that are unavoidable, like yearly pelvic exams, root canals and dates from hell. Why is it that I seem to have more of those things than other people?

Paul took pity on me. "Hey, I'll let you decide where we eat," he offered.

"Gee, thanks. How generous of you. I'll think on it."

He finally left me alone and I got back to work. Shortly after noon, I drove to my apartment. It was nice driving on the Parkway in the middle of the day. No traffic, so you could actually crank the car up to sixty-five.

When I pulled into the parking lot, the van for Natty Neatniks was already there. I parked the car and limped over. Three young Hispanic women climbed out of the car and smiled at me.

"I'm Lexi Carmichael," I said, holding out my hand to the one in front.

She shook my hand and smiled back at me shyly. "You let us in, yes?"

I nodded. "Follow me."

We trudged up the three painfully long flights of stairs where I unlocked the door and turned off the alarm. The three girls walked in and gasped at the mess.

"This isn't my fault," I said, but I don't think they understood.

The woman I had shook hands with whipped a cell phone out of her pocket and punched in some numbers. She spoke in rapid Spanish with someone and then hung up.

"Sorry," she said. "Big mess. Long time here. This cost extra."

My stomach took a dive. I had a feeling I'd be lucky to get out of this for under three hundred dollars.

"How much extra?" I asked warily.

"One hundred dollars."

"A hundred dollars *extra?*"

"Big mess," she repeated as if I were an idiot. Maybe I was. "Long time here."

I looked around. She was right. It was a big mess and one I didn't want to deal with.

"Okay," I said, suddenly afraid they might leave. They looked ready to bolt and seemed hopeful I'd change my mind. "I'll pay extra. But don't forget to do the laundry."

two girls. They took off for the bathroom and bedroom respectively while I whipped out my checkbook, added up all the extras and gave the woman her check.

"Just lock up before you leave," I said.

"What about alarm?" she asked. "You give me code?"

"Forget it. Just lock the door." Who did the alarm really keep out these days anyway?

I left my apartment, entered the McDonald's drive-thru and ordered a cheeseburger, large fries and a Diet Coke. I unfastened the top button on my skirt and ate in the car as I drove back to work. To hell with eating right. I was stressed out and depressed. It was no fun being in the poorhouse, having sore muscles and getting stuck with a guy who thought disco dancing was cool.

When I got back to my desk the message light on my phone was blinking. I pressed the button.

"Hi, Lexi. It's Elvis. Got the info you requested. Call me."

I picked up the phone and dialed his number. He answered on the first ring.

"Hey, Elvis," I said.

"I've got rather lukewarm news to report," he said. "There's not a whole lot of data available on Bouker other than he's the military attaché to the Yemeni Embassy in Washington. That means he's likely their spook. He was assigned to the post just over a year ago. He's married and has three kids ages eleven, nine and three, all boys. He lives in a condo on Massachusetts Avenue. His kids go to the Islamic Saudi Academy in Northern Virginia and are taken there by a driver every day. On the weekends, he frequents a Middle Eastern restaurant on Connecticut Avenue near the zoo called the Ali Kabab House. He's got an international driver's license and likes fast cars. As far as I can tell, he's traveled to Pennsylvania, California, Arizona and Florida, presumably on vacation since he's been in the country. Not surprisingly, the FBI keeps tabs on his movements. He looks pretty clean, meaning no known or obvious associations with terrorists. Seems to be your run-of-the-mill embassy guy."

Except for the fact that he broke into my apartment and threatened me with a gun. "Thanks, Elvis," I said. "Oh, and there's one more thing I wanted to tell you about."

I filled him in on my meeting with Finn Shaughnessy and told him what Slash had suggested about using Finn to plant a program in the company network that would give us immediate access to CGM.

"Cool. You think this Finn guy would do it?" Elvis sounded excited.

"I don't know. If you think it's a good idea, I'll ask him."

"It's a good idea. Hold on, Xavier wants to talk to you."

I waited until Xavier came on.

"You said you got a call from Basia yesterday," he said, "so I asked a friend of mine at the phone company for a favor and he tracked down the number for me. I don't know if Basia is still there, but the number came from a swanky restaurant in Stockholm."

"Stockholm? As in Sweden?" I asked in surprise.

"The one and only."

"That was good thinking, Xavier."

"And that's why they pay me the big bucks," he said and hung up.

The revelation startled me and I sat in my chair thinking. Another Swedish connection. I *was* on to something and he was big, blond and had a black belt. My gut instinct had been right. Lars Anderson was involved in this somehow because no way in hell did I consider this a coincidence. But how could I get him to talk? I didn't think my roundhouse kick would be threatening enough.

I placed my elbows on my desk and rested my head in my hands before nearly jumping out of my skin when I saw Paul standing quietly at the entrance to my cubicle.

"Now what?" I said crankily. I sincerely hoped he hadn't overheard anything important while I was talking to Elvis and Xavier.

"I came to see if you had decided where you want to go for dinner tonight."

That had been the last thing on my mind. I closed my eyes and suddenly had a brilliant idea.

"Actually, I have," I said, smiling. "I'd like to try a restaurant in D.C. that I've heard a lot about."

"This isn't going to cost me a fortune, is it?" Paul complained.

"I hear it's pretty reasonable," I replied, knowing nothing of the sort.

He brightened. "So, what's it called?"

"The Ali Kabab House. It's on Connecticut Avenue near the zoo."

"Ali Kabab?" he said, frowning. "It sounds Middle Eastern."

"Well, I wasn't feeling like Mexican," I said, shrugging. If I had to go out with Paul, at least I could try and see if I could accidentally run into Mr. Middle Eastern Guy again, but this time on a more even playing field.

"It sounds weird," he said doubtfully. "How about a steak house?"

"Come on, Paul, be adventurous."

"Excuse me," came a nasal voice from behind Paul. "Mail time."

Paul looked over his shoulder and frowned. "Come back later. Can't you see we're having a private conversation here?"

"Sorry," the guy mumbled.

"For God's sake, Paul, let him past," I said irritably, leaning back in my swivel chair. Paul could be such a jerk sometimes.

Paul scowled, but stepped aside. A guy wearing a baseball jersey, jeans and an Orioles baseball cap shuffled into my cubicle with a pile of mail. He kept his back to me as he dropped the pile on my desk.

"So, are we on or off?" I asked Paul.

"Come on, Lexi. What's wrong with good old American food like a hamburger or pizza? Why do you want to eat something so exotic?"

I held my ground. "Look, I agreed to go disco dancing. Humor me, here."

I heard a snicker and both Paul and I looked in surprise at the mail guy. He turned around to face me slowly. "I like exotic food," he said softly.

My mouth fell open. It was Slash, barely recognizable behind a pair of thick black-framed glasses, his dark hair stuffed beneath the cap. He had hunched his broad shoulders and looked short and stooped. But the same twinkle was in his smoky brown eyes, his chin was still partially unshaved. He smiled openly at me. The Italian accent was completely gone and I could have sworn I heard a nasal New York twang.

"No one asked you jack," Paul said.

"Paul!" I exclaimed. "What's your problem?"

"Sorry, I didn't mean to interfere," Slash said, turning away.

"No, wait," I said hastily.

Slash paused, looking at me over his shoulder. His eyes flashed a warning, reminding me to hold my tongue.

"Ah, where is the regular guy—you know, Herman?" I asked. Herman was a young man with Down's Syndrome who brought our mail around every day. He was friendly, efficient and dependable, and I never had known him to miss a day of work.

Slash shrugged. "Busy day, I guess. He needed some extra help. Besides, he owed me one."

I laughed. "Unbelievable."

Slash grinned again, tipped his hat and disappeared from my cubicle. I saw him go past, pushing the mail cart, still slouching his shoulders.

Paul watched him go. "What's with him? He must be new. Can you believe how he just interrupted our conversation? Just who did he think he was talking to?"

I rolled my eyes. Paul could be a snob *and* a jerk. "So are we in agreement about the restaurant or not?" I asked.

Paul frowned. "Oh all right," he said grumpily. "If you insist on the strange cuisine, I'll concede. I am a gentleman after all. Ali Baba it is."

"Ali Kabab," I corrected.

"Whatever. I'll pick you up at seven."

I nodded, barely even thinking about Paul anymore. I still couldn't believe Slash had strolled right into my cubicle. It meant he must have security clearances up the yin yang. Maybe he *was* who he said he was.

I reached over and picked up my mail, flipping through it. At the bottom of the pile, I pulled out an oversized index card. Written on the card in thick black ink were four words.

You can trust me.

NINE

At five o'clock I left work and drove home, my muscles feeling a little better and the headache finally gone. But there was a lot on my mind, especially now that I knew Basia had called me from Sweden.

The apartment smelled of lemon cleanser and polish. I walked through the kitchen, the living room, the bedroom and the bathroom. All the papers, knickknacks and junk had been picked up off the floor and the furniture gleamed. But best of all back in the bedroom, a huge pile of clean, folded laundry sat on the middle of my clean and made up bed.

Smiling, I stared at the laundry. This was the best thing that had happened to me all week. Still grinning like a happy idiot, I went to the bathroom and ran hot water in the sparkling white tub to soak my stiff muscles and relax before I had the date from hell with Paul.

I spent a good thirty minutes in the tub before turning on the shower to wash and condition my hair. After toweling off and blow-drying my hair as straight as possible, I slipped on a pair of normal cotton underwear and donned my new red dress again. Only Finn had seen it and I wasn't worried about running into him at the Ali Kabab House or the disco club.

To ensure my muscles stayed loose, I downed two more ibuprofen. I stared at my pale face in the mirror and, sighing, pulled out the make-up box again. I opened it, set aside the eyelash curler and found what I think was rouge. I scooped the cream out with my finger and rubbed it on my cheeks. I looked like Heidi with the red apple cheeks, but at least I had color. After some consideration I dabbed at my cheeks with a tissue until they took on a more natural hue. I wasn't bold enough to try lipstick, but I did get brave and used mascara on my lashes with minimal smearing. Finally I stepped into my red pumps and stared at myself in the full-length mirror.

Other than the flat chest, not too bad, I decided.

As I passed through the living room I noticed my phone message light was blinking. I pressed the button.

"Hi, Lexi, it's Finn. Call me on my cell phone as soon as you can. It's urgent."

I went to my purse, dug out his card and dialed his cell phone. The operator told me the number I had called was presently not available, but I could leave a message. So I did, telling Finn I'd be out for most of the evening but would try to call later. Actually I wasn't ready to talk to him yet because I needed to figure out a way to ask him if he'd be willing to plant the program in the company network. I wasn't sure of the ethical problems it would raise for him. Everything depended upon how desperate Finn was to discover the truth.

Because I had a few minutes to spare, I called the Karate Academy but got another answering machine with Lars's voice on it. I didn't leave a message because I wasn't sure what to say. *Call me. I think you know where Basia is.* Probably not the best approach to take with a guy built like Lars who could probably break my neck in two without even breathing hard.

At precisely seven o'clock, Paul rang my bell. He had showered and shaved and looked nice in a pair of khaki Dockers and a short-sleeved, light blue, button-down shirt. He looked at me and whistled.

"Wow, you look amazing."

He didn't say anything about my cheeks, so I took that as a good sign. "Thanks," I said, grabbing my purse and punching in the code on the alarm.

"What's with the new security?" Paul asked, looking over my shoulder.

I shrugged, trying to make light of it. "I just decided I needed to feel safer."

"Because of all this weird stuff going on."

"Exactly."

"Oh," he said, but didn't ask any more questions. Once Paul had been informed that my weird stuff was on a need-to-know basis and had the attention of the higher-ups in the agency, he pretty much followed the plan. He'd make a good foot soldier.

The Ali Kabab House was in a renovated townhouse. A neon sign blinked Open in one of the windows. The lawn was green and trimmed and someone had planted azaleas and pansies in a small garden. We climbed the steps to the restaurant and Paul opened the door for me. Guess chivalry isn't dead everywhere.

Inside we waited by a podium that said Please Wait to be Seated. It looked like there were two parts of the restaurant, an upstairs and a downstairs. Downstairs were a dozen small tables with white tablecloths, small flickering candles and gleaming silverware. The place was small, but cozy and clean. The walls were adorned with thick Turkish-looking tapestries and artwork featuring desert landscapes.

There were four people sitting at a table when the waiter serving them drinks spotted us at the door. He rushed over to greet us.

"*Masaa al-khair,* good evening," he said with a smile. He was thin and dark-haired, dressed in a crisp white shirt and black jeans. He held a small pad in his hand. "Table for two? Smoking or non-smoking?"

"Non-smoking, please," Paul said.

The waiter led us to a small table near the window and I chose the chair that would give me a view of the door. I didn't expect Rashid Bouker to waltz in the door, but sometimes luck is a funny thing, and it seemed like a good idea to be prepared just in case.

The waiter offered to get us something to drink and Paul ordered a glass of wine. The hangover still fresh in my mind, I ordered a club soda with a lime. I could tell Paul was disappointed. He was likely wishing I would get tipsy so he could take advantage of me.

The waiter gave us a few minutes to look over the menu. When he returned with our drinks, I told Paul I was ready to order. Paul's face was all scrunched up as he stared at the choices, and I could tell he wasn't finding much on the menu appetizing.

To help him out I went first, ordering the lentil and chard soup with rice, and some meat pastries with pine nuts called *sambousik*. Paul looked at me like I was from another planet. Maybe I was. But I smelled a yummy aroma coming from the kitchen, and besides, I felt like living my life a bit dangerously in case the end was near.

Paul hemmed and hawed until he reluctantly ordered the meatball soup and a roasted lamb dish. He didn't look thrilled about his choices, and probably was wishing a steak would magically appear.

The waiter brought our drinks and we chatted about nothing in particular until our soups arrived. About five minutes into the conversation I was reminded of why I had decided not to go out with him the last time we were on a date. There was no spark, no chemistry at all, and Paul liked to talk about himself. Before long my eyes began to glaze over and I felt depressed. I had the most pathetic love life on the face of the earth. My mother was right. I was an embarrassment in matters of the heart.

Before dissolving into a mush of self-pity, I set my napkin on the table and stood. "I'm going to find the ladies' room," I said abruptly.

Paul looked at me in surprise and I realized I had cut him off in midsentence. "Sorry," I mumbled apologetically. "I'll be right back."

I headed toward the stairs in search of the restroom. When I reached the top landing, a large room opened up to my left. The corridor went on straight ahead of me. I heard voices and laughter, so I peeked inside. A round table in a corner was filled with a half-dozen young men. A veil of smoke hung heavy in the air. I squinted, trying to see if I could make out Rashid Bouker when an arm from behind snaked around my neck and a hand clapped over my mouth. I was dragged backwards down the corridor, squirming and kicking my legs until my attacker whispered in my ear.

"Silence, Lexi."

I recognized the voice and stilled. Slash.

Even though I had stopped thrashing, he kept his hand firmly over my mouth. He dragged me to a room, opened the door and yanked me inside. Releasing me, he flipped on the light and glared at me.

We were in a small bathroom that contained a chipped porcelain sink and a single toilet. A roll of paper towels sat on the sink next to some liquid hand soap. The ceiling light was a single dull bulb.

I waited until my heart stopped doing the tango before I hissed, "Just what in the *hell* do you think you are doing?"

Slash was angry too, and for the life of me, I couldn't

figure out why. I was the one who had just been assaulted and dragged into a bathroom.

"What am *I* doing?" he repeated, his voice furious. "The question is what are *you* doing here?"

I noticed he was dressed in black, this time in a cotton T-shirt, jeans and a leather jacket. The jacket was an unnecessary fashion statement because it was eighty degrees out, but in any event, he didn't look anything like the mail guy in my cubicle today.

"I happen to be on a date," I said angrily. "You knew I'd be here."

"I did not," he snarled.

"You heard me talking about this restaurant with Paul in my cubicle today," I insisted. "You're stalking me."

I probably shouldn't have said that because a hot, red flush crept up his sexy unshaven neck and his eyes flashed daggers at me. But I was mad too, and he had nearly taken ten years off my life with his grab-and-drag stunt. I took a step back, but it didn't put a whole lot of distance between us given the fact that the bathroom was extremely small.

His hands clenched at his sides. "I'm *not* stalking you and I didn't hear you talking about *this* restaurant today," he said coldly. "If I had I assure you, you wouldn't be here. Just so you know, *I* was here first."

I laughed. "Yeah, right. Why on earth would you be here?"

"Because I'm part of a stakeout, damn it. And you walked right into it, dragging along that idiot boyfriend of yours."

"A stake-out?" I repeated in disbelief. "Do you think I'm dumb enough to believe that? Wait, don't answer that. And, by the way, Paul is *not* my idiot boyfriend."

Slash's eyes narrowed. "Then just who is he?"

"A colleague. I owed him a favor and he's collecting."

His expression darkened. "Collecting what?"

"That's none of your business," I snapped, trying hard not to look embarrassed which was difficult because my cheeks were likely a flaming crimson color.

"It's very much my business," he retorted.

"Why? Because you are on some kind of stakeout? How lame an excuse is that? I'm not a complete imbecile, you know." My voice had risen considerably.

"How cursed am I that you showed up here now?" he said, his voice matching mine.

For a minute we glared at each other until Slash finally leaned back against the wall and crossed his arms against his chest. The black leather jacket creaked slightly and I caught a faint scent of his expensive aftershave.

"I mean it, *cara,* what are you doing here?"

"I told you. I'm on a date."

"Why here?"

"Why not? The last time I looked, America was a free country."

His nostrils flared, but his voice came out calm and controlled. "You're digging around."

"Digging around?" I gave him innocent eyes. "Me?"

He wasn't buying it. "You found out that Rashid Bouker likes to frequent this restaurant, didn't you?"

I crossed my arms against my chest, mimicking his stance. "Maybe."

"This is serious, *cara.* Go home."

"Since when have I been any safer at home?" I snapped. "And where do you come off, telling me what to do? I thought you were some kind of computer genius for the NSA and now you tell me you're on a stakeout. What are you really, a spook for the CIA?"

His eyes narrowed. "I'm not CIA."

"A cop, then."

"No cop."

"Military?"

"No."

"Then who the hell are you?" I demanded. I was mad and scared. When I get mad or scared, I become pushy and sometimes use cuss words. It's my tough act.

"Don't ask questions you don't want answered," Slash warned. His face was impassive, but I saw a muscle in his jaw ticking and I knew he was trying to control his anger. Or maybe he was trying not to laugh at me.

"So you think this is the solution, *cara?* Strolling into the restaurant and sitting in the window so Bouker won't miss you? What kind of plan is that?"

I felt defensive. "Maybe I wanted to talk to him on neutral ground."

"He's dangerous. You could get hurt."

"It may come as a surprise to you, but despite the fact that I'm female, I can handle myself quite well, thank you. I already did so once with him without your assistance."

Slash closed his eyes, the expression on his face pained and angry. "You're not going to leave the restaurant, are you?"

"No."

"Then you should know. Bouker's already here. He arrived just before you did."

"He did?" I tried not to sound too surprised or scared. "*Si,* he did."

"Is he in that room I was looking into?"

Slash nodded. "I'm here for the same reason you are. I'm trying to find out more about Bouker. Who he meets and with whom he does business."

"Are you alone on this stakeout?"

"No more information…for your own good."

He put a finger on my lips and the contact sent a jolt of

heat racing through my veins. For one mindless, insane moment, I wished he would yank me into his arms and kiss me blind until I forgot about psycho guys with guns who kept breaking into my apartment and that I was on the date from hell with Paul. Then I remembered Slash was one of those strange guys who had magically appeared when all of this had started happening and it kind of ruined the moment.

"So, what exactly did you plan to say to Bouker if he spotted you tonight?" Slash asked, jolting me back to reality.

"How come you get to ask all the questions?"

"Behave, *cara,* and just tell me. What crazy plan did you have up your sleeve with Bouker tonight?"

I considered it. What would I have said to Bouker if I ran into him? Actually, I hadn't thought that far in advance. I shifted nervously on my feet. I saw Slash nod like that's what he had expected all along.

"Go finish your dinner and get out of here as quickly as you can," he finally said. "If Bouker sees you, pretend you don't recognize him."

Now I was feeling pretty stupid. Slash was right. I was in over my head. I had come here tonight with no plan, no strategy, no nothing. Amateur sleuth or idiot agent, take your pick, that was me. I should have left this whole mess to the professionals, whoever they might be.

I sighed. "Okay. I guess you're right. Paul is probably wondering what I'm doing in here for so long."

Slash snorted but said nothing.

"What is that snort supposed to mean?" I asked, narrowing my eyes. "You don't like Paul."

"Do you?"

"Not really," I said defensively. "But I'm allowed to say

"I see."

"No you don't. Look, Paul is an okay guy, but an awful date."

"Because he's not the man for you, *cara*."

"Oh, great. Now you sound like my mother. When did you become such an expert on my love life? You've known me for two days and now you think you know who is right for me?"

He smiled and reached out to touch my hair. "*Si, cara*. Italians are masters at matters of the heart."

The air in the bathroom practically snapped, crackled and popped with sexual tension. I was afraid to move or breathe for fear that if I did, I'd throw myself at him.

After what seemed like a thousand years Slash spoke softly. "Go on," he said.

I wasn't sure if he meant for me to go on and get out of the bathroom or go on and throw myself at him. Just in case, I decided to play it safe. I let out my breath and fumbled for the doorknob.

Before I turned it, I had one more question to ask. "How did you get to my side of the office at the NSA today?"

He looked at me steadily, those brown eyes intense. "If you believe I am who I said I am, then you already know the answer to that."

He was right. I let out a breath. "Well, what you did wasn't an easy feat, getting past all those security checkpoints. I suppose it means you have a lot more connections than I expected."

"I do, and you know I won't hurt you, *si?*"

"At the very least, I believe that."

"Good," he said, his voice softening. "Because I *am* one of the good guys."

"Yeah, well, I suppose that remains to be seen. I guess I'll be seeing you around."

"Very soon, *cara,*" he promised.

I threw him a hard look over my shoulder. "By the way, if you come to my place, knock first, would you?"

That mouth twitched again. "If you insist."

I opened the door and peeked out, looking down the corridor. I didn't see Rashid creeping around the hallway, but there was a very large woman in a blue-and-white flowered dress waiting patiently by the door to use the bathroom. I blushed.

"Sorry to take so long," I told her and then watched her expression turn to one of shock when Slash stepped out behind me and nodded politely.

She moved quickly past us and slammed the door shut. I could hear it lock. "You've forever ruined my reputation," I told him, rolling my eyes.

"All the women say that."

Now it was my turn to snort, but he probably didn't hear because he had taken a few steps in front of me and was blocking me from the view of the room where Bouker supposedly sat. When we reached the top of the stairs, he gave me a gentle push.

"Go on alone," he said.

"But where are you going to go?" I whispered.

"Don't worry about me, *cara.* I'll be where I need to be."

I turned and walked down the stairs. When I was halfway down, I looked back over my shoulder. Slash had vanished.

Paul was waiting anxiously for me. "What took you so long?" he demanded. Our food sat untouched on the table.

"I'm sorry," I said. "My nose needed a lot of powdering."

We started to eat, and the food was surprisingly tasty. Even Paul seemed impressed.

"This was a good idea," he said a bit grudgingly.

"Sometimes I have better ideas than other times," I said. It was the understatement of the millennium.

Just then the woman who had gone into the bathroom after Slash and me walked down the stairs. Embarrassed, I avoided looking at her. But to my horror she walked over to our table.

"Excuse me," she said. I hoped that maybe if I didn't look at her, she wouldn't look at me either. No such luck.

"Was that Enrique Iglesias?" she asked, her face splitting into a big grin. "I'm a huge fan."

I nearly choked on my food and grabbed my water and took a large swallow.

Paul looked at her, frowning. "What are you talking about?"

I waved my hand, my eyes watering. "Nothing," I interjected. "No, it wasn't Enrique Iglesias."

She looked disappointed, but thanked me and walked away. Paul turned his frown on me. "What was that all about?"

"There was some guy waiting to use the restroom who looked like Enrique Iglesias," I explained. "I guess she hoped it was him."

"How do you know it wasn't?"

That was a good question. "His nose," I said. "It was definitely smaller than Enrique's."

Paul's frown deepened, but he didn't say anything more. I guess he had finally come to the realization that I was one strange cookie.

We finished our dinner and I begged off dessert. Paul ordered a dish called *um Ali'* or Ali's mother. He gave me a taste and it was wonderful. It seemed to be some kind of pastry pudding with raisins and coconut steeped in milk. I was proud of him for being so adventurous.

Paul insisted on paying so when the bill came, he

whipped out his credit card. The waiter took it and disappeared. After a few minutes, he reappeared.

"Excuse me, sir," he said. "There is a problem with this card. Could you come with me for a moment?"

Paul and I exchanged surprised glances. "That's a perfectly good card," he protested. "I pay my balance every month."

"Of course you do, sir," the waiter said. "It's simply that we appear to be having some kind of problem with our machine. Please, sir, would you come with me for just a moment?"

Paul looked at me and I shrugged. He stood and followed the waiter back toward the kitchen where they disappeared behind a pair of swinging double doors.

I picked up my water and took a sip just as Rashid Bouker sat down in Paul's chair.

"Hello, Miss Carmichael," he said.

I froze in midsip and then smiled. "Excuse me, do I know you?"

Bouker leaned over the table and spoke in a low tone. "There is no time to play games," he said, his voice heavily accented. "You are in grave danger. You would do best to get out of town as quickly as possible. Vanish. The only reason you are still alive is that they still hope you can lead them to Miss Kowalski."

My heart had begun to hammer pretty darn fast in my chest and the hand holding the water glass trembled. "Who are *they?*" I asked.

"This is your last chance. Heed my words," he said and then stood. From the corner of my eye, I saw Paul returning to the table.

"Who was that guy?" he asked, walking up to me and jerking a thumb toward Bouker.

I swallowed hard. "The manager," I said. "He told me to try the lamb next time. Is everything straightened out?"

Paul nodded. "It was just a glitch. The damn machine was on the blink. It only took a minute to fix."

Apparently a minute was all Bouker had needed to pass on his warning. He'd already gone back upstairs. I looked around to see if I could see Slash, but he was nowhere in sight. I wondered if he had even seen the exchange, although I didn't see how that could have been possible since he was upstairs and we were downstairs.

Clueless to my building anxiety, Paul smiled. "Let's go dancing," he said cheerfully, taking my arm and leading me outside.

"Groovy," I said glumly. I really wanted to go home, but instead I had to go shake my booty.

Paul drove to Club 56, a sort of retro disco club in Silver Spring, Maryland. It was dark, packed and everyone there looked Paul's age. I felt nervous and out of place, which for me was pretty normal.

We made our way through the crowd until we found a small table. A huge revolving disco ball hung above the dance floor, throwing out flashes of red, green and white. K.C. and the Sunshine Band were singing loudly about the way they like it and I resisted the urge to cover my ears.

"How about a drink?" Paul shouted at me.

"Okay," I shouted back. If I was going to be in here for more than five minutes, I absolutely needed a drink.

"Great. I'll surprise you with something," he said and disappeared toward the bar.

Terrific, that was just what I needed in my life—more surprises.

Paul returned shortly with a tequila sunrise for me and a vodka and tonic for himself. I took a sip of the tequila and it went down pretty smoothly. I took another sip.

Maybe if I were tipsy, this disco dancing stuff wouldn't be so unbearable.

After a couple of minutes, Donna Summer began singing about her hot pants and Paul dragged me out onto the dance floor. My muscles were still kind of stiff, but the tequila was loosening them right up. I tried to imitate the other dancers around me but felt like a robotic puppet. Apparently the puppet dance was in because people smiled at me and Paul seemed satisfied with my efforts.

After several songs, including a slow one, I collapsed in my chair and Paul brought me another tequila. I drank that one and began to feel really good. For at least an hour I hadn't thought about Basia, Slash, Rashid Bouker or my life being in imminent danger. When the Bee Gees started to sing about staying alive, I jumped out of my seat and dragged Paul to the dance floor.

"They're playing my song," I yelled to him over the music.

Two and a half hours later, I was drunk and exhausted. Even Paul looked worn out.

"You're a hell of a dancer, Lexi," he said.

I smiled. Who knew I had talent at disco dancing?

He leaned over the table. "Come on, let's get out of here."

We pushed our way out of the noisy club. The outside air was hot, oppressive and sticky, but at least it was fresh. I filled my lungs, took a step and stumbled. Paul grabbed on to my arm, holding me firmly.

"The car is this way," he said.

As we walked toward his BMW, I noticed that a dark sedan at the other end of the parking lot had started its engine and begun to slowly drive toward us. The sedan didn't have its lights on and I thought that was strange.

"Look at that," I said to Paul, stopping in my tracks and swaying slightly. "No lights."

"Whatever," Paul said, pulling me along clearly thinking I was drunk and babbling about nothing.

Okay maybe I was drunk and babbling, but the least he could do was listen. Call it a hunch, call it female intuition, but I suddenly had a creepy feeling about that sedan.

I tried to stop Paul but he kept moving briskly and my foot slipped out of my pump. I yanked my arm free from Paul's grasp and reached down to grab my shoe when the sedan backfired and I felt a flash of heat slide across my bare back. Someone shouted and I straightened just as a dark form came flying out from behind a parked car and slammed into me.

"Get down, get down," someone yelled as I tumbled against Paul and all three of us crashed to the ground in a tangle of arms and legs.

There was a lot of shouting going on, most of it in my ear. From the corner of my eye, I saw the sedan flip on its lights and screech out of the parking lot with a nondescript brown van I hadn't noticed in hot pursuit. People were running outside from the club to see what was going on.

Someone pulled me off the asphalt and into a sitting position. I tried to shake off the buzz from the alcohol and catch my breath from the body slam so I could figure out what was going on. When my vision cleared, I realized Slash knelt next to me holding my hand. Paul was just picking himself up off the ground and dusting off his khakis.

"What the hell was that?" Paul shouted.

I was still looking in shock at Slash.

"A drive-by shooting," Slash said, pulling me to my feet.

Once again the Italian accent had vanished. "I saw the guy pull the gun and tried to warn you," he said in sort of a midwestern twang. "Are you okay, miss?"

My mouth fell open. "Miss?" I croaked out.

"You mean someone shot at us?" Paul said, horrified. "My God, what kind of sick people live in this country?"

"Did you call me miss?" I said to Slash again. Maybe I was more tossed than I thought.

A crowd had started to gather around us, including a couple of bouncers from the bar. "What's up?" one of the guys asked Slash. I guess he looked in charge.

"A drive-by shooting," Slash explained.

"Shit," one of the bouncers replied. He looked to weigh about four hundred pounds, had no neck and wore a Hawaiian shirt and shorts. Guess that was the disco fashion these days. "We haven't had one of those for six months. Anybody hurt?"

"It seems that everyone's okay," Slash volunteered.

Sure, easy for him to say. A bullet hadn't whizzed over his head.

"Should I call the police?" the other bouncer asked. He was thin and tall with a scraggly beard and mustache. A cigarette dangled between his fingers.

"Already here. I'm an off-duty police officer," Slash said, pulling a badge out from his pocket and flashing it at the guys. "The police are already in pursuit."

The no-neck guy looked relieved. "Lucky break for them," he said, nodding his head at Paul and me. Slash nodded.

The crowd from the club began to dissipate, most of them returning to the dance floor, apparently disappointed there were no bodies or gore to see. Ho, hum. Another drive-by shooting. Welcome to the nation's capital.

Paul looked over at Slash and then held out his hand. "Thanks for saving us, officer."

I was still standing there dumbly staring from Paul to Slash. Half of me was in shock that I'd been shot at. The other half was mad that Slash had followed me. Worse, Paul had no idea that the guy standing in front of him was the same guy who had shuffled into my cubicle earlier today carrying the mail.

Slash handed Paul a business card. "Call me tomorrow and you can file an official report about the shooting," he said. "Hopefully it will help put these guys away for a long time when we catch them."

"Yes, sir, I'll do that," Paul said, looking kind of shaken. "Thanks again." Paul held out his hand and Slash shook it.

"No problem," Slash said. "You kids take care."

Kids? Without even a glance at me, Slash turned and walked away across the parking lot. Numbly, I let Paul take my arm and head for the BMW. When we reached the car, Paul let out a stream of cuss words.

"Wait! Someone slit the tires," he practically screamed in my ear. "Officer, come back," he shouted at Slash.

Slowly Slash turned and walked back toward us. "What's wrong now?" he said, a concerned look on his face.

"Someone vandalized my car," Paul said and I thought he might cry. I guess this was turning into the date-from-hell for him, too.

Slash walked around the car and looked at the tires. "Rotten luck. Come on, I'll give you guys a ride home."

"But what about my car?"

"You can file another police report tomorrow. It should be covered by insurance."

Paul looked glum but he followed Slash across the parking lot.

I simply stood there, staring at the both of them. My brain, fogged by alcohol and the realization that someone had just shot at me, was having a hard time properly processing the events going on around me.

Paul turned and motioned to me irritably. "Come on, Lexi."

I wanted to stomp my foot like a two-year-old and demand answers to my questions. What the hell had just happened, why was Slash at the disco; and did someone just try to *kill* me? Instead I stumbled across the parking lot and caught up with them.

Somehow I wasn't surprised to see that Slash drove a sleek black SUV. Paul sat up front and I climbed in the back and sank into the soft leather seat. The car smelled nice, new and expensive.

We drove in silence until Slash dropped Paul off. He didn't seem to think it odd that Slash had taken him home first. I was just thankful that Paul seemed to have forgotten about the good-night kiss with the tongue he'd made me promise him. I guess it would have been awkward for him with Slash sitting there watching. Lucky for me, I guess the BMW was more important than a little tongue.

Paul seemed almost dazed as he got out of the car. "I'll call you," he said to me and I nodded without saying a word. "Thanks again, officer," he said to Slash.

As soon as Paul shut the door, I leaned forward toward the driver's seat. "Start talking," I warned Slash. "Or your ass is grass."

Slash turned around in the seat and looked at me incredulously. "My ass is grass?" he repeated. "Is this some kind of coarse American expression?"

"Cut the bullshit. You're not even Italian."

"I adore it when you are tough with me, *cara*. Keep talking dirty."

"This isn't funny," I shouted. "Someone just tried to *kill* me."

Slash ignored me and backed the car out of the parking lot. He didn't say anything else until we were on the main road headed for my apartment. "I know someone tried to kill you," he finally said. "It was a good thing I was following you, *si?*"

The Italian accent was back and I was mad at myself because I had missed it.

"You said you weren't following me," I cried.

"I wasn't until Bouker had his little chat with you. Then I got nervous."

"You heard what Bouker said to me? What are you, Superman with radar hearing or something?"

Slash abruptly pulled off on the side of the road and twisted around in the seat. "Lean forward, *cara,*" he said softly, crooking his finger at me.

"What for?"

"There is something I want to show you."

My heart stopped beating and my breath froze in my throat. He was going to kiss me. Every nerve in my body went on high alert. I should have done something like told him to go to hell or pushed him away, but instead I leaned forward and lifted my mouth to meet his. I felt Slash slip his hand around the nape of my neck and then trail his fingers down between my shoulder blades to the low dip of my dress. Anticipation thrummed through every pore of my body until I couldn't stand it anymore. Then he palmed something from the back of my dress and brought it around, dashing any hope I was going to experience a spectacular lip-lock.

He turned on the overhead light and I blinked. In the palm of his hand was a miniature listening device stuck on the back of what looked like a decorative button.

"You bugged me!" I shrieked.

Slash looked pained. "I was protecting you."

"You said you weren't a cop."

"I'm not."

"That's not what you told those bouncers back there. I saw your badge."

"I lied in the name of national security."

"What?" I screeched. "I saw that van chasing the people in the sedan that shot at me. If they aren't the police, then just who are they?"

"I can't tell you that."

The two-year-old in me suddenly made her appearance and I stomped my foot hard, rocking the SUV. "Why not? And don't give me that crap about a need-to-know basis. This is my life we're talking about."

Slash remained calm. "Hush, *cara*. I know you're frightened. But you're safe now. I'm with you."

With that, he turned around in the seat and eased the car back on the street. I sat in my seat, hands clenched in my lap, feeling bereft, cranky and mortified. I vowed to never *ever* talk to him again.

"You know," he said softly. "I really am who you think I am. I've been honest with you about that."

I broke my vow of silence almost immediately. I have zero willpower when it comes to vows, which means I would have made a lousy nun even if you don't count the no-sex part.

"I don't know *who* I think you are," I said staring out the window. The tires whooshed across the pavement and the engine hummed softly. "I don't know *anything* about you."

"I am the man the Zimmerman twins summoned, the man known as Slash. I'm also the person who can help you find your friend. Computer security is my expertise, among other things."

"What other things?"

He fell silent and I sighed. It was impossible to stay mad

at a guy who looked amazingly like Enrique Iglesias, especially when he spoke to me in that deep, husky, Italian accent. "All right, at least tell me this. Are you really protected around the clock by the FBI?"

"Si."

"It's true about you being some kind of national treasure?"

"That, unfortunately, is a burden not an honor."

"Then just where are these agents that are supposedly protecting you?" I still felt sulky.

Slash pointed in the rearview window. I twisted around in my seat and saw a set of headlights following us. "That's them?" I asked. "You didn't lose them?"

"Not tonight, *cara*."

His voice sounded tired and for a moment, I tried to put myself in his shoes. Would I be happy about having someone follow me around every minute of the day ready to kill me if I fell into enemy hands? Maybe being a national treasure wasn't all it was cracked up to be.

Slash drove to my apartment building and parked the SUV. I climbed out and stumbled, but Slash was by my side quickly and steadied me with a hand under the elbow. Across the street a dark sedan with the motor running and lights on had pulled over to the side of the road.

I looked at Slash. "The FBI?"

He nodded, so I lifted my hand and waved at them. To my surprise, the driver lowered his window and gave me the thumbs-up. Just your friendly neighborhood FBI agents. How weird was that?

"Come, *cara*, I'll walk you to your apartment," Slash said, shoving his hands into the pockets of his jacket. He looked unusually worried and thoughtful.

"Why? Do you think there is someone waiting for me there?"

"I doubt it. The FBI has been watching your place. It's clean."

"The FBI is watching *me* now?"

He didn't say anything and my apprehension mounted. A million questions were on the tip of my tongue, but I didn't ask them because I knew Slash probably wouldn't or couldn't answer them.

We climbed the stairs and I put my key in the lock, turning it. Slash let me disarm the alarm, but before I could step farther inside, he pushed past me, one hand inside his jacket. Suddenly I realized why he wore a jacket in eighty-degree weather.

"I thought you said the place was clear," I whispered loudly.

He shrugged. "I don't always trust the FBI to be thorough."

"Oh, that's comforting," I hissed. "They don't say that in public service announcements."

He rolled his eyes and disappeared into the dark of my apartment. In less than a minute, he returned and flipped on the hall light.

"It's secure," he said. Then he smiled. "I like what you've done with the place."

"It's called maid service," I said, shutting the door behind me. "But my place had better not get tossed again or I won't be able to afford it."

Slash leaned back against the wall, looking both sexy and dangerous in his black leather jacket. He was silent for some time before he spoke.

"I think we need to talk, *cara.* Do you feel comfortable doing this now?"

I dumped my purse on a chair and turned around. "Do I have to do all the talking or are you finally going to tell me something?"

"I'll tell you what I can. That's the best I can offer."

"Do I really have a choice in the matter?"

"No."

"Then why ask?"

He exhaled a deep breath. "Because I like you."

That made me feel a little bit better. But I was still cranky and more than just a little tipsy. "What about the listening device? Will the entire FBI be listening to our conversation?"

Slash slipped his hand into his pocket and pulled out the button. He snapped it in half between his fingers. "From now on, this is between you and me."

"How do I know you're not wired somewhere else?"

He spread his arms. "Do you wish to frisk me?"

As tempting as it was, I shook my head. "Just take off your jacket."

He lowered his hands and shrugged it off. Sure enough, he wore a black leather shoulder holster with a gun tucked snugly inside. He wore it with ease, as if computer hackers did this kind of thing all the time.

"Have you ever...you know, killed anyone with that gun?" I asked.

"Why is that important for you to know?"

"Seeing how you're starting to come around a lot, I think I'm entitled to know."

He walked closer to me and took my hands in his. His skin was warm against mine, his grip firm and reassuring. "If you must know, I have killed men. But mostly in self-defense."

Mostly. I noticed how he'd casually slipped that in. I wondered about the other times, but I was too chicken to ask.

"All right," I said, pulling my hands from his and trying

to ignore the chill that ran up my spine. "At least you're honest. I respect that."

"Come then, let's sit. Shall I make us some coffee?"

I raised an eyebrow. "Can you?"

He looked amused. "I assure you that I am a man of many, *many* hidden talents."

I wasn't going to touch that comment with a ten-foot pole, so I did the smart thing for once and kept my mouth shut.

Slash walked into my kitchen and I could hear him rummaging around, opening cupboards and looking for the coffee. I should have gotten up to help him, but I really needed a minute. I had a lot to think about. It was one thing to be threatened with a gun, but someone had actually shot at me tonight. If I hadn't reached down to fix my sandal, I could be dead.

How did Slash fit into all of this? Was he really Italian? Or American? Computer hacker extraordinaire or a talented con man? From a pure informational point of view, I didn't know much about him other than he had a hell of an expensive computer set-up, could slip silently past my alarm, had apparent run of the NSA, and looked comfortable wearing a gun he'd admitted using to kill people. How reassuring was that?

Despite everything that had happened, I was still no closer to finding Basia and extricating myself from this mess she'd gotten me into. Now the FBI was watching me, Yemen Embassy officials were warning me that my life was in danger and people were taking potshots at my head.

Not good. Not good at all.

I glanced over at the small table where my telephone sat and noticed my message light was blinking yet again. I pressed the play button and listened. All three messages were from Finn saying to call him as soon as possible.

The last time he threatened to buy me a cell phone himself. I reset the machine. I wasn't in any condition to call Finn now. He would just have to wait until the morning.

By the time Slash finally returned with two mugs of coffee, I felt like I had a slightly better grasp on my sanity.

"Do you take milk?" he asked.

I nodded. "It's in the fridge."

Slash walked back to the kitchen and returned carrying the milk. I poured a dollop in my coffee and offered him some.

He shook his head. "No, I take it black."

I should have figured as much. He sat down on the couch next to me, the gun just sitting there in its holster next to my hip. I moved away slightly, blowing on my coffee and holding the mug with both hands.

"So what do you want to talk about?" I asked.

He turned on the couch to face me. "Events are starting to move quickly and I want us to work together. I told you a little about the situation last time we spoke and I'm prepared to tell you more. But I need your help, as well. We need to find some measure of trust here, *cara*."

"Wait, can I ask you something before you reveal anything sensitive?"

"Of course."

"Is this some kind of NSA training exercise? Because if it is, I'd rather just take a failing grade. I don't have any grand ambitions to do undercover work and I'm obviously not cut out for this kind of thing."

He looked at me in surprise and it seemed genuine. Then again, he was a master of deception, so what did I know?

"Why would you think this is some kind of test?" he finally said.

"Well, Elvis said it was possible. And my boss knows

something is wrong. He warned me today not to play the prima donna. He said his unit was a team and under no circumstances should I engage in heroics, whatever that means."

Slash sighed. "Jonathan Littleton has been warned to keep an eye on you, but with a loose grip. He's being deliberately kept out of the loop and he doesn't like it. Undoubtedly he was trying to find out what you are involved in."

"I see."

"Now consider this. Rashid Bouker is an embassy official from Yemen. How likely is it that we could, or *would,* for that matter, involve him in some kind of NSA employee training exercise?"

Good point. "Okay, so this is the real deal, then," I said. "But if I find out this has been some kind of NSA character test, I'm not going to be happy. I'm happy with my character just the way it is."

"This is no NSA test. I promise you that. We both know this isn't standard operating procedure, but I don't have time to do it by the book. I'm going to read you into restricted access information right here. Everything we discuss from this moment on is highly classified. Are you okay with that?"

"Wow, I feel like I've been knighted or something. Are you sure you have the authority to read me in?"

"I'm sure. Are you ready?"

I exhaled a deep breath. "Ready."

"Excellent. Now let's go through the list of who we know Al-Asan has impregnated."

"Whoa, just a minute. Did you just say 'list'? Do you mean Al-Asan impregnated someone else besides Basia's cousin?"

"Si."

I didn't ask how or where he got the information, mostly because I didn't want to know.

Slash reached into his shirt pocket and pulled out a piece of paper. "Believe it, *cara*. There are seven women involved in this procedure. First we have Hilda Strauss, age twenty-two, from Munich, Germany. German intelligence noted a meeting between her and a member of Al-Asan's entourage a few months earlier in Heidelberg. She was in Genoa, Italy the same day Al-Asan's bodyguards were killed."

"Let me take a wild stab at this—she was visiting a medical establishment connected with Bright Horizons or other CGM staff."

"That is the most likely scenario."

"What about Judyta Taszynski? Was she in Genoa on that day, too?"

"*Si,* she was. And so was nineteen-year-old Lupita Lopez, a fashion model from Colombia; twenty-four-year-old LaTasha Brown, an art curator from Toronto; Khanatta Chraibi, a twenty-two-year-old optometrist from Morocco, Ito Yakusari, a twenty-three-year-old translator from Tokyo, and Sarah Cunningham, occupation unknown, from London. All were staying at the *Hotel Locanda di Palazzo Cicala* last December at the same time."

"Do we know who picked up the tab at the hotel for the girls?" I asked.

"Al-Asan."

"What a surprise. What else do we know?"

"Well, a quick examination of their bank accounts shows that a substantial amount of money was deposited exactly two months later in the women's accounts following the gathering in Genoa. All of the women were apparently also set up with their own apartments, cars and access to premier medical staff in their hometowns. I need to take a more thorough look at their finances to see if there is any more of a pattern."

I shook my head in disbelief. "I just can't believe what I'm hearing. This doesn't make any sense. Why would a wealthy Saudi prince go to all this trouble to inseminate a bunch of women of different nationalities? What's up with that?"

Slash took a sip of his coffee. "Honestly, I don't know. It's even more curious because Al-Asan already has nine children with his wife. Six of them boys."

I sat back on the couch trying to make sense of everything he had just told me.

"And what's the Yemen connection?" I murmured. "Why did Bouker threaten me to get those documents and then warn me about impending danger?"

"I don't know and as far as I can tell, the only link to Yemen is the CIA's suspicions that the hit on Al-Asan's bodyguards was the work of followers of Yemeni terrorist Samir Al-Naddi. But Yemeni government officials are adamant about separating themselves from the actions of Al-Naddi."

I set my coffee mug on the table with a thump. "Okay let's say that Al-Asan wants to get his jollies by impregnating a wide variety of women around the world. Only he doesn't do it the old-fashioned way, which, frankly speaking, would be a hell of a lot easier, more fun, and considerably less expensive than in vitro fertilization. Instead he invites them to Genoa, Italy, all at the same time, and has it done clinically. Why?"

"Maybe he's shooting..." Slash paused, groping for the right word.

"Blanks?" I offered.

"Ah, *si,* blanks. Perhaps he's shooting blanks."

I looked at Slash in exasperation. "You said he's got nine children. How blank can he be?"

"Perhaps he used them all up."

I rolled my eyes. "Who in their right mind could possibly want more than nine kids?"

Slash shrugged. "Well, perhaps it's something simple— a competition of sorts. He wants more children than his brother, for example. I don't know. Maybe he's just *bizzarro*."

"I'm leaning toward the bizarre theory. Anyway, wouldn't the children legally be bastards? I'm no expert on monarchies and all, but isn't proper lineage important to a royal family? Why, at the very least, wouldn't he try to impregnate Arabic women?"

"I don't know," Slash said wearily, rubbing his temples.

He'd probably already thought a lot about this. But I wasn't ready to give up yet.

"All right, you said that the CIA suspects Yemeni terrorists possibly linked to Al-Naddi assassinated two of Al-Asan's bodyguards in Genoa after they had delivered something to the Bright Horizons clinic. Do we know what the guys were delivering?"

Slash shrugged. "Semen, I presume."

I tried not to be grossed out, but I could feel my cheeks starting to heat. Was I really having a conversation about semen with a national treasure?

"Why the delivery? Why wasn't Al-Asan there in the clinic himself? Isn't he supposed to, you know, provide a fresh sample? I mean, isn't that why they stock the bathrooms with pornography and men's magazines?" My cheeks were flaming now, but I tried to act cool, like it was no biggie for me to talk about men playing with themselves in a clinic bathroom.

"Do you really think I know the answer to that?" he countered.

Well, well. Maybe Mr. National Treasure also felt uncomfortable discussing this matter. It was hardly surprising. We barely knew each other, and semen probably wasn't a regular conversation starter even for normal people. I tried to steer us back to safer ground.

"Then why did the shooters ambush the bodyguards *after* they made the delivery?" I asked. "Why not before?"

"Does it matter?" he said, still a bit cranky. "What would they do with Al-Asan's semen if they stole it?"

"Hold it for ransom?"

"Very amusing."

Just like that we were back to discussing semen again. I thought for a moment. "You're right. It doesn't make sense. But why kill the bodyguards at all if they didn't need the package?"

"A message or warning of some kind, perhaps?"

"You mean, like Al-Asan and Al-Naddi are archenemies?"

"*Si,* like that. Except that I haven't been able to find any direct link between Al-Asan and terrorist scum like Samir Al-Naddi. The Saudis have been very vocal about distancing themselves from Al-Naddi's group."

"Then maybe Al-Asan has some kind of secret political sympathy for Al-Naddi."

"Perhaps, but it's doubtful. Al-Asan appears to be one of the more moderate faces of the Saudi royal family."

"Maybe it's just a front."

"Perhaps."

I frowned, picking up my mug from the coffee table and taking a large swallow. "Oh, I forgot to tell you that Finn thinks Judyta is pregnant," I said. "So, I guess it worked."

Slash raised an eyebrow. "And what did he base this presumption on?"

"Neighbors of hers in the apartment complex in Warsaw. They say she was pregnant before she disappeared. If the procedure took place in Genoa in December, she should be pretty far along now. Do you know for a fact that these other women were also successfully impregnated?"

"We won't know for certain unless we get a peek inside CGM files."

"What about asking the other women? Can't you just track them down and ask them what's up?"

"If only it were that simple, *cara*. All of them have disappeared, including Judyta Taszynski."

I blinked in surprise. "Disappeared?"

"*Si*. Vanished."

"That can't be a good development."

Slash just looked at me and took another sip of his coffee. I stood and walked over to the kitchen and back. Maybe a bit of pacing would clear my head.

"Perhaps we're coming at this from the wrong angle," I said after a few minutes. "Maybe we need to see what the girls have in common."

"We've already thought of that," Slash said. "The girls have nothing obvious in common—they come from completely different nations, cultures and even religions. Their backgrounds, upbringing, language and education are all varied. The only thing that binds them is that they are relatively young women aged nineteen to twenty-four, which are excellent years for breeding, I suppose."

"Breeding?" I repeated, raising an eyebrow.

"Well, isn't that what Al-Asan's doing?" Slash said. He sounded rather disgusted.

Perhaps he was right to feel that way. Personally, I don't have anything against in vitro if people really want children. But Al-Asan seemed to already have his fair share at nine, and from what I could tell this in vitro procedure didn't involve his wife. I wondered what he would say to her when he brought the kids back to the palace. *Hi, honey, I'm home. And here are a bunch of new kids for the family. Just don't ask where I got them.*

Still, all the facts weren't in and there wasn't any point in being too judgmental yet.

I pushed my hair off my neck, closed my eyes and leaned back against the wall. The buzz from the tequila was beginning to wear off and my muscles were starting to ache again.

Slash set his mug down and walked over to me. His close proximity made every nerve leap to alert. He was so amazingly good-looking I could hardly breathe. How had I gotten so close to so many sexy guys in such a short time?

"Now it's your turn, *cara*," he said softly. "Talk to me more about this Finn Shaughnessy."

"What about him?"

"Did you ask him about Acheron?"

"Not yet," I admitted.

"Why not? Don't you trust him? I thought he was *nice*." He said the word *nice* with such derision in his voice that I pursed my lips.

"He *is* nice. And I trust him as much as I trust anyone these days. My gut instinct tells me he's a good guy."

"Then get him to agree to let us in from the inside."

I sighed. "I'm trying to figure out how to delicately ask him to plant the program."

"Well, make haste," he said. "The twins and I have finished the program."

"Wow, that was fast."

Slash shrugged. "It's important." He reached into his jacket and pulled out a clear case containing an unmarked gold CD. "All Shaughnessy has to do is insert it in his drive and click on the program. The rest is up to the twins and me."

"You had it with you all night?"

"*Si*. The twins and I did our part. Now the rest is up to you and Finn Shaughnessy."

I hesitated. "You know, I'm not sure this is the right thing to do. I guess I should mention that Basia said not to trust Finn."

He raised a dark eyebrow. "And just when did she say that?"

I sighed and set the CD down on the coffee table. "I forgot to tell you. She called yesterday and left a message for me on my answering machine." He didn't appear at all surprised to hear this and suddenly I understood. "But you already knew that, didn't you?"

He nodded. "*Si,* I knew. I also know she's hiding out somewhere in Sweden with Judyta."

I stared at him in shock and then shrieked in anger. "I don't believe it! You bugged my phone. What else have you done? Put hidden cameras in the bathroom, too? How *dare* you!"

"Calm down," Slash said in a pathetic attempt to soothe me. "It's not like that at all."

"The hell it's not. This whole conversation is a sham. Why even bother with me since you apparently have the entire U.S. national security apparatus at your beck and call, Mr. Whoever You Are?"

"It's not like that," he repeated. "I won't lie to you. You are being monitored. Judyta is the only girl on whom we have a lead and you are the link to her."

"Is that what *they* instructed you to say?" I said, still furious at him. "Are *they* feeding you your lines?"

He stepped forward, gripping my shoulders tightly. I

tried to shrink away but he wouldn't let me. "No one tells me what to say," he said firmly. "Your apartment is not bugged, just your phone. I have told you the truth, *cara*. I may have withheld information or provided it judiciously, but I have not lied. Never."

My eyes burned with tears. I felt betrayed, soiled. "You're using me," I whispered. For a girl with a high IQ, I had been pretty stupid not to wonder why such a hot guy had acted so interested in a geek girl like me.

"No. You came to me, *cara*. It was meant to be, our helping each other. I will admit this partnership has not been easy for me. I usually work alone, so perhaps I am not handling this as well as I would like. Forgive me."

"But you said you have other people working with you." I sniffed.

"Working *for* me. There is a difference when two people must work equally in synchronicity. I have never met a woman quite like you before, Lexi. You are capable, innocent and deliciously unpredictable."

I kind of wish he had said beautiful, sexy or intelligent, but I guess beggars can't be choosers.

He gently wound a strand of my hair around his finger. The gesture was intimate and unexpected. I held my breath, and for a moment we gazed into each other's eyes. I could see his pupils darken until I could hardly see them anymore. Then, to my acute disappointment, he abruptly dropped his hand and stepped back. Once again I'd thought he would kiss me, and once again, I was wrong. Apparently, I had no skill whatsoever in reading the sexual signals of men.

I wasn't sure I could take much more humiliation in my life. He *had* to have seen the desire on my face, the expectation. Yet he couldn't even bring himself to give me one lousy, little kiss.

"So why is someone trying to kill me?" I asked, trying to change the subject, clear the air or do anything but stand there stupidly.

He exhaled a breath. "Because they want to sever our only link to Judyta. I think it's that simple."

I didn't think it was simple at all, but then again, I'd never had anyone try to kill me before. Slash rubbed the back of his neck and then returned to the couch, picking up his mug again.

"When will you talk to Finn Shaughnessy?" he asked without looking at me.

I stood where I was, still feeling like a fool.

"He called me several times this evening and left messages," I said stiffly. "I'll give him a call first thing in the morning."

"Be careful of what you say on the phone," Slash warned. "It's not secure."

"What now? You don't want the FBI to know what we're doing?"

"Don't worry. I will keep the FBI, NSA and others appraised of any developments. But the FBI may not be the only ones listening in."

"Who else, then?"

"We don't know. Just be careful."

Oh, that was comforting advice. "Is Finn in any kind of danger?"

"Not yet, but we have him under surveillance, too. I'm having his background checked out as we speak." Leaning back on my couch, he took a sip of coffee. "Perhaps now you might tell me how Lars Anderson fits into all this?"

I sighed. My life held no secrets anymore. Not like I had any great ones to begin with, but still, I didn't like the fact that everything about me, warts and all, was now open to official scrutiny.

"I don't know how Lars fits into this," I said. "Basia signed up for karate lessons with him shortly before she disappeared. There may not be any connection."

"I don't consider it a coincidence that she shows up in Sweden and Lars Anderson just happens to be from there," he said. "There must be a connection."

"Well, if you have a theory I'd be happy to hear it."

"I don't have one yet. I ran a check on him and he appears clean. But there must be a link we are missing."

I thought the same thing, but had come up with no answers. "I'll let you know if I discover anything."

"Good." Slash ran his fingers through his hair and stood. "I must go now. There is much to do."

He didn't offer operational details and I didn't ask. Instead I glanced at my watch and saw it was past one o'clock in the morning. I sat where I was while he picked up his jacket and put it on.

"Set the alarm," he said, motioning toward the door.

I followed him to the corridor and dutifully punched in the code. He was careful not to watch, which was kind of silly since he could break into my place in under three minutes anyway.

"Well, I'll see you around," I said, waiting for him to open the door and leave. After all, he only had sixty seconds to depart before the alarm sounded.

Instead of leaving, he suddenly backed me up against the wall, placing one hand on either side of my head and trapping me there. He looked serious, sexy and more than a little dangerous. His gun pressed into my hip and I sincerely hoped it didn't go off.

"Watch your back," he said softly. "I don't want anything to happen to you. There are many matters that are yet to be resolved between us."

"What kind of...matters?" I squeaked.

He smiled mysteriously.

"You're married, aren't you?" I blurted out and then wished the floor would open up and swallow me, or more likely, that an armed assassin would break down the door and shoot me.

His lips twitched. "No, I'm not married. But I do not take advantage of women who have been shot at or drinking. Especially not both in the same night."

"That's terribly gallant of you," I admitted.

He pressed a soft kiss against my cheek. "Buona notte, cara," he murmured. "Sogno di me."

I foolishly pressed a hand to my cheek where he had kissed me. "That means 'sweet dreams,' doesn't it?" I asked, hoping he was impressed that I was picking up Italian so quickly.

A smile curved across his lips as he opened the door. "Not exactly, cara. It means dream of me," he said and then disappeared down the stairs.

As I closed the door behind him, I had a feeling that's exactly what I would do.

TEN

SATURDAY DAWNED FAR too early and I forced myself awake when the alarm went off at six-thirty. Typically I slept in on the weekends, but there was so much to do today that I gingerly sat up in bed, holding my throbbing head in shaky hands until I could open my eyes. Bright summer sunshine spilled through cracks in the vertical blinds and I squinted in order to bear the light.

I carefully swung my feet over the side of the bed and stumbled into the bathroom. Rummaging around in my medicine cabinet above the sink, I found the extra-strength Excedrin and proceeded to struggle for a full five minutes getting off the child-proof, adult-proof and idiot-proof cap. My hand trembled as I shook out the tablets and half a dozen went down the drain before I managed to catch two. I popped them into my mouth and cupped a handful of cold water to wash them down. The most important business of the morning completed, I stood in a shower as hot as I could stand for twenty minutes, letting the water massage my aching back and neck.

As I stepped out of the shower, the phone rang. I grabbed a towel and dashed to the bedroom to answer.

"Lexi?" a male voice said.

"Finn?" I replied. The connection was bad. He must be calling from a cell phone.

"Yes, it's me. Where have you been? I've been ringing your frigging phone off the hook."

"I'm sorry I missed your calls yesterday," I said. "I had

to go out last night. Did you get my message? I was going to call you first thing this morning."

"We've got to talk right away," he said and I could hear a car honking in the background.

"That's no kidding," I said. "Someone tried to shoot me last night."

I heard screeching tires. "What? Are you okay?"

"They missed. So, other than a blinding hangover, I'm just dandy."

"What happened?"

"It's a rather long and sordid story."

"Jesus, Joseph and Mary," he said. "Look, I'm headed your direction. I know it's early, but can I come by?"

I thought of the CD sitting on my coffee table that I was supposed to give him. "Sure," I said, calculating how long it would take me to get ready. "How far away are you?"

"About ten minutes," he said. "Give me your address."

I gave him directions and hung up. Darting back to the bathroom, I finger-combed my hair, bypassed the rouge and put on lip balm. I pulled on a pair of cut-off jean shorts and a sleeveless baby-blue blouse. My sandals were in the back corner of my closet, so I yanked them out and shoved my feet into them. I grabbed my wallet out of my purse and stuck it, my keys and Slash's CD into a tote bag. Jamming my sunglasses on my nose, I went down to the parking lot to wait for Finn. Even though Slash had told me my apartment wasn't bugged, I wasn't sure I completely believed him. And I certainly didn't want anyone listening to what I was going to say to Finn, partially because it involved an illegal activity like planting a program in his company's computer so hackers could break in.

I hadn't waited more than two minutes before I saw Finn pull up in a sleek dark green Jaguar convertible. I couldn't help but goggle—and not just at the car. He looked really different in jeans, a white T-shirt and dark sunglasses. Casual, sexy, yummy. I shook my head. I had started to feel increasingly disoriented as I bounced from one gorgeous guy to the next. How did normal women handle this?

I tried to look nonchalant as Finn screeched to a halt next to me, putting on my yeah-sexy-guys-take-me-for-a-ride-all-the-time-in-Jags expression. But he looked grim as he leaned across the front seat to open the door.

"Get in," he said. "Do you know a quiet place we can talk?"

"Dunkin' Donuts," I said, getting in and shutting the door. "The ambiance is lacking, but the food is good."

He didn't respond to my early morning stab at humor and instead put the car in gear, adeptly maneuvering out of the parking lot. I directed him to the site a mile away and he pulled into an empty spot.

Neither of us got out of the car. Instead Finn shifted toward me, hands gripping the steering wheel, the sun bouncing off his dark shades. I found it a bit disconcerting that I couldn't see his eyes, but then again, he couldn't see mine either. My gaze darted around the parking lot trying to see if I could spot a government tail, but I didn't notice anything out of the ordinary. That was probably the idea.

"What happened last night?" he said, his voice angry. "Who tried to shoot you?"

I gave him the abridged version, leaving out Slash's role in the entire fiasco. Finn made no comments, but his fingers squeezed the steering wheel so tight his knuckles were bloodless.

"We're getting damn close to something," he said. "Something big."

"That's not all," I blurted out. "Basia called me yesterday. She left a message for me on my answering machine."

Finn started in surprise. "Is she all right?"

"For the time being, I suppose."

"What did she say?"

"Not much. She's fine and safe and said I shouldn't trust you." I gave myself a mental head slap. Lexi Carmichael, master of subtlety.

Finn sighed. "I'm not surprised she said that. I officially belong to the company who may be responsible for putting her in danger. Did she say where she was?"

I shook my head, deciding not to mention anything about both Xavier and Slash tracing the call to Sweden. "But she said she was safe."

"Will she call back?"

"I don't know."

"Well, at least she's alive," he said, exhaling. "I sincerely hope she's with Judyta. Lexi, there's something else I need to tell you. Strange things have started happening at work."

"What kind of strange things?"

"I've been abruptly pulled from several big cases. There's always a good reason for it, like something unexpected has come up or I'm needed elsewhere. But I've got the distinct feeling that I'm being isolated for a specific reason. I don't like it."

"I'm sorry, Finn."

"There's more. I got an unusual phone call yesterday."

"From whom?"

"Chloe Small. Harold Small's wife. She was the one who found the contract in her husband's safety deposit box. She asked me to meet with her."

"Did you?"

"I did. Chloe told me she didn't think Harold's death was an accident and she wanted to know if the documents she turned over to me might in any way support that."

"Why did she think his death wasn't an accident?"

"Apparently she thought that from the start, but her concerns were dismissed by both the police and the higher-ups at CGM. She hoped I had discovered something that would confirm her suspicions."

"What suspicions?"

"She said Harold had been acting strange for months. He wasn't sleeping or eating well, and he got very nervous whenever they went out. He wouldn't talk to her about the source of his anxiety, but once told her something big was going down at work."

"That's all he said?"

"Unfortunately, he didn't elaborate."

"What did you tell her about the documents?"

"I told her the truth without going into detail. But I also told her that I, too, suspected Harold's death might not have been an accident."

I rubbed my eyes beneath my sunglasses. They felt raw and tired like the rest of my body. "You realize we're talking murder here."

"Bugger it, don't I know that," he said, his Irish accent suddenly slipping through. I realized he must truly be shaken.

"Chloe also said that about three months ago Harold received a significant amount of money. He told her it was an unexpected bonus from the company for his outstanding performance on a case."

"Did he name the case?"

"No."

"How significant a bonus are we talking?"

"Twenty grand."

I whistled. "Some bonus."

"And unusual, as well. I can't imagine anything legit he could have been working on that would earn him an extra twenty grand."

"Sounds to me like someone was buying his silence."

"But for what? What in the hell is the company involved in?"

My head had begun to throb. I needed caffeine to counteract the hangover and I needed it badly. I opened the door to the car. "I need some coffee in order to think. You want some?"

"I'll come in with you."

I ordered an extra-large coffee and a bottle of Diet Coke. Then Finn ordered a chocolate-covered donut with sprinkles, so I got one, too. We took the food and drink back to the convertible and ate in silence with the sun warming our heads and shoulders.

When I finished eating the donut, I wiped my greasy hands on a napkin and took a sip of coffee. "Finn, does the word Acheron mean anything to you?" I watched him carefully, but he seemed genuinely puzzled.

"No, should it?"

"It was written in code at the bottom of the contract you sent Basia."

"I didn't send her anything with a code on it."

"I didn't think so. She penciled it in for some reason. I'm trying to figure out why."

"Why didn't you tell me about this earlier?"

"I wasn't sure I trusted you."

He lifted his sunglasses to the top of his head and looked at me, his green eyes both troubled and serious. "What about now?"

"I'm doing the best I can, Finn. I want to trust you even though Basia told me not to. I just hope I'm not wrong about you."

He put the sunglasses back down and looked away. "You're not."

"Good, because I think if we can find out what Acheron means, we may be on to something."

"You think it means something to the firm."

"Yes. Maybe the name of a case or a file. It's worth a shot and we can find out for certain…if you help."

There must have been something unusual in my voice because he cocked his head to me. "Just what did you have in mind, Lexi?"

I unzipped my tote bag and pulled out the CD that Slash had given me. "This."

Finn looked at me for a long time. "What exactly is it?"

"Trust me. You don't want to know, *exactly*. All you need to do is open it on your computer. That's it."

He kept staring at me without saying anything. Then he took the CD and slipped it into his glove compartment.

"I'll be going by the office later today," he said, putting his hands on the steering wheel. "I'll let you know when it's done."

"Thanks," I said, feeling increasingly uncomfortable. As a lawyer he knew full well the possible consequences of what he was about to do and I felt like a criminal for asking, even though the cause was just and an employee of the NSA had instructed me to do it. But Finn didn't know any of that, so I felt badly that for him, the choice was morally gray.

"By the way, just to ensure that I can reach you from now on I got this for you." Finn reached into his shirt pocket and pulled out a tiny cell phone.

I looked at the phone and then back at him in disbelief. "You bought me a cell phone?"

He smiled. "Not exactly. Consider it a temporary loan. Given our present circumstances I thought it prudent that we be able to reach each other quickly. I'm sorry if I'm being presumptuous. You don't have to take it if you don't want to."

I thought for a moment and then took it. "Okay. It's a good idea. I'll consider it a loan."

Finn grinned at me with what looked like relief and then handed me a booklet and a charger. "Instructions are inside, along with your number. It's a piece of cake to operate. Just like a computer."

"Yeah right," I said, remembering the fiasco I'd had with his phone in the restaurant bathroom. "Thanks, I guess."

"Don't worry, you'll get used to it," he said, taking a sip of his coffee and returning it to the cup holder. "Just don't let your mum know you've got it."

"That's no kidding," I said as we got out of the car and dumped our cups in the trash. Then Finn put the Jag into gear and pulled out of the parking lot. With a stern warning to be careful, he dropped me off at home.

Upstairs, I tossed my tote bag on the coffee table and examined the new cell phone more closely. When I was convinced I understood the basics, I walked out onto the balcony and dialed the twins' number.

"Hello," mumbled Xavier. He yawned. Obviously geniuses had to sleep after all.

"Sorry to wake you," I said. "I just wanted to check something out."

"Sure," he replied, sounding a bit more alert. "Where are you calling from?" I guess the twins had caller ID.

"A new cell phone. Look, I just wanted to make certain you and Elvis had helped write a program with Slash that I was to pass on to Finn Shaughnessy at CGM."

"Affirmative. He did the base of the programming and we sort of refined his work a bit," Xavier said. "Tuned it up, so to say. It didn't need much. He is good, Lexi. Very good. A wizard in the extreme."

"Well that's comforting. Just so you know, I gave the program to Finn this morning. We should find out in a little while whether or not things worked out."

That seemed to wake up Xavier even more. "Cool," he said and I could hear him shuffling around. "I'll tell Elvis. We'll be monitoring it."

"Thanks. Let me know how it goes. And, Xavier, if you need to get in touch with me, will you call me on this number?" I rattled off my new cell number, but before I hung up, Xavier told me Elvis wanted to talk to me.

"Hey, Elvis," I said when he came on the line. "Nice job on the program."

"Thanks," he said and he sounded a bit sleepy, too. "Look, Lexi, I don't want to spook you or anything, but I came across something interesting about Slash last night."

"Slash?" I repeated. "What do you mean? Xavier said he was the real deal."

"He *is* the real deal—optimum to the letter. I have no doubt he is *the* Slash we thought he was. But it appears he's also got an interesting past."

I felt my heart skip a beat. "What kind of interesting past?"

"Well, I called in a couple of favors from some guys I know who did a little digging around for me."

"And?"

"Slash is definitely Italian and he had a rather interesting job before coming on board at the NSA."

"What did he do?"

Elvis paused for a minute. "You may be surprised."

"Try me."

"All right but don't say I didn't warn you. Slash worked, or perhaps even still works, for Vatican intelligence."

"What?" I screeched. "No freaking way."

"Way."

"You mean to say that the pope has his own intelligence service?"

"In a manner of speaking. Back in the 1800s, the Catholic hierarchy ordered various faithful groups to spy on heretics and report to the Church. In 1909 Pope Pius XII formed a more sophisticated version he called *Sodalitium Pianum.* A lot of people didn't like knowing the Church was involved in espionage, so in 1921 the Church announced that the group had been officially disbanded. Still, many experts believe that the group remains intact and is one of the most powerful spy networks in the world."

"You're saying Slash was, or is, a member of this *Sodalitium Pianum* group?" I said, struggling to contain my disbelief.

"Yes."

"Okay, I'm having a hard time picturing this." Slash just seemed too sexy and dangerous to be the religious type. Then I remembered the small gold cross he wore beneath his shirt and reconsidered.

"Did you happen to discover Slash's real name?" I asked.

"Not really. He has a list of aliases three pages long, all government provided. I'd venture a guess one of them is his real name, but I have no idea how to determine which."

"You trust your sources on this?"

"Implicitly. Lexi, I don't know how this plays into everything. It's just another thing to add to the mix."

I was hoping the mix would stay just where it was. I was no cook, nor did I have any desire to be promoted to head chef.

"Thanks, Elvis," I said, flipping the phone shut and

sliding it in my pocket. Things were definitely starting to heat up. There would be time to think about Slash working for the pope later.

Going back inside my apartment, I grabbed my tote bag again. I went down to the parking lot, looking around to see if I was being followed. Nothing unusual jumped out at me. On the other hand, it was a beautiful Saturday summer morning and there were lots of people out for a drive and walking around. So I probably wouldn't have a clue I was being followed unless someone held up a sign reading FBI Here.

I hopped into the Miata, put down the top and drove directly to Anderson's Karate Academy. The place was packed and I had to wait until Lars finished teaching a group of students with red belts before he finally walked over to see me.

"Hi, Lexi," he said cheerfully. He didn't even looked flushed, but his students were sweating and red-faced as though they had run a marathon.

"Hi, Lars," I said. "Basia is in Sweden."

There was a flicker of surprise in his eyes and then he shrugged. "Lucky for her."

"No more games with me. She's in serious danger. I need to find her."

Lars looked around at the parents who had begun to stare at us and then motioned for me to follow him. Without speaking, he led me to his office and shut the door.

"Why do you think I know where she is?" he said, sitting down.

I remained standing and crossed my arms over my chest. "Don't give me this crap about her being your student. I've known Basia for years and the idea of her taking karate is about as absurd as anything I could possibly imagine."

"And from that you extrapolate that I know where she is?"

"I know that for some misguided reason you think you're protecting her. But she's my best friend. You've got to trust me. She just called me and she's scared."

"If she just called you, why didn't she tell you where she was?"

"I wasn't home. She talked to my machine and didn't leave a number where I can reach her."

"Then how do you know she's in Sweden?"

"I have my ways," I said rather smugly.

His face hardened. "Good for you. But the bottom line is that I don't know what you're talking about."

"Look, just so you know, the stakes have been raised considerably. Someone tried to kill me last night. And that's not counting the two previous times I was accosted at gunpoint by people looking for documents Basia was translating. We are talking significant danger here."

His face remained impassive. "Then go to the police."

"It's not so simple."

"Sounds simple to me."

"I think you know better. A lot better. Look, I just need you to get a message to her."

I leaned forward and snatched a pen and a piece of paper off his desk and scrawled down my new cell phone number. "Have her call me as soon as she can. If I found out she's in Sweden, others will find her, as well. I have a feeling their intentions toward her will not be as altruistic as mine."

He stared at me, saying nothing, so I stalked out of his office without a backward glance. I drove home, feeling frustrated and discouraged, constantly peeking in my rearview window for the FBI.

The minute I got to my apartment, the phone rang. Stepping into the kitchen, I picked it up.

"Hello?"

"Hey, sis, it's Rock. I've got some of that info you requested."

"Great. Where are you?"

"At home. Why?"

"Don't go anywhere. I'll call you right back."

"Well, make it quick. I'm on my way out."

Maybe it was paranoia or maybe I just didn't want the government to know everything damn thing I was doing, but I reached for the cell phone Finn had given me, intending to use it instead. To my shock it started to ring just as I grabbed it, and I dropped it like a hot potato. I didn't have time to talk to Finn at this exact moment, so I left it on my couch where it kept ringing. Dashing next door, I rang Jan's bell and prayed she was home.

After a moment, the door flew open and Jan Walton's seven-year-old son, Jamie, stood there staring at me without saying anything.

"Hi, Jamie," I said. "Is your mom home?"

He looked at me, blinking rapidly, and then said, "Did you know the red spot on Jupiter is really a raging, burning storm?"

"Yep. I knew that."

Just then Jan came to the door, looking relieved to see me there. "Sorry, I was in the bathroom. Jamie, you know you're not supposed to open the door without me."

"Did you know that Jupiter is four hundred eighty-three and a half million miles from the sun," he said as if he hadn't heard her. "If you traveled at one hundred miles per hour, twenty-four hours a day, it would take five hundred and fifty-two years to reach the sun."

It took me several seconds to calculate that in my head,

and damned if he wasn't right. "Amazing," I said. "How about Saturn?"

"Eight hundred and eighty-seven million miles from the sun," he answered promptly. "If you traveled at one hundred miles per hour, twenty-four hours a day, it would take you one thousand and twelve years to reach the sun."

"I love this kid," I said.

"It's mutual," she said and then patted Jamie affectionately on the shoulder. "All right, buster. Go play on the computer."

Jamie darted away without a word and Jan ushered me inside. "Glad to see you, Lexi. I was beginning to think you had fallen off the face of the earth. What's up?"

"This is going to sound like a strange request, but can I use your phone?"

"What's wrong with yours?"

"It's a long story," I said. "It's kind of urgent."

"Of course," she said, looking puzzled. "You can use the one in the kitchen."

I went into the kitchen, sat down at the table and dialed Rock's number. He answered on the first ring.

"You want to tell me what's going on?" he demanded.

"Not right now. What do you have for me?"

"You were right about Bright Horizons almost going bankrupt a year ago. But they miraculously turned it around."

"How miraculous are we talking?"

"Forty million dollars worth."

I whistled. "Wow, some miracle."

"It smells fishy to me," said Rock. He has a pretty damn good nose for fish.

"My thoughts exactly," I said.

"Anyway, I emailed you a couple of articles from some business publications with a bit of background info on the company and press about the company's rejuvenation. You might find it useful. Check it out when you get a chance."

"Thanks, I will," I replied. "Any idea where the dough came from? I mean, is the infertility business really that profitable?"

"Profitable, yeah, but not to the tune of forty million. I think you may be on to something, Lexi."

If he only knew.

I suddenly had a thought. "Hey, Rock, does the word *Acheron* mean anything to you?"

He paused for a moment, thinking. "No. Should it?"

"If I were to tell you it might be connected to Greek mythology, would that ring any bells?"

"No. What in the hell are you talking about?"

"I'm not sure. I think the word or a certain meaning of Acheron might have some connection in all of this."

I could hear the scratch of his pencil as he wrote it down. "Just what have you got yourself into?"

"Well, that's the thousand dollar question these days," I said as lightly as I could manage. "Look, Rock, Acheron is supposedly a mythical river in the Underworld. Do me a favor and see what else you can come up with."

I could tell he had more questions to ask, but he knew me well enough to know I wasn't going to answer them. "Okay, I'm on it," he said. I knew if anyone could dig up something useful, it would be him.

I hung up and Jan walked into the kitchen, looking at me in concern. "Are you all right, Lexi?"

"I'm not sure."

"Is this a matter of national security or something?"

"Something," I said honestly. I had never officially confirmed it, but Jan pretty much knew I worked at the NSA like half of the population in Jessup. It didn't take a brain surgeon to figure that out.

"Is that why you can't use your phone? It's being tapped?"

"Yeah," I admitted. "Look, I don't want to say anything more so that if you're asked, you can honestly say you don't know diddly squat."

"I *don't* know diddly squat," she said in exasperation.

"Good. That worked for Ronald Reagan and Bill Clinton and it should work for you. Keep up the good work. I promise you the full story later."

I left her apartment and returned to mine. The cell phone Finn had given me was ringing nonstop where I had left it on the couch.

I picked it up and pushed the talk button. "Hello?"

"Where in the hell have you been?" Slash yelled.

My brain froze for a minute in confusion. "Hey, how did you get this number? I just got the phone about an hour ago from Finn." This was really starting to get annoying.

"Need you really ask, *cara?*"

"Jeez, is nothing sacred in America any more?"

"Not when it potentially involves terrorism."

I sighed. "Why are you calling?"

"I need to talk to you."

"So, talk."

"Come downstairs."

"What?"

"Look out your window," he said.

I went to the balcony and looked out. Slash sat there in his big black SUV, waving at me out the open window.

"I have no life," I muttered and hung up the cell phone, tossing it back on the couch.

I climbed down the stairs and out to the parking lot. Slash stood leaning against the car, crossing his arms against his chest. He wore jeans, a white muscle shirt and the darkest pair of mirror shades I'd ever seen. Remembering what Elvis had told me about Slash and his supposed connection to Vatican intelligence, I peered closer and saw the tiny gold cross tucked beneath his shirt. It made sense in this context, but could it really be true? A guy as sexy and dangerous as Slash seemed more destined to be on the dark side of things. Then again, when had I ever accurately read people?

"So, what's up?" I asked.

"We've got a big problem," he said grimly.

"Jeez, how much bigger can this problem possibly get?"

"Come," he ordered, leading me to a nearby tree that provided some welcome shade. He sat down on the grass, crossing his legs in a yoga-like position. I sat down beside him, with my legs straight out, knobby knees and all. They were still sore from all the pretzel sits I had done in karate and there was no way I was crossing them again.

"So?" I prompted after a few minutes had gone by and he hadn't said anything. He sat as still as a statue, calm and serene, almost like he was meditating. Since I couldn't see his eyes behind those shades, I had no idea if he was even awake or cared that I sat there.

"Dead," he finally said.

"Excuse me?"

"Six of the girls impregnated by Al-Asan have turned up dead. Murdered."

"Murdered?" I repeated in shock. "Oh, my God. How were they murdered?"

"Executed. One shot to the back of the skull each. No clues left. They were professional hits."

I felt sick. "The babies?"

Slash shook his head.

My stomach heaved and I swallowed hard. "What about Judyta?" I asked, my voice shaky. "Did you find her...too?"

"No. But I don't have to emphasize that she's in grave peril."

"But why would someone kill them?"

Slash pushed his fingers through his dark hair. His voice sounded tired and his cheeks sported a five o'clock shadow. "I don't know. But we have what could be a lead on the assassinations of Al-Asan's bodyguards in Italy."

"What kind of lead?"

"I reviewed the crime report this morning, including an interview with Al-Asan. According to the report, at approximately ten o'clock in the morning on December 17, Al-Asan's two bodyguards left the *Hotel Mediterraneé* en route for the Bright Horizons clinic. Al-Asan told investigators he was in Italy to undergo a medical procedure, but not surprisingly, didn't offer any more information. Apparently the weather was particularly bad. It was snowing hard and the visibility was poor. According to two employees at Bright Horizons, the bodyguards arrived at approximately ten-fifty, dropped off the briefcase and left the clinic. They were in the building for less than five minutes."

"How far is the clinic from the hotel?"

"About ten minutes."

"Even in poor weather?"

"In poor weather it would be no more than half an hour at the most, *cara*."

"So what were they doing for that extra thirty minutes?"

"This is what we need to find out," Slash said.

"Where were the bodies found?"

"According to the report, the bodies were discovered at approximately eleven-fifteen in an alley five minutes from the hotel, lying in their rental car."

"No one heard any shots or saw anything?"

"No. It apparently occurred in a blind alley, meaning no windows or doors open onto it."

"Isn't that convenient?"

"*Si,* and I believe it is no coincidence. The back of the rental car had been damaged. It looked like they had got hit from behind."

"A good reason to pull over," I mused. "Especially if the weather was bad. Accidents happen, right?"

Slash nodded. "One man was shot while he was in the car and the other while he was out of the car. Multiple shots on both of them. The Italian medical examiner wrote, however, that he was certain both men had been moved from their locations once they had been shot, but then later returned to the exact location where they were killed. Similar fibers found on both bodies indicate that the bodies were stacked somewhere together—most likely in a truck or a van."

I looked at Slash in disbelief. "How weird is that?"

"Very."

"But why hide the bodies and then return them to the spot of the crime?"

"I have no idea."

"What about time of death?" I asked. "How sure is the examiner of that?"

"Certain within an hour or two."

"That's not particularly helpful. What was Al-Asan's official reaction to the murders?"

"Shock, naturally. He said he had no idea who could have committed such an atrocity. Italian officials are leaning toward a robbery gone bad."

"Robbery?"

"Both of the men's wallets and watches were gone. The

polizia traced the identities of the men via the rental car, which led them to Al-Asan. But this was no robbery."

"I agree. But then what was it?"

"I don't know."

We were quiet for a moment, and I started to find the hot, humid air stifling. Then Slash turned his head toward me. "Did you give Shaughnessy the disk?"

I nodded. "I did it this morning. He said he'd take the disk to work today and do it. I already told the twins." It was on the tip of my tongue to ask him about his possible connection to the Vatican, but I didn't know how it mattered at this point. So I decided to keep it to myself until I had time to think about it more.

Slash stood and held out a hand to pull me to my feet. "*Eccellente.* If Shaughnessy has done his part, I've got work to do. I want you to stay at your apartment where I can reach you at a moment's notice."

"Why?"

"Because I don't like what's happening," he replied with a frown. "Women are showing up dead and someone took a shot at you last night. I want you to be safe, Lexi."

Without thinking, I looked over my shoulder. I saw my neighbor, Mrs. Wolansky, walking her dog in a big open area across from my apartment. Somehow the familiar sight calmed me.

"I'll be okay," I said, but my voice shook a little bit. "After all, the FBI is watching me, right?"

Slash smiled and touched my cheek. Without a word, he turned and walked back to his SUV. As he drove away I watched until I couldn't see the black speck anymore and then returned to my apartment. There was no way I was sitting around doing nothing, so I picked up my purse and cell phone before heading back out to my car. It took me just under five minutes to reach the twins' house.

I rang the bell and Elvis answered. He practically dragged me inside.

"Shaughnessy did it," Elvis said, pulling me into the command room and over behind Xavier who sat peering at a monitor. "He planted the program. Check it out, we're in CGM."

I peered over Xavier's shoulder, not certain what I was looking for. "Did you find anything interesting?"

"What do you think?" Xavier said, a smile in his voice.

"Just tell me you found a file called Acheron," I breathed.

"Bingo," Xavier said happily, twirling around in his swivel chair.

"Is it encrypted?" I asked.

"Hell, yes. But give us an hour or two and this baby is ours."

Elvis sat down next to his brother and they started talking in that language only they understood. I wandered into the kitchen to help myself to something to drink. I had just grabbed a Coke when the cell phone in my pocket began to ring.

I pulled it out and flipped it open. "Hello?" I said. There was a lot of static and I could barely hear anything. "Finn?" I asked. "Slash? Anyone?"

The crackle continued and then my heart stopped when I heard a voice say, "Lexi, are you there? It's me. Basia."

ELEVEN

I WAS SO shocked I dropped the unopened can of Coke. It fell to the floor with a clatter and then rolled across the linoleum, stopping against the base of the kitchen island.

"Basia?" I shouted into the receiver. "Where in the *hell* are you?"

"Lexi, thank God, it's you. I'm safe for now."

"Do you have any idea of the trouble you're in?"

"Yes, and I'm scared."

I knew exactly what she meant because my own heart was racing. "Is Judyta with you?"

"How do you know about Judyta?" she asked and then laughed hoarsely. "Oh yeah, you're with the NSA. Right."

"Basia, listen to me carefully," I said. "We don't have time for a lot of small talk. I'm pretty much up to speed on what is going on. I got the documents and I've figured out that Judyta is your cousin and she's acting as a surrogate mother for a Saudi prince named Mahir Al-Asan. But how in the world did you connect the translation you were working on for Finn Shaughnessy at CGM to Judyta?"

She blew out a deep breath. "Rather simple, really. Judyta sent me an exact copy of the contract I was working on. She wanted me to check it out to make sure the translation was on the up and up. In her letter, she told me she had signed up to be a surrogate mother for a Saudi prince to earn extra cash so she could study abroad. But she became suspicious when CGM refused to give her a copy of the contract for her own records. So she stole it from her files during a check-up when the nurse left it in the room for a moment."

"They had a copy of the contract in her medical files?"

"That and more. Judyta told me there was also a document that kept referring to her as part of Project Acheron. It sounded really weird and scared her to death. She didn't dare steal that document, too, so she just wrote to ask me if I could find anything unusual about the contract and whether or not Project Acheron rang any bells."

"So, that's why you penciled the word Acheron in code at the bottom of page three."

"I knew you'd figure it out! Do you know what Acheron is?"

"Not yet, but I'm working on it," I said grimly. "And I've got the twins helping me. Is there anything else of interest I should know about Judyta's contract?"

"Not that I can think of. I looked it over carefully. Other than naming the clients, Judyta and Al-Asan, it was word for word like the one Finn had asked me to translate. Do you remember Greg Santiago?"

"Vaguely. Wasn't he at Georgetown?"

"Lived one floor down from us in the dorm. He went on to law school at Yale and returned to D.C. to practice. He looked over my translation of the contract and said he thought it was worded very oddly. He's not an expert on surrogate pregnancy, but he thought the language was definitely irregular and considered it very suspicious that they wouldn't provide Judyta with her own copy."

"A nineteen-year-old girl," I murmured. "They thought they could manipulate her easily."

"Then the accident happened."

I looked up sharply. "What accident?"

"Judyta was driving in the outskirts of Warsaw when she was run off the road. She came within inches of plunging down a sharp incline and into a lake when a car she thought wanted to pass smashed into the side of her. She managed to spin the car around and stop with only one tire hanging off the incline. As she spun, she saw the car race by. It was a dark sedan with two men inside. She was really shaken."

"How was she so sure this was connected to her pregnancy?"

"She wasn't. But when she got back to her apartment, her neighbors told her men had come by asking about her. They were asking a lot of odd questions about her pregnancy and whether or not she had given birth to the baby."

"Polish?"

"No, Americans speaking Polish and not very well at that."

I breathed out a heavy sigh. "So she bolted."

"Immediately. She stayed with a neighbor for a couple of days while she contacted me and asked me to come help her get to safety somewhere."

"So, you went."

"Yes. I had no idea what the hell was going on. I had a feeling the contract and the word *Acheron* had something to do with it, but I no longer had the luxury of figuring it out."

"But I could."

"You were the only person I trusted. And I knew if someone could unravel it, you could."

"Look, Basia, I'm darn close to finding out exactly what Project Acheron is. But there's something else you should know. Judyta wasn't the only one implanted with Al-Asan's child."

"I know," Basia said. "Judyta met the other girls in Italy."

I winced. "Jeez, what was it, some kind of surrogate mother slumber party?"

"I know it sounds odd, but at the time it seemed an easy way for her to make a boatload of cash in a short period of time."

"Nothing is ever quite so easy. In fact, it's a lot worse than you can imagine. Brace yourself for this, Basia. For some unimaginable reason, all of the other surrogate mothers have been murdered. It looks like Judyta is the last girl alive."

"What?" Basia gasped. "Murdered? Why?"

"I don't know."

"Oh my God. Then it's true. Our lives *are* in danger. I thought someone was following us."

"Someone is following you?" I asked, my stomach turning to ice.

"Was." The connection suddenly sounded fainter as though I might be losing her. "Luckily, we know this area better than they do. I'm pretty sure we're safe for the time being. I guess I don't have to ask how you found all this out."

"No time now. But I do need to know how Judyta got hooked up with Al-Asan." There was a weird crackling noise and for a heart-stopping moment I thought the connection was lost. "Basia?" I shouted in panic.

"I'm still here," her voice came back faint, but still there. "She answered an advertisement online. She was contacted by Bright Horizons staff in Warsaw and then went through a rigorous health and psychological screening. The pay was incredible, more than she ever could have imagined. She didn't really consider what it all meant."

"I'm not being judgmental here. How is she feeling now?"

"She's fine but understandably scared. Things have changed for her. Lexi, she wants to keep the baby."

I blew out a breath. "Shit." A wave of static crackled

in my ear. "Jeez, Basia, what do you want me to do now? How can I help you?"

"Are you sure this phone is safe?"

I felt sick to my stomach. "No, it's not safe at all. There are likely others listening, at the very least, the FBI. You should also know Finn Shaughnessy gave me this phone. He could be listening in, too, for all I know. I know you told me not to trust him, but I think he's being set up in all of this, as well."

"I'm not sure I agree," she said. "Don't trust anyone except for Lars. He gave me your number."

"How is he involved in this?"

"It's not safe to tell you about Lars now." There was a long stretch of silence with a lot of static in between. "But don't worry, Lexi. I'm taking precautions," she finally continued. "This call will be difficult to trace. Judyta and I, we are well protected, at least for now."

I winced as the static crackled and I knew an end to the connection was imminent. "I've got to go," she said. "I'll contact you soon."

"How?"

"Not by this phone again. Another way. A safer way."

"What do you want me to do until then?"

"Help me figure out a plan to protect Judyta and let her keep the baby."

"Yeah, sure, piece of cake," I said, my voice shaking. "Good thing you're not asking me to do the impossible."

"That's what I like best about you, Lexi. A sense of humor in the middle of a life-threatening crisis."

"Well you'd better survive so I can kill you myself for what you're putting me through."

I heard her laugh, and was relieved to hear some humor to the sound. For a fleeting moment, she sounded like the Basia I knew.

"I knew there was a reason we're best friends," she said. "We can discuss this over margaritas soon. My treat."

Before I could answer, the noise on the line disappeared and there was dead silence.

"Basia?" I said frantically and then shook the cell phone, like that would help. "Basia?"

The connection was gone. I flipped the phone shut and leaned against the counter, shaking. For a good five minutes I stood there trying to absorb all she had said.

Still trembling, I returned to the twins' command room where they sat lost in their own world. They spoke in low voices while furiously typing away on their keyboards, presumably trying to hack into the Acheron file. I sincerely hoped whatever was in that elusive file would finally clue me in to what was happening in my own life. I wanted very badly to interrupt the twins and tell them that Basia had called but was afraid to break their concentration. I really needed to know what was in that file.

Then another, more disturbing thought occurred to me. If the FBI knew I had Finn's phone, I wondered how long it would take them to inform Slash that I'd received a call from Basia. I wasn't ready to talk to Slash just yet. I needed more time to think over the conversation.

"Lexi," Elvis said suddenly, breaking into my reverie. "I think this is something you should see."

"Are you in?" I asked, hurrying over.

"Not in Acheron yet. But I found something else in CGM's files you might find interesting."

I stood behind his chair, my hands resting lightly on the back of his seat. Looking over his shoulder, I studied the monitor.

"I broke into CGM's human resource records," he said. "Your friend Finn Shaughnessy seems to be more than just a lowly lawyer."

"What do you mean?"

"You tell me."

Weird, but I thought I heard a trace of jealousy in his voice. What could he possibly have against a guy he'd never met? Frowning, I peered over his shoulder at the screen. "What am I supposed to look at?"

"This document," he said, swiveling around in his chair and standing up. "Take a look."

I sat down in his chair. It was still warm, which was good because I was freezing with all the arctic ventilation from the air conditioner blowing on me and I'd forgotten to get a blanket.

I took a breath and started to read what looked like a typical personnel file. Finnigan Shaughnessy, age thirty, born in Cork, Ireland. He attended the National University of Ireland in Dublin as an undergraduate and double majored in business management and public health administration. He went to Georgetown Law School and earned a law degree.

There was a bunch more stuff about his academic achievements and papers. He'd done some research involving medical technology and the law, which made sense since he'd ended up at CGM. Then I read a sentence that stopped my breath. I reread it and then tapped my finger on the monitor beneath the sentence.

"Can this be right?" I asked Elvis, looking at him over my shoulder.

He smiled, apparently satisfied that I had picked up on the oddity. "Don't see why not. It's kind of strange, though, don't you think? A guy like him working at a place like CGM."

I turned back to the monitor and read the sentence for a third time.

Emergency contact: Father: Mr. Logan Shaughnessy (Shaughnessy Winery, Cork Ireland).

"Logan Shaughnessy," I repeated. "This can't possibly be *the* Logan Shaughnessy I'm thinking of."

"How many Logan Shaughnessys do you think live in Cork, Ireland and own a winery?" Elvis asked.

"Shit," I said, putting my chin in my hand. Logan Shaughnessy, the colorful and eccentric Irish billionaire, had topped Forbes' list of richest men in the world last year. His wine was way too expensive for my palate, but I'd had it at my parents' house once and it seriously rocked.

"Oh, man, you're right," I said, starting to breathe faster. "What could possibly be next? First Slash isn't who I thought he was, and now I discover that Finn is the heir to a wine fortune. Isn't anyone who they say they are these days?"

"The real question is what is a guy like Finn Shaughnessy doing at CGM?" Xavier said.

"Whatever the reason, I have a feeling I'm not going to like it," I moaned.

Xavier motioned to me and sat down in front of another computer nearby and starting typing. "Guess we should read the tabloids more often," he said, angling the monitor so I could see.

He'd pulled up *Celebrity Focus* magazine online. Still in shock, I leaned over and read the cover story about Finn being one of Ireland's most desirable bachelors. According to the article, he was currently dating Finnish supermodel-turned-actress, Claudette Hyvärinta, whose last name just happened to mean "good chest" in Finnish. The article also had pictures of him racing speedboats off the coast of Ireland, looking gorgeous with his hair tousled and his cheeks red from the wind.

Still in disbelief that Finn and this guy were one and the

same, I continued to read the article, feeling stupider by the minute. It wasn't so much that I'd met with him several times and had no idea he was a celebrity, but more that I felt betrayed he hadn't even mentioned it. He was under no obligation to do so, but it made me appear doubly idiotic since I work at the NSA and hadn't even bothered to uncover information about him. Now that I thought about it, why hadn't I checked out Finn more thoroughly?

Oh, yeah, I remembered why. Because Slash told me he had Finn checked out and nothing unusual popped up. Nothing unusual my ass, that SOB. I was certain Slash knew who Finn was. He probably thought it was a riot to keep me in the dark. That's me—stellar NSA employee who turns out to be completely clueless.

Elvis must have noticed I was upset, because he put his hand on my shoulder. "Don't let it get to you, Lexi. Perfect hair, chiseled muscles, well dressed…that is so not your type."

I glanced up at him in surprise. "I have a type?"

"Sure, we all have a type. Sometimes we just don't know it."

Elvis had a type, too? Just as I started pondering that, the shrill sound of my cell phone rang and I reached into my pocket to grab it. I started to open it and then changed my mind. Instead I pushed a button and turned it off.

Elvis looked at me in surprise. "Why'd you do that?"

"I don't want to talk to anyone just yet," I said. Mostly because if it was Finn, I needed more time to assimilate the information I'd just learned about him. If it was Slash, I needed to decide whether he was trying to help or hurt Basia and Judyta.

"Hey, guys, I've got something," Xavier suddenly exclaimed, his voice excited. "We're in."

I momentarily forgot my mortification about Finn

and leapt to Xavier's side, peering eagerly at the monitor. "In Acheron?"

·"The one and only," Xavier said gleefully.

Elvis's fingers flew across the keyboard. "Oh yeah, come to Daddy," he breathed as data suddenly scrolled across the screen.

"Are you downloading it?" I asked in a hushed voice.

"We'll have the whole thing in about three minutes," Elvis answered.

For the next three minutes the room was completely silent except for the whir and hum of the computers and the air conditioner. Then Elvis typed something and stood up.

"Another one bites the dust," he said and then stretched. "I think I'll have a beer."

Neither of the twins looked worried in the least, while I was on the verge of a heart attack. To the twins it was just another hack. To me, it was life or death.

Xavier sat in Elvis's vacated chair and perused the file. After a moment he whistled. "Not good," he said, his voice serious. "There is some pretty bad shit in here."

"Define shit."

"Are you sure you're ready for this?"

"Not really, but I don't see how I have much of a choice."

"Okay, then here goes. Bright Horizons isn't just doing in vitro fertilization procedures to help couples conceive."

"Like, *duh*. They're doing some kind of weird surrogate pregnancy deal, right?"

"Not exactly."

"What do you mean 'not exactly'?"

"I mean they're creating life all right. But not by traditional means."

"What other means are there?" A niggling finger of dread crept up my spine.

"We're not talking in vitro fertilization, hormone therapy

or surrogacy pregnancies, legal or otherwise," he said. "We're talking about something much more sinister here."

My stomach clenched. "How sinister?"

Xavier looked at me, his expression grim. "Bright Horizons is cloning human beings."

TWELVE

I FELT AS though he'd punched me in the gut. "Cloning?" I gasped. "As in reproductive human cloning? Impossible!"

Elvis walked into the room with three beers. He handed one to Xavier and me and then sat down beside his brother. "Backspace, dude. Did I just hear you say human cloning?" He looked as startled as Xavier, which was pretty amazing since I didn't think much of anything shocked the twins.

Xavier nodded, taking a swig of his beer and scrolling rapidly through the file. "Yeah, and from what I can tell this Al-Asan dude paid big bucks to try and get himself one."

"How big?"

Xavier's fingers flew over the keyboard. "Looks like about forty million dollars big. Probably just a drop in the bucket for a guy like him."

"Forty million dollars?" I exclaimed. "So that's how CGM was able to financially afford to turn things around. My brother Rock uncovered the same figure, except now we know it came from one source—Al-Asan. I wonder how many other potential clients CGM has got lined up."

"Probably plenty," Xavier said. "But presumably only if Project Acheron works out."

"The name makes sense now," Elvis murmured. "Project Acheron."

I backed into a chair and sat down, my legs suddenly weak. "Odysseus poured sacrificial blood into the confluence of the rivers Acheron and Styx to summon the ghosts of the dead," I muttered. "I get it, too."

"Actually, it's more like *resurrecting* the dead," Elvis commented. "Creating an immortal life, in a way, if one keeps cloning oneself forever. Grotesque and yet, dissonantly poetic."

"This is seriously messed up," Xavier said, shaking his head. "How in the world did a girl like Basia get mixed up in a mess like this?"

My stomach roiled. "Her cousin Judyta is one of several surrogates hired to carry Al-Asan's clone. The problem is, Judyta doesn't know about the cloning part. Probably the other women didn't either."

I quickly gave them the complete rundown, including my recent conversation with Basia, all the information Slash had told me about Al-Asan's bodyguards being murdered in Italy, and the young women presumably carrying Al-Asan's clone showing up dead across Europe.

Xavier whistled under his breath when I finished. "Are you saying someone tracked down these women and killed them execution style?"

"According to Slash, yes. All except Judyta. But Basia told me she thinks their lives are in danger. Judyta has already managed to escape one accident."

"Nasty stuff, if it's really playing out this way," Elvis commented.

"What do you mean, *if* it's really playing out this way?" I asked.

"Well, cloning is a complicated procedure," he explained, shrugging. "Cloning humans is likely to be even more difficult than theorized. Scientists aren't able to properly study or determine its safety without conducting a large-scale study. In laymen's terms, that means clinical trials on a mass scale. I just don't see that happening in the near future, at least not out in the open. And once you take the research and trials underground, the science itself becomes suspect."

"Jeez," I said, trying not to be disgusted. "Do you really think CGM has a good chance of getting a clone of Al-Asan out of this?"

Elvis shrugged. "It depends on the ability and the genius of the people involved, as well as the procedures they used. And I wouldn't discount a healthy dose of luck. But as far as I know, primates are especially difficult to clone for a wide variety of reasons, not the least of which is proper brain development. But if I were to make guess based on sheer mathematical supposition, the odds would be extremely low that CGM could get a healthy clone from this. Let me take a look at the file for a moment."

He moved over to another terminal and started scrolling through the Acheron file. A few minutes later, Elvis twirled around in his chair. "Well, from what I can see, it looks like CGM gave it their best shot. Their scientists, geneticists and doctors all appear to have solid credentials. They had the money, the equipment and the resources. Implementation took place last December in Genoa, Italy, using freshly harvested skin cells from Al-Asan who was also in Italy for the procedure. It looks like seven women were implanted at this time, all of varied nationalities. From what I can tell, this appears to be a deliberate action. The scientists wanted to see if any one nationality might have a stronger physical constitution over another that might help stabilize the fetus."

I swallowed hard. "First of all, *eeew.* Second of all, is Judyta definitely one of the seven?"

"Her name is listed in the file."

I inhaled a deep breath. "Okay. So, the odds are low,

but there is still a chance CGM could get a clone out of this, right?"

Elvis shrugged. "Of course there is always that chance. The mere fact that Judyta hasn't yet miscarried is a very good sign for CGM. Nonetheless that doesn't mean there won't be problems down the road for both her and the child even if it survives the birthing process. But just the birth alone could be a huge watershed for science."

I stood and started to pace. I needed to clear my mind, to look at this as coolly and objectively as possible. This was science and I had to remove my emotions and look at it in terms of the hard, cold facts. If I were to fully understand what I was up against, I needed to know exactly how the procedure worked.

"All right, so give it to me as simply as possible," I said. "How does one create a clone? I mean, you said they probably used skin cells from Al-Asan."

Xavier leaned forward in his chair. "Theoretically, it's a fairly straightforward procedure. A healthy, unfertilized egg is harvested from a female and the nucleus removed. Cells are then taken from the person who wants to be cloned. Typically those are skin cells, and at least one of the cells must contain all forty-six chromosomes."

"Then what?"

"Then the new cell with its nucleus is inserted into the egg," Xavier explained. "Chemical or electrical stimulation is used to divide the egg, just as if it had been fertilized naturally. Once the embryo is stable, it can be implanted into a uterus where it grows and develops."

"It sounds easy," I said. "What about that Scottish sheep, Dolly, who was cloned back in 1996? Didn't she turn out okay?"

"Not exactly," Elvis answered. "At first she looked all right, but scientists later found arthritis in her leg, which is a rare condition in sheep before ten years of age. She also showed signs of premature aging and lived shorter than the average life span of a sheep."

I rubbed my temples to try and stave off the headache that was starting there. "So Al-Asan paid forty million dollars to get himself a clone. How did CGM keep the money all hush-hush?"

Elvis shrugged. "Someone doctored the financial records. It seems to be the corporate rage these days."

I couldn't argue with that. "Does this mean it was a straight profit for CGM?"

"Not exactly," Xavier answered. "More like a long-term investment. Think of the potential income that could be generated for the company in the future."

I grimaced. "Break down the financial costs for me."

Elvis steepled his fingers together. "First CGM would have to find a half-dozen young, healthy women to donate eggs. Not all eggs are viable. Only about one-third of them would turn out to be usable embryos. To find just the right ones could get expensive."

"But it wouldn't matter what nationality, eye color or IQ of the woman donating the egg because all of her genetic material is removed during cloning," I said.

"Right. Then they'd have to find excellent candidates in superb physical shape to carry the babies to term since it would be a high-risk pregnancy."

"Just to see if there were a difference, they chose seven women of differing ages and nationalities. Except the women didn't even know just how dangerous the risks were going to be," I said.

"Exactly. Once the eggs were fertilized with Al-Asan's genetic material, they'd be implanted into the women's uteruses," Elvis continued. "The mothers would be monitored very closely because of the extremely high risk for miscarriage, abnormally large fetuses, severe birth deformities or any number of other problems we can't even begin to imagine."

I tried unsuccessfully to ignore the constant churning in my stomach. "Okay, so that's why the women had to sign the contracts promising to see specific doctors in certain locations. And that's probably why CGM spread the women out across the different continents so that there would be less of a chance they'd attract attention if things started to go wrong. And naturally CGM never told the women they were part of a reproductive cloning experiment."

Xavier nodded. "Additionally, I'd guess that CGM would keep a large reserve of cash to protect the doctors and scientists who worked on Project Acheron. They'd want to be compensated if it ever became known they were involved in cloning human beings. They would certainly risk losing their licenses, not to mention their reputations."

We fell silent for a moment, thinking over the magnitude of what we'd uncovered.

Then Xavier spoke up. "You said Basia called you on your new cell phone. How did she get your number?"

"Lars Anderson," I replied. "Her new Swedish karate instructor. He's helping her for some reason. I know he is in this up to his neck, so I marched over to his studio this afternoon and told him I needed to reach Basia and left my new cell number. He played dumb, but lo and behold, a couple hours later she called me. I guess it worked."

"Backspace a nanobyte. Did you say karate instructor?" Xavier looked flabbergasted. He seemed more shocked by the idea that Basia would take karate than the fact that CGM was cloning human beings. Actually, if I really thought about it, it *was* a close call in terms of shock factor.

"I know it sounds crazy," I said. "But for some reason

Basia signed up for karate lessons shortly before she disappeared. Lars has a karate studio over in Laurel and clearly knows more about her whereabouts than he is letting on."

"He's Swedish?" Elvis murmured. "And Basia and Judyta just happen to be in Sweden. Well, at least we have a connection."

"Yeah, but what? I had my brother Beau check him out in the police files and he's clean. He became a naturalized American citizen last year and has run the karate studio for three. No tickets, no warrants, no obvious skeletons in the closet."

"Everyone has something to hide," Elvis said firmly.

"Maybe Basia and Judyta are staying with his family somewhere in Sweden," Xavier offered.

"Too easy," I said. "Slash is on to Lars and you can bet he's already used all his resources to check out that possibility."

"That means we still don't know their connection," Elvis said. "You say Basia never mentioned Lars before, and we all agree that the mere thought of Basia doing karate is astonishingly absurd."

"I might point out that she didn't mention Finn Shaughnessy either," Xavier said.

"Well, not before she disappeared," I replied. "But afterwards she warned me not to trust him. In Finn's defense, though, I think it's just because he's connected to CGM. She didn't know his particulars. Personally, I think he's as much a victim in all of this as we are."

Neither Elvis nor Xavier looked particularly convinced, but I pressed on. "Okay, let's forget about Finn and karate lessons for now and focus on the big picture."

"Good idea," Elvis agreed. "Shall I give it a shot?"

"Please."

"Okay, so here's what we know. Mashir Al-Asan, a

Saudi prince, underwent a cloning procedure via CGM's clinic in Genoa, Italy, last December. Cloned fetuses were implanted in seven women of varied nationalities. As far as we know, six of the seven have turned up dead and executed, none having successfully given birth. One of the women, Judyta Taszynski, is still alive and, as far as we know, healthy and pregnant. Presumably she is hiding somewhere in Sweden, being protected by her cousin Basia, and a naturalized Swedish-American karate instructor. Why and from whom they are protecting her is a mystery. Now the NSA, FBI and possibly the CIA and Vatican intelligence are all vested in finding Judyta Taszynski for reasons we can only speculate upon."

I nodded. "Okay, that sums it up fairly well, except don't forget to mention that two of Al-Asan's bodyguards were murdered in Genoa at the same time the implantation took place. The hit was possibly a robbery gone bad, or if the CIA is to be trusted, possibly conducted by followers of *überterrorist,* Samir Al-Naddi. A high-ranking Yemeni intelligence officer has also taken an intense interest in the whereabouts of Judyta."

"I'm with you guys so far," Xavier said. "It also seems clear the NSA has sanctioned your participation in this, but for some reason you're being played blind."

"Except for the guiding hand of Slash," I said. "You know, this really bites. I mean, how do we even know for sure that Slash is working for the NSA? What if he is really still with Vatican intelligence and just cooperating with the NSA?"

Elvis shook his head. "Despite his connection to the Vatican, which I'd venture to say is a lifetime commitment, he's definitely working for the NSA."

Xavier nodded vigorously. "Yeah, Lexi, he's in. While we were working on the program to hack into CGM, he was in and out of places that one only goes if they are part of the NSA. Besides, if he weren't NSA, he'd never have got our message in the first place. He's the real deal, Lexi. You can take it to the bank."

I had high regard for the twins' opinions, not to mention their gut instinct. If they thought Slash was NSA, then that was good enough for me.

"Then how do we figure Slash into this?" I asked.

Elvis rubbed his chin. "My guess is that Slash and his team already knew or suspected CGM was cloning humans, but they needed a smoking gun."

"They needed you," I said, suddenly understanding. "Slash must have failed in his attempts to get in. Jeez, how could I be so stupid? They used me to get to you guys. For an expert hack."

"Um, we went to him, Lexi," Xavier pointed out.

"Maybe they planned it that way."

"Either way, there's no sense in crying over spilt milk," Elvis said. "They're in and we're in. At this point we know they desperately want you to lead them to Judyta."

"But for what end purpose?" I murmured.

"You've got to decide how to play Slash," Xavier warned.

"I've got a feeling Slash is going to be a problem," I said glumly. "I think we made a big mistake bringing him in on this."

"You wanted speed and he was instrumental in helping us get in," Elvis said bluntly. "Xavier and I could have done it alone, but with Slash we made time in a big way. If I remember correctly, that was a priority at the time."

"It was," I said, sighing. "Clearly I had no idea of the scope of the problem. Now I don't know who to trust anymore."

Xavier took a swallow of his beer and leaned back in

his chair. "Well, if you ask me, I'd say Basia should save her own skin. I'd urge her to go to the nearest American Embassy and ask for help."

"She won't do it," I said flatly. "She won't abandon her cousin. Besides Judyta wants to keep the baby."

Xavier whistled. "Do you think she'd change her mind after she heard the baby contained none of her own genetic material?"

"I don't know," I said. "But I think she should have the opportunity to choose."

The twins fell silent and I tried to settle the chaotic swirl of thoughts in my head. Typically I'm the kind of person who needs quiet time to ruminate and reflect in order to figure things out. Unfortunately the luxury of uninterrupted thinking time didn't seem in the cards for me anytime soon.

"Did either of you happen to notice any mention of anything to do with terrorism, Yemen or anything like that when looking through the Acheron file?" I asked the twins.

"No, but it's a huge file and we've only scanned it," Xavier said. "We'll keep looking."

Elvis shook his head. "Lexi, this is one hell of a mess. Still, it seems to me that you have a lot more to fear from the brass at CGM than just about anyone else. The execs are likely to go to extreme measures to protect themselves if they discover you're on to their profitable little secret."

I shivered. "You don't have to warn me. I've already had enough experience this past week with guns and threats of bodily harm to last me a lifetime. I'm only sorry I dragged you guys into this."

Xavier shrugged. "In my opinion, there are greater forces at work here. Either way, I'm okay with it. The question is what are you going to do now?"

I honestly had no idea. "Well, maybe things will become clearer if I approach this logically and analytically—like a math equation, I guess. The problem is the shifting and hidden variables. It seems like everyone has a personal agenda—the FBI, NSA, CIA, Yemen government, Al-Asan, CGM and possibly even Vatican intelligence. And that's not to mention Basia and Judyta herself. Who knows who else is vested in this? But what is the common denominator?"

Elvis and Xavier looked hard at me in silence.

I held up my hands. "Okay, other than *me,* what is the common denominator?"

Xavier lifted the bottle of beer to his lips and took a swallow. "Honestly, I'm not seeing one. But if we pick it apart, I guess I'd say that on one end, the U.S. government and the Vatican definitely want to put an immediate stop to the cloning."

"Yeah, but I'd venture a guess that their primary goal is to keep it quiet," Elvis offered. "I mean, think about it. If Judyta's pregnancy actually comes to term, the knowledge of a successful human cloning could potentially be more dangerous than the attempt itself."

I could see where they were going with this. Once the scientific breakthrough had been made, the floodgates would open. Any ethical, moral and religious concerns would be drowned in scientific excitement.

"Okay, now on the other end of the spectrum, where does a royal Saudi prince with a desire for a clone and the Yemeni government fit in?" Xavier asked.

"Well, that's the million dollar question, isn't it?" Elvis commented.

I pressed my fingers to my temples. "I don't get it. Why don't U.S. authorities just go in and shut down CGM? That would certainly put an immediate stop to the cloning attempts."

"That might have worked months ago," Elvis said. "But now it's too late. CGM has already implanted the clones. What's left is to track down everyone and acquire, or perhaps even suppress, the evidence."

That sounded pretty darn ominous to me. "Okay, I can see why no one wants it to get out that human cloning is taking place, the Vatican included. But I just don't buy the idea that the U.S. government, and especially not the Vatican, is systematically hunting down innocent women and executing them because they carried or are carrying, a clone of a Saudi prince. After all, the women weren't even informed of Project Acheron." I sighed. "Jeez, I just don't have a clue here. What am I going to do?"

Elvis put a hand on my arm. "You have to do the only thing you can do, Lexi," he said. "You have to play your advantage."

I looked up hopefully. "I have an advantage?"

"Of course. You're the only link between all of these groups and Judyta Taszynski. Basia isn't going to trust anyone but you, and every player in the game knows it."

"Then why did someone try to shoot me in front of the disco club?"

"Apparently someone wants to stop you from revealing Judyta's whereabouts."

"CGM?"

"That's the most likely candidate."

I squeezed my eyes shut and rubbed my forehead. Elvis was right. I did have an advantage and it was a big one. But how was I supposed to use it? This whole situation had gone so far beyond the scope of my expertise that it was breathtaking. I was nothing more than a junior techie who liked chocolate éclairs, doing crossword puzzles on my lunch break and drinking Diet Coke for breakfast. Excitement for me meant answering the final Jeopardy question correctly while eating my nuked dinner off a tray. Human cloning, terrorists and people with guns were for experienced field agents or movie stars, not a desk-jockey, geeky computer nerd/mathematician like me. Yet here I was. So what was I going to do about it? Whine and mope, or do something useful?

Think, Carmichael, think.

I resumed pacing and chewed at my fingernails. "All right, if I'm to use my so-called advantage to help Basia, I need to know exactly what I'm up against. Slash isn't talking and the NSA is apparently playing me blind in this. So that leaves me with only one course of action. I've got to stop being a doormat and start making things happen the way *I* want."

"Now you're talking." Elvis smiled encouragingly.

"What do you have in mind?" Xavier asked.

My heart pounded furiously and I wondered if real field agents nearly had a heart attack each time they were about to embark upon a dangerous and daring course of action.

"I've got to figure out a way to bring all the involved parties to the table, minus Judyta, of course," I said slowly. "It's kind of like when James Bond leads the good guys to the bad guys and then they have it out on a deserted island surrounded by lots of sharks."

The twins stared open-mouthed at me, so I smiled. "Just kidding. About the shark part, at least. But I really mean it about bringing everyone together. I've got a gut feeling that things will break wide open if I can initiate a surprise confrontation between all the parties involved. If every player is forced to show his or her hand, maybe I'll have enough data to determine who is out to help Judyta and who wants to hurt her."

"Sounds iffy," Xavier said doubtfully. "So many things could go wrong."

"These days, iffy is the story of my life."

"Actually, I approve," Elvis said, tapping his chin. "It gives you some measure of control."

Yeah, like I felt even remotely in command of this situation. But Elvis was partially right. It did give me at least the illusion of control. Either way, I preferred that a heck of a lot more than being manipulated every time I turned around.

Snatching a piece of paper and a pencil from a nearby table, I started to write. Elvis and Xavier peered over my shoulder. I scrawled:

$$S_S = R^* \, M \, C \, N \, F \, I_c \, V_t \, S_t \, Y_i$$

"S will equal the percentage for success of all parties meeting in Sweden at the same time," I explained. "First, we make a variable for each national and international agency interested in finding Judyta and estimate the probability for each to follow me to a showdown. I figure that to be relatively high." I scratched some more figures down. "Second, I'll insert a calculated psych average that people will do the expected under predictable circumstances."

"What's predictable about that?" Xavier asked.

"They all want to find Judyta. The difficult part is including the unknowns, like someone deciding to shoot or stop me along the way, or planes, trains or natural disasters putting the timing off. So, I'll weight that with a twenty percent margin of error." I took a moment to calculate that in my head and marked it down. "Then, taking into account all the known and unknown variables, I have a forty-three point eight percent chance of success in getting all parties to meet in Sweden at the same time. Not great, but doesn't suck either."

The twins studied it thoughtfully. "Quantum bogodynamics," Xavier said.

"Optimum," Elvis added.

I let out a deep breath. I always felt better when my world was defined by the rigid logic of mathematics, even if some of the variables were rather questionable.

"So, I'm thinking that we send an 'invitation' to some of the players, sort of like how you brought Slash into this in the first place," I continued. "The others I'll bring to the party myself. They're watching and following me, so presumably they'll go everywhere I go. Then, boom, we've got everyone together who has an interest in this thing. That's when I'll start the auction."

Elvis raised an eyebrow. "Auction?"

"An information auction. Those willing to put information on the table regarding their reasons for wanting to find Judyta might get some information in return. I can't begin to figure out how to best help Judyta until I know what all her options are. That includes knowing what each group plans to do with the baby if she births it successfully."

"Do you intend to bring Basia to the table, too?" Xavier asked.

"Absolutely. She's critical as she'll be representing Judyta in all this."

"How are you going to bring her here if she's in hiding somewhere in Sweden?"

I considered for minute. "I don't bring her anywhere," I finally said. "I'm going to take everyone else to her."

I saw the twins' eyes widen, but I could tell each of them was weighing the odds, and calculating the risk.

"So you bring all these groups together," Xavier said slowly. "What will stop them from shooting you or each other the moment they show up at this unexpected information auction?"

"Because they all want the same thing—Judyta Taszyn-ski. I'm not saying it will be pretty, but I think at the very least *I'll* be safe as long as the NSA is present."

"But you can't entirely trust the U.S. government," Elvis pointed out. "You have no idea what they want with Judyta. Will they permit her to birth the clone? And if so, will they want to study it, dissect it or eliminate it? Or possibly all of the above."

I shivered. "I know. It's risky as hell. Do you guys have any other ideas?"

The twins shook their heads and I nodded. "We go ahead. I've got a feeling we don't have much time. Judyta and Basia are not going to be able to avoid such a determined search for much longer. We have to put things into play while we still have the advantage."

"All right, I'm with you so far," Elvis said. "Details?"

I had already chewed my thumbnail to the quick, so I started on my pointer finger. My mind raced with possibilities as I determined, adjusted and discarded ideas.

"Okay, the key here is surprise," I finally said. "I don't want it to be too obvious that I know what I'm doing. So let's say I pretend to give those U.S. government agencies watching me the slip and head for Basia in Sweden. They already know she and Judyta are hiding there, so as soon as I disappear, that's the first place they'll look. Since I have no official training as an agent, my pathetic attempts at avoiding detection will naturally seem amateur."

"They *will* be amateur," Elvis pointed out.

"True," I said. "And all the better for me, I guess. The point is I *want* the U.S. government to follow me, but I *don't* want them to know I'm leading them."

"All right, keep going," Elvis said. "Presuming that you are able to bring the U.S. side to this illusory table of yours, how do you intend to bring along someone like Rashid Bouker?"

"Clearly I'll need to tip off Bouker somehow," I said. "He's critical to the plan because we have to figure out how Yemeni intelligence plays into this. We'll have to fashion his invitation carefully. I'll have to drop a clue, provide a tantalizing intelligence tidbit. You know, something subtle like that."

"I'm sure I'll be able to do that," Elvis said quickly. "It shouldn't be too difficult to hack into the embassy network and fabricate a piece of information to pass along to Yemeni intelligence."

"Jeez, hack into an embassy computer?" I said, shaking my head. "No freaking way. I've already led you guys far enough down the path to perdition. I'm a small fish, but both you guys have important reputations and brilliant minds to protect. Besides, this isn't your fight."

"The hell it's not," Xavier interjected angrily. "We helped Slash break into CGM, so that means we're already up to our necks in this situation."

"Still, it's not too late to back out. I appreciate you all serving as my sounding boards, but I really can't ask you to do any more."

"He's right, Lexi," Elvis said quietly. "We're in to stay. Save your breath on the arguments. Deal the cards and let us play our hands, too."

A lump formed in my throat. "Are you guys sure about this? It's not going to be pretty whichever way it turns out."

"We're good to go," Elvis said. "So let's get on with it."

Touched by his steadfastness, I threw my arms around him and gave him a big hug. When I pulled away, his face had turned bright red.

"Did I squeeze too hard?" I asked. "Lars said I was a natural at karate. Perhaps I don't know my own strength."

He shook his head quickly and Xavier laughed.

"Well, you guys are the best friends I've ever had besides Basia," I said, sniffling.

"Um, we're your only friends besides Basia," Xavier pointed out.

"That's true. Still, I don't know how to thank you for everything."

"I'm sure Elvis could think of a way," Xavier said under his breath, and Elvis turned even redder. Before Xavier could speak again, Elvis smacked his brother on the side of the head.

"No more fooling around," Elvis said sternly. "We're far from done here. We've yet to discuss Finn Shaughnessy's role in all this."

Indeed. And this was a much harder call to make, primarily because I was unusually attracted to him. We'd made some sort of weird connection, and I didn't understand it, let alone need my judgment clouded by such a nebulous variable.

"Finn," I sighed. "Truthfully, I think he'd be safer out of the loop at this point. I don't see him on CGM's side, but something about him doesn't add up for me, either. Perhaps the best course of action is to simply disappear without informing him of anything. Leave him in an operational blackout. That way, on the slim chance he is actually helping CGM, he's kept in the dark. If he's just a victim, then he can continue to remain blissfully ignorant."

"I agree," Elvis said just a little too quickly, and for a moment, I thought I heard a note of relief in his voice. Jeez, for some reason, he really had it in for Finn.

"Okay, it works for me, too," Xavier said. "But if something doesn't add up with Finn Shaughnessy, then it's time to find out what it is. If he's got a secret, I'll find it."

I didn't doubt that for a second. "Well, there's one more

thing, guys," I said. "I'll need at least three or four minutes alone with Basia before the gathering starts so I can clue her in to what's going on. Without my warning she might inadvertently play our hand too early."

"That's going to be a tough one," Elvis said. "Once you disappear, the U.S. will most likely be in full cooperation with Swedish authorities and might detain you the second you land in Sweden."

"Unlikely. Remember, I'm just a dumb kid. They want to watch me, not stop me. They're more likely to put a surveillance team on me, never suspecting I might notice such a team in the first place. And even if I did, they certainly wouldn't think I'd be able to ditch them."

"As long as you keep the element of surprise on your side."

I nodded. "Yes. It's painfully obvious that the critical piece in all this is timing. I figure we'll need at least a week to detail all the operation's plans. That way we'll have everyone in place, exactly where we want them, when I pull out my trump card."

"And that trump card will be?" Xavier asked.

I leaned forward, my determination growing. "The ultimate prize, of course. The whereabouts of Judyta Taszynski."

THIRTEEN

BEFORE I COULD say another word, the doorbell rang. "You expecting company?" I asked the twins with a raised eyebrow.

Elvis stood, shaking his head and heading for the door. Xavier and I followed, looking over Elvis's shoulder.

I guess I should have been surprised to see Lars Anderson standing there, but I wasn't. Maybe I had just used up all the shock my nerves were capable of in one day.

He seemed even taller outside the confines of the karate studio and wore a blinding white T-shirt, a pair of white shorts and tennis shoes. His bulging muscular arms were crossed against his chest. The man looked like a country club tennis pro instead of a Swedish karate instructor.

"Hey, Lexi," he said, ignoring the twins and looking straight at me. "I saw your car parked in the driveway. I need to speak to you right away."

I wondered if he always drove around town looking in driveways for other people's cars, but figured now wasn't the time to ask.

"Hey, karate man," I said, stepping past Elvis and onto the porch. "Thanks for passing on my number to Basia. She called."

"I know. That's why I have to speak with you."

"So, speak."

Lars narrowed his eyes. "Alone."

To my surprise, Elvis stepped in front of me. "Say

what you have to say right here. She's not going anywhere with you."

Lars bristled. "Back off, geek. This is for her ears only."

Elvis stiffened and Xavier stepped forward to stand beside his brother.

Sensing an unwelcome rise in testosterone, I held up a hand. "Whoa, back up just a minute, everyone." When no one moved, I frowned. "I mean it. All of you stand down." Jeez, the last thing I needed right now was a pissing match.

"Look, it's okay," I reassured the twins. "Let me talk to him alone. I'll be right over there in the driveway."

The guys all glared at each other for another moment and then Lars stalked off toward his car. I followed him across the lawn to the driveway where his sky-blue Ford Mustang was parked next to my Miata.

"What's up?" I asked.

Lars reached into his shirt pocket and pulled out a folded piece of paper. He handed it to me without a word.

"What? No small talk?" I quipped.

"Just read it," he answered. Evidently he wasn't in the mood for humor. I opened the note and scanned the brief, scrawled message.

Meet me on the Island of Djurgarden near Stockholm this Monday at 11:30 p.m. Come alone. Wait by the front entrance of the Nordiska Museet (Nordic Museum). I'll find you. Basia

"Is this some kind of joke?" I said, looking up incredulously at Lars. "This isn't her handwriting."

"No, it's mine. Memorize it."

"What?"

"You heard me. Memorize it. I'll give you fifteen seconds." And with that, he pulled a lighter out of his pocket

"Jesus H. Christ," I cried. "You're nuts!"

"Ten seconds."

Panicked, I glanced back at the paper and committed the information to memory just as Lars snatched it out of my hand and held the lighter to it. He waited until the flames licked his fingers before letting what was left of the paper flutter to the ground where he stomped it into ashes.

"What's with all the drama?" I demanded. "Been watching too many reruns of *Mission Impossible* or something?"

"Just be there," he said, turning away.

"Wait," I said, grabbing his arm. "I'm actually formulating a plan right now to help her. Can you get her another message?"

"She's not scheduled to contact me until next Thursday," he said. "Sorry."

"That's not good," I said, starting to panic. "Monday is too soon. I need more time. Please, Lars, it's urgent."

He looked at me for a long moment. "I'd do it if I could, Lexi," he finally said, and for some reason, I believed him. "She's really going to be out of contact until Thursday."

I started to breathe faster. "Oh, man. This isn't good. You've *got* to tell me how you're connected to Basia."

"That's up to her," he said, climbing into the Mustang and turning the key in the ignition. "Good luck."

He sped away, leaving me standing there in his dust. I watched him until the car faded out of sight. Then, utilizing all the cuss words I knew, which sadly weren't that many, I returned to the twins' house.

Xavier and Elvis stood stoically on the porch. "What was that all about?" Elvis asked, frowning.

"I've just had the timeline moved up. Lars said Basia

contacted him and she wants me to meet her in Sweden on Monday night."

He raised an eyebrow. "This Monday? It's already Saturday."

"I know. I told him I needed more time. But he says he won't be in contact with her until Thursday. I don't dare miss the meeting in case we don't have another opportunity."

"Do you trust Lars?" Elvis asked.

"Basia said I should. And he did pass on my number to her. I guess that means he's on the up and up."

"Why is he helping her?" Xavier said, leaning against the porch railing.

"I wish I knew. He's not talking and I don't think Basia wanted to give it away over the phone. It's not like I enjoy trusting him blindly, but at this point I don't see how I have another choice."

"Then you've got to get to Sweden by Monday night," Elvis said resolutely. "That means you leave ASAP."

"Yes."

"Well, you can't simply fly to Sweden from here. It would be too obvious," Xavier said.

"I know. That's why I'm not going to fly from the States."

"You're not?"

"Nope. I'm going to go out of Canada. It's possible the NSA will be electronically monitoring the airports there, but it's also possible they won't. Either way, it seems like a sensible, if not amateur, attempt to get to Sweden, all the while pretending to throw everyone off track."

"Not bad," Elvis admitted. "But it means you'll have to start out tonight and essentially drive all night. And *that* means we have a lot to do before you leave."

For the next several hours the twins and I hammered

out all the operational details of our plan. I would never
have been able to pull it off alone but with the twins on my
side, at least I had a fighting chance. There was no question
it was risky and had a better than good chance of failure,
but it was the best we could do on short notice. And if everything went *exactly* as planned, it might actually work.

I left their house just before five o'clock and noticed a
dark blue sedan I'd never seen parked on the street about
three houses over. The driver didn't seem to be trying to
hide. I would have gladly bet my thong underwear he was
FBI surveillance. Guess they had advanced from discreet
to overt surveillance. I drove home with the dark sedan
tailing me. The phone in my kitchen was ringing when I
walked in, but instead of answering it, I immediately unplugged it. The cell phone was still turned off. I couldn't
risk talking to Finn or Slash at this point. Anyone else
would just have to wait.

I tossed my keys on the counter and was heading for
the bedroom when there was a knock at the door. I froze
and then crept to the peephole. Slash stood there, his thick
arms crossed against his chest. He wore an olive-green
T-shirt, black shorts and sandals. His dark hair had been
slicked back behind his ears, and his shades were still on.

Crap. He was the last person I wanted to see right now.
I silently moved away from the peephole and leaned back
against the wall.

"Lexi, open the door," he demanded. "I just saw you
go inside."

"Go away. No one is home."

"I need to talk to you."

"I'm not in the talking mood."

"It's important, *cara.*"

I thought about walking back to my bedroom and refusing him entrance. He'd bypass my alarm and come

in anyway. Sighing, I opened the door a crack but didn't invite him in.

"What do you want?" I asked.

"Forgive me, *cara,* but I am worried about you. Why aren't you answering your phones?"

"Maybe I didn't feel like talking to anyone."

He frowned. "I need to know you're safe."

"So now you know. Goodbye."

I tried to close the door, but he wedged his foot in, blocking me. "Basia called you," he said.

I stopped trying to close the door and leaned against it. "Yes. And since I'm apparently bugged to high heaven, I knew you'd find out."

"You are angry with me. What happened? Do you no longer trust me?"

"Did I ever?"

"I'd like to think so. Please, may I come in?"

I sighed and then, against my better judgment, I opened the door and let him in. He followed me to the kitchen, where I leaned against the wall, my arms crossed against my chest. He stood too, leaning back against the sink. We stared at each other like two gunslingers ready to square off in the middle of Main Street, but neither of us made the first move.

"Well?" I finally asked. "Are we going to stand here and stare at each other all day?"

"Don't do it, *cara.*"

"Do what?"

"Whatever you are plotting in that lovely mind of yours."

"Why do you think I'm plotting something?"

"Because you wear your emotions on your face. Surely you aren't thinking you can help your friend on your own."

I stuck out my chin. "Why not? I do believe I have Basia's best interests at heart."

"You're so certain I do not? Do you really think I have cause to bring harm to her?"

"Do you?"

"No. Now please tell me what I have done to make you so angry."

I took a step forward, glaring at him. "All right, you want me to tell you why I'm royally pissed at you? You already knew about the cloning, didn't you?"

He let out a deep breath. "So, that's it. No, *cara,* we didn't know for certain about the cloning, but, indeed, we suspected it."

"Suspicions you conveniently kept to yourself," I said. "I thought we were on the same side."

"We are, but we had to know for sure about the cloning before we started making accusations about CGM and Bright Horizons. Now, thanks to you, the twins and Finn Shaughnessy, we know for certain what we once only suspected."

"You used me," I said coldly. "You used me to get to the twins and to Finn Shaughnessy. You'd probably been trying to hack into CGM for a while, but were unsuccessful."

His voice was calm and controlled. "*Si,* that part is true. But I did not use you. You and the twins came to me first. It was a stroke of good fortune, or perhaps destiny, that we found each other. Rest assured, *cara,* that my goal has always been the same as yours—to shut down CGM's Bright Horizons cloning operation and find out who is killing those young women."

I folded my arms against my chest. "So, how does *Sodalitium Pianum* and the Vatican play into all this?"

It was the first time since I'd met him that I saw a crack in his cool composure. He jerked as if I'd hit him in the chest. Then he slowly pushed his sunglasses to the top of his head, his dark eyes assessing me thoughtfully.

"How did you find out? The twins?"

I was surprised he didn't deny it or try to cover up with some plausible explanation. "I asked them to check you out."

"You are far more capable than I ever expected."

"Yeah, well, meet the real me."

He fell silent and I could see he was debating what and exactly how much to tell me. Then his jaw tightened. "The less you know about *Sodalitium Pianum,* the better."

"That's what I mean. If you're not keeping me in the loop, then why should I trust you?"

Slash rubbed his unshaven chin, looking decidedly uncomfortable. "I am bound by many oaths of secrecy, *cara.*"

"But the Vatican *is* involved," I persisted. "Why?"

"There are many people and organizations involved," he answered. "But think about it. You don't need me to tell you why the Vatican would be opposed to human cloning."

He had a point. "I guess I don't," I said, my anger abating.

Walking around the kitchen table, Slash stood in front of me, holding me by the shoulders. "I want to tell you something. It's been a long time since I've felt so protective of a woman. We are just starting what I hope will be a long and mutually beneficial relationship. If you try to do whatever you are plotting without my help you *will* be in terrible danger."

"I'm already in terrible danger."

"Imagine ten times that. I can protect you, but you must help me. What did Lars Anderson give you today in front of the twins' house?"

So he knew about that, too. The FBI surveillance team was earning its paycheck.

"Oh, that. Lars gave me his phone number. He wants a date."

"Then why did he burn it?"

"He's a good-looking guy. Guess he didn't want it getting around."

Slash's eyes darkened. "Don't play me, *cara.* It's not wise."

"Who's playing whom?" I retorted, my anger rising again. "Why are you so afraid for me? You hardly know me."

Slash gazed at me for a moment and then said quietly, "For a very smart woman, *cara,* you are incredibly obtuse in matters of the heart. That might work on another man, but not me." Grabbing a fistful of my shirt, he yanked me toward him. I think I yelped but the sound slid down my throat as his mouth crushed against mine in a flash of heat and speed. In an instant, my entire world turned upside down. I'd never, *ever,* been kissed like this and yet somehow, it seemed exactly right. I felt him pause, the briefest of hesitations and suddenly realized that he asked for permission to continue. He ran his fingers across my hair and murmured something against my mouth in Italian. I slid my arms around his neck, wound my fingers in his hair and kissed him back. I could feel the satisfied curve of his lips against mine as his tongue stroked inside my mouth. Blood pounded in my ears and my emotions whirled and skidded like a multi-dimensional number racing onward toward infinity.

When his mouth pulled away, I experienced a profound sense of disappointment. His lips brushed my brow and lingered against my cheek.

"That, *cara,* is my answer to you," he whispered.

Without another word, he released me and left the kitchen. He moved so quietly, I barely heard the door to my apartment click shut.

Dazed, I slid to the floor and sat with my back against the wall. I stayed there for at least five minutes still feeling the burn of my lips and the quiver in my stomach. The visit from Slash had utterly unnerved me, but it had also firmed up my course of action. His presence indicated that my plan was working and that was important. No matter what had just happened between us, I had to push it aside and focus on what needed to be done.

When I was certain my legs would hold me, I headed back to my bedroom and logged on to my laptop. I scrolled through my email, taking time to look through the information on Bright Horizons that Rock had sent me. Nothing new that I hadn't already known, but I forwarded it to one of the twins' dozens of email accounts for safekeeping. Then I went to a secret email of my own and typed a message to Rock: Reproductive Human Cloning. He was bright enough to figure it out from there.

I changed into a clean pair of jeans, a white T-shirt and a black-and-orange Orioles baseball cap. Next I counted out the hard cash I had on the premises, including the small emergency stash hidden in a fake deodorant can underneath my bathroom sink. The stunning total came to $227.39.

I stuffed a couple of clean panties, bras and T-shirts into my oversized black tote bag, adding my address book, keys and passport. Lastly, and most importantly, I added my laptop, two rechargeable batteries and the battery charger. I grabbed my car keys and drove back to the twins' house.

Elvis opened the door. "That was quick."

"I would have been faster but I had a visit from Slash," I said, coming inside and heading for the command room.

Elvis sounded surprised. "They *are* worried. The leash is tightening."

"Not for long," I said with a bravado I didn't feel. "Phase

A of the operation is about to go into play. Did you drive the truck to the mall?"

"Just got back. We weren't followed as far as we could tell. The blue sedan hightailed it as soon as you left."

"I noticed. He's parked outside again. So far, so good, I guess."

Xavier walked into the room and handed me a thick manila envelope and an electronic adapter.

"The adapter is so you can charge your computer while in Europe," he explained. "And there is an extra grand in the envelope just in case you need it."

I looked at the envelope in shock. "I can't possibly accept this."

"Consider it a loan," Elvis said, pressing it into my hands.

My throat thickened. "Thank you."

"Um, I hate to sound like the prophet of doom," Xavier said. "But what happens if the plan doesn't work?"

I didn't really want to think about it, but a good operational plan had to consider any and all consequences.

"I guess the worst-case scenario would be if I actually succeed in getting everyone together and no one is interested in talking or participating in my auction. That would be pretty awkward. People might start shooting and I could end up dead. But I've got a hunch that's not going to happen, especially with Basia there. If I can maintain the element of surprise, I think things are going to happen, and happen fast, as soon as the players start seeing each other."

"It sounds dangerous to me," said Xavier. "Are you sure talking is all they will want to do?"

"No, I'm not sure. But I'm hopeful. If I'm right, there's going to be a lot of pretty powerful people coming together. I can't see what they'd gain by shooting at each other."

"What about shooting at you?" Elvis asked.

"Yeah, I suppose that's a distinct possibility. I just hope there will be enough people present that believe it's in their best interest to keep me alive."

"So, what's the best-case scenario?" Xavier asked.

"Judyta remains safe and gets to keep the baby if that's what she wants, and everyone lives happily ever after. Including me."

Elvis looked at me. "Are you sure you want to do this, Lexi? At the very least you'll probably lose your job, no matter what happens."

I reached over and took his hand, squeezing it. "Basia needs me. Besides, if I don't end up dead or in jail, I can always start a new career as a cashier somewhere. You know, stellar math skills and all."

It was supposed to be a joke, but neither Xavier nor Elvis cracked a smile. So much for lightening the mood.

"All right," Elvis said. "We all know what we have to do and we're clear on the rules. Just *don't* deviate from the plan, not even an iota. We have to do this exactly the way we hammered it out. There is no room for mistakes. Got it?"

"Got it," I said cheerfully. "I will not deviate from the plan in any shape, form or manner, and absolutely, *positively,* no improvising. I can remember that."

Elvis nodded. "Good. Are you ready?"

I took a deep breath, as my heart started racing. I sincerely hoped I wasn't being delusional in thinking I could really pull this off.

"As ready as I'm ever going to get," I said, wondering if anyone noticed my hands shaking. "Is this phone secure?"

Elvis nodded and I tried not to look scared. "Okay, then let's do it," I said, picking up the phone and dialing it.

FOURTEEN

JAN WAS GAME for the plan after I assured her that Jamie would never be in any danger. She knew how much I adored him, and being a nice person, she agreed to help. As promised, it took her just under twenty minutes to arrive at the twins' house with Jamie in tow. She had dressed as I requested in faded blue jeans, a short-sleeved red T-shirt and a floppy straw hat. Slung over her shoulder was her favorite extra-large, multi-color tote bag. She held hands with Jamie until they reached the front steps, then the seven-year-old bounded up the stairs and rang the doorbell at least fifteen times in rapid succession until Xavier let them in.

Jamie had met the twins several times before and the three of them were comfortable together in a weird, genius sort of way. While Xavier took Jamie off to show him something cool on the computer, Jan and I stepped into one of the twins' empty bedrooms. They apparently used it as a storage room because one side of the room was stacked floor-to-ceiling with labeled white banker boxes full of computer equipment, while the other side of the room was home to an enormous heap of tangled cords and wires. There was no rug on the hardwood floor, no pictures hung on the wall, not a bed in sight. This room would definitely not win a prize for interior decoration.

"Lose the shirt," I said, pulling off my own T-shirt and holding it out to her. "And make it quick."

"Well, at the very least I expected a movie and dinner," Jan quipped as she slipped out of her red shirt and handed it to me.

I pulled the shirt over my head and shoved my arms in. "I owe you big time."

"I know. But I suppose you aren't going to enlighten me any further on what you're doing."

"Nope," I said, pulling my hair back into a ponytail exactly like Jan wore. "I would, but I swear, the less you know about any of this, the better. Trust me on this."

"I do trust you. That's why I'm here. I'm just worried about you."

"I'm worried about me, too," I said truthfully. "But things will work out. I hope."

I transferred the contents of my black bag to her tote and then jammed the straw hat on my head. She put the baseball cap on her head and posed. I studied her critically.

"Not bad from a distance, but you're shorter than me. I just hope the FBI isn't paying close attention."

"I'll try to keep my head down," Jan said, holding out her car key. "You, too."

I took the key and we returned to the command room where Xavier and Jamie were playing an online game. We had to wait until the game was finished and then Jan explained to Jamie that he was going to go to the shopping mall with Elvis and me. To my surprise he nodded and immediately headed for the door. Elvis followed him.

"That was easy," I whispered to Jan. I knew autistic kids typically didn't like changes in their routine.

"We went over it three times before I left the apartment," she whispered back. "Besides, he knows you and Elvis, so it's not going to be a problem." Then she took my hand and squeezed it. "Good luck, Lexi."

I gratefully squeezed back and then hurried after Jamie and Elvis, throwing a last glance over my shoulder at Xavier. He gave me the thumbs-up sign and I smiled back at him with a bravado I didn't feel.

As promised, I kept my head down as I made my way to Jan's car. Jamie climbed right into the back seat and I was touched to see Elvis help him carefully fasten his seatbelt. I hopped in the driver's seat and started the car. Elvis got in and I pulled out of the driveway. I dared a glance down the street and saw the dark sedan parked four driveways down. I didn't look for long because Elvis said the driver was watching us.

"Are you ready to rock and roll?" he asked.

"As much as I'll ever be," I answered truthfully.

"Then let's go."

I took a deep breath and we drove down the street. I made a few unnecessary turns and detours, but as far as I could see no one was tailing us.

"Do you think the FBI bought it?" I asked.

He shrugged. "We'll see."

It wasn't a terribly inspiring comment, but at least it was honest. When we got to the mall, I parked the car in the prearranged spot in the garage and all three of us went inside. We walked to the video arcade and Elvis popped some quarters into a pinball machine for Jamie.

When Jamie was busy, Elvis turned to me. "It won't take them long to figure out you've taken our truck. But it will give you the illusion of an earnest, attempted evasion and that's what we're after. Here's the key."

I took it from him. "You and Xavier are the best," I said. "How can I ever possibly repay you guys?"

"Get Xavier a date with Basia."

"He doesn't need me for that. He should just ask her himself."

"He won't."

"All right, then consider it done. How about you?"

He looked at me for a long moment and then turned away. "I'll tell you what—I'll think about it. Now get going and be careful. And remember our all-important mantra. *Don't* deviate from the plan."

"Got it," I said. "No deviation whatsoever."

"Not one iota, Lexi. I mean it."

"Not one. And thanks."

With one last look at Elvis, I turned and left. As promised, the truck was parked at the pre-determined location in the mall parking lot. I quickly pulled out of the garage and headed north on the freeway. As far as I could tell, no one followed me. Then again, I wasn't James Bond, so how would I know? Deciding to be happy in my ignorance, I turned the radio to full blast and sang along with a classic rock station as the sky darkened.

About three hours later, somewhere in rural Pennsylvania, I was in dire need of gas and a bathroom. I took the very next exit that had a gas sign, but unfortunately had to drive about two miles to find the station. It was one of my pet peeves, having to drive miles from the interstate to get gas, so I was kind of cranky when I finally found it.

Once there, my heart sank. The tiny run-down station was dimly lit and had one barely-standing pump. Crap, that meant no EZ-Mart with microwave burritos, bad coffee or a decent bathroom. There were no other cars being serviced and for a moment I wondered if it were even open. Thankfully light shone in the window of the adjacent building and I could see a crooked neon Open sign flashing orange. I pulled up in front of the pump and prayed that at the very least there was a bathroom for public use.

I was relieved to see an overweight, middle-aged guy sitting behind the counter, watching television. I pulled open the door and a little bell on the knob rang. He stood and assessed me, pushing his red ball cap back on his head and pulling a toothpick from his mouth. His other hand rested below the counter and I was one hundred and ten percent sure he had a shotgun there.

Apparently he decided I wasn't a robber, because he removed his hand from under the counter and smiled at me. He had a wide gap between his two stained front teeth.

"Good evenin', little lady," he said. "How much gas you want?"

At five foot eleven I hardly considered myself little, but decided not to debate the point with him.

"Twenty dollars' worth," I said, laying a twenty on the counter. "You got a bathroom here?"

"Out in back," he said. "Here's the key."

He handed me a key dangling from a chain that had a plastic replica of Pamela Anderson dressed in her low-cut, red *Baywatch* bathing suit. I held it away from me and stared in fascinated horror.

"It's for the girls' bathroom," he said, snorting. "Get it?"

Yeah, I got it all right. This guy was seriously twisted. "Uh, thanks," I said, quickly heading back out into the night.

It took me a good two minutes to work the key into the rusty keyhole and I felt decidedly uncomfortable squeezing Pamela's plastic boobs while doing it. When I was just about to give up and use the bushes, the key turned and the door opened.

Once I finished my business and washed my hands in the rusty sink, I headed back to the truck to fill up the tank. I put my hand on the nozzle when a dark form abruptly stepped out in front of me.

"Hello, little girl," Beefy said.

It was a good thing I had just gone to the bathroom. I screamed and dropped the nozzle. It fell on top of Beefy's shoe, splashing some gasoline onto the leather. He glanced down and frowned.

"I'm going to smell like gas now," he said.

That was the least of my problems. "What are *you* doing here?" I asked, my voice unnaturally high and terrified.

He crossed his thick arms against his chest. "It's a nice, balmy night, isn't it? I thought perhaps we could take a drive together, deep into the woods for a little chat. What do you say?"

"Gee, as romantic as that sounds, I think I'll pass."

He pulled out a gun and pointed it at me. "I urge you to reconsider."

I swallowed hard and looked at the gun. "Well, if you put it that way."

"She's not going anywhere," came a voice from around the side of the station.

To my utter shock, Finn Shaughnessy stepped out of the shadows. He, too, had a gun and pointed it at Beefy. Apparently everyone in the entire universe except me owned a firearm. Maybe it was time I changed that. In fact, morphing into a female Rambo was suddenly looking mighty attractive at the moment.

I started to hyperventilate. Oh, my God, the plan was falling apart before it had hardly even started. Finn was supposed to be in an operational blackout and Beefy, well, he hadn't even been considered worthy of discussion. Big mistake. I made a mental note to never, *ever,* discount a minor variable the next time I planned clandestine action.

Jeez, I had to dump them both, and quick, or Elvis would skin me alive for breaking Rule #1—No Deviating From The Plan For Whatever Reason. Unfortunately, if I were to dump them successfully, I'd have to break Rule #2—No Improvising. Elvis would just have to understand that we all do what we must in moments of unexpected operational chaos.

I lifted my hands. "Okay, everyone just relax," I said firmly, pretending that I actually had some semblance of control here. "How did you guys find me?"

Neither answered. Apparently it was a rhetorical question. How obvious did it have to be that I had no skills whatsoever at evasion, even by amateur standards? I might as well have driven around town with a Here I Am neon sign flashing on my forehead for everyone to see. Well, everyone except the FBI. Now the plan to ditch them until I got to Sweden wasn't looking so good.

Beefy and Finn continued to ignore me, keeping their guns pointed at each other in a weird kind of standoff. I felt like a B-movie actress, standing by helplessly while the men shot it out over me. Of course, to a girl like me, this had a bit of appeal in a primitive, warped kind of way. On the up side, as long as they weren't shooting at me, maybe they'd disable each other and I'd be able to escape unscathed. But I didn't condone violence, even if it worked in my favor.

"Drop the gun, Harry," Finn suddenly ordered, causing me to jump. His Irish brogue was thick and he was probably nervous as hell. Actually, I was nervous as hell, too, but instead of developing an accent, I had to pee again.

"Your name is Harry?" I said, looking at Beefy.

"I should have killed you when I had the chance," Beefy growled.

"He tried to kill you?" I asked Finn in disbelief. "You mean you *know* each other?"

No one answered me.

"Do you even know how to use that gun, Irish?" Beefy said. "Your hand is shaking."

"Oh, *contraire*. Your vision is blurred with fear."

"Um, excuse me," I interjected. "It's not like I want to interrupt this very mesmerizing conversation, but can't we all just get along?"

Unfortunately, instead of promoting peace my Rodney King speech brought out the violent tendencies in both men. Before I could draw another breath, Beefy grabbed me around the neck and yanked me to his chest. Finn shot a bullet right over our heads. I almost peed on the spot, shocked that Finn had actually used the gun.

"You missed!" I half shouted, half gasped the obvious because by now Beefy was pretty much choking me. Then he shoved the gun hard against my neck where it found a cozy little niche right against my jugular vein.

"Back off, Irish," he snapped and then squeezed me tighter. "Drop the gun and I won't hurt her."

"Oh, jeez," I managed to utter despite the chokehold. I hoped Finn wouldn't do it. I'd seen enough of those cop shows on television to know that as soon as Finn dropped the gun there was a 99.9 percent chance that Beefy would kill us both anyway. If Finn kept the gun, at least we'd have a fifty-fifty chance.

"Don't do it, Finn," I cried, my voice garbled on account of the fact that my windpipe was being slowly crushed by Beefy's forearm.

For a moment we all simply stared at each other in the dim light. I shifted on my feet and crossed my legs hard because I really had to pee now. Then, as if in slow motion, Finn began to lower the gun. In response Beefy lessened his hold around my neck.

"What are you doing?" I screeched at Finn once I could breathe again. "Haven't you ever seen a police drama? Don't you know the good guys are never *ever* supposed to give up their guns no matter what?"

"I know what I'm doing, Lexi," Finn said, carefully

tossing the gun to the ground in front of him. "Now let her go."

"In good time, Irish," Beefy said, moving the gun from my temple and aiming it at Finn.

"Oh, my God," I moaned. Finn was obviously no connoisseur of American television, and therefore had no idea of the colossal mistake he'd just made. What could I do? Maybe I'd pass out, wake up and discover this had all been a horrible dream. Then again, if I passed out, Beefy would probably kill Finn and then take me for a torture-and-maim session in the woods.

I was knee-deep in kimchee. Not that I wasn't in deep kimchee to begin with, but things had just moved from deep to downright subterranean. Jeez, what would James Bond do?

Well, he certainly wouldn't stand around dithering about it, I told myself sternly. Saying a small prayer under my breath, I summoned all my strength and slammed an elbow into Beefy's gut, loosening his hold around my neck. Then, because I *wasn't* James Bond with a secret dart gun in my watch, I used the only weapon I had at my immediate disposal—my mouth. I opened it and took a great big chomp out of Beefy's forearm. Blood filled my mouth and I started to choke.

"Umffff!" Beefy grunted and he fired a shot wide and to the left of Finn's head.

I guess Finn had known what he was doing after all because I saw another gun magically appear in his hand. He must have had some plan I had just thrown a royal crimp in. Now he couldn't shoot without hitting me, so he launched himself forward, plowing into Beefy and me and knocking the gun from Beefy's hand. We all fell to the ground, shouting and grunting in a tangle of limbs.

I got an elbow in the windpipe and it knocked the breath

out of me. My left wrist bent unnaturally under someone's hip and an excruciatingly hot pain shot up my shoulder. I howled, wanting to clutch my wrist to my chest, but I could neither move nor breathe with two men rolling around on top of me. Suddenly the crushing pressure on my chest disappeared and I realized Beefy and Finn were now grappling around in the dusty road for control of the gun.

I struggled to my knees, my injured wrist cradled against my chest, and looked over at the men, grunting and punching. "What do I do now?" I shouted in panic to no one in particular.

I looked around wildly and saw the pale face of the gas station attendant peering out at us through the window.

"Call the police," I screamed and his face disappeared.

I was still trying to figure out what to do next when Beefy stood triumphant, holding the gun and pointing it at Finn who lay on the ground with blood smeared on his mouth and left cheek.

Trembling, I stood on shaky legs and walked closer to Beefy. "Leave him alone," I pleaded. "Look, I'll do whatever you want."

Beefy didn't look at me, but I noticed he was breathing hard and his face was bright red from the exertion of the fight.

"You certainly will *not* do what he wants," Finn said, coming to his feet and wiping the blood off his mouth with his sleeve.

"You're in no position to stop me, Irish," Beefy said. "Face it, you're the weaker man."

"Kiss my arse, you *gobshite*," Finn snarled.

I wasn't exactly sure what *gobshite* meant, but I was fairly certain it wasn't a glowing compliment in Ireland.

For a moment we all stood around breathing heavily and

staring at each other as if unsure what to do next. Then Beefy turned unexpectedly to me.

"You bit me," he said, frowning.

"Ah, yeah," I stammered. "Sorry. It was a spur-of-the-moment, my-life-is-in-mortal-danger kind of thing."

"Don't ever do it again."

"Okay," I agreed.

"You've been a lot more trouble than we ever expected," Beefy said. "I should have finished you off in front of that disco club. Actually, maybe I should have shot up the club while I was at it. I hate disco."

I contemplated that in stunned silence. First, that Beefy was the one who shot at me in front of the disco, and second, because we actually had something in common.

But first things, first. "You shot at *me?*" I asked him incredulously.

"You should have taken that incident seriously."

"Believe me, I *always* take people shooting at me seriously. Why'd you do it?"

Beefy rubbed the back of his neck. "I didn't want you giving away the whereabouts of Judyta Taszynski to anyone except CGM. And that still holds. Either you tell me where she is or you'll die."

"Um, are those options mutually exclusive?"

"Damn, I like you, Lexi," Beefy chuckled. "I don't want to have to hurt you or your boyfriend. So, please, spare me the trouble and just tell me where I can find Judyta Taszynski."

"Jeez, what is with everyone?" I said indignantly. "Finn is *not* my boyfriend."

Beefy rolled his eyes. "Whatever."

"Don't tell him anything," Finn warned.

Desperate, I glanced over my shoulder, hoping to see the gas station attendant marching out with his shotgun.

Unfortunately he was nowhere in sight. I hoped like hell he'd at least called the police and they'd be here momentarily. That is, if they even had police out here in Nowheresville, Pennsylvania.

"I'll give you one more chance, Lexi," Beefy said, his finger tightening on the trigger. "Where is Judyta? If you don't answer, I'm going to shoot the Irishman in the knee. After that I'll shoot his arm, shoulder, back, both hands and then his neck. At some point, he'll be begging me to shoot him in the head. I'll make you watch until you tell me where Judyta is hiding. Or you can tell me now. This is your last warning," Beefy said, his eyes narrowing. "One."

"Wait!" I screeched.

"Two."

As panic gripped me by the throat, I shifted my weight and, using all the strength I had, gave him the best karate roundhouse kick I had ever performed. The kick hit him square in the lower back. I think the sheer surprise of it knocked him forward a couple of steps.

Unfortunately the arm holding the gun didn't waver or budge. Not one single iota.

Instead Beefy started to laugh. "You've got to be kidding. Is that the best you can do?"

"Nope," I said, panting. "How about this?" I leapt onto his back shrieking as if I were a crazed maniac, clawing at his face. Not very James Bond-like, but we are who we are.

Beefy kept laughing and threw me off with barely any effort. I nearly fainted from the pain in my wrist when I hit the ground hard. Unfortunately, throughout all of this, Beefy didn't seem alarmed in the slightest. Instead he laughed even harder, tears starting to stream from his eyes. His entire body began to shake and I thought he'd shoot Finn by accident before he could do it on purpose.

I started to silently say my prayers because I was afraid Finn and I were about to become serious toast.

Suddenly Beefy began to cough and choke. As Finn and I watched in astonishment, the gun dropped from his fingers and he keeled over face-first onto the ground. I scrambled to my feet and then Finn leapt over and kicked the gun away, rolling Beefy over onto his back. He was out cold.

"Are you hurt?" Finn asked me.

"Just my wrist," I shouted. When I get scared, I shout to hide the clawing, embarrassing fear. "I don't think it's broken, but it hurts like hell."

"What did you do to him?" he asked, looking down at Beefy.

"Nothing. He just keeled over."

"Shit," he said, dropping to his knees. To my horror, he abruptly ripped open Beefy's shirt to the white T-shirt beneath.

"What are you doing?" I shouted.

"Stop yelling," Finn said, wincing. "What does it look like I'm doing? He's had a bleeding heart attack, lass. I've got to start CPR. Go see if that useless attendant called the police. Tell him to call for an ambulance, as well."

Holding my throbbing wrist to my stomach, I ran into the station. The chair where the attendant had sat was empty. I went around the counter, picked up the phone and called 911. I found the gas station address on top of a receipt on the desk and requested police and an ambulance, then hung up despite the operator insisting I stay on the line. I ran back to Finn who was still administering CPR and told him what I'd done.

"We're going to have company soon," he said.

"I know. Well, I guess I'd better be going."

Finn looked up at me. "And where might that be?"

"Anywhere but here."

Finn leaned down close to Beefy's face. "Dammit, he's not breathing."

"Too bad," I said, lifting my hands.

"You're going to have to help me," he said, resuming the chest compressions. "Give him mouth-to-mouth."

I looked at Finn, flabbergasted. "Are you freaking nuts? No way are my lips touching his."

"He's dying, Lexi."

"He just tried to kill us!"

"Do you want to stoop to his level?"

I took a step back. "Frankly, it's looking like a pretty attractive option at the moment."

"Lexi!"

"Oh, jeez," I said, trying to calm myself. "All right, all right. Can't I do the pushing part?"

"Do you know how?" he asked as he steadily continued the compressions.

"Not really."

"Then lock lips and start blowing."

"This can't be happening," I moaned, kneeling down next to Beefy. Grimacing, I turned his pudgy face toward me with my good hand.

"Check to make certain he hasn't swallowed his tongue," Finn ordered.

"Sure, easy for you to say."

Finn helped me pry open Beefy's mouth and I got an unpleasantly close-up look at his front gold tooth. Trying not to appear squeamish, I grasped his tongue and pulled it straight. "There, at least he's not choking on it."

"That's the spirit, lass. Start the breathing and don't forget to pinch his nose shut. Listen for my count during the compressions. When I'm done, you start."

"Oh, God, oh, God," I murmured as I leaned over

Beefy and pressed my mouth to his. His skin was cold and clammy. His mouth smelled faintly of onions.

I did the breaths as instructed and lifted my mouth. "Now what?" I asked.

"Keep going," Finn instructed.

Finn made me keep up the pace for what seemed like forever, but was really only a minute or so. To my surprise, Beefy suddenly took a huge, gasping breath.

"Oh, my God, you did it," I said in amazement. "He's alive."

"*We* did it, and he's just barely alive," Finn said grimly. "See if you can find something to keep him warm. Then we've got to get the hell out of here."

I rushed into the station again, but still no sign of the attendant. I yelled for him and heard a noise in a back room. I ran over and tried to yank the door open, but it was locked.

"Open up," I shouted. "I need a blanket."

"Get out of here," he screamed back at me. "Get out, get out, GET OUT or I'll shoot!"

I totally, utterly believed him, so I left him there screaming and desperately searched the room for something that would serve as a blanket. I saw the attendant's jacket hanging from the back of his chair, so I snatched it and ran back to Finn.

"It's the best I could find," I said, out of breath.

"It'll do," he said, covering Beefy and then standing. "Let's go."

"Is it safe to leave him?" I asked.

"Do you want to wait for the police?"

"Not really."

"Then we don't have any choice. The police and paramedics will likely be here any minute."

I thought of Basia, Judyta, my mission. "You're right.

Well, thanks again for all your help, but I guess this is where we part ways."

"Like hell it is," Finn growled. "You aren't going to drive anywhere with an injured wrist. You need my help. We go together."

"No way!"

"Look, we don't have time to argue. The FBI already has an APB out on the truck you're driving. Once they've confirmed you're in the area, the state police will haul you in before you can even get out of Pennsylvania. With me, you'll at the very least have a better chance to get where you are going. No one will know I'm involved unless Harry here regains consciousness and tells them. Given the condition he's in, I'm betting we'll have a good head start."

"Crap," I said because I knew he was right.

"So we do it my way," he said, brushing the dirt off his jeans and quickly retrieving his guns. "My car is around back. Get in. Now."

I wanted to argue but could hear the faint wail of sirens. "Okay," I said, making an executive decision and grabbing my purse and bag.

We left Beefy where he lay and the Jag peeled out of the gas station. Finn drove a little way and quickly pulled off onto a dirt lane. He drove into the shadows of the trees and then cut the lights. We sat there in the dark until the emergency vehicles passed us by.

"We're out of here," Finn said, smoothly thrusting the car into gear and pulling back out. "Where to?"

"North," I said simply.

"A little more information would be helpful."

I exhaled a deep breath. I couldn't see how I had much choice. In my opinion, the plan was still salvageable; it just required a tiny bit of improvisation. Maybe Elvis would overlook the small deviation given the fact that I had just survived a near-death experience.

"Buffalo, New York."

If Finn was surprised, he didn't show it. Instead he drove without speaking until we reached the interstate. Then he asked, "How's the wrist?"

"Other than the excruciating pain, it's fine. At least I'm alive."

"We're going to have to stop and get some painkillers or you're not going to make it far."

I agreed with him but didn't say so aloud. I didn't want to appear weak and needy, even if that was exactly how I felt.

"Are you going to tell me how you found me?" I asked.

"Sheer dumb luck, actually. I was following Harry. I tried to warn you by cell but for some unfathomable reason, you had turned it off."

"It's being tapped by the FBI and I didn't want them to know my every move."

"The FBI? Are you joking?"

"I wish. How did you know Beefy's name?"

Finn ran his fingers through his hair. "He works for CGM. You were right. He's a hired thug."

"How did you find out?"

"A little sleuthing. Unfortunately he caught me red-handed, snooping around on my boss's computer. He politely informed me we were on the same side and I needed to keep my nose out of matters that didn't concern me, or else."

"Or else what?"

"He'd kill me."

"He said that? Nice guy. His name is Harry?"

"Harry Jorrell."

"Even the name sounds beefy."

"Well, he was once a P.I., but had his license pulled for so-called unorthodox practices."

"Why am I not surprised? Then I guess the real question is how did Beefy track me here?"

"He's a pretty good ex-detective, I guess."

"And you?"

"Okay, so I was playing detective, too," Finn admitted. "After our little chat in my boss's office, I decided to check Harry out. I followed him to your place in Jessup. When he didn't find you there, he drove around the town looking for your car. When he found it, he parked a short distance away and began his surveillance. Then I noticed someone else in a dark-colored sedan was watching you, as well."

"That would be the FBI."

"They're tapping your phone *and* following you? What's going on, Lexi?"

"You tell your part first," I insisted.

He didn't look pleased but continued. "Well, I was curious why Harry was staking you out, so I stayed with him. For several hours I watched him keep an eye on your car. So I was surprised when he suddenly perked up when a man, young woman and kid left the house and climbed into a beige Toyota."

I sighed. "That would be me disguised as my neighbor."

"I didn't get it, but Jorrell was on to you from the start. He followed the Toyota to the mall, and so did I, despite the fact that I thought it strange he'd left you at the house uncovered. We watched you switch to the truck and that's when I realized Harry had made you. I guess he just waited for the first opportunity to strike. That, apparently, came at the gas station."

"Well, I guess that makes Harry a lot smarter than he looks. Except he didn't make you tailing him."

"Maybe he did," Finn said thoughtfully. "Maybe he

figured he could kill two birds with one stone. I mean that literally."

"Great. I suppose that means the only surveillance team I fooled was the FBI."

Finn looked over at me. "What the hell is the FBI doing involved in all of this?"

I didn't answer and instead slouched down in the seat, pressing my aching wrist against my stomach. The adrenaline from my near-death experience was wearing off, and the steady hum of the tires across the pavement was lulling me into sleep.

"Come on, Lexi," Finn said. "You've got to tell me what's going on."

"Why does it matter?"

"Give me a good reason for going along with whatever insane plan you have for rescuing Judyta and Basia or I'm driving you straight away to a hospital."

"Why are you so sure I have a plan? And by the way, I'm offended by the use of the word *insane*."

"I reserve the right to use the word *insane* until I hear your plan. You need me and you know it. It's not rocket science, Lexi."

I sighed. "Okay. I admit that maybe, *just maybe,* I could use your help."

"Then fill me in. What's happening? What is this Project Acheron?"

I decided to tell him like it was—straight up. "CGM is cloning humans."

Swearing, Finn swerved across two lanes and pulled over in the emergency lane, slamming on the brakes. My skull banged against the headrest and I yelped as my wrist bounced against my knee.

"What did you say?" he demanded, looking at me with a mixture of disbelief and shock.

If he was acting, I had to give him credit. He looked pretty shaken.

"It's just what I said. CGM is cloning humans and getting big bucks for it."

I gave him the brief version of all I knew up to now, including how the twins had helped me, but minus the contents of Basia's note and omitting any mention of Slash. I don't know why it seemed so important to protect a guy I didn't even really know, but our kiss had changed things even if I wasn't sure exactly how.

Finn ran his hand through his hair. "Jesus, Joseph and Mary," he said under his breath. "I can't believe it. Human cloning. I had no idea it was even scientifically possible yet. But I don't understand. Who is killing the young women?"

"I don't know. But the U.S. government, including the FBI, would like to know."

He pressed a hand to his forehead and I noticed his arm was trembling. "I guess it's all starting to make sense in a repulsive sort of way. Harold must have known about the cloning. He probably drew up the secret contracts for CGM. That's why they gave him the bonus—to pay him off. He apparently got nervous about it and left me the generic contract in the safety deposit box, just in case."

"But who killed Harold?" I asked. "Someone at CGM?"

"I'm having a hard time believing that. But after our encounter with Jorrell back at the gas station, I can't discount the possibility."

For a minute we sat in silence as the cars on the highway whizzed past us. Then, without another word, Finn maneuvered the Jag back on to the interstate. He got off at the next exit and drove into the parking lot of a small gas station EZ-Mart.

"You go get some painkillers and something to eat, and

I'll see if I have anything in the trunk that can serve as a makeshift sling."

I nodded and entered the almost deserted EZ-Mart, where I bought necessities such as ibuprofen, Diet Coke, coffee, chips, chocolate, crackers and some breath mints. By the time I returned to the car, Finn had taken what looked like an old rag and fashioned it into a sling. It smelled a bit like wax and gasoline, but it would do. He helped me get my arm into it and I breathed a sigh of relief when my wrist was cradled comfortably against my stomach.

While Finn pumped gas into the Jag, I washed down several painkillers with some Diet Coke and topped it off by eating a few peanut butter crackers and a chocolate bar. For some reason, I felt immediately better. Probably it was the chocolate. Then I felt the bump in my jeans pocket and remembered I still had the Pamela Anderson key. I pulled it out of my pocket and stuck it in Finn's glove compartment. I wondered what he'd think when he found it, and smiled.

"Can I drive?" I asked, opening the door and sticking my head out. "I've never driven a Jag."

"Not a chance, lass," Finn said, screwing the gas cap back on.

"Jeez, you're not one of those men who is all touchy-feely about his car, are you?"

"Is there any other kind?" he said, but I saw him grin as he climbed in.

We drove for a while in silence, sharing the junk food. Finn turned the radio to a soft jazz station and kept the volume low. "Aren't you tired?" I asked Finn after an hour had passed. "We can take a break, you know."

"I'll let you know when I need one."

"It's about six more hours to Buffalo."

"What's in Buffalo?"

"I don't have the foggiest idea," I answered. "Do you have your passport?"

He gave me a wry, sideways glance. "I take it that means Buffalo is not our final destination."

"Yep. So, do you have your passport?"

"Actually, I do."

"Well, I guess that's convenient."

"But you're still not going to tell me exactly where we are going."

"No. Not yet."

He sighed. "At this point, there's no point in keeping secrets, Lexi."

"Okay. You spill first."

He stared at me. "What's that supposed to mean?"

"Why don't you start by telling me who you really are?"

"You know who I am."

"Do I?"

"Dammit, Lexi, what are you going on about?"

I popped a cracker into my mouth and ate it. "Why didn't you tell me you were some kind of frigging celebrity?"

Finn fell quiet for a moment. "Oh, you found out, did you?"

"Better late than never. That doesn't mean I'm not embarrassed for being in the dark for so long."

"It's not a big secret. It just didn't come up in conversation."

"Well, it just came up now."

He lifted his hand from the steering wheel and rubbed the back of his neck. "What's the big deal? So I didn't volunteer information on my family background. Sue me."

"My point exactly."

"What point?" he said and I could hear the exasperation in his voice.

"The point is you're asking me to trust you, with my life and lives of others, and I don't really know the first thing about you. What's a guy like you doing at CGM in the first place? And what other important information about yourself have you conveniently forgotten to mention because it, uh, didn't come up in conversation?"

I could almost feel his Irish temper rise. "Okay, Lexi, you want me to spill, so I'll spill. If you really must know the truth, I'm at CGM because I needed a break from Ireland, my father and my notoriety, in that order. I wanted to find a quiet place to get established on my own as a lawyer. I'm interested in many things—the law, business, computers and biotechnology—and CGM seemed like a good fit at the time. There, now that you know I'm a frigging celebrity does it change your opinion of me?"

"In some ways it does. It adds a new dimension to you. You're a lot more high profile than I expected. But what bugs me the most is that I feel blindsided."

"Blindsided?"

"You could have told me."

"Christ, Lexi, you expect every guy to spill his guts to you after just a few meetings?"

"Hey, we went to dinner at least twice. That's significant, I think."

He swore under his breath. "And women wonder why men think they are bleeding nuts. Okay, I'm officially sorry I didn't spill my guts sooner. There, I have been the bigger man and apologized. Does that make things better?"

"A little," I said, slightly mollified. "The bleeding nuts comment wasn't particularly helpful, though."

He shook his head and then laughed. "No one would believe what has happened to me since I met you. Trouble follows you around like a little black cloud."

I couldn't exactly argue with that, so I changed the subject. "So you really came to the U.S. to get away from your family's notoriety?"

"Is that so hard to believe?"

"Maybe. I would think being a celebrity is fun."

"It sure as hell isn't," he said. "Not if you're born to it, anyway."

I sensed some deeper issues here, but decided now wasn't the time to explore them. "Well, I guess I'm living proof that you achieved at least a margin of that anonymity," I said grudgingly.

"Aye, and I actually kind of liked it."

"Well, don't think that just because you appear in *Celebrity Focus,* that's going to make me go all gooey eyes over you."

He glanced sideways at me, a grin on his face. "I'm devastated. Guess you'll just have to like me for my rapier wit and intelligence."

I sat up straight. "Speaking of intelligence or lack thereof, what the *hell* were you thinking when you dropped the gun back at the gas station? Are you a complete idiot?"

"Hey," he protested. "I had another gun, you know."

"You're a lawyer, not Dirty Harry."

"That doesn't mean I don't know how to use a gun."

"Sure and by the time you pulled it out, we'd have both been toast."

"Yet here we are, safe and sound. Chalk one up for the lawyer."

"Excuse me, but I saved *your* life. Need I remind you that I'm the crazed, shrieking maniac who jumped on his back?"

"From that you deduce you're the one who saved our lives?"

"Damn right. Gave him a heart attack, didn't I?"

Finn started laughing and the tension that had been

building between us lessened. To my surprise, I was relieved. As wary as I was of trusting Finn, I realized I was even more nervous of getting to Sweden alone. In a way, I was kind of glad to have him along. Even if it did temporarily screw up the plan.

I watched the dark landscape rush past as we drove. "Do you know when you're nervous or mad, your Irish accent returns big time?" I said.

"I'm not surprised. It's hard to concentrate on perfecting an American accent when I'm pissing mad or my life is in peril."

"Why change your accent at all?"

"I don't like to stand out."

Right. A gorgeous, intelligent guy like Finn would stand out no matter who or where he was, his celebrity status notwithstanding. Shame on me, that I didn't see that at once.

"Tell me what Ireland is like," I said, taking a sip of coffee. "I've always wanted to see it. Is it really as green as everyone says?"

Finn chuckled. "It's green because it rains a bloody lot. In terms of the countryside, there are narrow and winding roads, deep bogs, sharp, jutting cliffs and lots of loose chippings."

"Chippings?"

"Rocks sharp as nails. The way the lorries and the tour buses all tear around the roads of Ireland these days, it's a wonder there's a working tire in the whole country."

I noticed that when he started to talk about Ireland, his voice changed, becoming dreamy and poetic with the softest hint of a lilt. I liked it.

"I suppose you play soccer there, too."

"We call it football, but yes, I play. Just for fun. But my first love is hurling."

"Gross!"

He laughed. "Hurling is a game similar to hockey. It's played with a small ball and a curved wooden stick. It's Europe's oldest field game, created by the Celts."

"It sounds fun, I guess. Do you miss it?"

He paused. "I do. But I don't miss the rag photographers who follow me around night and day when I'm in Ireland. It becomes tiresome quite fast."

"Why don't they follow you around here?"

"Oh, they did at first. But once I settled into my dull and predictable routine, it wasn't so fun for them anymore. I get up, go to work and go home. It took them less than three weeks to die of boredom. They need far more colorful people than me to sell papers. Thankfully, we seem to have reached a mutually satisfactory balance and I try to give them their fill of me when I'm home on holiday. These days they're fixated on my younger sister, Maureen. She's pursuing a career as a pop singer."

He fell silent, so I stared out the dark window, barely able to keep my eyes open. The steady sway of the car and the excitement of the day were catching up with me, and not in a good way. I yawned. My eyelids felt like they weighed a hundred pounds.

"So, tell me more about your sister Maureen," I said, blinking. "What's she like?"

"She's a bloody pain in the arse. But I'm crazy about her. She just turned twenty-one and thinks she's hot shit."

"Hot shit, huh? I bet you thought you were hot shit at twenty-one."

"I *was* hot shit," he said, chuckling. "Had the world at my feet." He turned and smiled at me. "I haven't felt like that in years...until tonight. You know, Lexi, you make a lad feel like he could do anything."

"I'm taking that as a compliment because I'm too tired to argue."

"I *meant* it as a compliment."

"Just checking. You know, if guys like you hung around geek chicks like me more often, you'd be surprised at what you could learn."

"So I'm discovering," he said and I could hear the smile in his voice. "How about you close your eyes for five and I'll wake you when I'm ready to take a break."

"What? No more desire for small talk?"

He shook his head and turned up the radio slightly. The soft jazz sounds were soothing and my head fell back on the headrest.

"Okay, maybe I'll just take five," I agreed.

"Brilliant."

I closed my eyes and let my thoughts drift off. Just as exhaustion claimed me, I thought I heard Finn murmur, "This lass puts the heart crossways in me…"

FIFTEEN

I MUST HAVE slept for more than three hours because when I woke, a quick glance at the dashboard clock said it was already twenty-six minutes past three o'clock in the morning.

I moved my wrist before remembering it hurt and then winced when hot pain shot all the way to my shoulder.

"How'd you sleep?" Finn asked.

"Fine," I said, trying to stretch my legs. "Why did you let me doze off for so long?"

"You needed it."

"You need a break, too. Where are we?"

"I-90 in New York."

"Want to pull over for coffee and a bathroom break?"

"Sounds good. I could use some real food. We'll see if there's anything worthwhile off the next exit."

We found an all-night trucker's diner and Finn parked the Jag next to a beat-up Toyota truck. I got out of the car slowly, my entire body stiff and sore like it had been used as a punching bag. Finn was walking a bit funny, too, and I thought he was probably feeling the effects of his tussle at the gas station with Beefy.

After using the restrooms and cleaning up a bit, we sat down in a scarred silver-chromed booth with red plastic seats. I ordered scrambled eggs with sausage and a biscuit, and Finn ordered three poached eggs, two sides of toast and a bowl of oatmeal. The waitress was about fifty, plump with bleached blond hair, and she brazenly flirted with Finn while we ordered. Her red-and-white plastic nametag read Layla. I rolled my eyes when she purposely dropped her pen in his lap, but Finn gallantly retrieved it and gave her a smile that caused her to blush and scurry off.

"How can you stand that?" I asked him.

"Stand what?"

"Women falling all over themselves to get your attention."

He grinned. "It's a tough life, but someone has to live it."

I snorted derisively, but he just shrugged it off. When the food finally came we devoured it like people who hadn't eaten in weeks. Neither of us spoke a single word. Even Layla looked over at us a bit strangely as we shoveled mouthfuls of food in without stopping. When my stomach was finally full, I gulped down some more painkillers and leaned back in the booth to digest my meal.

Finn finally put his fork down and leaned back, as well. "I'm pretty sure this is the best food I've ever eaten."

I wrinkled my nose. "When was the last time you ate at a truck stop?"

"Never. That's what I like about you, Lexi," he said with a slow smile. "You sure know how to show a lad a good time."

I rolled my eyes and then gingerly shifted my wrist against my stomach. Finn's smile faded.

"It still hurts?"

"Some," I admitted. "But I'll live. I hate to admit it, but I'm glad I have you around to drive for me." I leaned forward on the table, cupping a hand around my steaming mug. The coffee was strong, bitter and most likely brewed hours earlier. I drank it just the same. "Why are you really so determined to help me? And don't say it's because of my stellar personality."

His mouth twitched, but I also noticed how tired he

looked. His chin was shadowed with a day's growth of beard and his eyes were rimmed red. How he could still look wickedly handsome was a mystery, and a part of me hated him for it.

He sighed. "Truthfully? Right now my life isn't worth a fiver. You know what they did to Harold Small. We both know bleeding well he didn't die in a car accident. Now that CGM's cloning operation has been compromised I'm a loose end, especially since they know Harold passed on that sample contract to me. The same goes for you, too, you know."

He was right, but that didn't mean I was going to trust him. I'm a cautious person by nature, and there was something about him that didn't quite add up right for me. Nonetheless his presence could be useful to me up to a point, and the plan was still viable *if* I could get to Sweden in time to put it into action.

"All right, Finn," I said. "I'll tell you what. I'll let you in on some things, but first I need to check my email."

"They have wireless access here in a truck stop?"

I pointed to the door where a small poster hung. "Why not? It allows to the truckers to check in."

I pulled out the laptop, pushed aside the dishes and set it on the booth table. After booting up, I entered my password and connected to the internet, pulling up my mail. I had thirty new messages. I deleted the ones that promised to enhance my penis by three inches and pay my mortgage, making a mental note to install a better spam filter if I got out of this mess in one piece. The rest of the mail included an email apiece from my brothers, three urgent messages from my parents, two messages from the twins and ten messages from a variety of addresses I didn't recognize.

I started with the twins' messages. Both of them were in code, so I jotted them down one at a time on a napkin and got to work. We had pre-arranged a code to use for all communications, so it only took me about three minutes to decode the first message, and another two to decode the second. Anyone monitoring my mail would have to spend a good chunk of time on decoding only to discover they revealed nothing of interest to anyone but me.

"What are you doing?" Finn asked curiously, seeing me scrawl away on the napkin.

"Decoding," I said, not looking up. "The FBI is tapping my phone, so there is no reason to assume they're not monitoring my mail."

"Won't they be able to break the code?"

"Sure," I said. "But it will take some time and result in no pay-off. The twins are pros. The messages will be very nonspecific."

And indeed they were. The first message simply said that all travel and lodging arrangements were completed and exactly as we discussed. The next message said they had received a visit from Slash who was very angry about my stealthy disappearance. But they had played dumb, which was so hilarious I couldn't help but laugh aloud. I hoped Slash would try to decode this message, although he probably wouldn't be as amused as I.

The most important things taken care of, I read the message from Rock. He said the FBI, who was madly searching for me, had contacted him, Beau and my parents. Mom and Dad had been frantic before my dad went into his lawyerly mode, saying whatever it was I had supposedly been doing, I had been coerced, kidnapped or forced into it against my will and he would prove it in court. I smiled at that, even though I felt guilty as hell for worrying them. Although Rock didn't say anything specifically about working on the CGM story, I knew he was hot on it because he thanked me for my "tip" and said things were heating up.

I briefly scanned the messages from Beau and my parents because I already knew they'd be panicking and trying to figure out what was going on. I didn't want to answer them just yet, so I looked through the mystery ten messages.

As I'd suspected, all of them were from Slash from a variety of different accounts. He was furious and urged me to call him and stop any foolish plans I had to rescue Basia myself.

I ignored them and sent back a quick message to the twins in code, explaining I had to do a tiny bit of improvisation and asking them to make identical travel arrangements for Finn. I told them I'd explain everything later, but for now the plan was still intact even though, for the time being, Finn would be tagging along.

Finn sat patiently sipping his coffee while I did all this. Finally I logged off, snapped my computer shut and returned it to my tote bag. Then I sat staring at him for a full minute. He lifted an eyebrow at my perusal but said nothing.

"Okay, I've decided you can come along. I'll tell you a little of the plan at a time. Are you cool with that?"

"Do I have a choice?"

"No."

"Okay, then I'm cool." He leaned back in the booth. "Why don't you start by telling me where we're going?"

I drank the dregs of the bitter coffee and winced. They burned a hot trail all the way to my stomach.

"Toronto International Airport," I said. "We'll have to ditch your guns before we get there."

To MY RELIEF we had no problem at the Canadian border. We left Finn's guns wrapped in newspaper and safely ensconced at a bus stop locker in Buffalo and then sailed through the checkpoint. The border guard glanced at our passports, did a perfunctory look through the car and our bags and then waved us through.

When we finally reached Toronto International Airport, Finn found the long-term parking and pulled the Jag into an empty spot. He got a small navy blue duffle out of the trunk and I slung Jan's oversized tote bag over my shoulder. We were traveling light.

"No checked luggage and what I presume will be one-way tickets," Finn said. "You realize we'll be stopped by security at least a hundred times before we ever get to the gate."

"That's okay," I said. "We've got time. I don't mind as long as I don't get strip-searched."

Finn grinned. "Be still my beating heart. Could I watch?"

I looked at him, puzzled. "You'd want to watch?"

He sighed. "Sometimes you kill me, Lexi. Look, now that we're at the terminal, aren't you going to tell me where we are going?" He stopped and opened a door for me, motioning me to go through.

"Stockholm," I said, deciding it was time to accommodate him. "Via Prague."

"Is that where Basia and Judyta are?"

"Yes."

"Why the drive to Canada?"

"I couldn't just buy a ticket to Stockholm and fly there with everyone following me. It will be harder for everyone to track me if I go out via Canada. I'm not foolish enough to think that this maneuver gives me a lot of time. Just a bit of a head start. And that's all I need."

"To do what?"

"To talk with Judyta and Basia before we have company. To find out what they want."

He gaped at me. "That's it? There is no other plan?"

"Hey, it's a good plan."

"I'm not sure I believe that. You seem smarter than that."

"I'm going to try really hard to pretend I didn't hear that."

He shrugged. "Okay. You're the boss."

Despite our early arrival at the airport, we were able to check in at the Czech airline counter. My ticket was waiting and the twins had received my email and secured Finn a ticket, as well. I couldn't even imagine the conversation the two of them must be having about Finn's sudden insertion into the plan, but I was grateful that they trusted me.

The gate didn't open for another six hours for our five forty-five p.m. flight, so Finn and I had a lot of time to kill. We strolled around the airport, browsing through the expensive duty-free stores and buying some extra pain-killers for the flight. A bit later Finn treated me to lunch. I didn't eat much because I was pretty nervous. Any minute I expected to be apprehended by the FBI, although what I could be busted for, other than an NSA employee traveling abroad without permission, escaped me. I supposed I could be charged with interfering in a government investigation, although I was still quite unclear exactly how the U.S. government was involved in all of this in the first place.

To calm my nerves, Finn bought a pack of cards. We played gin rummy for several hours, and I killed him in forty-six consecutive games. After all, if you really think about it rummy is largely just one big mathematical equation with a little luck thrown in. Still, Finn was stubborn and didn't want to give up until he won at least once, so I let him score big on the forty-seventh game because I was sick of playing. I think he knew I let him win, but he didn't say anything.

We were first in line when the gate opened. Whether it was a miracle of fate or science, the plane actually left on time.

The flight to Prague was long, but uneventful. I dozed for a couple of hours, and Finn slept like a log for most of the flight. I envied him the ability to sack out like that but was glad at least one of us was getting some much-needed rest. The few times he woke to eat or drink, the flight attendants flirted shamelessly with him. That, for some reason, made me crankier than ever.

I flinched each time I went into the airplane bathroom and saw my reflection in the mirror. Totally unfair seeing as how Finn looked ready for a magazine cover shoot. My hair was in serious need of washing, my chin had broken out and my teeth were fuzzy. My wrist had swollen and turned purple, so I kept it tucked safely in the sling. I tried to do some damage control by brushing my teeth and hair, and scrubbing my face with airline soap. But nothing could hide the huge black circles under my bloodshot eyes.

We arrived just after seven-thirty in the morning, Prague-time. Our flight to Stockholm didn't leave until half-past noon, so we wandered around the airport again, had an early lunch and played a dozen hands of poker, all of which Finn lost.

"That's it," he said, tossing down his cards in frustration. "I understand that math plays a role in cards, but you have to factor in luck, as well. It's unfathomable that you continue to win every time."

I shrugged and took a sip of bottled water. "I guess I'm lucky *and* smart."

He shook his head. "Well, bugger that. If we get out of this alive, I'm taking you to Vegas."

I'd never been to Vegas and taking on the odds with Finn by my side sounded exciting. "You're on," I agreed. I could wear my red dress and pretend to be a Bond girl.

Finally we boarded the next leg of our flight and the plane took off. Within two hours, we landed at Arlanda Airport in Stockholm.

"I presume you've got reservations at a hotel somewhere in the city," Finn said as we headed out to the taxi stop. "It's tourist season, you know."

"Stop worrying so much," I said. "If anyone should be allowed to worry, it's me. Do I look remotely worried? No. That's because I've got everything under control."

At least I hoped so. Secretly, I *was* damn worried. Not about the hotel reservations, which I knew were taken care of, but about my need to ditch Finn and soon so I could put the rest of the plan into play.

We quickly hailed a cab and headed off to the hotel where my reservations were secure under the name Mrs. Susan Jaffe. Since the hotel didn't require identification and I was paying in cash, I figured I was anonymous enough, at least for now. Unfortunately the hotel was small, just three floors, and they were booked solid. That meant Finn, I mean Mr. Jaffe, would be sharing the room with me. He didn't seem too upset about it, but it was another unforeseen complication for me. I'd just add it to the list of things I had to work out by the seat of my pants.

We trudged up to the third floor and unlocked the door. The room wasn't huge, but it was clean. One bed, one small table with two chairs, and a wooden wardrobe. The loo, I was told, was down the hall. It wasn't The Ritz, but it would do.

"Guess the one bed means I'll be sleeping in the chair," Finn said. "Unless, of course, you'd like company."

"We can sleep in shifts," I suggested.

"You sure know how to bring a lad's ego down a notch," Finn said.

I glanced at him in surprise. "Why? I'll let you go first."

He let out a loud breath. "Never mind. Want to get something to eat?"

"Later," I said, dropping my bag on the bed. "I need to check my email first."

Finn shrugged. "Okay, I'll go change some money and check things out a bit. When I come back, we'll go eat."

"Sounds good," I said, pulling my laptop out of my bag and setting it on the table. He left as I plugged the adapter into the wall and booted it up. As it hummed I leaned back in the chair, closing my eyes and rubbing the back of my neck. My entire body felt sore and achy, not to mention my throbbing wrist. I would have loved to stretch out on the bed for a solid eight hours of sleep. But I had to meet Basia this evening and had a lot of work to do before then. I presumed someone on Slash's team had picked me up at the airport and tailed me here since I'd used my real passport to enter the country. But Bouker was another story entirely. I needed to find out whether he had taken the bait the twins had dropped and was on his way to the party.

Once I logged on, I accessed my mail and saw two emails from the twins, both marked urgent. I opened the first one and quickly decoded it.

The fish took the bait, headed out last night. Will arrive 1800 hours Monday and should be in place by 2300. You have a green light.

I breathed a deep sigh of relief. That had been the part of the plan I worried most about. Now that Bouker would be in Sweden in about two hours, the rest would hopefully fall into place.

I closed that message and pulled up the next one. The message was short—just one sentence. It took me about a minute to decode it. My blood turned to ice. I stared at the words as if they were written in a foreign language and then blinked.

"Impossible." I carefully copied down the message again, this time taking extra time to decode. But the words didn't change.

Finn Shaughnessy working undercover for MI-6.

"Shit!" I cried, standing up abruptly and knocking the chair over. "I *knew* he couldn't be trusted."

Why Finn, an Irishman from Cork, would be working for the British equivalent of the CIA was a mystery. But somehow, it fit. Something had bugged me about Finn from the get-go. He had seemed too capable, too smooth. And hadn't it been damned convenient how he showed up at the gas station, wielding not just one, but two guns, just in time to save my butt? I hadn't suspected British intelligence, but that was probably the point. This was a tricky development because it meant Finn had likely been keeping British intelligence, and possibly by extension, the Americans, apprised of my every move. Feelings of betrayal and anger swept through me. It hurt more than it should have because in a small way, I'd let Finn have a glimpse of my inner self. Worse, I'd been dumb enough to think we'd made some kind of deeper connection. All the time, he'd probably been laughing his head off at the clueless geek girl. God, he'd even kissed me to further his mission.

For a minute I paced the room, my hand pressed tight to my forehead, thinking. Neutralizing Finn was going to be more challenging than I'd anticipated. *Stay calm, Lexi.* If I removed my emotions from this unnerving development and looked at this objectively, uncovering Finn's secret life didn't change much. I'd planned to ditch him anyway. The key was to keep him thinking I was clueless so I could use this to my advantage. And playing clueless just happened to be one of my more impressive strengths.

I shut down the computer, scooped up the papers where I had worked the code and methodically ripped them into tiny pieces that would flush down the toilet. I'd develop a plan to neutralize Finn, but first I needed a hot shower and some clean clothes.

I stripped and soaked my aches in the bathtub before soaping up and shampooing my hair with one hand. Then making the water as hot as I could stand, I used the detachable showerhead to rinse off.

Afterwards I combed out my hair, leaving it loose so it could dry, and pulled on the wrinkled white T-shirt and jeans. My wrist felt better from the soak, and I was able to flex my fingers a bit. I refastened the sling and went back to the room where Finn had still not returned. Good, because I hadn't yet figured out how to keep him from mucking up my plans.

I sat down on the side of the bed and then realized my throat was dry. Maybe I'd take walk around a bit and see if I could buy a bottle of water somewhere.

I grabbed the room key and walked out the door, nearly running over my next-door neighbor exiting her room. She had platinum hair with pink streaks and was dressed in a spiked collar and black leather dress, with a pair of handcuffs dangling from a belt around her waist. A row of earrings dotted each ear and a matching one glinted in her right nostril. When she opened her mouth, I saw a stud on her tongue. As I stood there staring at her dumbly, a whole crew of punks spilled out into the hallway, laughing and jostling each other. It was just my luck that I'd booked the only hotel in Stockholm that was apparently hosting a punk convention.

"Uh, hi. Do you speak English?"

"Sure, I went to Oxford," she said in perfect clipped English with only the faintest trace of a Scandinavian lilt.

"Do you know where I could get a bottle of water and some ice?"

"You must be American."

"Is it that obvious?"

"Oh, yes. The café at the corner will probably have some if you're willing to pay."

She smiled as one of the other guys came up beside her. He was tall and skinny, and like the others, dressed completely in black leather. His hair was dyed magenta, and he had two stud rings in his nose, a large silver hoop in one ear and a collar with metal spikes around his neck and both wrists. It was a good thing he was smiling all friendlylike because if not, I'd have run screaming the other direction.

"This is Manfred," the girl said. "I'm Annika."

"Um, nice to meet you," I said. "I'm Lexi."

Manfred clicked his boots together and saluted me, and as he did it, he jingled. I saw he also wore a pair of handcuffs attached to his belt. I wondered if they carried them to make a fashion statement or wanted to be prepared for some kind of weird, kinky sex.

A light bulb popped in my head. Weird kinky sex! That was it. It would be the perfect idea to neutralize Finn. But first I had to part one of these young punks from their handcuffs, and I wasn't certain it would be an easy thing.

I pasted a bright smile on my mouth. "This may sound like a strange request, but would either of you be willing to sell me your handcuffs?"

They looked at me as if they hadn't heard me right. "Handcuffs?" Annika finally asked.

I pointed to the pair attached to Manfred's belt. "Would you be willing to sell those to me?"

Both she and Manfred kept staring at me in open-mouthed amazement. I could tell by their expressions they didn't make me as the type who used handcuffs.

"Have you ever used them before?" Annika asked me.

I put one hand on my hip and tried to look cool, knowledgeable and relaxed...a handcuff connoisseur. "Sure...sort of."

"It will be difficult with your hand hurt," Manfred finally said.

I looked down at my wrist and flexed my fingers. "Actually, it's feeling better. And the cuffs aren't for me anyway."

Manfred said something to Annika in what I assumed was Swedish and she shrugged. "Fifty dollars," she said.

"Fifty dollars? Are you nuts?"

"It will be worth every dollar," Manfred promised me. "He will like them very much. Mine are extra long and not so easy to find."

I couldn't help it; I blushed. Yeah, I was the real handcuff master all right. "Twenty," I countered.

"Thirty and we deal."

"Okay," I said. "Wait here. I'll be right back." I returned to the room, peeled off three tens and returned to Annika and Manfred. He'd already taken the cuffs off his belt and they dangled freely in his hand. Annika took the cash and Manfred handed them to me, along with a small key.

"By the way I saw your bloke in the hall," Annika said, winking. "Quite a bobby-dazzler. I think he'll have fun."

I didn't know what a bobby-dazzler was, but nodded like I did. "Uh, yeah, and that reminds me," I said. "There is a chance that my bobby-dazzler may, ah, complain a bit at first when I use them. You know, yell for help or something. But if you hear anything, just ignore it. I'll take care of him. It will be all part of the game."

"Cool," Manfred said, looking at me with what I was pretty sure was admiration. I felt my stomach go a little queasy and hoped I wasn't giving him the impression that all Americans were as perverted as me.

"We won't be around anyway," Annika assured me. "Tonight is the big concert with Rancid Duck. We'll be out all night. Have fun."

They waved and walked down the corridor. I took my thirty-dollar handcuffs back to the room and attached one side to the bedpost and hid the other side down behind the back of the bed, the cuff open. I sincerely hoped Finn wouldn't find the cuffs, but even if he did, I could play dumb. Like maybe they came complimentary with the room or something.

Finn returned about thirty minutes later, probably from giving his bosses a full report on our activities. I suppressed my desire to smack his handsome face because it was imperative he not notice my feelings toward him had changed. His lengthy absence had actually been welcome since in addition to the handcuffs, it had given me time to get water, a map of Stockholm and directions to Djurgarden Island.

"Anything interesting on email?" he asked, sitting down on the bed.

"Not a thing," I lied. "Where'd you go for so long?"

"I took a walk and got some fresh air. Are you hungry yet?"

"Actually I'm famished."

"Good, let's go get something."

We headed out the door and Finn locked up. "So now that we're here, what's the next step?" he asked.

"I guess it wouldn't hurt to let you know that I'm meeting Basia tomorrow evening," I said even though I was actually meeting her tonight.

He looked surprised. "You've been in touch with her already?"

"Not here. When I was back in the States. She set up a rendezvous point."

"Where?"

"Sorry, that's on a need-to know basis. No more questions for the time being, okay?"

He didn't look happy about it but to his credit, he didn't press.

We found an outdoor café not far from the hotel. Finn had the fishballs, called *fiskbullar* in Swedish, and I tried the crayfish. It was delicious.

"I take it you've been to Sweden before," I said, setting my fork down and leaning back in my chair.

"Several times. I like it very much."

"I'm clearly not as cosmopolitan. This is only my second trip abroad. My first time was an eighth-grade trip to Paris."

"You speak French?"

"Only if I need to find a bathroom."

He laughed and we chatted as we drank some excellent Swedish wine with dinner. Finn, of course, picked it out. Now that I knew his family background, I was interested to hear what he could tell me about wine. To my delight, he told me about his family's winery in Ireland and about the wine-making process. I realized although he may not have wanted to work in his father's business, he had definitely picked up the know-how.

After dinner we took a leisurely stroll along Strandvagen Road where I discreetly noted the tram stop across the bridge to Djurgarden Island. My back-up plan had me taking a ferry across, but I typically didn't do well on boats, so that would be a last resort.

When we finally returned to the hotel room, Finn disappeared down the hall for a bath, and I strategically put some of my junk on the side of the bed without the cuffs. That way if Finn wanted to rest for a bit, he'd have to lie down on the side with the cuffs. I sincerely hoped that a full stomach, clean body and jet lag would conspire to put him out just long enough for me to snap a cuff on his wrist and chain him to the bed.

After that I logged on the computer again to see if I'd received any further messages from the twins. There were none, which I presumed to mean all was well. I sent a quick message back to them in code updating them on the developments. Finn returned when I was in the middle of typing the message, so I casually urged him to stretch out on the bed for a while. To my relief, he didn't argue and promptly lay on the side of the bed with the handcuffs.

I congratulated myself. So far, so good. Plan A of what I was now calling "Neutralizing Finn" was moving along nicely.

I surfed the web some more, checking out weather conditions for this evening in Stockholm and reviewing an online map of the city so I had a back-up plan to get to the rendezvous point in case something happened.

Thirty minutes passed and I heard Finn's steady, even breathing. A glance over my shoulder showed that his eyes were closed, hands folded atop his stomach. I looked at my watch and saw it was nearly ten o'clock. That meant an hour and a half before game time. I wanted to make sure I had plenty of leeway, so I decided I had to make my move now. I slipped the sling off and flexed my fingers. My wrist was still swollen and an angry black-and-blue color, but I could move my fingers and hand, and that would be critical for what I needed to do next.

Still sitting in the chair with my back to Finn, I unbuttoned the top two buttons on my blouse and fluffed up my hair. I didn't think it would be necessary, but just in case Finn awoke before I had the cuffs on him, I needed to be ready. I slowly stood, my stomach churning with nervousness. Seduction was a game I'd never played and I was pretty sure I wouldn't be good at it. But we all do what we have to do when lives, not to mention national security, are at stake. Still, actual seduction was Plan B of Neutralizing Finn, and whereas I was one hundred percent certain it would be a pleasurable experience, at least for me, I hoped I wouldn't have to go that far.

Putting Plan A into effect, I quietly knelt down beside the bed. Finn didn't move and there was no change in his breathing. I leaned over and groped blindly for the handcuffs. It wasn't as easy as I had expected and I had to lean over so far, my hair fell slightly onto his chest.

Just as my fingers closed around the handcuff, Finn's eyes snapped open. I was so frightened, I nearly screamed.

"Lexi?" he said, blinking and apparently confused. "What are you doing?"

"Uh, um, I…" I stammered idiotically, frozen half-poised over his body. My hair rested on his chest, my face mere inches from his, but I didn't move. There was no way in hell I was letting go of the cuffs now that I had them in my grasp. My heart thundered as Plan A evaporated in a puff of smoke, but I tried to remain calm as I moved into Plan B.

Seduction.

Oh, God. I wasn't sure I could do this.

"Just relax, Finn," I said in the huskiest voice I could manage. "I think you'll like this."

Gathering up my courage, I leaned over and mashed my lips against his. He gasped and then I realized he wasn't kissing me back. Mortified, I pulled away, knowing he was ready to bolt in about five seconds if I didn't do something. That meant moving to Plan C. There was only one problem. I didn't have a Plan C.

"Finn, I'm...sorry," I stammered. "I just couldn't, uh, control myself."

"What's gotten into you?" he said, starting to sit up, but I pushed him back down on the bed with an elbow to his chest.

He looked really surprised now. Great, not only did he think I was a slut, he probably made me as the dominatrix type, as well. Jeez, wait 'til he saw the handcuffs.

"It's the...uh, close proximity to you," I said breathily, pretty sure I was starting to hyperventilate. Sweat had started to trickle down my back. My shoulders ached from the uncomfortable position of half sitting, half lying across him and I thought I might sneeze.

"Or it could be the, uh, jet lag," I stammered. Holy crap, I wasn't making any sense whatsoever.

Think seduction, I urged myself. *Be sexy, slinky and ooze sensuality.*

I tried to shake my chest a bit, because I was pretty sure boobs turned on most men. But because I still had a death grip on the cuffs, all the shaking probably only made me appear spastic. God, Finn was looking at me like I was having a seizure. *Focus.* Slowly I lifted the cuffs until they were even with the bed. I just needed to grab his hand and cuff it. It would take all of two seconds, but timing was everything. I couldn't afford to fumble, despite my injured wrist, because Finn was bigger, stronger and more agile than me. I'd have one chance, and one chance only, to snap them on right.

Finn's eyes were so wide I thought they might pop out of his head. "You're trying to seduce me?" he sputtered in disbelief. Instead of looking turned on, he seemed kind of freaked.

"Yes, I, ah, like your big muscles," I stammered stupidly. *Shit.* Apparently I was the master of sexy conversation. *Not.*

But for some unfathomable reason, my nervousness seemed to relax him. I got a big break when he folded his arms behind his head, just inches from the cuff.

"Well, now, lass, this doesn't mean you're going to start talking dirty now, are you?" he said with a smile.

I looked at him in horror. "Talk dirty? Me? Well… ah…okay, I can do that. Um, spank me hard, big daddy, then I'll—"

Before I could finish, Finn slid a hand around the back of my neck and yanked me down hard against his mouth. He gave me a wickedly hot, electrifying, open-mouthed kiss. The room spun and I'm pretty sure I forgot to breathe. I might have even had a small heart attack. Yet a tiny part of my brain, probably the part living in fear that my life was on the fast-track to death, somehow remained detached.

Though my body was ready to get naked and do the horizontal tango, I realized I had just been presented with a golden opportunity. As Finn deepened the kiss, I slid the cuff across the pillow to where his other hand lay and snapped it on his wrist.

He stilled immediately and I guess it took him about three seconds to realize what I'd done. I used those precious seconds to tear my mouth from his and leap out of reach.

"What the bloody hell?" he yelled, sitting up and yanking on the handcuffs. To my enormous relief, they held magnificently. "Lexi, what is this about?"

"I'm sorry, Finn," I said apologetically. "Really sorry. But I have to meet Basia. Alone."

The look in his eyes was murderous. "Unhook me, lass."

"I'm afraid I can't do that."

"Bugger it, Lexi. Let me go."

My mouth still burned from his kiss. I'd never, *ever,* been kissed like that, and I was pretty sure I'd never experience such heat again. I had this wild urge to throw myself back in his arms and see just how kinky I could get with extra-long handcuffs. Who knew if I'd get another chance in this lifetime? He looked so damn sexy with mussed-up hair and that wild, dangerous Celtic look in his eyes. I wanted to give it a go.

Jeez, maybe I was a pervert.

He yanked again on the cuff and I held my breath that the bedpost would hold. It did.

"Ye don't know what ye are doing," he said, his Irish accent thick.

"On the contrary, I know exactly what I'm doing," I said.

"Ye can't do this alone. Ye need me."

I raised an eyebrow. "I need you or I need MI-6?"

It was just a second but I saw surprise and acknowledgement flash in his eyes. It was all I needed.

"I don't know what ye are talking about."

"Sure you do. Look, I don't blame you for having your own agenda. I have mine."

"Lexi, unhook me and I'll explain everything."

"I'm sorry, but I'm in a hurry right now. I'm sure you understand. However, I'm not without heart. If I don't come out of this alive, your cell phone and the key to the cuffs are over here on the dresser. Someone will find you eventually."

He pulled on the cuffs again and swore at me in a steady stream of English and Gaelic. "Ye're going to get yourself killed without me," he warned.

I rolled my eyes to the heavens. "That seems to be the consensus going around these days. Guess what? Bugger *that!* I'm not a helpless idiot. It's really starting to piss me off."

"Lexi," he growled. "Don't be foolish. This is bigger than you can imagine."

"I can imagine pretty big. For a girl, that is." I smiled sweetly. "Don't worry about me, *Agent* Shaughnessy, I can take care of myself. Oh, and I guess I should also tell you that I happened to mention to our punk convention floor-mates that we might be having wild, kinky sex in here with said handcuffs. Yelling or screaming isn't going to help."

"Don't do this, lass."

I shoved some money into my tote bag along with a map, a sweatshirt and a baseball cap. Then I carefully put the sling back on my arm because my wrist was killing me again after all the excitement.

"Lexi, you don't have to go this alone."

"Yes, I do. I'm sorry it had to end this way between us, Finn, because I had really started to like you. Who knows? The world is a crazy place. Maybe our paths will cross again some day." I permitted myself a sad smile.

He yanked on the handcuffs again to no avail. "That will be unlikely if you're dead."

"Then let's hope a little of your Irish luck rubbed off on me. Goodbye, Finn."

As I left the room and carefully locked up, I heard him swearing after me in Gaelic.

SIXTEEN

IT WAS A quarter past ten by the time I exited the hotel. The sun was still shining, the birds singing. It was weird, but in the summer in Sweden, I guess the sun never really sets. I don't know how people got used to it. Still, it played in my favor since I was able to see my surroundings more clearly.

As expected, I quickly spotted a surveillance team just outside the hotel. A bald man sat on a bench across from the hotel entrance reading a newspaper, and a thin, blonde woman was sipping coffee at a café a few meters away. I knew they were together because the moment I exited the hotel, the man gave me a startled glance and then hastily looked over at the blonde. They both seemed pretty shocked to see me, so I guess Finn had informed them that we'd be in for the night. The element of surprise definitely worked for me because I sincerely doubted they would have so obviously given themselves away without it.

I strolled down the sidewalk, pretending I didn't notice them following me. I kept track of them by monitoring their reflections in the store windows. They followed me at a careful distance, one on each side of the street. They didn't seem to be taking too many precautions to hide themselves, which likely meant they thought I hadn't spotted them. Why should they suspect I had? I'm a twenty-five-year-old computer desk jockey, never trained as an agent, who'd been abroad only once before in her entire a lot easier. Right now my job was temporarily eluding them so I could have a minute or two alone with Basia before the party started. I definitely didn't want our little gathering to start until all parties were present. That made timing the trickiest part of the plan.

As I continued down the sidewalk, I noticed a young couple in front of me. The woman whispered something to the man and he scooped her into a hug, laughing. It seemed innocent until he glanced over at me. For the briefest of seconds, we made eye contact and I turned away, my heart racing.

Shit! They had put another team on me. I don't know how I knew for sure, but I just did. My gut had made them, and I'm a big believer in gut instinct. So that made four agents tailing me, two more than I expected. That threw me for a serious loop because I hadn't expected to be so well covered. I probably had Finn to thank for that.

Panic swelled in my throat. Now I wasn't sure I could pull this off. Ditching one surveillance team would be hard enough, but there was no way in hell I'd be able to shake both teams.

Think, Carmichael, think.

I walked ahead blindly, not noticing that someone had come up quickly behind me until he threw an arm of iron around my shoulders and squeezed hard.

"Keep walking," he said in a low voice before I could say a word. "You have two teams of two watching you. Whatever you do, don't scream or act frightened. I'm an unexpected variable so they won't make a move unless I appear to threaten you. My best guess is that we've got about three, possibly five, minutes before they move."

My mouth gaped open in shock, but I managed to keep walking. "Elvis! What in the hell are you doing here?"

"Saving your hide."

"What?" I hissed. "Are you nuts? What happened to Rule #1—Absolutely, *Positively* No Deviating From the Plan?"

"Look who's talking, Ms. Queen of Deviation," he hissed back. "Where's Finn Shaughnessy?"

"Handcuffed to a bed."

"What?" he practically screeched. "You were using handcuffs?"

"Jeez, Elvis, it's not what you think. I mean, it's not about sex." I remembered the kiss. "Um, not exactly. Anyway, I handled him just fine."

"I'm not worried about him. What happened to your arm?"

"It's my wrist and a three-hundred-pound thug fell on it. Don't worry, I handled him, too. Sort of."

"We have to abort the plan. There have been some new developments."

I glanced in a shop window as we passed and I saw the blonde woman talking frantically on a cell phone. The young couple was whispering to each other and neither looked happy. The bald man was nowhere in sight. Apparently Elvis's unexpected appearance had freaked them out and now they were all trying to figure out what they were supposed to do next.

"We can't abort," I said. "We're too close."

"We have to. Samir Al-Naddi is putting a wrench in our plan."

"Al-Naddi the Yemeni terrorist? What does he have to do with this?"

"A Yemeni businessman was murdered last night in Munich, Germany. All his ID, including his passport and credentials, were stolen. Someone used his passport to enter Sweden this afternoon. I got a tip from a friend at the NSA who says the hit on the businessman smelled to high heaven of Al-Naddi's work. But here's the kicker: the U.S. thinks it's Al-Naddi himself here in Sweden, masquerading as the businessman."

"Here?" My mind raced furiously. "Slash said the CIA suspected that Al-Naddi had something to do with the murder of Al-Asan's bodyguards in Genoa, but we couldn't finger the connection. Now it looks like Al-Naddi could just be another player at the table."

Elvis's expression was grim. "He's not just another player, Lexi. He is *the* player."

"What do you mean?"

"I mean I've discovered his connection to all of this. He's interested in Judyta Taszynski because she is carrying *his* clone."

I stopped dead in my tracks, despite Elvis's direction to keep walking. My blood turned to ice. "What did you say?"

"Keep walking," Elvis urged and pulled me along by the arm. "Look, once I was in Bouker's computer, I decided to do a little browsing around. Slash's connections in the CIA were right. Al-Asan's bodyguards were hit by followers of Al-Naddi."

"But why? It doesn't make any sense."

"It makes perfect sense. They stole Al-Asan's DNA and replaced it with Al-Naddi's."

I pressed a hand to my mouth, my thoughts racing. Pieces of the puzzle fell into place. "Oh, my God," I breathed. "The terrorists hijacked Al-Asan's DNA *before* the cloning procedure took place. Then they somehow delivered it to the doctors at Bright Horizons without letting on that anything had happened."

"They must have used look-alikes of the men who were killed."

"Which would explain why the bodies of the men were hidden for a short time and then laid out again to be found,"

I said. "Slash said the Italian medical examiner couldn't figure out the anomaly. Their bodies couldn't be discovered *before* the delivery had been made. It also means the doctors unwittingly implanted Al-Naddi's clones into the women without anyone knowing."

"Everyone except Al-Naddi and his followers."

"But who's killing the girls?"

"Yemeni intelligence. They've been making sure that no clone of Al-Naddi's exists. President Al-Fulani of Yemen is an archenemy of Al-Naddi. It's no secret. He's made it his number one goal to eradicate the man and his terrorist operation from Yemen soil."

"But the girls didn't know they were carrying Al-Naddi's clone," I protested. "Why kill them?"

"To ensure that none of them carried to term."

I swallowed the nausea that rose in my throat. "Except Judyta is still alive and pregnant. Oh, man, this is seriously bad." I glanced in a shop window and realized I'd been so distracted I had lost the location of all the members of the surveillance teams.

"So, you can see why it's too risky to continue," Elvis said. "It's one thing to bring together members of different governments. It's something entirely different to add a terrorist to the mix. Especially one as volatile as Al-Naddi."

"How do you think he found out about the rendezvous?" I asked anxiously.

"Possibly a sympathizer in the Yemeni Embassy. But I have an even more ominous supposition."

"Which is?" I asked, not certain I wanted to know.

"It's possible the U.S. government or even Vatican intelligence tipped Al-Naddi off to your whereabouts on purpose."

"A set-up for Al-Naddi," I breathed. "Here. Basia and I are the bait."

"As noble as it may seem to you, being bait for a terrorist, we can't possibly continue. Al-Naddi could blow us all to kingdom come."

My thoughts were spinning. I took several deep breaths and then stopped, clutching Elvis's arm.

"No," I said, trying to organize my thoughts. "Al-Naddi wouldn't hurt me or Basia. We're the only ones who can lead him to Judyta."

"He might not kill you, but he could capture and then torture you until you coughed up the information."

I winced. "Okay, good point. Especially since torture is *not* on my list of things to experience in this lifetime. Certainly Al-Naddi should be considered unstable and dangerous. Normal rules of conduct don't apply to him. But what would happen if we abort the plan? Al-Naddi disappears and regroups for another day. Judyta and Basia have to remain in hiding because they will still be hunted by Yemeni intelligence, the U.S. government, MI-6, Vatican intelligence and Al-Naddi's followers, although for radically different reasons. My life and that of everyone connected to me in this matter remains at risk. I could get picked off at any time just for knowing too much. No thanks. I'd rather not be looking over my shoulder for the rest of my life wondering when and from whom I'm going to buy it. I want to finish it now."

Elvis looked really worried. "Lexi, I've got a bad feeling about this."

"Me, too. But think about it. You know I'm right. Aborting the plan at this stage carries its risks, too. If Al-Naddi is here, he might get lucky and locate Judyta and Basia even without us. Look, we could do this and still stay in control. I just need a few minutes with Basia alone to clue her in to what's going on."

Elvis didn't appear convinced. "There are so many chances for things to go wrong."

"I know. But we've also got everyone in place. I've got to trust that the U.S. has enough invested in this to protect Basia and me. I'm going ahead with the plan. Are you in?"

He exhaled loudly. "You'll have to lose both surveillance teams."

"I think I already have. Do you know where they are?"

He pulled me into a hug and put his head close to mine, like we were conversing intimately. "Talk to me," he ordered, scanning the street over my shoulder. "Make it look like we're having a heartfelt discussion."

"We *are* having a heartfelt discussion."

"Well, keep talking in a heartfelt way then."

"I'm too nervous. Want me to recite the periodic table?"

"You sure know how to turn a guy on."

The quip surprised me because I never imagined Elvis as a guy who could be turned on. I don't know, I guess I just pegged him as a genius too elevated to bother with everyday things like dating, social skills and sex. Maybe I was wrong.

"Okay, let's see," I murmured. "Hydrogen, helium, lithium, beryllium, boron, carbon, nitrogen, oxygen, fluorine—"

"Found them," Elvis interrupted. "As far as I can tell, we're still being watched by two teams. They've apparently been told to hold position. I bet they want to figure out who I am and what you're going to do now."

"Good question. What *am* I going to do now?"

"You know the tram schedule to Djurgarden Island?"

"Yes. Every fifteen minutes on the hour."

He glanced down at his watch. "We've got five minutes. Let's do it."

"Do what?"

"The new plan."

"You've figured it out already?"

"That's why I get paid the big bucks. Thinking on the fly does have its advantages."

"I'm officially impressed."

"Good to know."

He leaned over and brushed his lips against mine, soft, tender and totally unexpected. My heart gave a little jump. I had no earthly idea what was going on. Three kisses in the past forty-eight hours with three extremely different guys. That was definitely a record for me. In fact, it would probably stand as a lifetime record, seeing how I might not live much longer. It was fascinating data and the analytical part of my brain wanted to examine each one. But now wasn't the time to try and figure out what it all meant. Besides, Elvis had already begun to move again and I had to hustle a couple of steps to keep up.

"Listen carefully," he said and quickly outlined his plan.

It was astoundingly simple, which meant it had a fair-to-decent chance of working since I was the one who had to put it into play.

Nonetheless, as we headed for the tram stop my heart was thundering so hard in my chest, I thought I might have a heart attack. Sweat oozed down my back and I was glad I wasn't holding hands with Elvis because my palms were slick with moisture. I wasn't cut out for this secret agent stuff.

I glanced in a window and saw our teams were again in place and that they trailed along behind us now, no longer bothering to act discreet.

"They know we've made them," I observed.

"Yes," Elvis agreed. "But it doesn't change anything."

"Guess not." Then trying to lighten the mood, I said,

"Did I mention I like the fedora? Kind of reminds me of Indiana Jones. But what's with the trench coat?"

He smiled, likely just to put me at ease. I noticed his brown hair was squished flat under the hat and his glasses were slightly askew. He looked pale and exhausted and I realized he must have flown all night and then hightailed it to the hotel to save me.

"Always wanted to play secret agent," he said lightly. "In my opinion, no better way to do it than in a black trench coat."

I smiled back. "*The Matrix* fantasy. Yeah, I get it. It's ace. No, *you're* ace."

"Sure, that's me," Elvis said, grinning, and then glanced again at his watch. "Tram is late."

"Maybe your watch is fast."

"Maybe."

Just as he said that, I saw the tram come into sight down the street. There were three passengers waiting at the stop—two young women and a kid about six years old.

"Good luck," Elvis whispered.

"You, too," I said.

I calculated the distance and the time I needed to make a dash for the stop. Six seconds. It was an iffy estimate, a bit tight considering how out-of-shape I was, but I could make it. Barely.

"Keep walking. And don't stare at the tram. Take judicious glances."

"Okay," I said, my chest feeling tight.

A tremor shook in my leg muscles and my breathing had become shallow as if I'd already been running for miles. I forced myself to calm down. Relax, focus and concentrate. All I needed was six frigging seconds. I could do it.

The tram pulled up to the stop, the doors opened and

some people got off. The young woman with the little boy climbed on.

My hands clenched into fists and I ground my teeth together.

Wait...wait...wait.

Sweat slid down my temples, plastering my hair to the sides of my cheeks.

Don't screw it up, Carmichael. There's a hell of a lot riding on you.

I waited until the last woman lifted her foot to climb on to the tram. "Now," I breathed.

At exactly the same moment, Elvis and I made our moves.

SEVENTEEN

I HEARD THE warning shouts behind me, but adrenaline surged through my veins as I swung aboard the tram with one second to spare before the doors closed. I dared a glance out the window and saw that Elvis had done exactly what he had said he would and blocked the path of the closest agent—the young man who was half of the cute, giggling couple. Elvis had stepped into his path, neatly tripping him and sending him sprawling face-first into the pavement before effectively disappearing into the gathering crowd. The pretty young woman raced after the tram, but she was too far behind to catch me.

At this point all the agents following me had abandoned any pretense of discretion and were either running or shouting. The thin blonde woman was shouting into a cell phone and I spotted the bald man dashing toward a parked car. But the tram picked up speed and there was nothing they could do but watch as we sped out of sight. They now knew I was headed for Djurgarden Island, but it was a big place with lots of tourist attractions, so it would likely take them some time to find me. It was all the head start I needed to talk with Basia. I only prayed she'd be on time for our rendezvous because if she wasn't, things would start to fall apart fast.

I got off at the stop for the Grona Lunds Tivoli Amusement Park directly in front of the ferry docks. Even though it was nearly eleven-thirty at night the crowd was young, and it was a good place for me to blend in. I pulled my blue sweatshirt out of the tote bag and over my head and then tucked my hair up into a ball cap. It wasn't a sophisticated disguise and it certainly wouldn't hide me forever, but it might give me a few extra minutes.

I made my way toward the Nordic Museum, staying as much as I could with the crowd. I didn't spot anyone tailing me and hoped that would hold for a while longer. The museum was the most conspicuous building on the island. I made a circle around the structure, but didn't see anyone. A glance at my watch indicated it was eleven-thirty on the dot.

"Come on, Basia," I breathed and leaned against a door on the east entrance, which was partially obscured by some bushes.

Exactly one minute later, I saw a lone figure in jeans and a green blouse walking toward the front steps. The size and shape of the figure was right, but the hair was too short and light blond. It was the way she walked that gave her away.

I stepped out from the side of the museum. "Basia!"

She turned quickly and then broke into a run. Before I had taken no more than two steps toward her, she had already collided with me at full force, her arms thrown tight around my neck.

"Lexi," she said. "Oh my God. I've never been so glad to see anyone in my entire life."

"You dyed your hair." As if I didn't have anything more important to say like "I'm glad you're alive," or "We're in serious trouble."

She stepped back, her face pale and drawn. Tears shimmered in her eyes. "I wasn't sure you'd be able to get here in time."

"Hey, a little faith, please. I work for the NSA, remember?"

She had lost a lot of weight and the blouse hung from

her petite form in a way that kind of scared me. "Did you come alone?"

"More or less," I said. "I left Finn Shaughnessy handcuffed to a bed in the hotel. But that's a story for another time."

Her eyes widened and then she noticed the sling. "What happened to your arm?"

"A three-hundred-pound thug fell on it while trying to kill me."

She gasped. "Oh, God, Lexi. I'm so sorry to have dragged you into all of this. I didn't know who else to turn to."

"It's okay. Look, we don't have a lot of time for chit-chat before things go down." I glanced at my watch and saw we had about two minutes until the party started. "Is Judyta safe?"

"Yes, for the time being. What do you mean 'before things go down'?"

"You'll see. You just have to trust me and follow my lead. But whatever you do, absolutely, positively and under *no* circumstances are you to give away Judyta's whereabouts until I give you the go-ahead. Got it?"

Panic started to creep into Basia's eyes. "Lexi, what's going on?"

"A hell of a lot more than Judyta bargained for," I said, steering Basia toward a bench and motioning for her to sit. "How is she?"

"Mentally, she's frightened. Physically, she's fine. Lexi, Judyta had the baby yesterday."

My mouth fell open. "Yesterday?"

"Yes. She gave birth to a little boy."

"Okay," I said, breathing fast. This changed things. "Was it healthy?"

"As a horse," she said, smiling. "He's a big baby. Judyta named him Tadeusz, or Tadek for short."

My heart started to thud uncomfortably. I had no idea how to break the news to her or how to soften the blow. "Basia, look, I don't know of an easier way to say this to you, so just prepare yourself."

"Prepare myself for what?"

"Tadek is not an ordinary baby."

"What do you mean?"

I held my breath then expelled it with a whoosh. "Judyta gave birth to a clone."

Shock melded with complete disbelief on her face. "A *what?*"

"A clone. Judyta was implanted with a clone. She was a surrogate for what may be the world's first successfully born human clone. That's what this whole mess is about."

"But I saw him. He's just a tiny little baby."

"Yeah, that's the whole idea." I tried to soften my tone. "Where did she deliver? I mean, you didn't take her to the hospital, did you?"

Basia shook her head. "No, we didn't dare risk it. The family we are staying with knows a midwife. She helped Judyta deliver."

"This family—are they friends of Lars Anderson?"

"Yes."

"I knew he was up to his neck in this!" I exclaimed. "Why is he helping you?"

Basia looked down at her hands. "Lars and I have a history."

"A history? Like you dated him?"

"Sort of."

I blew out an impatient breath. "We don't have time for ambiguity, Basia. Spill."

She chewed her lower lip and I had never seen her look

so sad or miserable. "Well, remember our first year at Georgetown? The following summer I went to Poland to do some translation work for the Polish military. They were conducting joint exercises with U.S. and Swedish special ops teams and I served as a three-way translator. The captain of the Swedish team was Lars."

"And?"

"I fell for him. Hard. I was nineteen, young and stupid. I knew it wasn't a good idea to fool around with a participant, but I was nuts about him. We managed to keep our affair a secret, but we were caught."

I shrugged. "So what? It's not like he was your superior or anything. You were two consenting adults after all."

"It's not so simple. Lars and I were so embarrassed, but that's not the worst part. Lexi, Lars was married."

"Oh, crap."

"According to Lars, he and his wife were on the verge of breaking up but I swear I didn't know. He didn't tell me until after we'd been found out. I felt used and betrayed. Somehow I finished up the translation job."

"Why didn't you tell me about this? I thought we were best friends."

"Because I was ashamed. I was the other woman. I didn't want you to think badly of me. Lars contacted me during our second year at Georgetown, but I didn't respond. He divorced his wife, resigned from his special ops unit and moved to the U.S. to start a new life. He's been calling me periodically over the past several years, but I never responded until all of this stuff with Judyta started happening."

"And you responded by signing up for his karate class?" I asked in disbelief.

"No. We just used that for cover. After everything with Judyta started going down, I needed a safe place for her to go. I immediately thought of Lars. I wanted to get her out of Poland, and Sweden is close. Lars agreed to help, so we're staying with an old military buddy of his out in the country."

"I bet the affair was never made an official military part of Lars's record," I murmured thoughtfully. That's probably why Slash hadn't made the connection between Lars and Basia.

On the other hand, Slash had never offered me the information that Lars had once been part of a Swedish special ops team. I was positive he had dug that deep into Lars's background, although I bet that little tidbit had intrigued, as well as greatly worried, him. I would venture a guess it had also helped Judyta and Basia evade detection for so long. Lars was a pro.

"Lexi, how can you be so certain Judyta's baby is a clone?" Basia asked. "Maybe this is all a big mistake." Yet even as she said the words, I could see the truth of the situation sinking in for her.

"I wish it were a mistake," I said, sighing, and then glanced at my watch. Bouker was late. I didn't see anyone else arriving either, but time was getting tight and I expected things to go down any minute.

"Look, Basia, I need to know what Judyta wants. Do you think she'd still want to keep the baby after learning about this?"

Basia gripped my hand and squeezed so hard I winced. "Lexi, Judyta loves that baby. It's hers now. I can guarantee it won't matter to her who or even *what* Tadek is. You have to promise me that you'll help figure out a way to let her keep him."

"Okay. I'm working on it."

"So, what's the plan?"

"Well, hopefully I've led everyone who has any interest in the whereabouts of Judyta Taszynski to this exact spot. My game plan is to break the whole thing wide open by holding an information auction of sorts."

Basia looked at me in surprise. "An information auction? Here?"

"Yes. Time isn't on our side, Basia. You have some of the world's best intelligence agencies looking for you. It won't be too long before they find Judyta. If we want to settle this on her terms, it's going to have to be here and now."

"Oh, God. Are you sure this is a good idea?"

"Actually, I'm having second thoughts, but it's too late now. The interested parties are scheduled to start arriving any minute."

Basia closed her eyes and I thought she was a lot more composed than I would have been in her situation. "I didn't even know human cloning was possible," she murmured.

"Science has been on the verge for many years. Honestly, it was only a matter of time before it happened. It still doesn't make it any easier to swallow. And, Basia, I'm sorry, but things could get worse."

"Worse? What can possibly be worse than this?"

"Well, Bright Horizons, the clinic where Judyta was impregnated, almost went bankrupt until someone apparently found a way to provide a decent cash infusion by offering clones to the very rich and very discreet. But someone else also got a whiff of Bright Horizons' cloning operation and had the brilliant idea to use it for furthering a political cause."

Dismay and fascination clouded her expression. "What kind of cause?" she asked almost fearfully.

"Do you know who Samir Al-Naddi is?"

"Isn't he some terrorist nutcase?"

"Yes. Well, he apparently had his followers assassinate the two bodyguards carrying Al-Asan's DNA samples for the cloning procedure and then switched it with his own. His followers delivered the sample containing Al-Naddi's DNA to the clinic, where it was eventually planted into the surrogate mothers."

Basia shook her head vigorously, horrified disbelief etched on her face. "Oh, no. No, no, no. You can't possibly mean to say Judyta just gave birth to a clone of a...a *terrorist*."

"Unfortunately, that's exactly what I mean."

"Then who is trying to kill her?"

"We are."

He had moved so quietly that I hadn't even heard him. I gasped and whirled around on the bench to see Rashid Bouker standing behind me with a small revolver in his hand. I put a hand to my heart to steady the gallop.

"Jeez, what took you so long?" I asked. "You're late. Sit down."

He blinked in shock. "You're *expecting* me?"

"Yes. You're the first of many people I'm expecting. So, put the gun away. You won't need it."

"What are you talking about?"

"Just what I said. We're about to have an interesting little party."

His face was incredulous. "You set me up?"

"You and everyone else. You don't really think the tip about my rendezvous with Ms. Kowalski here in Sweden at exactly this time was just a stroke of good fortune, do you? I need you here, Bouker. I want to know exactly why you are so anxious to find Judyta Taszynski."

"I warned you to stay out of this," Bouker threatened. "You would have been wise to take my advice, Miss Carmichael."

"Who *is* this?" Basia interrupted, her eyes riveted on the gun in Bouker's hand.

"Basia, meet Rashid Bouker, military attaché of the Yemeni Embassy in Washington," I said.

"Yemen!" Basia exclaimed. "Wait. Isn't that Al-Naddi guy from Yemen?"

"Samir Al-Naddi is scum. His name should not be mentioned in the same sentence as my country," Bouker growled.

"Look, we know about Al-Naddi's DNA switch," I told Bouker matter-of-factly. "I also know you're under direct orders from your president to extinguish Al-Naddi in all his forms, including his clones. You're the one killing the surrogate mothers."

Bouker looked at me in astonishment. "You know about the switch?" he said, searching my expression as if he could figure out where I'd discovered that. "How?"

"Hard work, sweat, blood and tears," I said, shrugging. "It's the American way."

"You mean *your* government is the one killing the surrogate mothers?" Basia asked, stabbing her finger at Bouker's chest, seemingly forgetting that he still held a revolver pointed at us. "Why?"

Bouker's eyes narrowed. "Al-Naddi, the scourge of Yemen, is trying to replicate himself. He, in all his forms, must be utterly extinguished."

"Those women were innocent, for God's sake!" Basia said angrily. "Not a single one of them knew they were carrying Al-Naddi's clone."

"It's unfortunate, but all loose ends that lead to Al-Naddi must be permanently eliminated."

"That's just nuts," I yelled. "And *you're* nuts, too. Haven't you read any of the scientific literature on cloning? Children are molded not only by DNA, but also by environment, education and upbringing. Be realistic here. No one lives twice. Not even some psycho terrorist."

"Do you really care to test that theory with the clone of Al-Naddi?" he asked.

I didn't, but I wasn't going to concede that point just now. "I am confident enough that Judyta Taszynski would not raise another Al-Naddi," I said, raising my chin.

"And if Al-Naddi's followers ever get their hands on the baby?" Bouker asked grimly. "How will his education, upbringing and environment be any different than that of his father?"

"They won't find her or the baby," I said with a conviction I didn't feel.

"Yes, they will," he countered, his voice chillingly cold. "You cannot hide her forever. As long as Judyta Taszynski is alive, they will find that baby."

"I don't care. I'm not going to let you kill her," I said firmly.

Bouker stared at me for a long moment and then his voice softened. "I know the executions seem a harsh step, but trust me, in the end we will have saved many, many more lives. Perhaps even American ones. We must balance the good of the whole against the needs of a few."

Basia slapped Bouker hard across the face. The crack of her open palm hitting his cheek stunned both Bouker and me because for a moment, we just stared open-mouthed at her.

"Bastard," she hissed at him. "Don't you *dare* try to justify murder to me."

Bouker frowned and for a moment, I thought he might hit her back. Then his eyes narrowed into tiny slits. "Are you dumb, woman? I am holding a gun to your heart."

"You won't shoot me, because I'm the only person who has exactly what you want," she said hotly.

Bouker nodded and then turned the gun on me. "True. But I could shoot her."

I gulped. "Okay, let's all calm down. You're here, Bouker, because I fed you a tip. In minutes, if not seconds, the rest of the players who received similar tips will arrive. Then we'll all talk. Peacefully."

At least, I sincerely hoped so. I glanced at my watch. What the hell was taking Slash, the surveillance team, MI-6, the Swedish authorities and whoever else had decided to crash the party so damn long to show up? I couldn't have been *that* good at evading all of them. Or had I? If they didn't show up soon, I was in real deep kimchee. I had counted on them to protect Basia and me.

"You're a fool," Bouker said to me. "I have no intention of waiting for anyone else to show up. Do you think I came here without a plan of my own?"

He grabbed Basia by the shoulder, hauling her up from the bench. He slid the gun under his windbreaker and pressed it into her back. "Let's move," he said.

"Now wait just a minute," I started.

"Move or I'll kill you both and take my chances," Bouker said grimly.

I came to my feet. "Where are we going?" I asked, trying to stall as he pushed us ahead of him.

"Just move."

My mind raced as we walked around the back of the museum and headed down the sidewalk. I couldn't figure out what had gone so wrong with the plan. Slash and the surveillance team should have spotted me long ago. In fact, when Bouker appeared, they should have immediately made their move, if for no other reason than to protect me and Basia—their only link to Judyta.

So, where the hell were they?

As we moved toward the tram stop, I glanced around. There were very few people walking about now and no one gave us a second glance. Nervously I looked up and noticed a glint coming from the branches of a tree. I frowned, wondering why metal would be in trees, when the answer hit me like a punch in the stomach.

Slash and the others weren't still looking for me. Oh, they'd found me all right. They were up in the trees, probably on top of the museum, in fact, likely everywhere, waiting. But waiting for *what?* Well, whatever it was, I sure hoped they got to it soon because things were going downhill a lot faster than I expected.

As the three of us approached the street, a white van suddenly pulled up in front of us and screeched to a halt. The side of the van had black-and-red lettering that said *Nordiska Museet.*

"Uh, oh," I said. "I don't like the looks of this."

"Get in," Bouker said, pushing us forward as the side door slid open.

I hesitated. "Um, did I mention I get carsick in vans?"

"Don't argue with me, Ms. Carmichael. You're expendable."

"Well, if you put it like that," I said and started to climb in.

Before I could get in, I heard a loud crack. I flinched on reflex and then understanding dawned. The crack was a single report and I'd been shot.

I clutched my abdomen, but when my hand came away there was no blood, no nothing. In fact, I couldn't feel anything, not pain, heat or cold.

Just then Rashid Bouker staggered forward and fell into my arms, causing me to lurch backwards into the rear fender of the white van, holding onto him as if we were dancing. I smelled the scent of blood and realized it was Bouker, not me, who had been shot.

Basia had apparently been as stunned as I and started screaming as two armed figures jumped from the van.

One was a tall, thin man with a black mustache, and the other a slender, pretty, dark-haired woman. Basia started to run, but the man caught her by the back of her blouse and hauled her into his arms. The grim-faced woman yanked Bouker from my grasp and pushed him to the ground. Then she grabbed me by the fleshy part of my upper arm, trying to pull me into the van.

I resisted, kicking and shouting at the top of my lungs. In the distance I saw a dark figure run up behind the man holding Basia and tackle him, sending all three crashing to the ground in a tangle of flailing limbs. The gun flew from the tall man's hand and landed on the ground a few feet away.

"Elvis!" I shrieked when I saw the black trench coat and realized who was trying to save us. "He has a gun!"

The woman holding me was temporarily distracted, so I used the moment to shift my weight and smash my elbow into her face as hard as I could. Blood spurted from her nose as I slid my hand out of my sling and grappled for the gun, trying to point it away from me. I managed to force her arm above her head, and she accidentally discharged the weapon. She snarled and tried to bite me, so I slammed her into the van, using my weight as a weapon.

She head-butted me hard in the face and I felt my nose crack. But I hung on as she twisted her body and together we fell to the ground, still fighting for control of the gun. As we rolled around on the pavement, I saw out of the corner of my eye that Elvis was in big trouble. The tall man was seconds from recovering his gun, although Elvis desperately held on to his leg, using all of his geeky one hundred and thirty-five pounds to keep him from moving. Basia sat in dazed shock on the pavement, undoubtedly paralyzed with terror.

In the meantime, the dark-haired woman had rolled

me onto my back and started screaming at me in what
sounded like Italian. My strength was quickly ebbing and
I wasn't certain I'd be able to hold on to her wrist with
the gun much longer. She kneed me twice in the stomach
and despite my determination, my grip began to loosen.
Grunting, she finally wrenched her wrist free and lifted
the gun. Just before pulling the trigger, her head seemed
to explode and she fell over on top of me, the gun falling
from her fingers to the ground. I screamed and frantically
tried to push her off me. Gasping for breath, I rolled to the
side just in time to see the tall man aiming his gun at Elvis.

"No!" I shrieked.

Seemingly from nowhere, a man sailed through the air
in front of Elvis just as the gun was fired. The man took
the bullet square in the chest and fell hard to the ground.
Then another crack sounded and the tall man aiming the
gun at Elvis abruptly fell forward toward Basia, his arms
outstretched. Basia screamed and crawled toward Elvis,
where he lay on the ground. His trench coat was torn and
the fedora nowhere in sight. Sobbing, Basia reached him
and he rose to his knees, pulling her into his arms. Then,
to my astonishment, the man who had taken the bullet in
the chest for Elvis sat up, drew a gun and knelt over the
fallen man.

Suddenly dozens of people materialized out of nowhere,
sirens were wailing and everyone was shouting and running. My strength was completely gone, so I lay on the
hot pavement, panting for breath, covered in the blood and
gore of the woman who still lay half on top of me.

People were issuing orders in several different languages and the acrid smell of gunsmoke burned my lungs.
I felt like coughing but wasn't even sure I could draw
enough air into my lungs to make the effort worthwhile.
My eyes were blurry with tears, my nose throbbed, and

the pain in my wrist felt like sheer agony. I was pretty sure my wrist had been completely broken this time, and maybe my nose and a couple of ribs along with it. Still, I guess it was better than a bullet to the brain.

The man who had protected Elvis walked over and knelt down on the pavement beside me, pushing the woman's body off with a contemptible grunt. He gently smoothed the hair off my face and slid a steady hand under my head, lifting it up.

I got my first good look at his face as he asked, "Are you okay, *cara?*"

EIGHTEEN

My ANSWER WAS to turn my head to the side and throw up. I couldn't stop until I had nothing but dry heaves. Each contraction of my stomach sent an unbearable pain through my wrist and nose, and when I finished I lay back panting in exhaustion. Slash stayed with me the whole time, murmuring comforting words to me in English and Italian, wiping my mouth and face with a soft cloth. I heard him call for a medic and some water and soon I felt a cup being pressed against my lips. I greedily drank a few sips.

"What the hell took you so long?" I finally managed to croak.

Slash was dressed in fatigues, a dark T-shirt and heavy black vest. A pistol rested against his boot. A variety of ropes, knives and other assorted tools hung from a thick belt around his waist.

"Sorry," he said, helping me into a sitting position and handing me a cloth to press to my bloody nose. "Things didn't go exactly as we had expected."

"Tell me about it."

"We had marksmen in place, but you were in too close proximity to shoot them safely."

"Well, next time do me a favor and take your chances."

"Are you injured anywhere?" he asked, his hands slipping across my chest, abdomen and legs, gently feeling, searching and pressing.

"Are you asking that just so you can cop a feel?"

He smiled. "Maybe."

"No, I don't think I'm shot anywhere. But I'm pretty sure my wrist is broken and maybe some ribs. Something happened to my nose. It feels squashed. I think there's gore in my hair. But I'm not complaining. I'm alive."

He leaned over and lightly pressed a kiss against my cheek. "You are one damn lucky lady. So, this was your plan, *cara?*" he asked, waving his hand across the bloody scene.

"Actually, no. I had envisioned a lot more civilized talking and a lot less shooting."

He clucked his tongue softly. "I told you no heroics. You did not listen to me."

"Hey, I didn't plan on the heroic part. It would have worked out a lot better if people would have acted the way I expected."

"Rule number one in undercover operations—expect the unexpected. People are not computers, *cara*. They will, more often than not, act illogically."

I sighed. "I calculated a twenty percentage margin of error on that. Note to self, next time, make it fifty percent. Slash, I know about Al-Naddi's clone. It would have been helpful if you had clued me in earlier."

"I didn't *know* earlier. Things happened more quickly than we expected. I knew you'd try something, but I didn't think it would be something quite so bold. You forced us all into action."

"That was the idea."

"Well I admit it was a clever move, bringing in Bouker. That all but guaranteed we'd see Al-Naddi here."

"Is that him?" I asked, looking over at body of the tall, mustached man who had almost killed Elvis. "Mr. Super-terrorist himself, Samir Al-Naddi?"

"*Si.* We'll do DNA tests to make sure, but I'm certain that it is, indeed, him."

He didn't look so threatening lying there on the ground, his arms still stretched out in front of him. Still, I sensed evil and shivered.

"Is he dead?"

"*Si*. A single shot to the head."

I turned away, feeling sick to my stomach again. I wondered if I'd ever feel normal again. Just then a guy dressed in fatigues similar to Slash's walked over to us. He had a buzz haircut, a gun and a weapon's belt identical to the one Slash wore.

"Nice work, Agent Carmichael," he said to me. "Are you all right?"

"*Agent* Carmichael?" I repeated with a raised eyebrow, looking at Slash.

"Consider it a field promotion," he said, his lips twitching slightly.

I shook my head and it hurt. "Who are you?" I asked the other guy in my scratchy voice.

"Agent Russo," he said, straightening. "I'm in charge of this operation."

"What operation?"

"Operation Rebirth."

"And that would be?"

"The shutting down of CGM's cloning operation and the capture or deaths of two of the world's most-wanted terrorists, Samir Al-Naddi and his first lieutenant, Alessia D'Agostino."

"Is that D'Agostino?" I asked, pointing to the woman's body, which was now surrounded by medics and what looked like military photographers.

"Si," Slash replied. "We think D'Agostino masterminded the hit on Mashir Al-Asan's bodyguards in Genoa."

"Is she Italian?" I asked. "Because I'm pretty sure she was screaming at me in Italian."

"Her father was an Italian diplomat, her mother an Arab," Russo explained. "She became involved in Al-Naddi's cause during a tour her father had in Yemen when she was just a teenager."

"She served Al-Naddi's cause in many ways," Slash continued. "Besides being his lover, she also ran his terrorist network out of Europe."

"Is she dead, too?" I suppressed a shiver.

Slash nodded. "We would have preferred to take her alive, but we had no choice."

"She would have killed me."

"Si."

"What about Bouker?"

"He's still alive, but just barely. The other two Yemeni agents who accompanied him are dead. Al-Naddi and D'Agostino killed them and hijacked the van."

"So Bouker was expecting his people in the van, but instead he got Al-Naddi's," I said.

"That's right," Russo said. "Bouker had also secured a boat for escape, but we had it covered. We waited because we were hoping Al-Naddi would show before we moved in on Bouker. However we hadn't expected him to be in the van, so that took us a bit by surprise."

"A bit?" I repeated. "That *bit* of surprise nearly cost us our lives."

Agent Russo held up his hands. "At least it turned out all right."

I looked around at the dead and injured people and wondered just how he had come to that conclusion. Slash was right. People were too unpredictable, which is probably why I sucked at social skills, and apparently by extension, covert operations. Give me computers, algorithms and logic, and I shined. Give me people, and I couldn't talk my way out of a paper bag.

I folded the cloth and pressed it to a fresh spot on my nose. Looking around, I saw Basia and Elvis were being treated by medics. "Are they okay?" I asked Slash.

"*Si,* they are shaken, but alive. You have very brave friends, *cara.*"

"They're the best. And speaking of friends, you took a bullet for Elvis."

He shrugged. "I was wearing a bullet-proof vest." He unfastened it and pulled it off, dropping it to the ground. He gingerly rubbed his ribs. "I will be sore for a few days."

"Jeez, Slash. What if they were using armor-penetrating bullets? What if he had shot at your head instead?"

He reached under his shirt and pulled out the tiny gold cross from around his neck. "Ah, *cara.* Your concern touches me deeply," he said, taking my hand and pressing it to his heart. "But you shouldn't have worried. I had someone else looking out for me, as well." He kissed the cross and tucked it back inside his shirt.

I smiled in spite of myself and then saw that Basia and Elvis were being helped to their feet. Once upright, they limped toward me, Elvis with an arm thrown around Basia's shoulders. Basia's face was smeared with dirt and grass and her hair stood straight up on the left side of her head. Elvis had lost the trench coat and his mouth was bloody and swollen. I didn't want to even *think* about how I looked.

"Who are all these people and what's going on?" Basia asked me, coughing. "Is this part of the plan? And what are *you* doing here?" she asked Elvis.

"Trying to save both of you," he said. "And apparently not doing a very good job of it."

Using Slash's steady hand to support myself, I stood up, wobbled toward Elvis and gave him a one-armed hug.

"You are my hero," I said. "Next time you don't have to play secret agent to impress me."

"Me either," Basia said, giving him a slurpy kiss on the cheek. "You are one fab guy."

Elvis flushed, looking pleased, but said nothing.

"Oh, that reminds me, you owe Xavier a date," I said to Basia.

Basia nodded, nothing seeming to faze her now. "I can see there's a lot more to this story than meets the eye."

"You have no freaking idea."

"Um, sorry to interrupt this happy little reunion, but there are still important matters to attend to," Agent Russo interrupted.

"Who *are* you people?" Basia asked. "Is anyone ready to tell me just what the hell is going on?"

"Basia, this is Agent Russo and Agent… Slash," I said. "They're from the U.S. government."

"We need to know the whereabouts of Judyta Taszynski," Russo said.

To my surprise, Basia put her hands on her hips and got right in Agent Russo's face. All five feet two inches of her.

"For what purpose does the U.S. government need to find Judyta Taszynski?" she asked. She sounded pretty cranky and I didn't blame her after all we'd just been through.

"I'm sorry, ma'am, but I'm not at liberty to say."

"Look, Agent Russo," she said. "Either you start enlightening us or you get *nada*. We'll all just go our separate ways."

Russo looked offended. "You've got to be joking. I'm an agent of the U.S. government."

"I know who you are," Basia retorted. "Now you know who I am. Start talking and make it fast."

Russo glanced over at Slash who stood saying nothing,

his arms crossed against his chest in an almost yoga-like calm and his expression inscrutable.

"Look, all we need is some information here," I said to Russo. "What do you intend to do with Ms. Taszynski and her baby once you find them?"

"You have my word that Ms. Taszynski will not be harmed," Russo promised.

"What about the baby?" Elvis asked.

"It's not *her* baby," Russo said. "It's Al-Naddi's clone."

"It's *her* baby to her," I said. "What do you intend to do with the infant?"

Agent Russo had the grace to look uncomfortable. "It will be dealt with discreetly and properly by the U.S. government."

"The baby is not an *it,*" I said, folding my arms against my chest like Slash. "No."

"No?" Russo said, quite shocked. "No, what?"

"Judyta Taszynski wants to keep the baby."

"Impossible!" Russo exclaimed. "Look, we can get her another one."

I looked at Basia. "Did he really say that?"

"I'm afraid so," she answered.

"Do I need to spell it out, Russo?" I said. "Judyta wants to keep her baby. She won't care that he's a clone of a now-defunct terrorist. Figure out a way to make it happen."

"Have you all lost your minds?" Russo gasped, clearly aghast. "You should all realize that by withholding her whereabouts you are interfering in a matter of national security."

"We're talking about a baby, not a bomb," I said calmly. "Besides, Judyta has already had the baby and they've bonded."

Russo looked as though I had smashed a fist in his stomach. His mouth opened like a fish on a hook and he clutched his chest, gasping for air. He looked young and fit, so I sure hoped he didn't have a heart attack. Causing one heart attack a week was my limit.

"Oh," he breathed. "Is it normal?"

"The baby is a he, but does it make a difference?" I snapped. "You're not taking her baby."

"Well, I guess this changes things," Russo said between gritted teeth. "What do you want?"

I had my answer ready and could now only pray it would work. My heart thumped painfully against my chest as I faced the moment of truth.

"Witness protection for Judyta and the baby," I said in a surprisingly calm voice. "A new identity, a new place to live and a decent stipend for both of them. Leave her and the baby alone. No scientists hovering about, no weird examinations, no press conferences and no harassment. In return, she will promise to keep the true identity of the baby and its unusual conception under wraps forever." I looked over at Basia to see if she thought Judyta would agree to the plan and was relieved when she smiled at me.

"Are you crazy?" Russo exclaimed. "I can't agree to that."

"Well, that's the deal. Take it or leave it."

"If I don't deal?"

"Judyta and the baby disappear."

"We'll find her."

"First? Maybe, maybe not. We all know there are others looking for her. Are you willing to risk failure, Agent Russo? This way you're guaranteed to have Judyta's cooperation and have the ability to keep her and the baby under tabs."

"I don't think you understand what you're asking," Russo seethed. "Or who you're dealing with."

I put my good hand on my hip and got right in his face.

"Either show me you can make the deal or we'll go elsewhere to ensure Judyta's and the baby's protection."

I was bluffing like an SOB but glowered at Russo like I meant it. From the expression on his face, I figured he was supremely worried that his promotion was on the line if he screwed this up.

We stared at each other fiercely until Slash broke the silence. "Give her the deal, Russo."

Russo blinked in surprise and then turned his glare on Slash. "Have you lost it, too? Can't you see she's blackmailing us?"

"She's protecting her friends. But more importantly, she's right. Al-Naddi is dead and no one else needs to know Judyta Taszynski successfully gave birth to a cloned child. If needed, we can issue disinformation that the infant and mother died during birth. The deal is a fair one. Give it to her."

"You know I'm not authorized," Russo protested.

"Then get the authorization," Slash said simply.

Russo glared at me for another minute and then stepped away and began talking rapidly in a cell phone.

Basia gave me a quick hug. I winced at the pressure on my ribs. "So, um, who is he again?" she asked, pointing to Slash.

"His name is Slash," I said. "Slash, meet Basia."

"Slash?" she repeated. "Is that your real name?"

Smoothly sidestepping the question, Slash reached out and took her hand in his. "Basia Kowalski," he said in his deep sexy voice. "We meet at last. You're as enchanting as I expected. The pleasure is all mine."

He pressed his lips to her hand and I heard Basia inhale a sharp breath. When Slash looked away, she raised an eyebrow and fanned herself.

Elvis stepped forward and thrust out his hand. ".You saved my life, dude," he said to Slash. "I owe you."

Slash shook his head. "Actually, it is in the reverse. It is I who am indebted and I'm not a man who forgets his debts. You and your brother are not only brilliant but courageous, as well. We wouldn't have been able to break into Acheron without you. I sincerely hope that we shall have many more opportunities to work together."

Just then a medic walked up to Elvis. "I'd like to look at your leg, sir," he said, leading Elvis to a nearby bench as Agent Russo returned.

"All right, we'll deal," he said and tossed a cell phone to Basia. "But first call Miss Taszynski and confirm she'll agree to the plan."

Basia smiled sweetly. "Thanks, but I'll get the message to her in my own way and *after* I have the deal in writing, recorded *and* double-checked by my lawyer."

"Nice touch," I said admiringly.

Russo actually looked worried. "Well, there are some additional details we'll need to hammer out," he started and the two of them began talking. Basia could take it from here, and I really needed to sit down, so I walked a few steps to a bench and collapsed.

Slash joined me, moving a long knife out of his way so he could sit comfortably. He didn't speak to me, just sat there looking sexy, dangerous and oddly amused.

"So, just who are you anyway?" I finally asked. "You do a hell of a lot of dangerous stuff for a computer hacker slash national treasure."

"Actually, I am starting to think that perhaps you wish to usurp my position," he said with a hint of a smile. "You pretty much single-handedly plotted an operation that eliminated two of the world's most dangerous terrorists and shut down a human reproductive cloning site."

"I had a lot of help, you know. And nice try at avoiding my question. Who are you, really? You don't look or act like any computer hacker I've ever known."

He chuckled. "Consider me a man of the new millennium."

"Nice image. When did you figure out what I was trying to do?"

"When you tipped off Bouker. We were watching him and knew the only way he would have figured out you were headed for Sweden was that he'd gotten a tip from the inside. But *we* knew you were headed for Sweden long before you disappeared. You knew that, though, didn't you, *cara?* You planned a gathering of all the interested parties—quite an intriguing idea. We had to scramble to change our operational plans once we finally figured out what you had in mind."

"Yes," I said simply. "I knew you'd come and bring the posse. The twins and I also guessed you'd probably use me as bait for luring Al-Naddi to the gathering."

Slash shook his head in disbelief. "It was a bold move for a woman like you—untrained and untested. You took us by surprise in many ways, *cara*. We never thought you'd purposely lose your FBI tail and run. We also hadn't counted on Harry Jorrell following you and nearly kidnapping you out from under our noses. Luckily Shaughnessy was on assignment tailing Jorrell and managed to salvage what could have been an operational catastrophe."

I felt my insides tighten at the mention of Finn's name. His deception still hurt like a fresh wound and I didn't have the strength to face it now.

"So Jorrell didn't work for you," I said, trying to keep my voice neutral.

"No, he worked for CGM just like Shaughnessy told

you. They wanted to find Judyta as much as we did. And you were their only lead, as well."

"Did you know it was Jorrell who tried to kill me in front of the disco club?"

Slash nodded. "We figured. Better dead than leading us to Judyta."

I sighed. "Great. I supposed it helped that Finn conveniently kept you informed as to my whereabouts until I put him out of play at the hotel. What were his orders?"

"He was to watch your back. Protect you from exactly what just happened." Slash touched my shoulder gently. "That was my job until you bolted. I'm glad you were not hurt worse, *cara*. Shaughnessy was foolish to let his guard down. You should have trusted me. Unlike him, I would have never allowed anyone to harm you."

"Um, speaking of Finn, he's back at the hotel in a sort of compromising situation."

"Not anymore. Might I say, the handcuffs were a naughty touch."

I lifted an eyebrow. "I presume that means he got loose."

"As soon as you lost your surveillance teams here, we sent someone to the hotel to check on Shaughnessy. That's when we found him handcuffed to the bed, red-faced and quite angry with you."

I felt a savage bit of satisfaction. "Did the NSA recruit him to contact me?"

Slash shook his head. "He'd been recruited by MI-6 long before you came on to the scene. In fact, we had no idea MI-6 had any interest in the cloning operation until Shaughnessy contacted you and we started digging. MI-6 had to reveal his cover to us. Your introduction to Shaughnessy actually brought our two agencies together."

"So I was the unwitting bridge between MI-6 and the NSA?"

"Don't be angry, *cara*. We couldn't fill you in on everything and have you play the part so convincingly."

Bitter resentment rose in my throat. "What part? Oh, you mean the unsuspecting, expendable, bait part?"

His tone softened. "It wasn't like that. I was there to protect and guide you. Besides I never thought you'd strike out on your own, nor be so surprisingly good at it."

A nice thought, but they'd still used me and it seriously ticked me off. "Did you know about the DNA switch before we broke into the Acheron file?"

"No. We still hadn't figured out the connection between the hit on the bodyguards and the cloning operation. I told you the truth. More importantly, I couldn't break the encryption on the Acheron file quickly enough. Then, as if it were a gift from heaven, I received the invitation from the twins."

I looked over at Elvis. "Elvis could have been killed," I said, my heart aching. "Because of me."

Slash shook his head. "No. That responsibility would have been mine. I never expected him to follow you here."

"Me, neither."

"You seem to inspire an impassioned devotion in those whom you meet," he murmured. "Myself included."

"So that's why you decided to lie, deceive and kiss the hell out of me." It was like a knife to the heart, and I didn't want to believe it. His kiss had been so full of passion and heat, I'd been sure it had meant something to him. I shook my head. "Thanks, but that's not the kind of devotion I want."

"That kiss has nothing to do with this," he growled.

"It had *everything* to do with this. From this moment on, I don't ever, *ever* want you to mention that incident again."

He opened his mouth to say something, but I held up a hand. "Never," I insisted.

He sighed and leaned forward, resting his elbows on his knees. "I know you are angry with me now, *cara*," he said. "But I am a determined man. I *will* find a way to make it up to you."

Gently he took my good hand and lifted it to his lips. The warmth of his mouth against my skin made me jolt and I quickly snatched my hand away.

"You saved Elvis's life," I replied. "That's enough for me. Let's just call it even."

Slash shook his head. "As I told Elvis before you, I am a man who honors his debts. We're not finished yet, *cara,* and we both know it."

I didn't have the strength to argue, so I just sat back on the bench and watched the scene around me. Medics, soldiers, Swedish policemen and others walked about, talking on cell phones, taking photographs, and moving bodies into black bags and carting them away. It seemed surreal to be watching it all unfold in front of me.

"Jeez, people cloning terrorists," I said wearily. "What has the world come to?"

"I'm sorry, *cara*. Some days this business can be more than just unpleasant."

Still hurt by his and Finn's deception, I didn't answer and instead looked over at Basia and Agent Russo who were arguing fiercely. I had no doubt Basia would come out ahead, national security notwithstanding. She was smart and when her protective instincts kicked in, she was indomitable. I shifted and a hot pain sliced into my ribs. My wrist throbbed, my nose hurt like hell and the adrenaline of the past hour had started to fade, making my injuries all the more painful.

Just then a young man knelt in front of me and identified himself as a medic. "Are you injured, ma'am?" he asked.

His calling me "ma'am" was enough to make me experience severe emotional distress, but I just sighed. "My wrist, my nose and possibly my ribs."

"If you'll come with me, I'll take a look at them."

Slash helped me to my feet. He put an arm lightly around my shoulder and said, "You've proven yourself a valuable asset. Would you believe me if I told you that you could probably name your heart's desire? A promotion in the NSA's InfoSec Department? A move to covert operations?"

I turned to look at him. "Seriously? Whatever I want?"

"Name your heart's desire."

"What I really want is for Agent Russo to hold up his end of the bargain with Judyta. No funny stuff. Can you promise me he'll do that?"

Slash smiled. "Right now, *cara,* I'd promise you the world. I will personally oversee the bargain. You have my word on it. Trust me?"

He leaned over to kiss me, but I turned my head and his lips brushed my hair instead. He sighed and I turned my face toward his. I hadn't expected him to look so sad. Sighing, I reached up and touched his cheek. "For once, Slash, I think I actually do."

NINETEEN

THE GOOD OLD American sun streamed through my window as I woke. It was nice to be home again in safe, boring Jessup, Maryland and not have to worry about things like thugs, psychos and terrorists singling me out for target practice.

I got out of bed, showered and dressed in jean shorts, a white blouse and sandals. I rewrapped the soft new bandage around my sprained wrist like the doctor had shown me, glad to see the swelling had subsided. My nose was broken, though, and I had two shiners and a strip of white tape across the purple bridge to show for it.

Although I'd been back in the States for just under a week, I slept most of the time, with small waking periods to surf the net, eat and watch the news on television. I also visited several times with my frantic parents, my brothers, the twins and Jan. This morning I planned to take a trip to the mall and pick up a few thank-you presents for Jan, Jamie and the twins. Friends don't forget about friends. Especially those who come through in desperate times of need.

The sudden absence of sexy and daring men in my life was a bigger letdown than I'd expected. Now that all the danger and life-threatening moments were over I was back to being plain, old, ordinary me. The excitement I'd experienced during the past week seemed to have been little more than a temporary fantasy, heightened by the ever-present threat of death. Perhaps without the drama and danger clouding their vision, I wasn't that appealing to men.

At least I still had my job at the NSA. Despite what I considered a near-disastrous debacle in Stockholm, Slash had been right about the higher-ups considering my actions favorably. Director Thompson of the NSA had personally sent a flower arrangement to congratulate me. My boss had called three times and left messages telling me to take as much time off as I needed. Even more bizarre, I'd been told that the president would call me today at three-thirty sharp. I had inquired just which president we were talking about, but his secretary apparently thought I was joking and got a good laugh out of it.

I knew full well it was a tactic to smooth over the fact that the NSA, FBI, CIA and assorted other agencies had somewhat bungled the job and they wanted to ensure my everlasting goodwill and cooperation in regards to the operation.

Whatever.

There was no getting around the fact that my life had been changed irrevocably. What had once been a stable, boring and mathematically predictable existence had been altered forever. It scared the beejeebies out of me because I'd had a taste of exotic field work and now it was in my blood. What would that mean to my future?

During my debrief on the plane back to the States, I was told that my involvement in Operation Rebirth, and that of the NSA, MI-6 and other assorted U.S. government agencies, was to be considered top secret. No details of the operation were to be released to the media. The NSA Office of Public Affairs would handle any related inquiries.

Basically it was a lot of legal mumbo jumbo, which meant I had to keep my mouth shut around my journalist brother. On the up side, it wasn't national news so I didn't have to contend with television crews camped out in front of my apartment or media requests for interviews.

The press still had a field day exposing CGM and Bright Horizons for the cloning debacle. My big brother was at the forefront. His front-page article for the *Richmond Gazette* broke the story and it had been picked up by all the national and international media outlets. Although I'd been sworn to secrecy on the terrorist connection and would never be able to fill Rock in on that particular angle, I figured the cloning scandal alone would win him a slew of prestigious prizes and perhaps that coveted job at *The Washington Post*.

Not surprisingly, I didn't see a thing in the paper, in the news or on the internet about the terrorist shoot-out on Djurgarden Island and I wondered how the FBI and Homeland Security would eventually handle announcing the deaths of the terrorist leaders Samir Al-Naddi and Alessia D'Agostino to the world.

I strolled into the kitchen and ate a banana for breakfast before downing some ibuprofen and heading out to my car. I stopped cold when I saw Finn Shaughnessy in the parking lot, sitting in a black Corvette convertible and drinking coffee from a Dunkin' Donuts cup. He was dressed in a baby-blue T-shirt stretched tight against his chest, jeans and dark shades. My mouth started to salivate and I wasn't sure if it was because of Finn, the donuts or the coffee.

"Glad to see you got free of the handcuffs," I said, trying to be as nonchalant as possible.

He tipped his cup to me in a salute. "It wasn't easy. In fact, if you must know, it was bloody humiliating. I let my guard down around you and it was a mistake."

"A mistake you won't ever have to worry about making again." I eyed the Corvette. "New car?"

"It's a rental until I can retrieve mine from the airport in Toronto."

"Oh, and don't forget to retrieve the guns from the locker in Buffalo," I reminded him. "I'd imagine MI-6 doesn't look too fondly on agents who lose their weapons."

Finn sighed and then leaned over and opened the passenger side door. "Contrary to popular belief, not everything I said to you was a lie. Get in, Lexi. I owe you an explanation."

"You don't owe me anything," I said tightly.

"Please, I want to talk to you and you haven't been taking my calls."

"Why should I? The operation is over. We've been debriefed and are now free to go our separate ways."

He reached into the car and held up another cup of coffee and a chocolate-covered donut with sprinkles. "I bought it for you."

I rolled my eyes. "Oh, please. Do you really think you can coerce me with a cup of coffee and a chocolate donut?"

"How about two donuts?" he said, holding up another one.

I eyed the donuts and then the coffee and hated myself because I felt my resolve vanish in a swirl of chocolate glaze.

"Well, I guess it wouldn't hurt to listen," I said, climbing into the car and sitting down. Finn handed me a napkin and one of the donuts.

"I like the new look." He gestured toward my two shiners.

I bit into the donut. "At least I don't need to wear mascara to make my eyes pop. Now you've got my full attention, so say whatever you want to say and make it snappy."

He let out a breath. "All right. You were right to trust your instincts about me. I wasn't telling you the entire story about my involvement in the case. But it's not as sinister as you think."

"I'm thinking pretty sinister."

He sighed. "I was already working at CGM when MI-6 recruited me through my father. As you may have guessed, he's rather well connected. MI-6 had become suspicious of a double hit in Genoa several months earlier and believed it was somehow connected to Al-Naddi's terrorist group. He had a pretty active cell in Italy and MI-6 didn't like the look of the murders. But what in the hell was the group doing killing the bodyguards of a member of the Saudi royal family? MI-6 started sniffing around and found out Al-Asan was in Italy to visit the Bright Horizons clinic. When they started investigating Bright Horizons they became suspicious of how the company managed to so quickly pull itself out of imminent bankruptcy."

"And you figured in how?"

"MI-6 smelled something rotten and wanted someone on the inside to check it out for them. When they told me CGM was possibly involved in reproductive human cloning, I was pretty damn shocked."

I took a sip of my coffee and closed my eyes. It was heaven in a cup. "Pretty brazen of MI-6 to just spill the beans like that," I said. "What if you were in on the whole thing?"

Finn shrugged. "They took a risk, yes. But it paid off for them. I wasn't involved."

"I see. So just like that, you graciously agreed to spy on CGM."

"Hell, no!" Finn exploded. "Do you think I even believed it at first? I was offended, dazed. Human cloning at the company where I worked? It was bloody unthinkable. I had no reason to suspect it was true, and besides, it's not like I implicitly trust what MI-6 says. I am Irish after all."

"But you didn't tell your bosses at CGM of MI-6's suspicions."

"Not right away. I decided to poke around, just for my own peace of mind. My colleague Harold Small had been acting strangely, so I befriended him to see if he'd tell me anything of interest. He never did reveal anything, but in the end, he left me the smoking gun in his safety deposit box."

"The contract. So why didn't you run with it to MI-6?"

"Because I couldn't read it. It could have been harmless and I would have looked like a bloody idiot. I needed it translated. I ended up being in hot water for not taking it to agency translators to start with, but I wasn't a trained agent, so what could they do?"

"You gave the contract to Basia."

"Yes. She'd done translation work for the firm before, so it seemed a natural choice. But a few days later when she disappeared along with the contract, I knew something was very wrong."

"That's when I entered the picture."

"Yes. I was desperate to find her. I hoped at the very least you could give me a lead on her whereabouts."

I took another sip of coffee and stared out the front windshield. Mrs. Wolansky was walking her dog like she did every morning precisely at nine o'clock. She saw me sitting in the convertible and waved cheerfully. I waved back, but not so cheerfully. In a way, a part of me mourned for the days when I'd lived my life in blissful ignorance of stomach-churning realities like human cloning, terrorist shoot-outs and people using me for their own gain.

"So, when did you tell MI-6 about Basia and the missing contract?"

"After you gave me the CD. I passed it on to MI-6 to make sure what was on it. They analyzed it and realized at once it was the work of the NSA. MI-6 immediately contacted the agency and was told an operation was already in progress."

"Gee, why am I always the last to know these things?"

"Well, they figured the NSA was working you blind. In a way, I was working blind, too. I had very little information to go on. After all, I wasn't a real agent, just a recruited one. I didn't know how Al-Naddi's group figured and I certainly had no idea that young women were being murdered."

"They let us muddle along together."

"Yes, and in a way, we played right into their hands. They needed you to get the cooperation of the Zimmerman twins to come up with a bloody brilliant hack to get into CGM's files, and me on the inside to plant it."

It still hurt to hear that, especially because I had not only allowed myself to be used, but the twins, too. "And once that was accomplished, they decided it would be helpful to use me as terrorist bait."

Finn ran his fingers through his hair. "It looks that way now, doesn't it? Truthfully, they're just bloody happy that they got what they wanted, which was to shut down the cloning operation and nab Al-Naddi and his lieutenant. Then, as an added bonus, we also came out of this alive somehow. Hurrah for the home team and all that."

"If this was such a delicate matter, why did they let you handle me?" I asked. "Why didn't they pass me off to a more experienced agent? Or did you tell them you're good at handling women?" I hadn't intended to say that, but I had, and now it lay between us.

He literally winced. "Ouch. I guess I deserved that. By no means was I their first choice, Lexi. But events were moving quickly and they thought I could manage you because we seemed to be in this together. We *were* in it together. But just in case, the Americans said they had another man on the inside to guide you. You never mentioned anyone else, though, unless it was one of the Zimmerman twins."

"It wasn't," I said glumly. It was Slash. They'd surrounded me, an ordinary, predictable, not-so-pretty math major, with handsome, dashing men, hoping I'd fall for at least one of them and spill my guts. In fact, I'd fallen for both of them, and in the end neither had been trustworthy. I guess it was a lesson well learned.

I closed my eyes and leaned back against the headrest. "You saved me from Harry Jorrell. Was that a set-up, too? To get me to trust you more?"

"No bloody way!" he exclaimed. "If you must know, that fiasco took me ten years closer to my grave. Your surveillance was left to the FBI, who thought you were an easy mark. Only they mucked it up royally. Everyone underestimated you, including me. No one considered you'd risk your job at the NSA to try to rescue Basia alone. It was truly a stroke of luck that I happened to be watching Jorrell. It was doubly good fortune the bloke had a heart attack before he could kill us or I had to shoot him."

"How did the NSA or MI-6 eventually make the connection between Al-Naddi and CGM?" The NSA had been stingy with details and I hoped to get more information out of Finn.

"The CIA was pretty sure the hit in Genoa was the work of Al-Naddi's followers. But they wasted a lot of time trying to connect Al-Naddi to Al-Asan and the Saudi royal family."

"When the only connection was that Al-Naddi switched his DNA with that of Al-Asan to get himself some clones free of charge," I mused. "Macabre, but pretty ingenious."

"Bloody disgusting, in my opinion."

"Yeah, in mine, too." Having lost my appetite, I set the chocolate donut aside and wiped my mouth with a napkin.

"The break came when the young women supposedly impregnated by Al-Asan started showing up dead," Finn continued. "One of the hits was on a young British citizen, Sarah Cunningham, who was one of Al-Asan's volunteers for what she thought was a surrogate pregnancy. Her murder and that of the other women were professional hits, but it was puzzling because MI-6 was convinced those murders were *not* the work of Al-Naddi's followers. That's when they started to take a completely different look at the events."

"It was Bouker and his Yemeni agents conducting the hits," I said. "They somehow found out about the cloning and that Al-Naddi had switched DNA samples with Al-Asan. More than likely, they have their own plant among Al-Naddi's followers. Then they started eliminating the young women one by one."

"Until there was one woman left. Judyta Taszynski. And you were the only lead to find her."

"So, as we headed for Sweden, you kept MI-6, and by extension, the NSA abreast of my whereabouts." I glared at him.

He sighed and looked away. "Yes. I'm sorry I had to deceive you, Lexi. I was just trying to protect you. This was bloody rotten stuff and I didn't like the fact they were working you blind."

"Yeah, just another day at work," I scoffed. "What about Al-Asan? Did he ever find out his DNA had been hijacked?"

"Apparently he's been informed. Understandably he doesn't want word of his involvement to get out. Needless to say it would prove quite embarrassing to the Saudi royal family."

"And as a result, the U.S. and British are keeping it a secret to preserve the important and delicate ties between our three countries."

"I couldn't have said it better."

I took another sip of coffee. "What about Harry Jorrell? Did he survive his heart attack?"

"He's alive and singing to FBI agents. He'll help nail the coffin shut on CGM's cloning operation for good."

"One can only hope," I said. "But I guess we both know it's only a matter of time before some other firm starts cloning humans and this whole mess will start all over again."

"I know," Finn said wearily, pushing his fingers through his hair. "But at least we've done our part to put a stop to it for now."

I put my hand on the door handle. "Well, thanks for the explanation. I guess that ends that."

"Not quite," Finn said. "Lexi, there's something I want to say to you. But I'll be damned if I'm not as nervous as hell."

Before I could say a word, he abruptly leaned over and kissed me on the mouth. Unlike the electrifying, hungry assault I had experienced at the hotel in Sweden, this kiss was soft and tender, but just as sensual. When he lifted his mouth, I blinked in shock.

"What was that for?" I managed to say.

"It's my way of saying I'm sorry, Lexi. For everything. Will you give me another chance?"

"Finn, the gig is up. You don't have to pretend to like me anymore."

"I wasn't pretending. Not during the operation and not now. Somewhere along the line, I really fell for you."

I looked at him in disbelief. There was no way a guy

like Finn would ever really be interested in a girl like me. I should have known that from the beginning.

"Right. What does your girlfriend think about you kissing other girls?"

"What girlfriend?"

"The Finnish model with a big chest named Paulette or Claudia or something like that."

"Claudette? Claudette's last name is Hyvärinta, which in Finnish coincidentally happens to mean 'good chest' not 'big chest'. I saw her at a party last summer and someone snapped a photo of us when we both went out onto the balcony to get some air. I don't think I've even exchanged more than ten words with her."

"So you're not dating her?"

"No." Leaning over, he carefully cupped his hand around my chin. Then he smiled that dazzling smile of his and I felt my stomach get all fuzzy.

"Do you think you could forgive me?" He pushed his sunglasses to the top of his head and kissed me again. His hand gently cupped the back of my neck and his lips were achingly tender. It took me all of a nanosecond to realize if he kept doing that, I'd forgive him not only for past transgressions, but for any future ones, as well.

I was just about to fling my arms around his neck and tell him he was completely and utterly absolved when he abruptly pulled away and swore under his breath. "Shit."

"Shit?" I said, touching my lips. "Was I *that* bad a kisser?"

He rolled his eyes. "No, it's not you—there's a photographer in the trees over there. He's taking our picture."

I squinted over my shoulder at the trees and saw the sun glinting off something. "Who is it this time? The NSA, CIA or MI-6?"

"More likely the *Star Icon*."

"The *Star Icon?* What's that?"

"A tabloid. And now our pictures will likely be plastered all over Ireland."

"Oh," I said, shrugging. "Does this mean I'm going to be famous, too, at least by association?"

He laughed. "Just the back of your head, lass."

"Figures," I said, leaning back in the seat. "Look, Finn, I don't want to ruin your reputation or anything. Maybe we should think this over. After all, there is no danger, terrorists or shooting to heighten your attraction to me."

He looked at me incredulously. "I don't need terrorists or danger to heighten my attraction to you. It's been hard enough for me to keep my hands off you all this time."

"Really?" I said, feeling a little giddy.

"Yes and it's a new experience for me. I'm not used to liking a woman who has such a…sharp intellect."

"Sharp intellect?"

"Well, you were the one who said I should start hanging around geek chicks more."

"True."

"Then why do you sound disappointed?"

"I'm not. Not really. A part of me hoped that you wanted me not only for my brains, but for my body."

His mouth curved into a smile. "Didn't I mention the part about being barely able to keep my hands off you?"

"Actually, you did," I said, feeling happier than I had in days. "You know, this is all new for me, too."

"How so?"

"Well for starters, I never had my picture taken kissing someone quasi-famous before."

Finn looked amused. "Quasi-famous? I like that. So, how was it?"

"How was what?"

"The kiss with someone quasi-famous."

I pretended to ponder it. "Well, on a scale of one to ten, I'd rate it a fifty. Not that I want to give you a big head or anything. Keep in mind I'm not that experienced."

He laughed. "So where does this put us, Lexi?"

"Put us?"

"I'd like to take you on a real date."

"Define real."

"A date where we don't have to discuss life or death issues, including, but not limited to, terrorism, cloning or executions of any kind."

"It sounds very lawyerly."

"I figured I'd better put my best foot forward."

I smiled. "Okay. Then maybe we'll go out sometime and see where it leads."

"I can work with that."

I put my hand on the door handle and pushed down. "Well, all this kissing and date negotiating have been exhilarating, but I've got errands to run."

To my surprise, Finn reached across me and closed the door. "Wait. There's something else I've been meaning to talk to you about, Lexi. Would you mind hearing me out a wee bit more?"

I sat back against the seat, looking at him curiously. "All right. What's up?"

"Well, I have a rather interesting proposition for you."

I raised an eyebrow. "I bet you say that to all the girls. Especially after a kiss like that."

"No, not *that* kind of proposition."

"Oh," I said, trying not to sound too disappointed.

He took a deep breath and I was surprised to see he seemed nervous. That, of course, piqued my curiosity even more.

"I'm going to start my own company," he finally said.

"Law firm, you mean."

"No, I mean a cyberintelligence security firm. I've been thinking about it for a long time and it seems that now is the best time in my life to do it. I've got the start-up capital and I intend to be competitive with other firms in this area. After what just happened, I figured there is no time like the present to pursue my dream."

"A cyberintelligence security firm?" I exclaimed in shock. "But you're a lawyer, for God's sake."

"Who's always wanted to be on the cutting edge of technology. Why do you think I took all those tech classes at Georgetown? Think about it, Lexi, my background in law will come in handy for this kind of work."

I sat there stunned, not knowing what to say.

"I'd like you to be on my team," he continued in a rush. "Will you consider it?"

Somehow I found my voice. "Team?"

"Well, I'm friends with Ben Steinhouser and we've been bandying about this idea of starting our own company for some time. He's got several excellent contacts in the field and he knows some good players he could bring aboard. He's agreed to be my co-director. You've heard of Ben Steinhouser, haven't you?"

Had I heard of Ben Steinhouser?

Everyone in security intelligence knew Ben Steinhouser. He was brilliant, highly successful, revered in both hacker and InfoSec circles. He'd started off as a programmer with the very first computers and worked his way up in the private sector in computer security and cyberintelligence. He could write programs to combat computer viruses that were so superior, he'd even gained the grudging respect of most hackers.

For eighteen years he'd ruled the NSA's InfoSec Department with an iron fist. He was proud of saying there had been no intrusions under his reign, not that there hadn't been a hell of a lot of close calls. I wondered how in the world Finn had met him and what he had offered a legend like Steinhouser to lure him out of retirement.

Crap. Although I didn't want to admit it, I was dangerously intrigued by the offer.

"You should know that I just got offered a promotion," I told Finn.

"I'll double your salary," he said promptly.

Tempting. But then I thought about the note of congratulations I'd got from Director Thompson and the calls from my boss. I remembered the phone call I'd be getting from the president of the United States at three-thirty this afternoon.

"You just kissed me," I reminded him. "Not to mention the fact that I handcuffed you to a bed. How would that affect a working relationship?"

"We'd figure it out. I like a challenge. In regards to the handcuffs, I consider it an action done in the name of national security."

"Yeah, that's what I thought, too," I said. Guess I wouldn't tell him about the kinky sex fantasy.

"If you come to work for me, there will be no travel restrictions and better benefits," Finn added. "You'll have more freedom and responsibility. You'll get to help Ben develop and craft the InfoSec Department from the ground up. And I intend to ask Basia to join the company, as well. We could use a good translator on staff."

The offer was incredibly attractive, but what about patriotism and serving my country? Could I do that from the private sector? More importantly, could I work for a man I might want to sleep with?

"Working for a private firm will give you more of a chance to stretch your wings," he added. "You'll have several new opportunities to explore avenues that might be closed to you at the NSA because of security concerns. I want you on my team, Lexi, because I want the best. Take a leap—you might find it exhilarating."

"I could also break my neck."

Finn reached out and touched my hand. "At least promise me you'll consider it."

I looked up at the baby-blue sky where nary a cloud was in sight. I was alive and my once ho-hum life had never seemed so filled with exciting and endless possibilities.

I shaded my eyes and looked over at Finn. "Okay, Finn," I said, giving him a nod. "You've intrigued me. I promise to think about it."

And I would. After all, Lexi Carmichael, Secret Cyber Agent, did have an awfully nice ring to it.

ABOUT THE AUTHOR

JULIE MOFFETT IS a bestselling author and writes in the genres of historical romance, paranormal romance and mystery. She has won numerous awards, including the prestigious PRISM Award for Best Romantic Time-Travel and Best of the Best Paranormal Books of 2002. She has also garnered several nominations for the Daphne du Maurier Award and the Holt Medallion.

Julie is a military brat (Air Force) and has traveled extensively. Her more exciting exploits include attending high school in Okinawa, Japan; backpacking around Europe and Scandinavia for several months; a year-long college graduate study in Warsaw, Poland; and a wonderful trip to Scotland and Ireland where she fell in love with castles, kilts and brogues.

Julie has a B.A. in political science and Russian language from Colorado College and an M.A. in international affairs from The George Washington University in Washington, D.C. She worked as a journalist for the international radio station Radio Free Europe/Radio Liberty in Washington, D.C., for eleven years, publishing hundreds of articles before "retiring" to be a stay-at-home mom and full-time writer.

Julie speaks Russian and Polish and has two sons. She enjoys interacting with readers at her website, www.juliemoffett.com, or on Facebook at www.facebook.com/pages/JulieMoffett-Author/123804877633091.

REQUEST YOUR FREE BOOKS!
2 FREE NOVELS PLUS 2 FREE GIFTS!

♦HARLEQUIN®

INTRIGUE

BREATHTAKING ROMANTIC SUSPENSE

YES! Please send me 2 FREE Harlequin® Intrigue novels and my 2 FREE gifts (gifts are worth about $10). After receiving them, if I don't wish to receive any more books, I can return the shipping statement marked "cancel." If I don't cancel, I will receive 6 brand-new novels every month and be billed just $4.74 per book in the U.S. or $5.49 per book in Canada. That's a savings of at least 12% off the cover price! It's quite a bargain! Shipping and handling is just 50¢ per book in the U.S. and 75¢ per book in Canada.* I understand that accepting the 2 free books and gifts places me under no obligation to buy anything. I can always return a shipment and cancel at any time. Even if I never buy another book, the two free books and gifts are mine to keep forever.

182/382 HDN GH3D

Name	(PLEASE PRINT)	
Address		Apt. #
City	State/Prov.	Zip/Postal Code

Signature (if under 18, a parent or guardian must sign)

Mail to the **Reader Service:**
IN U.S.A.: P.O. Box 1867, Buffalo, NY 14240-1867
IN CANADA: P.O. Box 609, Fort Erie, Ontario L2A 5X3
Are you a subscriber to Harlequin® Intrigue books
and want to receive the larger-print edition?
Call 1-800-873-8635 or visit www.ReaderService.com.

* Terms and prices subject to change without notice. Prices do not include applicable taxes. Sales tax applicable in N.Y. Canadian residents will be charged applicable taxes. Offer not valid in Quebec. This offer is limited to one order per household. Not valid for current subscribers to Harlequin Intrigue books. All orders subject to credit approval. Credit or debit balances in a customer's account(s) may be offset by any other outstanding balance owed by or to the customer. Please allow 4 to 6 weeks for delivery. Offer available while quantities last.

Your Privacy—The Reader Service is committed to protecting your privacy. Our Privacy Policy is available online at www.ReaderService.com or upon request from the Reader Service.

We make a portion of our mailing list available to reputable third parties that offer products we believe may interest you. If you prefer that we not exchange your name with third parties, or if you wish to clarify or modify your communication preferences, please visit us at www.ReaderService.com/consumerschoice or write to us at Reader Service Preference Service, P.O. Box 9062, Buffalo, NY 14240-9062. Include your complete name and address.

HI15

REQUEST YOUR FREE BOOKS!

2 FREE NOVELS
FROM THE SUSPENSE COLLECTION
PLUS 2 FREE GIFTS!

YES! Please send me 2 FREE novels from the Suspense Collection and my 2 FREE gifts (gifts are worth about $10). After receiving them, if I don't wish to receive any more books, I can return the shipping statement marked "cancel." If I don't cancel, I will receive 4 brand-new novels every month and be billed just $6.49 per book in the U.S. or $6.99 per book in Canada. That's a savings of at least 19% off the cover price. It's quite a bargain! Shipping and handling is just 50¢ per book in the U.S. and 75¢ per book in Canada.* I understand that accepting the 2 free books and gifts places me under no obligation to buy anything. I can always return a shipment and cancel at any time. Even if I never buy another book, the two free books and gifts are mine to keep forever.

191/391 MDN GH4Z

Name _____ (PLEASE PRINT) _____

Address _____ Apt. # _____

City _____ State/Prov. _____ Zip/Postal Code _____

Signature (if under 18, a parent or guardian must sign) _____

Mail to the **Reader Service:**
IN U.S.A.: P.O. Box 1867, Buffalo, NY 14240-1867
IN CANADA: P.O. Box 609, Fort Erie, Ontario L2A 5X3

Want to try two free books from another line?
Call 1-800-873-8635 or visit www.ReaderService.com.

* Terms and prices subject to change without notice. Prices do not include applicable taxes. Sales tax applicable in N.Y. Canadian residents will be charged applicable taxes. Offer not valid in Quebec. This offer is limited to one order per household. Not valid for current subscribers to the Suspense Collection or the Romance/Suspense Collection. All orders subject to credit approval. Credit or debit balances in a customer's account(s) may be offset by any other outstanding balance owed by or to the customer. Please allow 4 to 6 weeks for delivery. Offer available while quantities last.

Your Privacy—The Reader Service is committed to protecting your privacy. Our Privacy Policy is available online at www.ReaderService.com or upon request from the Reader Service.

We make a portion of our mailing list available to reputable third parties that offer products we believe may interest you. If you prefer that we not exchange your name with third parties, or if you wish to clarify or modify your communication preferences, please visit us at www.ReaderService.com/consumerschoice or write to us at Reader Service Preference Service, P.O. Box 9062, Buffalo, NY 14240-9062. Include your complete name and address.